There was something else.

She had seen it in his eyes . . . a warmth that

reached out, yet kept you at bay somehow.

She watched him walk away, over the bridge and

on, up the hill, until she could no longer see him.

"A man with troubles," she deduced quietly.

But, she shook herself, she was not here

to get involved with another man . . .

# JOSEPHINE COX

## THE BEACHCOMBER

AVON BOOKS

*An Imprint* of HarperCollins*Publishers*

AVON BOOKS
*An Imprint of* HarperCollins*Publishers*
10 East 53rd Street
New York, New York 10022-5299

Copyright © 2003 by Josephine Cox
ISBN: 0-06-052546-0
www.avonbooks.com

First Avon Books paperback printing: October 2003

Avon Trademark Reg. U.S. Pat. Off. and in Other Countries, Marca Registrada, Hecho en U.S.A.
HarperCollins® is a trademark of HarperCollins Publishers Inc.

Printed in the U.S.A.

10  9  8  7  6  5  4  3  2  1

This book, and every book I will ever write,
is for Ken, a man amongst men,
my soulmate and inspiration forever.

# CONTENTS

# THE BEACHCOMBER

# PART ONE

Midsummer 1952

## Quiet Stranger

# One

_____

WHAT THE HELL DOES HE THINK HE'S DOING!" AS THE
car lurched forward, Tom fought to keep control. He
had been taken by surprise when the car following seemed
to deliberately crash into his bumper.

"He's coming at us again, Daddy!" The two children in the
back were thrown hard against the seat-backs by the first
bump. They screamed a warning as the other car surged toward
them a second time. There was a moment of chaos before the
impact sent them hurtling toward the clifftops. "JESUS!" He
couldn't hold it! They were going over . . . dear God, they were
going over, and there was nothing he could do!

In that split second as he tried desperately to swing the car
round, Tom glanced again through his rear-view mirror,
needing to know who his attacker was, why he would want
to hurt them. The car was a blue Hillman Minx, he thought,
and the driver was crouched over its steering wheel, with a
Homburg hat pulled low over his forehead and dark glasses
hiding his eyes. It was impossible to get any idea of what he
looked like. "Crazy bastard . . . back off. BACK OFF!" In
response Tom felt the violent impact as they were hit again,
and again. Wrenched out of his hands, the steering wheel
seemed to spin out of control.

"God help us!" His wife's frightened voice penetrated the
chaos of his mind. "Children! Get down behind the seats!"
she ordered fearfully. He heard the pitiful whimperings of
his two children as they clung to each other. He saw his
wife, strangely silent now, her face shocked with disbelief as

she glanced back at their attacker. "My God!" Suddenly she was on the seat, frantically attempting to reach the children, but it was too late.

When the car rammed them yet again, they lurched forward, the windscreen shattering all over them, the other driver showing no mercy. Determined, he stayed with them, revving up, sending them forward toward the edge, fast and furious.

Everything was happening so quickly . . . a matter of seconds, no more. There was no time to escape. By now the car was badly dented; the doors were jammed tight. Tom had tried everything in his power and it wasn't enough. All manner of powerful emotions swept through him: disbelief; helplessness; and now sheer horror as the car became airborne.

There was a moment of eeriness, when the car appeared to pause in midair before the nose dipped and they fell into a downward plunge toward the rocks below. "Oh, dear God!" Throwing himself across his wife, he yelled for the kids to "STAY DOWN! HOLD ONTO EACH OTHER!" He could hear them sobbing, and now the soft, shivering sound of his wife's voice in prayer. *Death was only a heartbeat away.*

He would not remember the thud as they bounced onto the rocks and rolled over and over, crashing and breaking toward the beach; nor would he recall the screams of people who scattered in all directions as the car skidded at breakneck speed toward the sea-edge. The clanging bells of the ambulances and police cars as they rushed to help fell on deaf ears. Like his wife and children, he was beyond all that.

The next thing he knew he had awoken in the hospital. Bruised and battered, both his legs were broken and his neck was in a brace. When he woke it was with a scream for the children to "GET DOWN, KIDS . . . HOLD ON!" In that unbelievable moment, his mind was alive with the memory of what had happened.

"It's all right . . . ssh!" Gently the nurse settled him down again, her heart aching for what he must soon learn.

Later they told him that there was nothing they could have done to save Sheila or the children. "We tried and failed," the surgeon told him, hands outstretched and an expression of hopelessness on his kindly face. "I'm so sorry."

The car had turned over on top of them. Tom himself had been thrown clear . . . lucky to be alive, they said. But he wasn't "lucky!" He was angry, seething with a need to kill. Then he was sobbing, crippled with utter loneliness.

*All through that terrible night the questions had burned bright in his mind. Who was the madman who had run them off the road? Why did he do it? WHY?*

There were no answers, because in the months that followed, in spite of the police relentlessly pursuing even the minutest clue, the driver of that car was never found, nor was the car itself. Tom had described both as accurately as he could, but it was as though they had vanished off the face of the earth. They had spoken to owners in the area whose cars had been stolen around the time of the accident, but until and unless they found the vehicle itself, that wasn't of much help.

When eventually Tom was released from the hospital, he too made every effort to trace the man who had taken his family and ruined his life. Time and again in the following months, he returned to the scene, speaking with anyone who would listen. All to no avail. *The evil that had visited him and his family seemed to have gone as swiftly as it came.*

But the consequences of that fateful day would never leave him. Neither would the hatred he felt.

Now, almost a year later, all that was left for Tom was the awful nightmares when, in his deepest sleep, he would reenact the terrifying scene, hearing his children screaming, and Sheila, at first strangely silent, then frantically reaching out to protect her children . . . and all of them, helpless.

The dreams were so real and vivid, he would often wake up, arms flailing, yelling for the children to, "Get down on the floor, kids! FOR GOD'S SAKE, HOLD ON TO EACH OTHER!"

"Are you all right?" a gentle voice inquired. Tom opened his eyes, shocked and ashamed when he realized where he was.

"You were having a bad dream." The elderly woman seated beside him could see the sweat shimmering on his face and the look of pain in his eyes. "Can I get you something?"

He shook his head. "I'm all right, thank you. I didn't mean to fall asleep," he apologized. "It's just that trains always make me nod off." He smiled to ease the tension.

The woman nodded. "I was worried, that's all." She lowered her voice. "You were moaning . . . upset."

He grimaced. "It was just a bad dream." When she smiled and looked away, he found refuge in his newspaper.

But there was no refuge in his heart.

The woman frowned to herself. A lot of young men had come back from the war in a terrible state. Poor chap; it must be that.

As the train chugged onward, the billowing steam outside his window blocked his vision. His mind came alive with thoughts of how it used to be. He saw them all in his mind's eye: the woman he had loved, small and slim with big bright eyes and a smile that could light up a cloudy day. And the children: Ellie, quiet and reflective with a gentle nature, and Peter, the younger one, wild and willful, with a free, adventurous spirit. So different, yet so alike, in their kindness and generosity.

Reaching into his pocket he took out his wallet, pulling out a small photograph of them all . . . Bournemouth Sands, June 1951. His heart fell like a stone inside him. It seemed incredible to think that that wonderful holiday was just a year ago, and now, God help him, there would be no more.

"Is that your family?" The kindly old soul pointed at the photograph as he returned it to his pocket. "I always wanted a daughter, but was never blessed with another child."

Gesturing to his pocket, she added, "Lovely-looking children." Giving the cheekiest of winks, she whispered, "Mind you, I can see how they might be handsome, with a father as attractive as you."

Smiling and embarrassed, he wasn't quite sure how to answer that, so he glanced out the window and pretended to be interested in the shifting landscape.

The woman saw his embarrassment. She thought him too good-looking for words. Discreetly observing the dark blue eyes, and the thick shock of golden-brown hair, she was sent back to her youth, when she could have had the pick of any young man. Sadly those days were gone and now, gray and old, she had too many regrets to contemplate.

"I don't mean to embarrass you," she apologized, "but when I'm anxious, I tend to talk a lot." Her face crumpled into a frown. "I must admit I hate these trains—noisy, dirty things. And I mean . . . you're not in control, are you?"

"We're *never* 'in control,' " he answered thoughtfully. He knew all about that. He knew from experience how one minute everything was perfect, filled with love and joy, and, before you knew it, your whole world was turned upside down.

The steam whistle blasted noisily as they entered a tunnel. "Ooh!" The old woman shivered. "I'll be glad to reach London. I know I shan't relax till then."

He nodded. "You're doing fine," he answered; then turned away to concentrate his thoughts.

Thinking she was becoming a nuisance, she tutted. "I'm sorry . . . keep chatting away . . . I hope you don't mind?"

"No. You talk away, if it helps," he suggested with a smile. "I really *don't* mind."

"Only, you've been so quiet since I sat beside you, I thought you might be one of those people who like to be left alone?" She giggled like a schoolgirl. "My son warned me not to be a nuisance. He knows how some folks don't want to be bothered. You will tell me if I'm being a nuisance, won't you?"

"I promise, you're *not* being a nuisance." He shook his head. "It's just that I never find it easy to strike up a conversation."

Encouraged, she chatted on about the new Queen, and when a short time later she started to nod off, he began to relax. When he relaxed, however, it was inevitable that he should be overwhelmed by the faces of the woman and children in that photograph. He had loved them with a passion that frightened him. Now, they were gone and all he had left was memories . . . of when they were walking in the park, he and Sheila laughing at the children's antics, and afterward eating in that pretty little café by the riverside, where they would throw leftovers to the ducks.

The memories rolled through his mind like the reel of a film. For one precious minute they made him smile; *then they were breaking his heart.*

"Do you think it will be long before we get there?" The elderly woman woke as suddenly as she had nodded off. "I've never been to London before. I wouldn't be going now, if my only son hadn't taken his family and moved down there." She continued wistfully, "I've got four beautiful grandchildren. I've missed them."

Attempting to reassure her, he replied confidently. "Won't be long now," he said. "And London's fine. After a while you get used to it. I work for a big development corporation there," he confided.

She gave a wry grin. "I would have gone with them," she admitted. "My son wanted us to, but my husband is a cantankerous old sod. The farthest he'll go is to the bottom of the garden and back."

He smiled pensively. "I envy him."

"Why's that?" She was genuinely surprised by his statement.

"Why, because he sounds contented." He would have given anything at that moment to be "contented."

She gave a sorry little smile. "Unlike me! I've always been *discontented!* All the years we've been wed, I was the one who loved the dancing and going out—especially during the war, you know—but he was never that way inclined. He was an ARP warden. I expect that was enough excitement for him. If he could he'd be happy to sit by the fireside of a winter's night, and potter about in the garden in the summer. I always put it down to laziness or lack of enthusiasm, but now I think about it, you could be right."

His remark made her wonder. "Happen he's just been 'contented' all along." She gave a long, weary sigh. "It's sad really. We've always been so very different in what we want. But he so depends on me, you see."

When the tears rose in her eyes and she abruptly returned her attention to her book, he felt desperately sorry for her. He could imagine how this dear old woman and her husband might be mismatched; he assumed there were many couples like that: having stayed too long together, it was now too late for any chance of a new life for either of them.

Looking away, he peered out to where the countryside resembled a giant eiderdown, with misshapen patches of browns, yellows and melting shades of green. In the far distance, beyond the cotton-wool puffs from the train's funnel, he could see a lake, shimmering and twinkling. At other times that beautiful sight would have gladdened his heart, but not now.

His own thoughts invaded the quietness. *He had tried to go on, but it was impossible. This latest trip had been sheer hell! He found he could no longer conduct his business in that sharp, decisive way he used to. Too many things played on his mind. Dear God! Would there ever be any peace?*

Right now, he didn't even want to think about it. He wanted to wake up and find it was all a nightmare, that all was well and his family would be waiting at home, just like always. He laughed softly, a hard, cynical emotion cutting through his heart like a knife. It *was not* a nightmare, and he would not wake up from it; not for a long time; maybe never. Anger invaded his senses. A feeling of utter hopelessness swept through him. Life was a cruel master!

The last he saw of the old woman was in the train terminal. She looked a sorry sight as she trundled after the porter who carried her tiny suitcase. "I hope things turn out all right for you," he whispered and, almost as though she had heard, she suddenly turned to smile at him. He gave a small wave, she nodded, and in a moment was gone from his sight.

Hurrying to the taxi rank, he climbed into the first cab in the line. "Where to, sir?" The cabbie was a rough-and-ready fella, going gray and slow in his step. Tom couldn't help but notice the long scar running down the side of his face. "Got from running wild as a kid," he explained, anticipating Tom's curiosity. "I've an interesting tattoo of a snake an' all—" he gave a hearty laugh—"but you wouldn't want to know about that." Opening the cab door, he gave a cheeky wink. "I were drunk at the time . . . regretted it ever since."

His imagination running riot, Tom didn't dare ask. "We've all done things we regret," he answered with a friendly smile.

"Not *you!* A man like yousel'? By! I should think you've got the world at your feet." When Tom made no comment he closed the cab door and climbed into the driver's seat. "It might help if I knew where I were going," he quipped good-naturedly.

Having given him the address of his flat in Hammersmith, Tom leaned back in his seat. He suddenly felt incredibly weary . . . tired of his job; tired of trying to piece together his life. Tired of being so alone.

The cabbie discreetly regarded him through his mirror. "If you don't mind me saying, guv, you look like you could do with a good night's sleep." Suddenly swerving to avoid a delivery boy on his bicycle, he let loose a volley of abuse at the rider. "Watch where you're going, mate!" Leaning out the window, he screamed at the frightened fellow, who had done nothing wrong. "If you're fed up wi' life, throw yousel' off a bleedin' railway bridge!"

Having been flung clear across the seat, Tom righted himself and sat tight.

Completely oblivious to the chaos he'd caused, the cabbie asked, "Away on business, was you?"

"Yes," Tom acknowledged.

"I expect you glad to be 'ome, eh?"

"Right again." But what was he coming home to? No family. No real home, and nothing worthwhile to look forward to. His life was work and more work. These past weeks he had been seriously wondering if he should give it all up. Now, as the idea loomed large in his thoughts, it seemed to overwhelm everything else.

"What is it you do?" the cabbie asked.

"I'm one of three architects in a big development organization. We build office blocks, factories, large housing developments, that sort of thing. There's never two jobs the same." Wasn't it strange, he thought, how you naturally imparted your business to a cabbie. Probably it was because you never expected to see him again.

Turning a corner, the cabbie grinned at him through the mirror. "By! You must lead an exciting life? Plenty to build an' all, now the country's back on its feet."

Lapsing into silence, Tom let him chat on.

"I've allus wanted to travel, but never had the time nor money. I've got six kids and a wife who spends like money's gone outta fashion. I work six days a week, from seven of a morning till late at night. What chance 'ave I got to see the bleedin' world, eh?"

He gave a loud, raucous laugh. "Matter o' fact, I can never understand where I found the time to make all them bloody kids! Come to think of it, I can't even remember enjoying mesel at it, neither!" Taking his eyes off the road to peer through the mirror at Tom, he added, "D'you know what, matey? I've often wondered how many o' them kids belong to that smarmy bleedin' milkman!"

"Well, for what it's worth, *I* think you're a lucky man." In truth, Tom envied him.

"Oh! You reckon, do you?" Astonished, the cabbie afforded himself another glance at his passenger. "Here's me . . . a poor ol' chap, working all hours God sends, and like as not them two having it off behind my back. An' you say I'm a lucky man?" He laughed aloud. "Hey! Happen you're right. Happen he should tek her an' the kids off me 'ands, and leave me to enjoy mesel."

Tom defended his comment. "What I meant was . . . *any* man who's got a wife and children who love you . . . has to be a lucky man."

"Ah! But how do I know if they're *my* kids?" His tone grew serious. "No man likes being cheated on."

Sensing the cabbie's abrupt change of mood, Tom wisely avoided being drawn into the subject too far. "Look! The traffic's building up." He gestured to the road ahead, and the many vehicles vying for space. Since petrol rationing had ended, traffic had increased.

Swinging his taxi around a crawling trolleybus, the cab-bie cursed, "Bleedin' drivers! At least we've seen the last of the trams!"

Having got in front of the trolleybus, he refocused his cu-rious gaze on Tom. "It's a busy time o' day, as you must well know, guv . . . you living 'ere an' all that."

After a while the cabbie lapsed into a pensive mood, and it wasn't long before they reached Hammersmith. " 'Ere we are, guv!"

Drawing his cab into the curb outside a large, handsome building, the cabbie remarked with a whistle of appreciation, "Nice flats these . . . cost a pretty penny too, I shouldn't wonder." He clicked his tongue in admiration. "I wouldn't mind living in a posh place like this . . . all on me own where the brats and the missus can't find me."

Climbing out, Tom had his fare at the ready, which he handed to the driver, together with a generous tip, and a word of friendly advice. "You wouldn't like it," he said. "You'd be lonelier than you can ever imagine."

His words appeared to hit home, because suddenly the cabbie was deeply thoughtful. "You could be right," he an-swered. "Besides, what about that bleedin' milkman, eh? If I weren't there to keep an eye on him, Gawd knows what he'd be getting up to wi' my missus!" His loud raucous laugh echoed down the street. "By! He'd want to be deliver-ing more than the milk . . . if he ain't done already!"

Shaking his head, and with a wide grin on his face, Tom watched him drive off.

He was still chuckling as he entered the lift; though by the time he had reached his flat on the sixth floor the smile had slipped and the same idea that had haunted him these past weeks began to invade his thoughts again. "It's time," he murmured. There was no doubt in his mind now. "Time to leave it all behind."

Letting himself into the luxurious, soulless place that he now called home, he felt a wave of relief that the decision was made. "I need to get away from London . . . and all the bad memories." *If he didn't leave soon, he suspected he might go crazy.*

After a bath to wash the grime of the journey from his bones, he threw pajamas and a robe on, poured himself a whiskey and soda and stood looking out of the window. In the growing twilight, silhouetted against a moody sky, the skyline of London was a mesmerizing sight.

When the weariness took a hold, he threw off his robe, climbed into bed, and fell into a long, fitful sleep.

*Though even now, there was no respite from the shocking memories. Day or night, asleep or awake, they were etched on his soul.*

In the early hours, finally driven from his sleep by the dreams that haunted him, Tom got out of bed and began pacing the floor, unaware that he was being observed.

From the apartment block opposite, having been too restless to sleep, Kathy Wilson was looking out of the window, her gaze roving the front of the splendid building across the street. For one lingering moment her eyes rested on the window where, inside a softly lit room, a man was striding back and forth, head bent as he paced up and down, occasionally running his hands through his hair. Now he paused a moment, only to begin again, faster, more agitated . . . backward and forward, like a soul in torment.

Sensing his distress, she gave a whimsical little smile, at the same time softly commenting, "It seems I'm not the only one who can't find any peace."

When, in that moment, in the semi-darkness, a hand fell on her shoulder, she almost leapt out of her skin. "For goodness' sake, Geoff . . . don't creep up on me like that!" Swinging round, she regarded the man with surprise. "I thought you were still asleep."

Giving a wry sort of smile, the man gripped her by the shoulders. "I missed your warm body beside me." He kissed her on the neck, not seeming to notice when she flinched beneath his touch. "You look especially lovely tonight. Come on!" he urged. "Come back to bed, sweetheart?" Sliding his hands under her dressing-gown, he stroked her firm breasts.

When his fingers crept downward toward the softness of her inner thighs, there was no doubting his intention.

"No!" Frantic, she pushed him away. "It was a mistake . . . tonight was all wrong . . . I . . ." But when he pressed her lips with his, she felt the shudder of need ripple through her.

"Come back to bed, Kathy." Taking advantage of her hesitation, he collected her into his arms and carried her away from the window and across the room where, ever so tenderly, he laid her on the bed. In a moment he had slipped off her dressing-gown, leaving her naked before him; eyes wide with lust, he gazed down, his own desperate need obvious as his eyes roved over her petite, slim figure with its perfectly round breasts and tiny waist.

Her eyes, though, were her best feature: golden-brown, with long curling lashes and perfectly shaped eyebrows. "I do love you," he muttered, then, stretching his arms up to the bed head, he neatly straddled her. Leaning his head to kiss her on the mouth, he relaxed his body to fuse nakedness with nakedness.

It took less than five minutes for him to satisfy himself and, when it was over, it was she who drew away first; though he was so elated and fulfilled, he didn't even notice.

For a long moment she looked at him from the bottom of the bed; at his uptilted face. He gave a soft, low laugh. "I'm sorry it was so quick, but you shouldn't have kept me waiting!" Suddenly he was sitting up, staring back at her. "Was it all right for you, sweetheart?" It seemed to be of paramount importance to him.

Kathy smiled, a reluctant smile that appeared to pacify him. "Yes, Geoff," she lied. Up until then she hadn't realized how little she found attractive about him. She didn't even like him very much.

He glanced at the clock. "Oh, damn! It's still only six o'clock. You shouldn't have woken me so early! Come on . . . come back to bed . . . we've another hour yet."

She nodded. "I need a drink first."

He smiled. "What? You mean I've made you thirsty with all that lovemaking?"

She looked away. "Something like that."

"Well, *you* can stay up if you want, but I need my sleep." With that he drew the covers over him and, spreading himself right across the bed, he was soon asleep.

Seeing him like that, knowing how she had shared a bed with him, Kathy felt dirty, degraded. It had been a mistake. "It doesn't look like there'd be any room for me even if I *did* come back to bed!" Tonight, she had begun to wonder what she had ever seen in him.

In the half-light she made her way to the window, noisily tripping over the pillow he had thrown off the bed. "Who's that?" Peering over the covers, he stared at her, his tone impatient, all tenderness gone. "Are you coming back to bed, or what?"

"No! Like I said . . . I need a drink."

"Well, don't wake me up when you get back in!"

Lingering by the window, she looked across to the other building again. The light was still on, but there was no sign of the man now. "Poor chap," she murmured, "I wonder why he couldn't sleep? Divorced maybe . . . can't get used to it." She sighed. "I know what that feels like!"

Feeling sad and suddenly weary, she put the kettle on; while that was brewing she visited the loo. Afterward, looking in the mirror, she addressed herself in bruising tones, "You're a mess, Kathy Wilson!" Looking back at her image in the tiny oval mirror, she saw how the life had gone from her face; the golden-brown eyes weren't so bright anymore, and her brown hair was lank about her shoulders. "In the last year you've let yourself go. It's no wonder men have begun to treat you like the dirt under their feet. All right! So you were married and he left you because he'd found somebody else." Dan and she had been happy enough for a couple of years, but the war had taken its toll on him, as it had on so many other young men. She gazed at her image a moment longer. "Men! Who needs 'em?"

She allowed herself a smile. "You did have some good times though, didn't you, eh? And when he walked out, it was only natural that you felt worthless. So what! That was over a year ago, and you're still not over it. You're moody and bad-tempered. You almost lost your job because you were absent so often they thought you'd emigrated, and now, here you are . . . making a mistake with the first man who came along and was kind to you."

Casting a disillusioned glance toward the bedroom, she shook her head in dismay. "Geoff isn't for me! He may be handsome and well spoken, but deep down he's a bully, and he really fancies himself. I just let myself be carried along by the dates and the flattery."

She wagged a finger at herself in the mirror. "She might be the worst mother on God's earth, and there are times when you'd be better off without her interfering, but she's right!" she groaned. "It *is* time you got yourself together. You're not the first woman to lose her husband and you won't be the last." They were her mother's words, and they had never been truer.

She went to the kitchen, where she fetched a glass of water. As she sat sipping it and musing, she came to a conclusion. "Right! I've had enough of his hands all over me, ordering me around: 'Do this' . . . 'Get me that.' " She mocked him to perfection. ". . . And if he never kisses me again, it'll be too soon!"

It took all of two minutes for her to sneak into the bedroom, collect her clothes and sneak out again. Five minutes later she was ready to leave. One last peep at his sleeping figure on her side of the bed and she was tiptoeing out of there, to the merry tune of his snoring. "Sleep well, you bugger!" As she went, she deliberately slammed shut the door.

Having got up early, shaved and dressed and ready for off, Tom saw the young woman from his window. She was hatless, her shoulder-length brown hair flying out behind her. He watched as she bounced along with a spring to her step; he saw her deliberately stride out into a busy street and hail a taxi-cab, the traffic swerving around her. When, in order to avoid hitting her full on, the driver of the black cab screeched to a halt, she calmly climbed aboard and waved him on.

Tom laughed out loud. "*That's* what you call a gutsy woman!"

Just then the telephone rang; it was his brother Dougie. "Just checking you got back all right," he said.

"Got back . . . had a bath and an early night, and now I'm raring to go." What he was "raring" to do was to organize his life at last.

"Good trip?"

"Good enough."

"Right! See you at the office. I'll be late, I reckon . . . got a frantic call from Joe Nightingale . . . some planning difficulty or other, it's a damned nuisance. Still, I'm sure it's nothing we can't get round."

"Dougie, wait!" Now that his mind was made up, he needed to tell the world. "What time will you be back, do you think?"

"Not sure. You know what it's like. When Joe can't have his own way, he tends to get het-up. Then you have to take him out and discuss the finer points over a pint. I don't suppose I'll get away much before what . . . three . . . four? Why?"

"But you *will* be back at the office today, won't you?"

"Sure thing, but what's the panic?"

"No panic. There's something I need to talk over with you, that's all."

"Can't it wait till tomorrow?"

"No."

"Okay. I'll try and get away by two. How does that suit?"

"Okay. See you then. Give my regards to Joe."

"Hmh!" Dougie gave a laugh. "Knowing how difficult it can be to drag yourself away when he's got a bee in his bonnet, I'll probably have him in tow."

"Naw. You'll deal with it. See you at two then!"

"Can't wait!"

A moment later, having seen that his cupboards were bare, Tom threw on his jacket and made his way out of the building. He quickly hailed a cab, though not in the same cavalier way as the young woman before him. "Can you take me to the best greasy spoon you know?" he asked.

The cabbie acknowledged his request with a grin. "I know just the place," he said. "Sausages, mushrooms, and thick fried bread like you've never seen. Two slices o' bread and marge, and a pot o' tea to go with it." He winked in his mirror. "How does that sound, guv?"

Tom was impressed. "Sounds like the nearest thing to heaven to me," he said. Settling comfortably in his seat, he shut his eyes and ears to the traffic and let his stomach dictate.

Even now, early though it was, London was a bustling medley of trolleybuses, bicycles and motor cars. But the cabbie was as good as his word. "Baker's Caff," he declared, drawing into the curbside, "owned and run by my own dear mamma . . . name of Lola. Looks like the devil, cooks like an angel!"

At that minute a woman emerged. All smiles and white teeth, she was ample in every way; obviously of Italian origin, with her black eyes, and her dark hair tied in an elaborate knot at the top of her head. "Come in! Come in!" she urged.

Opening her dimpled arms, she embraced him with surprising strength. "Nice to see you, handsome man. You wanna the breakfast?" As she spoke she nodded, her smile growing so wide it almost enveloped her face.

The cabbie laughed. "Course he wants 'the breakfast!' Why do you think I brought him, eh?" Winking at Tom, he suggested mischievously, "Matter o' fact, I'm beginning to feel a bit peckish myself."

"No, you can't!" She wagged an angry finger at him. "I don't feed you no more today! You be a good boy . . . get away and bring me more customers."

Laughing, he deposited Tom into her care and drove off.

Lola's breakfast was as good as it got with rationing still in place: two huge sausages; a heaping of mushrooms; four crinkly cooked tomatoes; even a fried egg, and the whole plate swimming in juices and fats, which Tom eagerly mopped up with his chunks of fresh-baked bread. Afterward there was a cup of scalding hot tea to wash it all down.

Lola scooped up his plate. "You want *more?*"

"Good God, no!" Tom struggled out of his chair. "That was more than enough to last me the whole day, thank you. I've never tasted a breakfast like it!"

"So, you come back another time, yes?" Lola's round face was a picture of joy.

He nodded. "I'll be back," he promised. "Just try and keep me away!"

A few moments later, as he donned his wool coat and hat and left the café, he turned to wave; quietly amused when Lola blushed crimson.

His offices were only a short distance from the café. For a moment he debated whether to take the trolleybus or walk. He had been a minute at the bus stop when he decided against it. "On second thoughts, I'd best walk!" He patted his stomach. "It'll do me good."

As usual the office was a hive of activity. "Nice to see you back." As he walked through the gauntlet of typists and clerks, he was greeted with genuine affection.

Turning into his own office, he was not surprised to see the vase of flowers on his window-sill; it was a kind of ritual on his return from a trip. "Welcome home." Invaluable assistant and secretary to two of the architects here, Lilian was of pleasant appearance with pretty dark eyes. As always for work, her long auburn curls were neatly pinned back in a bun. She had been a good friend to Tom, he reflected.

Coming into the office, she placed the tray on his desk. "Like the flowers, do you?" That very morning she had taken ages choosing them.

"They're splendid, as always." He took another glance at the vase full of yellow carnations. "Thank you, Lilian, that was really thoughtful of you."

Resting his hands on her shoulders, he smiled down at her. "What would I do without you, eh?"

He observed his office with its neat filing cabinets and long, polished desk, the sun pouring in through the window, and for one aching moment he wondered if he had made the right decision after all. "Everything in order as usual . . . but then I shouldn't expect anything less from you."

He and the young woman had worked together these past eight years, and never a cross word. "You do tend to keep me at it, though." He glanced at the desk, its entire surface bedecked with neat piles of papers and rolls of plans. "You're not about to let the grass grow under my feet, are you, eh?"

She smiled confidently. "You'll find all the schedules typed up for your current projects; your 'urgent' messages, and a dozen appointments for this coming week." Her smile broadened. "Enough to keep you out of trouble, I'd say . . . Oh, and I've brought you a pot of tea to keep you going." She crossed the room but paused at the door. "Give me a call when you're ready to start dictation. Is there anything you want before I get on?"

He shook his head. "Not right now, Lilian." He meant for her to be one of the first to know of his decision. "Look, I think it might be a good idea for us to talk—" he glanced at the desk and groaned—"after I've waded through this little lot."

She seemed pleasantly surprised. "Talk? What about?"

"Not just now, Lilian . . . Like I said, when I've dealt with a certain matter." Which wouldn't be easy, but it had to be done.

"Okay." She turned to leave but then remembered. "Oh, and the boss asked to see you the minute you got in."

"Tell him I'm on my way."

With the door closed behind her he poured himself a tea. Taking a gulp, he scanned briefly through the papers on his desk, then another gulp or two, and he was out of the office and running up the stairs to John Martin's more private offices.

A tap on the door and straight in; though with caution when he saw that the "boss" was talking on the telephone. A big man with a big heart, John Martin had started these offices some ten years ago and never looked back.

On seeing Tom he quickly concluded the conversation. "Well, of course we want the contract, but there's more talking to be done before I sign on the dotted line. You know me, Arthur, I won't accept anything until I'm absolutely satisfied everything's in order, and you've a way to go before I'm satisfied on this one. Yes. Right. Talk to me then. Thanks, I will, yes, don't worry. You too!"

Replacing the telephone in its cradle he got out of his chair and shook Tom by the hand. "You did a good job, son. I knew it wouldn't be easy. That's why I sent my best man . . ." He winked. "But that's between you and me, if you know what I mean?" Feeling he needed to qualify his remark, he quickly added, "Oh, they're all good men and they know their trade . . . your Dougie especially. But *you've* got that certain knack of getting people to see reason, without banging their heads together." He sighed. "From what I understand, you had some real tough problems up there?"

Tom nodded. "It's running smoothly now, though," he reassured him. "When it came right down to it, there was nothing that couldn't be put right."

"That's exactly what I mean. Look, sit down. You've got a minute I'm sure." Rounding his desk, he took up a sheaf of papers and waved them in the air. "There's another difficult one coming up . . . a major project with several interested parties. Prime stuff . . . running into millions. It's in Glasgow—I'll need you there in the next week or so . . . a month at the outside. That should give you time to catch your breath."

Tom shook his head. "I can't do it, John. There's something I—"

The other man intervened. "I know! It's been one trip after another, and I had hoped to give you some time off. But you really are the best I've got. After this, I'll make sure you can keep your feet on the ground for at least a year, I promise."

Tom didn't know how to tell him, but it had to be said, and without the trimmings. "I'm handing in my resignation, John."

"WHAT!" Leaping out of the chair, his boss came around the desk, eyes bulging as he looked down on Tom. "What the devil's brought this on? I've already said . . . this job, then a year on home ground. I mean it . . . I know how hard I've pushed you, but after what happened I thought it might help . . ." Cursing himself, he paused. He had made it a rule never to raise the matter of the tragic incident that took Tom's entire family. "Look, I'm sorry, Tom, but I can't let you go. You're too important to me . . . to this whole outfit, for God's sake!"

Tom was equally adamant. "And *I'm* sorry, John," he replied calmly, "but the resignation stands . . . it'll be on your desk within the hour. I've had plenty of time to think about it, and my mind's made up. The truth is . . . if I don't leave now, I'll crack!"

"I see." Realizing how determined Tom was, and knowing his reputation for sticking to his guns, John understood the argument to be already lost, but he made one last try. "Don't be too hasty, son. Let's not talk 'resignation.' " He couldn't afford to lose Tom. "Take a long leave of absence . . . I don't have a problem with that. I can cope if I have to." He gave a half smile. "Though of course I'd prefer you to change your mind altogether . . ."

Getting out of the chair, Tom looked him in the eye. "Thanks all the same, but like I said, my mind's made up. I'll work out the month if you want me to, but to tell you the truth, I'd rather go *now* . . . right this minute."

For a long moment the older man regarded him, then, after a moment, he asked kindly, "What will you do?"

"I've decided to sell the flat and move away."

"Where will you go?"

Tom had not thought that far ahead. "I'm not sure," he answered truthfully. "Somewhere I'm not known . . . somewhere I can put my life into perspective. A quiet place, where I can find peace, and the time to sort out my life."

The older man began to sympathize. He could see the pain in Tom's eyes. He nodded. "I understand," he murmured. "You've been so driven this past year . . . maybe it's what you need."

Tom nodded. "It is."

"All right, Tom, I won't hold you to a month, but I will need you to pass on your schedules to a colleague . . . talk him through every aspect. Lend him the expertise to deal with it all in the way you yourself would." He threw out his hands in a gesture of helplessness. "It has to be a smooth transition . . . all loose ends tied up. I don't need headaches. You do understand what I'm saying?"

Tom understood exactly. This was big business. There was no room for errors. "Don't worry. I'll deal with it," he promised. "I won't let you down."

John nodded appreciatively. "I wouldn't do this for anybody else," he said, "but you've given me everything you've got to give and it's only fair I give some back."

"Who do you want to take over my schedules?"

"Your brother Dougie. Oh, I know he's still got a lot to learn, but he's doing well now. He's out of the same mold and he'll have the added incentive to do you proud. Yes! Dougie's your man."

Shaking hands, they said their piece. "And don't forget to keep in touch!" John warned. "When you're ready to get back in the saddle, your job will be here waiting for you."

A few minutes later Tom was back in his own office, slightly dazed and a little shaken by the enormity of what he was doing. Yet, amongst all the niggling doubts, he felt instinctively that he was doing the right and only thing.

After three days of being ensconced in the office with Dougie who, though a little nervous, seemed confident about the workload he was taking on, Tom said his goodbyes. There was a small leaving party; the good wishes of his colleagues, and, inevitably, tears from Lilian, who had taken his news very hard. "We'll miss you," she murmured, dabbing her eyes with her hankie. And he thanked her for all the years she had looked after him.

When it was over, he left the building with Dougie by his side.

They walked to the pub on the corner where they sat down with a pint each. Tom stretched his legs out and closed his eyes, a sense of relief washing over him. His brother's voice interrupted his thoughts. "I'm still not sure you're doing the right thing." Like Tom, Dougie was lean of build, with the same color hair; but his eyes were a clear shade of green, and when he laughed he laughed heartily. He wasn't quiet and thoughtful like Tom, nor did he have that same lazy smile. Instead, when he smiled, his face crinkled like a puppy dog's.

But he wasn't smiling now. Instead he seemed worried. "I wish you'd tell me where you're going."

"I'm not sure myself yet," Tom confided. "You'll know when I do, don't worry. Besides, you've got enough on your plate without fretting about me. Look, I'll be fine." He tried to smile reassuringly.

Dougie wasn't convinced. "I wish I could believe that."

"You'll just have to trust me. It's what I need to do. Until I get it all out of my system, I can't move on with my life."

Dougie nodded. "I can understand that. But you will let me know how you're doing, won't you?"

"I promise," Tom said. "When I'm settled."

The following morning, after placing the flat and all its furniture in the hands of an agent, Tom packed his bags and left. His first stop was the florist, where he collected a pre-ordered bouquet, a pretty thing with bright-colored summer flowers in a cradle of green leaves. It was a luxury in a country governed by austerity, but that didn't matter to him. It was the sort of thing he knew Sheila would have chosen herself.

Sited nearby, the churchyard was speckled with shrubs and trees of all blossom and variety and, far enough from the hustle and bustle, it was a place of solitude and beauty.

Tom laid the flowers beneath the headstone; he read the inscription and softly cried. It told of how a mother and her two children were laid there, taken by a tragic accident. It showed their names and ages, and at the bottom were written the words that Tom had requested:

*My dearest loved ones.*
*May God keep you safe*
*until we meet again.*

The tears filled his eyes. There was a moment of contemplation, and all too soon the time had come for him to leave—for now.

As he walked away, he saw a young woman laying a wreath not far from where he had been. Almost at once he recognized her as being the same woman who had run out into the street in search of a cab. She didn't look up. Instead, she blew a kiss toward the grave and walked slowly away, out of the far exit.

As before, Tom was intrigued. "Strange," he mused aloud, "to see her twice in such a short time."

As he drove off, he wondered about her. Then, as always, his mind returned to the other, more pressing thoughts plaguing him. Behind him, the stranger watched Tom depart before, with stealthy footsteps, emerging from the undergrowth. At the place where Tom's family was laid to rest, the stranger paused a while, then reached down to snatch up the bouquet left by Tom. In an angry, callous gesture, the flowers were slung aside, and a new, grander bouquet left in its place.

A few words of regret, a blown kiss. And the stranger was gone.

# *Two*

---

WHILE ON THE TROLLEYBUS TRAVELING BACK TO HER modest flat in Acton, Kathy had time to reflect. Every weekend for the past year, she had gone to the churchyard and laid a posy to remember her father. He had been a good man, a loving father, and she missed him more with every passing day.

The pain of losing that dear man was made worse by her mother's admission that she had never really loved him. In a terrible outburst, Kathy's mother Irene had claimed that her husband was not the innocent, caring man Kathy believed him to be. Moreover, she had told Kathy that he was selfish and domineering, in that he had always held Irene back in whatever she wanted to do. She said that, throughout their marriage, he had been the bane of her life . . . always at work; never adventurous enough for her. When he had suddenly fallen ill, she had made it quite clear that she was not prepared to dedicate her life to looking after him.

As it turned out, though, his illness was short and fierce. He was gone in a matter of weeks.

Distraught, Kathy had never forgiven her mother for the things she'd said. Her sister Samantha, however, was quick to defend Irene. It had always been that way: Samantha and her mother on one side; Kathy and her dad on the other. To make matters worse, Irene had almost seemed to enjoy setting her daughters against each other, always suggesting that Samantha was the prettier, more talented one of the two. There was no denying that, with her long, slim legs and a figure too perfect for words, Samantha was devastatingly attractive; the absolute apple of her mother's eye.

One particular evening stuck in Kathy's memory. In front of visitors, Irene had openly chided young Kathy for not caring enough about her appearance. "You've always been a slovenly creature," she complained. "You take after your father, more's the pity, whereas Samantha takes after me. She's smart and intelligent. She'll make something of herself. As for you . . . I don't know where you'll end up. Or who will want to marry you. Still, what does it matter? I dare say you'll be quite content."

Later, when her mother was busying herself elsewhere, Kathy tearfully confided in her father. "Why does she hate me so much?"

Brushing aside his wife's remarks, he quietly pacified the sobbing child, saying how Kathy mustn't be upset, that her mother didn't "hate" her. He suggested that maybe Samantha got more attention simply because she was the firstborn by nearly two years. He constantly reassured her that she was loved and wanted, every bit as much as her sister.

It was all of little consolation to Kathy. Time and again in the years that followed, she was made to feel rejected and isolated. In fact, if it hadn't been for her father and his quiet love for her, her life would have been unbearable. "You must never feel second-best," he would say. But, with a sister who could do no wrong, it was hard not to feel inferior.

Inevitably Kathy and her father grew closer over the years, and when his expanding business ventures took him away for days on end, she would pine at the window, watching for him hour after hour, "like a puppy dog!" her sister teased, but by now Kathy had learned to shrug off such cutting remarks. Though it hurt when her mother described her in barely concealed undertones as "the plain one." In her heart and soul, and in spite of her father's reassurances, Kathy knew she could never be the natural beauty Samantha was. Small-built, pleasantly pretty with chubby legs and a hearty laugh, Kathy spent ages looking at herself in the mirror and comparing her modest attributes with those of her more glamorous sister. It made her smile; made her sad. In the end, she shrugged it all off and, safe in her father's love, simply got on with her life.

She had proved her mother wrong: someone had wanted to marry her. Her wedding to Dan had been a quiet, wartime one, snatched during his leave, with no time for a pretty dress or a party. The two of them had fun at first, in the short, intense bursts of leave, but the long absences had taken their toll. They had never really got to know each other properly. Since the end of the war, Kathy had tried to be a wife to him, but with no children to care for, and a husband who was hardly at home, it had proved difficult. Dan had grown more and more distant, and had finally left her for another woman just before her father became ill.

And now he too was gone and she was alone, except for a sister and mother who treated her with contempt. Oh, but there was still darling Maggie, a very special friend who over these past few years had become more like a sister to her than Samantha could *ever* be.

"Your stop, miss!" The conductor's voice cut through her thoughts. "I thought for a minute you'd gawn off to sleep."

Kathy laughed. "Chance would be a fine thing," she replied with a grin. "To tell you the truth, I could sleep on a clothes-line!"

He waited for her to disembark. "What? Boyfriend been keeping you out late, has he?"

Kathy thought of her last encounter and laughed out loud. "I'm done with all that," she told him, and meant it.

Tucked away behind a row of shops, Kathy's flat boasted one tiny bedroom, a kitchenette, a sparkling white bathroom, and a surprisingly spacious living room, whose wide window looked down over the hustle and bustle of the locality.

Furnished with a brown, second-hand sofa, a little oak dresser carved with roses, a couple of seascapes hanging on the wall, and other market bric-a-brac placed here and there to make it more like home, the flat didn't have much in the way of luxuries. But it was clean and functional and suited her for now.

She had decided to rent it after she and Dan had split up.

It had been a struggle on her salary, but with Dan's small monthly check, she could just afford it. She couldn't have stayed in their old home. This place had given Kathy that sense of freedom and independence she had sorely needed. It was her sea of calm after the storm, and she loved it.

Relieved to be home, she pottered around the flat, her voice softly humming to the tune of Doris Day's "A Guy Is a Guy." She had spent a small fortune playing that song on the jukebox at the Palais, but it never failed to make her smile, as it did now. She danced across the room; she was looking forward to the usual Saturday evening at the Palais with Maggie. Saturday night was the one time they could really let their hair down; they could lie in for as long as they liked on Sunday morning.

Kathy picked up her bag, and ran down to the payphone in the hall. Her toes were still tapping as she waited for the connection. While she waited she launched into another rendition of "A Guy Is a Guy," her arms and legs jerking in time with the rhythm.

It seemed an age before Maggie answered. Kathy was about to replace the receiver when Maggie's blunt Cockney voice finally answered, "Yes, who is it?"

Kathy gave a sigh of relief. "It's *me,* who d'you think it is?" She suddenly felt tired to the bone. "I was just about to put the phone down," Kathy told her. "Where *were* you?" She grinned. "Hey! You haven't got a fella there, have you?"

At the other end of the line, Maggie continued drying her hair. "No, worse luck. I were in the bathroom."

"So, you haven't forgotten we're off to the Palais tonight, then?"

"No chance! I'm looking forward to it."

"Bad day, was it?"

Maggie groaned. "You *could* say that. I've never known the salon so busy. Eight bloody hours, an' I never even got a proper chance to sit down. Honest to God, Kathy, I don't know why I'm looking forward to the Palais, 'cause I'll not be able to dance even if I'm asked. Me back aches like it's been through a wringer, and me feet feel like two over-baked puddings."

Kathy was used to Maggie's moaning. It was all part and parcel of her colorful personality. She'd met Maggie at work, when she'd come in as a replacement receptionist. Maggie's outspoken style and vibrant outfits meant she hadn't lasted long—but long enough for the two of them to become good, if unlikely, friends. "We needn't go to the Palais if you don't want?" she suggested slyly. "We could go to the chippie instead, then come back here afterward. You can help me paint that bathroom wall . . . I've been meaning to do it for ages."

"What!" Incredulous, Maggie yelped down the phone. "You asking me to help you paint the bathroom wall . . . on a Sat'day night of all things?"

"Well, if you *really* don't feel like going down the Palais, I thought it would be a good idea. Besides, I finally bought a tin of paint last week . . . that lovely lavender color I told you about. And I know I've got two brushes . . ." She smiled mischievously. "It'll be fun. What do you say?"

Maggie was shocked. "Bloody hell, Kathy, have you gone bleedin' mad or what! *You* can paint if you like, but, pudding feet or not, *I'm* off to the Palais!"

Kathy laughed out loud. "That's more like it! Now stop your moaning and get ready. Eight o'clock as usual, outside Woolies."

Maggie sounded relieved. "You and your painting. You were just having me on!"

"It worked though, didn't it?" Kathy laughed. "See you later." Eager now to be ready, she replaced the telephone receiver and nipped back up to the flat.

Kathy glanced at the clock. It was just coming up for five. "Time enough yet," she muttered. "Tea and crumpet sounds good." Leaping off the sofa, she busied herself in the tiny kitchen area, filling the kettle and switching it on. She put two crumpets under the grill.

In a matter of minutes she was seated at the table, a steaming hot cup of tea in front of her, and alongside that two golden toasted crumpets. After a moment's hesitation, she added a scraping of precious butter from her weekly ration. "It's an end-of-week treat," she told herself.

Hungrier than she'd realized, she soon devoured the crumpets. Washing them down with the tea, she cleared away and went into the bathroom, where she ran a hot bath, stripped off, and gently lowered herself into the soapy suds. It felt wonderful. "Just what the doctor ordered!" She sighed and lolled, and closed her eyes to dream about her perfect man; only to groan with disappointment when she realized there was no such thing on God's earth.

"One of these days, I might get swept off my feet by the man of my dreams," she muttered, "though I'll probably be old and gray, and he'll have no teeth!" The image in her mind made her laugh out loud.

Ready to submit to a full hour of soaking in the tub, she stretched out her legs and, draping her arms over the side of the bath, began to sing; not the rock-and-roll stuff Maggie was so fond of, but a quiet, romantic Nat King Cole song, "When I Fall in Love." It was one of her favorites. She always loved to swell her voice up to that high note. She could imagine she was Alma Cogan, in sexy high heels and one of those frilly, swingy creations.

Her romantic rendition was brought to an abrupt halt when suddenly the doorbell rang. "Oh, *now* what?"

Slipping and sliding, she struggled out of the bath, grabbing a towel to wrap around her nakedness. It was her neighbor. "There's a telephone call for you. Says it's urgent," he told her. Dripping wet and disappointed, Kathy pulled on a dressing gown, went back downstairs and took up the phone. "Hi, Maggie." She couldn't resist a tease. "Don't tell me you've changed your mind about painting the bathroom walls?"

"It's not Maggie. It's me . . . Samantha. We need to talk."

The familiar voice of her older sister instantly darkened Kathy's mood. "What do you want?" She must want something, Kathy thought. It was the only time her sister ever called her.

"It's Mother."

"What's she up to now?" Kathy's mother was a law unto herself, though she hardly ever did anything that might hurt her darling Samantha.

Now, though, Samantha sounded anxious. "It's best if you come over," she suggested hopefully. "She's about to do something very silly."

"Such as what?" Kathy no longer had much patience with her mother's selfish antics.

"Please, Kathy. Come over. I can't talk about it on the phone."

"What . . . *right now?*"

"Please! I've tried talking to her, but she won't listen."

"Good God, Sam! If she won't listen to *you*, she's hardly likely to listen to me, is she?"

"If you don't help me, I won't be responsible for my actions. I mean it!"

Kathy had never heard her sister so frantic. "Where are you now?"

"At Mother's house."

"Does she know you've asked me to come over?"

"She *wants* you to. Be quick as you can. I just can't deal with it."

Kathy was intrigued. "All right. I'll be there soon as I can. Now if you don't mind . . . I'm soaked through and catching my death of cold."

When a moment later she replaced the receiver, Kathy leaned for a minute on the wall by the telephone. "What the devil are they up to now?" There was no telling with those two . . . one was every bit as devious as the other.

Back in the flat, she quickly dried herself off. After pulling on clean underwear, she then slipped on a pretty blue blouse, together with a calf-length dark skirt, which she thought made the best of her not-so-slim legs. Lastly, she pushed her tiny feet into a pair of smart brown shoes with a slender heel. A quick brush of her shoulder-length brown hair, a dab of lipstick, and she was ready; though a casual, passing glance in the mirror made her pause. "Just look at yourself, Kathy Wilson! It's time you did something worthwhile with your miserable life . . . you're losing your figure—as if you ever had one in the first place . . ." She gave a long, sorry sigh. "You've got to take a hold of yourself before it's too late."

Disillusioned, she turned away. "It's time you stopped pretending. You're in your mid-thirties and you've lost your way." It was a sobering thought.

Before leaving she gave Maggie a call. "I'll try not to be late," she promised, "but Samantha just rang. Apparently Mother's up to her antics again."

There was a pause before Maggie asked what the problem was.

"I don't know," Kathy confessed. "Samantha wouldn't say over the phone, but it sounds like trouble! I should let her stew in her own juice, but she was frantic. I'd best go and see what's happened. Like I say, I'll try and get to you on time, but if I'm not there by ten past eight, go on without me and I'll catch up."

Maggie was none too pleased, but agreed, with one reservation. "I don't like going on without you, so I'll give it a good half-hour."

"Okay." Kathy had a bad feeling about getting involved in whatever was happening between her mother and sister. "I'll be as quick as I can," she vowed. "Maybe Samantha's got it all wrong." Somehow though, she didn't think so.

When Kathy reached her mother's house, the dark mood was still on her. Even as she clambered off the bus, she was unsure about being here at all. It didn't feel right. It never did. But her instincts told her there was something going on that she should know about. So, putting all her doubts aside, she strode determinedly down the street.

A pretty four-bedroomed place, her parents' house was in a nice part of Kensington, situated in a tree-lined road where the houses sat well back amongst beautifully tended gardens; though if Kathy's memory served her right, her mother had never lifted one finger to the soil. Her father, Robert, was the one who had loved the garden, but since he'd been gone her mother had paid a man to come along once a week to tend and maintain the grounds.

Approaching the house, Kathy took a minute to consider

if she was doing the right thing. She came to a halt, her troubled gaze looking toward the house. She felt small and insignificant. She had lived in this house with her parents for many years—some of them good, some of them not so good. Her mother was a formidable woman; not the easiest creature in the world to get on with.

For one heart-stopping minute as she glanced toward the house, she could see her father standing on the doorstep, waving a welcome, his smile enveloping her like sunshine after rain.

In that moment of deep emotion, she turned away. Suddenly, to face her mother now seemed too much of an ordeal.

*"Kathy!"* Samantha had been watching for her.

Kathy looked up. Having seen her turn away, Samantha had opened the window and shouted. It was enough. Reluctantly, Kathy started toward the house.

As she approached the front door it was flung open by a woman in her late thirties, tall, slim and with her dark hair swept up in a handsome swirl. "I'm glad you didn't go away," she said accusingly. "I've done the best I can but she's impossible. I hope *you* can talk some sense into her!"

Propelling Kathy into the living room, she deposited her before the hostile stare of the older woman. "Speak to her, Kathy. Tell her she's being selfish." Digging Kathy in the back, Samantha urged, "Go on, Kathy! She won't listen to a word I say."

"I probably won't listen to *you* either, Kathy my dear, but I suppose you might as well have your say." Her mother's sharp brown eyes rested curiously on Kathy's upturned face. "Whatever you have to say won't make the slightest difference."

Out of the same mold as Samantha, Irene was taller and slimmer than Kathy. With her smooth auburn locks, bobbed by the most expensive hairdresser in town, and those exquisitely painted brown eyes, she was unnervingly attractive. Her fingers dripped with expensive jewelry, bought by Kathy's father over many years. She was magnificent yet intimidating: a woman you either admired or avoided. Bathed in a cloud of perfume, she had style and confidence, and today was no different. Dressed in a smart light-brown two-piece with straight skirt and fitted jacket, she was obviously ready to go out.

Kathy's thoughts were of Maggie and how she had promised to be as quick as she could. "I don't know what's going on here," she said, "and to tell you the truth I don't really care. I only came because Samantha was frantic . . . she said that I should get over here right away." Seeing her mother in all her glory, Kathy felt foolish. "The way she was going on, I thought you might be about to kill yourself!"

Irene laughed out loud. "Really? And you came to rescue me, is that it?"

When she trained her brown eyes on you as she did now on Kathy, there was something chilling about her manner; some fearful coldness that froze your heart. "All the same, it's as well you're here."

Kathy didn't trust her. "What game are you playing?"

"I don't need to play games." Her expression was calm. "I've made my decision and I'm happy with it. But there are things you both should know, and as I told Samantha, it's best that you're both here. Afterward, for all our sakes, I hope there'll be an end to it."

Moving through the haze of sweet-smelling perfume, she walked across the room to the dresser. "She's getting married!" Samantha whispered fiercely. "I didn't even know she was *seeing* anybody." Samantha was concerned only about one thing. "When you marry, isn't it true that everything you've got becomes half-owned by the other person? Where does that leave us, that's what *I* want to know."

"Married!" Shutting her ears to Samantha's rantings, Kathy felt as though she'd been knocked to the ground. "But she *can't!* It's not long enough . . . since Dad . . ." It was a shock, and for a minute she couldn't get to grips with it.

Returning with a small leather document case, Kathy's mother laid it face down on the table close to her. Turning to Samantha, she told her, "You're right, of course. When I marry, things are bound to change. You thought you would be getting all my jewelry after I was gone, and as for you,

Kathy—" Bestowing a generous smile on Kathy, she went on, "I know it was your father's dearest wish for you to have this house, but the truth is, I have other plans for it. Everything I shared with your father will be got rid of: house, furniture, even the jewelry he gave me. It's only fair on my new husband that I make a clean sweep."

Kathy had never cared about what might come to her after her parents were gone, but she had adored her father, and now that he was being swiftly discarded along with the house and everything in it, she felt physically sick. "Who is he . . . this man you're about to marry?"

"You know him well," her mother said with a cool smile. "You *both* do. His name is Richard."

Samantha gave an audible gasp. "Not *Richard Lennox?*"

"Clever girl, yes, you're absolutely right."

Kathy was shocked. "But he's a terrible man. You know Daddy hated him! He tried time and again to ruin his business. He undercut his trade so much, there was a time when Dad almost went under. Then, when he was succeeding again, that man wanted to buy him out."

"Nonsense. Your father was capable of seeing anyone off. He was in merchandising long before Richard moved into the business. Besides, Richard has quite enough of his own work, without taking on anybody else's."

Samantha too was shocked by her mother's choice of man-friend. "All right! You've told us often enough how well he's done. He was a coalman and now he owns fleets of lorries and mines in the North. But it still doesn't make him decent. I can't believe you're marrying him. Good God! He must be seventy if he's a day!"

"Not quite."

"But why? You could have any man you wanted." Samantha had expected something better for her mother. "I can't believe it. How could you bring yourself to marry a man like that?"

Kathy knew straight off. "It's *money,* isn't it? You're marrying him for his money!"

"Well, why not?" Seeing the look of incredulity on Kathy's face, Irene demanded, "What's wrong with looking after my future? In another few years I'll be sixty. Oh, I know your father left me well off, and I've got that all tucked away. But it won't last forever. Anyway, I don't enjoy being alone. I need a man in my life, someone to take me out and about. I want to travel the world . . . I need the very best of everything. Unlike you poor things, I've never had to work, and I never want to. I've always been used to the finer things in life, thanks to a generous legacy left me by your great-grandfather. Then, of course, when I married your father, he wouldn't even hear of me working, and of course, I didn't mind that at all."

Savoring the moment, she went on with a calm smugness that irritated Kathy and filled Samantha with admiration. "I intend to look after number one from now on." She pointed an accusing finger at her youngest daughter. "And I'll thank you not to look at me as if I'm some kind of monster."

Samantha remained in a sulk. "I thought you cared about me, but you don't. You're nothing but a grabbing, selfish bitch. All you care about is yourself! You couldn't care less what happens to *me*."

Infuriated, Irene rounded on her. "Is it my fault if you've both made a mess of your lives? At least I stayed married long enough to see my husband off. Look at the pair of you. It's pathetic! Neither of you married. You don't even own the roofs over your heads." Waving her arms to embrace the room, she declared triumphantly, "Look at what I've got to show for my efforts. Doesn't it make you feel ashamed?"

"You cow!" Samantha's temper was a match for her mother's. "You always promised you'd look after me, and now here you are . . . walking out with everything . . . feathering your nest again, and to hell with everybody else."

"How dare you!" In two strides Irene had Samantha by the shoulders. "You're the biggest disappointment of my life. It didn't matter about Kathy making a mess of her life . . . it was only what I expected. But *you*!" Shaking her hard, she let out a torrent of abuse. "I told everyone my daughter Samantha would make something of herself, but you let me down! You humiliated me in front of all my friends. You and her—" she thumbed a gesture in Kathy's direction "—you make me sick! Failures, the both of you!"

Suppressing her anger, Kathy's calm voice cut through her mother's cruel words. "You're right," she said. "It's true our marriages didn't work out. But you're as much to blame as anyone else. Always interfering . . . nothing was ever right. Constantly picking fights with Samantha's husband and mine . . . causing no end of trouble, excluding them from family; deliberately hounding them, until in the end they had no choice but to leave us. No man on God's earth would put up with what they had to put up with."

"That's not true!" Samantha now defended her mother from Kathy's anger. "Mother's right. They were weak and cowardly, or they would have stayed with us, no matter what." Samantha had married an American GI at the end of the war in a whirlwind romance. When Samantha had refused to go to Germany with him after the war, the marriage had stood little chance.

"I'm glad they didn't stay." Irene's feathers had been ruffled but now she composed herself. "They were wrong from the beginning, those two."

"It's all in the past, Mother." Kathy could never forgive her, but there was nothing to be gained by being at each other's throats. "You said you had something to tell us?"

Looking from one to the other, Irene took a deep breath. There are things you should know—" she glanced at Kathy "—about your father." Clearing her throat, she collected the document-case papers from the table. "In here are keys and the deeds to Barden House. It's a place in West Bay, Dorset."

Her face stiffened. "I didn't even know it existed until I was looking through your father's papers. I also found letters—intimate love-letters; hordes of them—from some woman who signed herself as Liz."

Bristling with indignation, she directed her hurtful words to Kathy in particular. "The truth is, your father was not the innocent you thought he was. He and this woman apparently had an affair and, judging by those letters, it went on for some considerable time. When he was away from home— when I believed he was working—he was with her, in that house! The two of them . . . in their little love-nest!"

Shocked and confused, Kathy was stunned into silence, while Samantha began to laugh. "The old so-and-so . . . carrying on behind your back. Well, I never!"

In a gesture of disgust, Irene thrust the folder at Kathy. "What do you think of your precious father now? He wasn't the caring man you always thought he was. Instead, he was a cheat and a liar, and I want nothing that was his! Go on, take them: the house, the letters, too. They're yours. Sell the house, burn it down, I don't care."

In an almost inaudible voice, she made a confession. "I went there . . . to West Bay. I was curious. I thought maybe it was *her* he'd bought the house for . . . that she was still living there. But it seems the house stood empty for months on end before I turned up. I learned a lot when I asked about. You'd be amazed how much people know in a small place like that."

Her voice trembled with emotion. "At first I thought I might be able to sell the place. I suspected it would be a grand house, filled with expensive furniture that she'd cajoled him into buying. I was wrong. It's just a horrid, poky little place, filled with cheap, rubbishy things I wouldn't even put in my shed. The gardens are all overgrown, and the windows are already beginning to rot. I have no use for it, just like I had no use for your father."

A look of regret crossed her features. "Besides, when I took a closer look at the deeds I realized I couldn't sell it anyway . . . You see, he bought the house in your name! I was furious. I locked the deeds and letters away and tried to forget about it. Now, though, I want rid of everything that reminds me of him."

"It's not fair!" Samantha was beside herself. "What about *me?*" she demanded. "She gets a house by the coast. But what do *I* get?"

Ignoring her, Irene was intent on Kathy. "I want you to go now," she told her in a cold, quiet voice, "and don't bother coming back."

Shaken by events, Kathy looked up; at this woman who was her mother . . . her tormentor, and she felt a wave of relief that somehow it was over . . . all the pain and heartache she had endured because of this heartless creature. It was over and, for the moment, it was all she could think of.

Kathy turned to Samantha, that haughty creature who was her mother in the making. Suddenly she pitied her. "Take care of yourself, Sam," she said.

Samantha didn't answer. Instead she deliberately looked away. But it didn't matter. Not anymore.

As she stood in the hall pulling on her coat, Kathy heard her mother reassuring Samantha. "You know I would never let you down. Once I have Richard's ring on my finger, this house will be yours. It's all agreed . . . ready to be signed and sealed. I don't need it—nor my jewelry—everything your father ever bought me. I've got plenty of money tucked away, and Richard will take good care of me. The jewelry's worth a small fortune, my dear. Sell it all," she urged, "and you'll be a rich woman."

Anxious now to get away, Kathy quickened her steps, the sound of Samantha's laughter echoing in her troubled mind.

Maggie was already walking away from the spot where they were supposed to meet. Kathy picked out her distinctive black hair and yellow coat. "MAGGIE . . . WAIT!" Chasing after her, Kathy was relieved she'd caught her. The last thing she wanted right now was to be with a crowd.

Maggie was delighted to see her. "I wasn't sure whether you'd have gone straight to the Palais by now."

Kathy shook her head. "I'm not in the mood for going," she confessed. "I thought I'd come here on the off-chance you might still be waiting . . . otherwise I would have gone to the Palais and begged off."

"Well, it's a good job I waited another ten minutes, ain't it, gal?"

"I'm sorry it took so long, Maggie." As Maggie continued with her to the bus stop, Kathy drew her to a halt. "Look, Mags, if it's okay with you, I need to talk." When it came right down to it, she had no one else but Maggie to confide in.

Maggie didn't hesitate. "Okay by me." She had already noticed how anxious Kathy seemed. "What's wrong?"

Hooking her arm in Maggie's, Kathy walked her along the street. "There's that quiet little pub on Albert Street," she suggested. "We can talk there."

🐚

Being Saturday night, there were more people in the pub than Kathy would have liked. "We'd best sit over there." Maggie pointed to a table by the window; on its own and some way from the bar, it seemed an ideal place to talk. "You go and sit down. I'll get us a drink . . . half a pint o' shandy, is it, gal?" she asked. "Same as usual?"

Kathy nodded. "Thanks, Maggie."

While Kathy settled herself at the table, Maggie brought the drinks. There y'are, gal . . . get that down you."

Maggie settled in her seat, took a swig of her Babycham, and asked, "Your mother been giving you trouble again, has she?"

"You could say that. She's full of herself as usual. Planning to marry an old business rival of Dad's. She says she's lonely, but I think she's hoping he'll 'pop his clogs' soon after so she can inherit his vast fortune. The upshot is, Samantha is being given the house and everything that's worth anything."

"Well, the old cow! No wonder you're down in the dumps."

"No, Mags. You've got it all wrong." None of that mattered to Kathy. "It's not important. It isn't that I need to talk about."

Maggie pointed to the document case lying on the table. "It's to do with that, ain't it, gal?" She had seen how carefully Kathy handled the case, laying it in front of her and never taking her eyes off it.

Kathy nodded. "*She* gave it to me."

Opening the case, she drew out the house deeds, but left the letters inside. "Look at that." Handing the deeds to Maggie, she waited for her reaction.

After perusing the document, Maggie was delighted for Kathy, but confused by the meaning of it all. "It's a house!" she exclaimed. "In *your* name. But that's wonderful." Seeing that Kathy seemed a little sad, she asked lamely, "Ain't it?"

Kathy told her the whole story . . . of how her mother had taken great delight in tearing her father's memory to shreds. She told her about the house in West Bay, and the woman called Liz, and the love-letters that her mother had read and that she herself could never read. She explained how she still found it hard to believe that her father had kept a secret lover for such a long time, and that she never even suspected. "Oh, Maggie, why didn't he tell me?"

"Because he loved you, that's why." Maggie hated what Kathy's mother had done to her: whenever she came into Kathy's life she always seemed to take delight in turning it upside down. "He knew how much you loved him, and he didn't want to spoil that. Happen he thought you would think badly of him, or he felt ashamed in some way that he had the need to go outside his marriage for love and affection."

Reaching out, she laid her hand over Kathy's. "Look, gal. I know this must all have come as a terrible shock to you, but don't let it spoil all them special memories of your dad. He was a lovely man. All right! So he set up a love-nest with this 'Liz' . . . and he never told anybody, not even you. But it doesn't mean he couldn't trust you."

Kathy had already told herself all that. "I know," she said, "and I don't blame him for what he did . . . any man would if he had my mother to put up with!" The hatred of her mother trembled in her voice. "Whatever he did, *she* drove him to it, and if that was the only happiness he could find, then I'm glad for him."

When the tears began to smart in her eyes, she took a minute for the emotion to subside. "She won't spoil my memories. I won't let her."

Maggie understood. "I'm sorry, gal." Maggie's heart went out to her. "But he never stopped loving you, did he, eh? 'Cause he even bought the house in your name. That tells you summat, don't it, eh?"

Kathy had wondered about that, and she voiced her questions to Maggie. "Why would he do that? If he found happiness and comfort with this . . . Liz, why didn't he buy the house in *her* name?"

Maggie shrugged. "Who knows? Maybe she's rich and doesn't need it. But for what it's worth, I think he was trying to tell you something." She dropped her voice to a whisper. "I think he was trying to tell you how happy he was with her. I think he wanted you to have the house . . . because he hoped you might go there and maybe find the same happiness he had."

Kathy smiled. "I thought that too," she admitted. "On the trolleybus coming over, I tried to make sense of it all, and I thought the same as you: that he wanted me to have the house, because he loved it so, and because he hoped I might love it too." Close to tears, her heart swelled with love for him. "I'm not upset or angry with him," she said, "I'm just so glad he found happiness, because I know he didn't have that with Mother."

She gave a wry little smile. "It was just such a shock. I never knew he had it in him to do something like that. In a way I admire him . . . more than ever. It shows he had the guts to take the chance of happiness when he saw it."

She recalled how her mother had gone to West Bay, looking for the woman. "She said the house was a 'poky' place . . . filled with rubbishy furniture she 'wouldn't even put in her shed.' "

"Ah, well, that's your mother, ain't it, gal? If summat didn't cost a bleedin' fortune, it ain't worth having."

"Apparently there was no sign of the other woman."

Maggie laughed. "Just as well an' all, if you ask me! I reckon there'd have been a right cat-fight if them two had got together."

Kathy didn't agree. "No, Maggie. She would have kept her distance and torn her to shreds with her vicious tongue. *That's* Mother's way. And I should know, because she's done it to me often enough."

"Will you try and find this Liz woman?"

"I don't think so." Kathy shook her head. "To be honest, I

would like to," she answered, "if only to thank her for the happiness she so obviously gave my father. But, to tell you the truth, I don't think she *wants* to be found." She had given this woman a great deal of thought and had come to that conclusion. "Maybe it's best to let sleeping dogs lie."

"What will you do . . . with the house, I mean?"

"I'm not sure yet. It's all too soon." She assured Maggie of one thing. "I won't *sell* it. I couldn't do that." She thought of her father and smiled. "It would be like selling his dream."

Maggie raised her glass. "Here's to your dad," she toasted.

Kathy clinked glasses. "And his dream," she added softly.

That night, when she was all alone with her thoughts and memories, she browsed through the deeds, feeling closer to her father as she turned the worn pages. She touched the letters one by one, but didn't open them. "What was she like, Dad?" she murmured to his smiling photograph. "I would have loved to have met her."

She cradled the letters and thought of when her father was alive, and sobbed until her heart ached.

It was a long time before she fell asleep, but before she did, her mind was made up. "It's time to make some changes. I'll give up my job and go to West Bay," she murmured to herself.

And, having decided that, she felt more at peace than she had done for a very long time.

# PART TWO

July 1952

*All Things New*

# Three

IT WAS EIGHT O'CLOCK IN THE EVENING ON FRIDAY JULY 12, 1952; the sun was beginning to drop in the skies and, along the coast, a rising breeze cooled the air.

After a long drive taking some six and a half hours, Tom headed his little two-door Morris Minor into the sleepy seaside hamlet of West Bay.

Drawing into a curve alongside the road, he slipped the car out of gear and left the engine ticking over while he looked at the directions that he'd scribbled down. John Martin had stayed down here just after the war, and had recommended both the place and a guest-house. "Turn left when you come off the main road . . . follow the signs to West Bay. You'll find 'River View' on your right . . . there's a big sign at the gateway. If you come into the harbor, you've gone too far."

Looking about him, Tom took stock of his surroundings; from where he was parked he couldn't quite see the harbor, but there were seagulls everywhere, and somewhere in front of him the tops of sailing masts bobbed up and down against the skyline. There was a fishmonger's to his left and a pub to his right, but not a soul in sight. "Where the devil am I?" he wondered aloud.

Taking another look at John's instructions, he groaned. "I've missed the guest-house," he realized. "I'll have to go back."

He almost leapt out of his skin when an old man tapped on the window. "Got lost, 'ave yer, son?" With a shaggy beard, a drooping mustache and a flat cap that covered almost all the top half of his features, the man resembled an old sheep-dog. His face was weathered and jolly, and his expression endearing.

"I 'ope yer don't mind, only I saw yer lookin' at yer map." His merry blue eyes crinkled into a smile. "Where is it yer looking for?" His homely Lancastrian accent was a pleasant surprise. He obviously wasn't from around here originally.

Weary and peckish, Tom was grateful for any help he could get. "Thank you, and yes, it seems I *have* got lost." Pointing to the paper in his hand, he told the old fella, "I'm looking for 'River View,' only I seem to have missed it." Holding up the paper so the old man could see the writing, he went on, "It says here, if I can see the harbor, I've gone too far."

"I see!" Showing a row of crooked white teeth, the old fella laughed. "Well if yer looking for 'River View,' you'll be a long time afore yer find it, 'cause it ain't there no more."

Tom was horrified. "Why? What do you mean?"

"Ah, well now . . . I can see you ain't got *that* in them-there directions, so yer can think yersel' lucky to 'ave come across me. You see, whoever told you to head for that place couldn't know it were burned down three year back. Afterward, the ground was sold off, they cleared the old building and built a pub. But they do board and lodgings, if that's what yer looking for."

Tom was relieved. "Thank God for that! I'm starving hungry." He explained, "I've just driven all the way from London . . . stopped at Brownhill for drinks and a bite to eat, but I could really do with a bath and a proper hot meal." Moreover, he ached through every bone in his body.

The old fellow dashed his hopes straight off. Pursing his lips, he tutted and sighed and warned in a low, ominous voice, "They do say as folks only ever stay one night there . . . summat about—" he rolled his eyes—"*ghosts.*"

Tom laughed. "The way I feel right now, I don't think *ghosts* would worry me one bit."

Disappointed, the old chap straightened up. "Please yerself, son. Are you planning to stay a while?"

Tom nodded. "I hope to," he said. "Only, I need a few days' grace, so I can look around to find a place to rent—long-term—until I sort myself out."

"Well, I never!" The old chap gave a kind of whoop. "That's it, then! Your troubles are over."

Intrigued, Tom questioned him. "How d'you mean?"

"Why! Cliff Cottage, o' course. It's a pretty little place right atop the hill there, warm and cozy, and you'll wake up to the sound of seagulls calling and a view straight from heaven . . ." Pointing toward the far side of the harbor, he explained, "It's owned by a lady who spends most of her time in Ireland . . . or is it Scotland?" He scratched his head and pondered, but his memory wasn't what it once was. "Anyroad, now she's gone away . . . put the place up for rent, she has. I swear, you'll not get a prettier place to live, if you tramped the world twice over."

Excited, Tom got out of the car to shake his hand. "It sounds perfect!" he said. "Who do I see about renting it?"

The old man puffed out his chest. "You see *me,* son, that's who yer see. *I'm* the fella yer want!" Holding out his hand in greeting, he told Tom proudly, "The name's Jasper . . . Jasper Hardcastle. I'm working hand-in-glove with the agent. I'm entrusted with a key to the property, so I can take you there now if you've a mind?"

The old chap was so naturally friendly, Tom had taken to him straight off; in fact, he began to feel as if he'd known him for years. "Right then! It sounds good to me. You'd best climb in the car."

As they drove through the harbor and along the promenade toward the upper ground, Tom commented on the beauty of West Bay: the harbor filled with boats of every size and color, the curving promenade, and that wonderful view out to sea. "It's just what I need," he confessed. "A year or so away from the hustle and bustle of London . . . some time to myself, a place where I can get things into perspective."

"That's the very reason I came here forty-five year ago." The old fellow gave a colorful account of himself. "I lived me younger days in Darwen . . . in the North," he revealed.

"I were twenty-eight year old, been wed just a year when I lost me darling wife—pneumonia, it were." His voice dropped as though he was talking to himself. "Wicked business! She were seven month gone with our first babby."

Tom could feel his pain; it was much like his own. "I'm so sorry," he murmured.

"Aw, no!" Jasper bucked up. "It were a long time ago. But, like I were saying, I'd been to West Bay as a lad with me mam and dad . . . had the time o' me life, I did, an' I never forgot. Well, I just kinda wandered back, if yer know what I mean . . . got casual work wherever I could: helping the fishermen; serving at the pub; a bit o' gardening 'ere and there. I were a handyman then, an' I've been a handyman ever since. Helped out where I could during the war, being as I were too old to fight in it." He chuckled. "An' I've never regretted one minute of it. The more I stayed, the harder it got to leave. There's a kinda magic about the place that wraps itself around yer. Teks a hold on yer heart an' won't let go." He laughed. "Mind it don't get *you* the same way."

"Right now, I wouldn't care if it did," Tom confessed. He glanced at the old chap, thinking he looked extraordinarily well for his age, and he told him so.

"Ah, well, that's 'cause I'm allus on the go. Seventy-three year old, an' I've never once had to see the doctor . . . except to register, o' course, an' I broke a toe once but it soon mended."

"You're a lucky man, Jasper, to be so content." Tom had forgotten how that felt.

Jasper's response was a question. "You never did tell me yer name, sir?"

Tom laughed. "Well, I can tell you one thing," he chided, "it's not 'sir!' " Taking one hand off the steering-wheel, he grabbed Jasper's outstretched hand. "The name's Tom Marcus, and I'm ready for some of that 'magic' you were just talking about."

The old man pointed ahead. "There she is: Cliff Cottage; pretty as a picture."

Tom looked, and what he saw took his breath away. With thatched roof and white-painted walls festooned with masses of climbing roses of every hue and color, it looked enchanting. "My God! It's perfect!" The cottage was bigger than he had thought, and as they drew up in front of it, he could see the well-tended gardens stretching back as far as the eye could see.

Getting out of the car, Jasper led Tom through the small white gate, and along the flower-lined path. "I know this place inside out," he imparted proudly. "I tend the gardens . . . clean the windows, and last summer I painted the whole house from top to bottom."

The more Jasper told him, the more Tom thought how, like the cottage, the old fellow was amazing.

"Right then, Tom Marcus, let's see what yer think o' the inside." Taking a key from his waistcoat pocket, Jasper slotted it in the lock and, turning with a flourish, he swung open the door. "In yer go!"

Stepping back to allow Tom by, the old fellow followed, giving detailed commentary as they went from room to room. "This 'ere's the living room," he said. "Not so big, mebbe, but like I said, it's cozy and warm, and of a winter evening the glow from the fire throws out a cheer . . . an' there's a whole supply o' logs in the woodshed . . . small-chopped and neatly stacked."

Tom's gaze roved over the room; with two windows, one facing west, the other south, the light poured in and filled the room with evening sunshine. Surrounded by clean blue tiles, the fireplace contained a vase of fresh-smelling flowers. "That's my doing, is that." The old man caught the look in Tom's eye. "Picked 'em this very morning . . . must'a known yer were coming."

He gave a wink, and Tom smiled. "I bet there isn't much you *don't* know," he declared.

The furniture was good: there was a brown leather sofa on one side of the fireplace, and a matching armchair on the other. The big green rug in front of the fire set the whole room off a treat. Against the back wall stood a small oak dresser, with nothing on top but a large, round china bowl.

The curtains were of plain beige color but "expensive material," according to Jasper. "The lady had good taste," he told Tom. "A quiet soul she was," he imparted fondly, ". . . kind-hearted too." He added quietly as an afterthought, "She had *her* troubles too, poor soul." When he realized Tom was waiting for him to expand on that remark, he swiftly moved on. "Right then, son, here's the kitchen."

Tom followed dutifully, sensing that whatever the old chap had been about to say with regard to that "kind, quiet lady" he had thought better of, and that was all right by Tom. He knew from experience that, occasionally, and for whatever reason, there were some things best left unsaid.

The kitchen was small but functional: there were pretty floral curtains at the window, and a smart white kitchenette with drop-down front and glass doors at the top. On the shelf near the window there was a stack of recipes and cookbooks by favorites such as Marguerite Patten. "Used to pride herself on being an excellent cook," Jasper revealed.

Both upstairs bedrooms were finished in the same subtle colors. The largest one had a theme of green: smart pink-and-green patchwork eiderdowns, apple-green curtains to match; a dressing table and wardrobe of adequate size.

The second room was done out exactly the same, though finished in blue.

Between the two rooms was a tiny bathroom, which was small but adequate. This too was a light, airy room. Emanating from a small dish of broken blossom in the windowsill, the sweetest of fragrances filled the air.

There was soap and towels already laid out, as if Jasper really had been expecting a visitor. "The thing is," he said after Tom made the comment, "I wanted it to look nice in case I had to show anybody over." His face creased into that wonderful, homely grin. "Though, if yer happy with it, I'll not be showing nobody else, will I, eh?"

Outside, in the twilight, the garden reflected the same love and care. There was a lawn surrounded by flower-beds and corner shrubberies, a delightful summer-house and orchard farther down, and from the terrace there was the most magnificent view imaginable.

Tom stood at the end of the terrace, lost in the scenery. The endless sea shimmered and danced in the flickering light and, as the sun was beginning to dip in the heavens, the whole sky was marbled with rivers of red and yellow. "It's the most beautiful sunset I've ever seen." He could hardly tear himself away.

Raising a thumb upward, Jasper suggested mischievously, "I had a word with 'im upstairs and asked him to show yer what he could do."

Quietly smiling at Jasper's outlandish remark, Tom still had the look of wonder on his face. "I know what you mean now," he said, "about the 'magic' taking hold." Already his soul was beginning to quieten. Here, in this seemingly timeless place, he was experiencing the first real joy since the day of the tragedy.

"So, does that mean you'll stay?" Having taken a liking to Tom, Jasper wouldn't let go.

Tom didn't even hesitate. "I'll need the cottage straight away," he answered, "if that's all right? I mean . . . do you need to contact anybody . . . will the agent want to see me before I take on the tenancy? I can stay at the pub if that's the case." He hoped he wouldn't have to. Somehow he felt as though he belonged in this delightful, cozy cottage.

Jasper had no doubts. "Look, it's the weekend, and as far as I'm concerned, you're already the new tenant. There'll be time enough to tell him on Monday. I expect he'll be around to have a chat with you . . . checking you out, like . . . papers to sign, that kinda thing. But I'm sure he'll agree with me that you'll do fine. So don't you worry, son, it'll be all right."

Grinning from ear to ear, Jasper handed him the key. "I'm away now, but I'll be back in about half an hour." He began talking to himself. "Let me see, you'll need bread . . . milk too, an' tea if you take it. Oh, an' you'll want to start a fire . . . it's an old cottage . . . gets a bit chilly when the sun's gone down, even in summer. I'll need your ration book, if that's all right. Give me a list of what you'd like."

He carried on talking as he went out the door, addressing Tom in fatherly tones. "You'll find everything works . . . electric, water . . . there's a bulb gone in the back bedroom, but I dare say you'll be sleeping in the front one so it won't matter. All the same, I'll have one fitted afore you know it."

He clapped his hands and softly chuckled. "Glad to have you aboard," he said, and left whistling.

Following him to the door, Tom watched the old man walk down the hill and away out of sight. "It seems I've found a friend," he mused, "and a home." It was a good feeling.

After collecting his portmanteau from the car, he first hung up his clothes in the wardrobe: four shirts—two short-sleeved, two-long-sleeved; two pairs of trousers; a casual tweed jacket and a formal suit for the odd occasion he might need it. All the smaller items, such as underwear and every-day bits and bobs, went into the drawer beneath. Shoes and plimsolls went under the bed.

When all that was done, he emptied out the toiletries, and a few personal items, which he laid on the bed. The photo-graph of his wife and children he placed on the dressing table. That finished, he put the case on top of the wardrobe.

After taking the toiletries into the bathroom, he made his way downstairs to the kitchen.

By the time he'd boiled the kettle and found teapot and cups, the old chap was back. "If yer mekking tea, I'm gasp-ing after that long trek up the hill." He gave a cheeky wink. "I'm a glutton for me tea with a spoon o' sugar if yer please. You'll find spoons in that there drawer." Pointing to a small drawer alongside the cooker, he placed his box of goodies on the table.

Taking the items out one by one, he counted them off. "Sugar, tea, toilet roll . . . can't do without that. Now then, let's see what's next. Oh yes . . . loaf o' bread, marge, a pinta milk, and a tin of spam." Dropping the empty box to the floor, he sat in the chair and waited for Tom to bring his tea. "I reckon you've enough groceries to be going on with," he told Tom.

He gratefully accepted his mug of tea. Tom seated himself at the other end of the table. The old man slurped at his cup and wiped his mustache. Tom laughed and shook his head; Jasper was a real gem. "Where did you get all this stuff any-way? I didn't see any grocery shops down there."

The old fellow explained. "There's four shops altogether:

the fishmonger's, and next door to him the fishing-tackle shop. Then there's the baker's—she bakes her own bread every day; it's allus fresh and crusty. An' around the corner there's the little shop as stays open a bit longer. It's run by a right nice lady, name of Amy Tatler. She sells everything from matches to newspapers. By! She's been running that shop for as long as I remember. I reckon she must be even older than what I am. Fit though . . . and smart with it."

He scratched his chin, gazing up to the ceiling as if working out the years. "She never wed as far as I can mek out, but she's a kind, quiet little woman, never lets on what she's thinking. All on 'er own, she is. By! It's a crying shame . . ."

For a minute, the old chap's thoughts seemed elsewhere, before he visibly shook himself. "She pretends to close at five o'clock like the rest of 'em, but you've only to knock on the door and she's there at yer beck an' call."

Tom sensed the old man's fondness for this woman. "Sounds to me like she might be lonely?"

Jasper shook his head. "Naw! Not Amy. She knits and sews, and keeps herself busy." Again, for a fleeting minute, he lapsed into that odd silence. "I can never understand why she never got wed, though . . . She were allus a pretty woman as I recall, and even now she's pleasant to the eye, an' pleasant in nature." He shook his head. "Seems a waste, but there y'are."

Tom nodded. "You really like her, don't you?" That much was painfully obvious.

Shocked that another man had found out his secret, Jasper blushed bright pink. "Gerraway! What would *I* do with a woman at my age, eh?"

Tom said no more. He knew when to keep quiet, so for a time he sipped his tea and the old man did the same, and all that could be heard was the ticking of the mantelpiece clock, until suddenly Jasper was on his feet and slapping Tom on the back. "I'm glad the cottage found its rightful tenant." He took a piece of paper from his waistcoat pocket and handed it to Tom. "I'll be here in the mornin' to mek sure yer all right. Meanwhile, here's me address if yer should want anythin'."

"I won't, thank you all the same."

"Well, just in case, yer can find me easy enough. Yer go down the hill and over the little bridge; turn left at the pub. Yer can't go wrong. My humble little home is right at the end of George Street, next to where they park the boat-trailers."

"I'm sure I won't need to trouble you," Tom assured him. "But thanks for all your help. You're a lifesaver."

"Fine, but don't forget now . . . I'm there if yer need me. I'm a light sleeper, so just tap on the window." He laughed. "Don't tap too hard, though, or that yappy dog next door will wake the whole bloody street!"

He bade Tom goodnight and was gone.

Afterward, Tom sat at the table for a while, sipping his now-cold tea and reflecting on his actions. "I'm beginning to think I've done the right thing after all," he mused aloud. "Coming here . . . leaving it all behind."

During the lengthy journey here, he'd had nagging doubts, but they were gone now. After meeting Jasper and finding this cottage, he felt in his heart that everything would come right.

A moment later, when the sleep weighed heavy on him, he cleared away the cups, made sure the house was locked up, and went upstairs.

First, he took a long, lazy bath. Afterward he climbed into bed and was asleep almost before his head hit the pillow. It had been a busy day.

Over the coming week, Jasper was a godsend.

Tom had settled into the cottage as though he was born to it, and the two men became firm friends. Though he would have liked to cut himself off from the world, Tom knew there were practical things he must do, such as letting his bank and other agencies know his change of address, and sorting out the rental agreement for the cottage. He had thought about applying for a telephone to be installed. Having a telephone line to the outside world went against all Tom's plans—and it would be expensive. But he worried about whether he should have a line for emergencies, and for keeping in touch with his good friend Lilian and his brother Dougie. In the end he decided to wait and see. There was a payphone just down the road.

"I expect you'll want to arrange deliveries of milk and newspaper too," the old man suggested, but Tom refused that idea. "I think it would be better if I walked down to Amy's and collected them," he decided and, for once, Jasper agreed.

By the evening after his arrival in West Bay, Tom had managed to get most of the practicalities dealt with and out of the way. To celebrate, he and Jasper paid a visit to the pub, where they drank a pint of best bitter and chatted to the locals.

Afterward, Jasper introduced him to Amy. "Any friend of Jasper's is a friend of mine," she said. Tom was astonished at how tiny and vibrant she was. Looking into her deep brown eyes and noting the sunshine of her smile, Tom could understand what Jasper had said. Yes, he thought, she has a goodness that shines out. And, like Jasper, he was filled with admiration.

The next morning, Tom was up early. For whatever reason he had found it difficult to sleep. "Must have been the beer," he groaned, rubbing his stomach with the flat of his hand.

As he couldn't sleep, he got washed and dressed and made his way downstairs, where he searched the cupboards, greatly relieved to find that Jasper had allowed for all occasions. The bicarbonate of soda in a glass of water was just what the doctor ordered.

While the kettle was boiling he threw open the back door and stood watching the sun come up. "Looks like it'll be a glorious day," he murmured. Already the air was warm and the skies blue, with no hint of a cloud anywhere. "Makes a man feel good!" He had not even spent forty-eight hours in West Bay, and already he was beginning to relax.

He drank his tea, and a few minutes later he had put on his jacket and was making his way to the cliff tops. High above the world, striding through the fields and on toward the sea, he felt like a man out of his time. It was a weird and wonderful feeling.

Down below in the hamlet, Amy was sorting the newspapers, with the help of Jasper, who every morning insisted on lifting the heavy bundles as they came in. "Look!" Amy had caught sight of the man at the top of the cliff. "It's odd for someone to be walking the cliffs at this early hour, don't you think?"

Curious, Jasper looked up. "It's that Tom chap." He recognized him straight away: the long, lean figure and that mop of hair, made unruly by the wild air-currents that swirled up from the beach below. "Poor devil. Looks like he couldn't sleep."

Amy suspected that Tom was a man with troubles but, like Jasper, she asked no questions. Now, though, she was curious. "Whatever's he doing up there, at ten to six of a morning?" A terrible thought crossed her mind. "He's not going to throw himself over, is he?"

"Good God no!" Jasper chided. "What little I know of him, I wouldn't say he were the sort to throw himself over a cliff!" Though it would not be the first time a man had leaped from the cliff tops to end it all.

Jasper studied Tom for a moment longer, quietly satisfied that he would come to no harm up there. All the same, he could tell that Tom was deeply troubled; from the way he sat hunched on the boulder, so still, his head bent low to the ocean, as though deep in thought.

"What's he doing?" Like Jasper, Amy was concerned.

"He's searching, lass."

"Searching . . . for what?"

Jasper shrugged. "Who knows?" He shook his head. He wondered what might be going on in Tom's mind at that minute. He remembered the way it had been with him, and his heart went out to that young man. "He's looking for what we all want," he murmured. "Contentment . . . peace of mind, call it what yer will."

Something in his voice made Amy reach out to touch him. "Let's hope he finds it then," she said softly. "You too, Jasper."

The old man squeezed her hand. "Yer a lovely lady," he said.

She laughed at that. "Flatterer!"

Drawing away, she wagged a finger at him. "We'd best get on with these papers, or they'll not be delivered by this time next week!"

As they worked, Jasper occasionally glanced up to where Tom was, high above the world, away from all things painful. "After a time it won't hurt so much," he murmured. "It'll get easier, son, you'll see." He gave a long, shivering sigh. "Whatever it is that haunts yer, it'll get easier, I promise."

He hoped there would come a day when Tom might confide in him. After all, everybody needs a friend, he thought. As for himself, he had been fortunate in finding one in little Amy.

Up on the clifftop, Tom was oblivious to the interest he had caused. He thought about his wife and children, and he smiled. "I wish I'd brought you here to this lovely place, when I had the chance," he whispered, "but you're here in my thoughts and in my heart." Before, when he thought of them, he had found it hard to breathe for the pain, but now, when he thought of them, it was with a strange sense of joy. "I've been a lucky man."

He looked straight ahead, as though speaking to a physical presence. "I've had the love of three wonderful people, and I've shared their lives. That's something that can never be taken away."

There was something else, too, and the hatred was like a bad taste in his mouth. "You might be hard to trace, you murderous bastard!" Instinctively clutching his fist until the knuckles bled white, he spoke in a whisper. "But I'll find you and, when I do, you'll rue the day you took my family from me."

Time and again he had searched his mind for a reason, and each time he was forced to surmise that the person who ran him over that cliff-edge must have been out of his mind. But it made no difference. "Madman or fool, you took three lives that day . . . and ruined another."

A terrible sense of rage overwhelmed him. "You'll pay for it. When the time is right, I'll take up your trail and make you pay for what you did!"

He stood up and strode away, his face set hard as stone as he walked toward the cottage and a measure of sanctuary. For now he must give himself the time he so badly needed. But the day would come when he would heal. His mind would clear and he would be able to think straight.

On that day, he would set out to find the killer.

And he would not rest until he found him!

# Four

"FOR GOD'S SAKE, KATHY!" TRYING UNSUCCESSFULLY for the umpteenth time to fasten the portmanteau, Maggie sat back on her knees and groaned. "What the hell have you got in here . . . the kitchen sink?" Suddenly free of her weight, the portmanteau heaved a sigh and up popped the lid. "Oh no . . . not *again!* Throwing herself flat on the floor, arms outstretched and eyes closed, she told Kathy, "That's it, gal. I give up!"

Up to her neck in scattered clothes and half-filled boxes, Kathy threw down the saucepan she was carrying and walked across the room. Leaning over the prostrate figure of her friend, she suggested invitingly, "What say we stop for a cup of tea?"

Looking up through one weary, open eye, Maggie wanted to know, "Is there any o' that fruitcake left?"

Kathy rolled her eyes. "Oh, I dare say I can find us a piece . . . but only *if* you can stop swearing and moaning long enough to eat it!"

Maggie scrambled up. "Go on then, gal. Go to it."

While Kathy busied herself at that, Maggie made another attempt to close the portmanteau lid, whooping and hollering when it finally clicked into place. "But *you* can carry it down the stairs!" she warned Kathy as they sat at the table with their tea and cake. "I've got a date on Thursday." She chuckled naughtily. "I'd rather not turn up ruptured . . . if you know what I mean?"

Kathy gave her a warning in return. "As long as you don't end up *pregnant* instead!"

Maggie was indignant. "No chance. I'm not *that* stupid!"

"All the same, be careful. You know as well as I do . . . blokes are only ever out for one thing."

"Not this one."

Replacing her empty cup on the table, Kathy was curious, "Who is he, then?"

"Just a bloke." Shrugging her shoulders, Maggie bent her head to the tea in front of her.

Realizing, Kathy groaned. "Oh, Maggie! It's not that cunning devil who kept bothering you the last time we were at the Palais, is it? The one who kept combing his hair and winking every time you turned round?"

Maggie went on the defensive. "It might be."

Sitting back in her chair, Kathy sighed. "Maggie! Maggie! Will you never learn?"

Wide-eyed and accusing, Maggie stared back at her. "What's wrong with him, that's what *I'd* like to know?"

"Well, for starters, he's vain and arrogant, and for another, didn't you see his snidey 'mates,' sniggering and carrying on behind him?"

*"So?"* Now she was really on the defensive.

Undeterred, Kathy spelled it out. "So . . . they were egging him on. You said that yourself." She was convinced. "I reckon he's trying to get off with you for a bet."

"I asked him that and he denied it," Maggie answered sulkily.

"Oh, did you now?" This was something Kathy had not been aware of. "So, you thought the same, did you? You never told me."

Maggie didn't like being cornered. "All right, it did cross my mind that he just might be trying it on for a bet, but he wasn't." Leaning forward, she gave Kathy one of her "leave me alone" stares.

Kathy got the message. "Okay, I won't say another word."

"Good!" Sighing loudly, she told Kathy, "I really like him. Anyway, I know how to look after myself."

"Fair enough." Not wanting to upset her, Kathy backed off. "Just be wary, that's all I'm saying." Her own mistake with Geoff was in her mind.

Secretly, Maggie still had her own doubts about her date,

but she was feeling lonely already, and Kathy hadn't even gone yet. "What about *you?*"

"What d'you mean?"

"Are you sure you're doing the right thing?"

Kathy gave a half-smile. "No."

"Then don't do it."

"It's too late now. I've broken it off with Geoff, I've left my job, my flat's been rented out to someone else and, thanks to you, I'm already packed." Glancing at the portmanteau, she laughed. "If it bursts open on the train, I'll pretend it's not mine."

At that, Maggie laughed with her, before making a serious suggestion. "If you change your mind, you know they'll give you back your job, because they said so. And you can always bunk in with me until you find another flat."

Kathy thanked her, but, "This is something I have to do, Mags," she replied thoughtfully. "I believe that house at West Bay was left to me for a purpose. Dad wanted me to have it, and I need to go there."

"Well, yes, I understand that, but why can't the pair of us go together . . . just for a week, to get the lay of the land. There's no need to throw away everything, not when you're not sure what you might be walking into."

Kathy didn't see it that way. "We've been through all this, Mags, and I'm still determined to go . . . though I wish you were coming with me, at least for a holiday." Lowering her voice, she tried to explain how she felt. "I've no family to speak of . . . except you. I work hard and pay my bills and sometimes I can't see the point of it all. I'm not happy, Mags . . . I haven't been since Dad . . . well, not for a long time, and what with Mother always on my back, and Samantha whining and moaning at every little thing, I think I'd have gone crazy if it wasn't for you."

"But look, Kathy . . . packing up and moving to a strange place . . . to a broken-down old house you've never even seen?" Pausing, she let the words sink in. "It's such a drastic step."

Kathy was unmoved. "But I've got nothing to lose." She gave a smile that was meant to put all Maggie's doubts aside. "I'll be all right, you'll see."

Maggie was still not convinced. "It's just plain daft if you ask me! Look at what you're doing. You've got two weeks' wages and a week's holiday pay, and a few savings—that ain't gonna last long, is it? And from what your mother told you about the place being 'derelict,' you could be walking into a right dump."

Kathy laughed. "Don't exaggerate."

Maggie persisted. "But how do you know, eh? You haven't even seen it. What if it's so bad you can't even live in it, then what? All right, you could check into a hotel, but then your money will be gone faster than you can catch the next train back . . . that's *if* you've got the fare."

She was desperately worried. "Think again, Kathy. Give me a few days and I'll get time off to go with you. It's at the coast so there must be caravans there. We'll rent one for a week and get the house sorted out at the same time. It'll be fun. Oh, Kathy! Say you will?"

Kathy was half tempted, but on reflection her resolve hardened. "My mind's made up. I'm catching the half past ten train and I'll call you when I get there." She loved Maggie and didn't want her worrying. "Look, if you like you can still ask for time off and follow me down. I'd like that."

"I'm not staying in no 'derelict' house, though!" Maggie was adamant. "I'm not as daft as you."

Kathy laughed. "No, you're dafter, or you wouldn't be going out with that bloke."

Maggie gave her a playful thump. "We'll see."

Kathy asked hopefully, "Do you think you *will* be able to get time off?"

"I'll have a damned good try."

Returning to stand the case on its end, she groaned when trying to lift it. "Like I said . . . I'm not carrying this thing down the stairs."

"Stop moaning, *you* don't have to," Kathy explained. "I've ordered a taxi. The driver can take it down the stairs, and the porter will carry it for me at the station."

Maggie gave a sigh of relief. "Thank God for that. Let *them* get the ruptures!"

There was still a lot more to do before the taxi arrived.

"These are the boxes to be collected for the charity shop." Kathy closed the last box. "And the rest is to be left for the landlord." Pointing to a piled-up sofa, she told Maggie, "He paid me a few bob to leave all the curtains, bedding, rugs and towels . . . oh, and a few ornaments I don't have use for. He wants to keep it all for his next tenant."

Maggie tutted. "Tight git! You'd think he'd at least get some new stuff."

Kathy agreed, but said, "He's tight-fisted with his money. That's why he's rich and we're not."

"No, it's not," Maggie retorted. "He's rich because he bought two houses along the street for next to nothing, and made them into eight flats." She pulled a face that made Kathy laugh out loud. ". . . *And* because he's a tight git!"

"You're right." Kathy had to agree. "We'd best get a move on or I'll miss the train." She began checking each room. "Best make sure everything's all right before we leave," she told Maggie. "I don't want him to think I keep an untidy, dirty place."

Maggie followed her. "If he wants to see untidy—" she was not surprised to note that every room was neat and clean as a new pin—"he'd best come and see *my* place."

They were startled when a man's voice boomed out behind them, "Taxi for the station. Would that be you two?" A large man with a beer-belly and a thick, gruff voice filled the doorway. "Well? Did you order a taxi or didn't you? I ain't got all day."

"It's me." After the initial shock of this big man with the booming voice, Kathy leapt into action. "If you could please take the portmanteau down, I need to collect a few things. I'll be right behind." She straightened her jacket and picked up her hat and gloves from the side.

As he walked toward the portmanteau, Maggie dodged into the bedroom. Without delay, Kathy followed, the pair of them peeping around the corner as he lifted the article. "Jesus, Mary and Joseph! What the bloody hell's she got in 'ere?"

"See, I told you it was heavy!" Digging Kathy in the ribs, Maggie was bursting to laugh. "I bet you've ruptured the poor devil!"

Red-faced and grunting, he carried it across the room and out the door, moaning and groaning as he bounced it down one step after another. "I wish he'd be careful," Kathy declared as they emerged from their hiding-place. "He might break it."

"Yes, and he might 'break' your bleedin' neck if you say anything."

A knock on the door announced the arrival of the charity people to collect the boxes. "Every little helps," the bottle-blond said with a grateful smile. "We have all kinds of people who come into the shop and buy this kind of bric-a-brac."

Maggie had a naturally suspicious nature. "If you ask me, they were a dodgy pair!" she said as they left. "I bet you they'll be straight around the market and flog the bleedin' lot."

"Don't be so cynical," Kathy chided. "These people do a good job."

Maggie didn't answer: she knew what she knew and that was that.

As the two of them left the house, the irate driver rounded on Kathy. "I hope you realize this meter's ticking?" he asked pointedly. Before she could answer, he grabbed Kathy's bag and threw it in the back. "I recall somebody saying they had a train to catch, and it won't be my fault if she misses it!"

Behind him, Maggie was laughing.

When it was time to leave, Kathy hugged her friend tight. "I'll call you when I get there," she promised. "Remember what I said . . . take care of yourself."

Maggie's bottom lip began to tremble. "You too," she muttered. "I'll ask for time off, so's I can come and help you settle in."

As Kathy climbed into the taxi, Maggie apologized. "I really should be coming to the station with you."

Kathy dismissed her worries. "There's no use you coming with me," she said. "I'll be on the train as soon as ever I get there. Besides, you've had three warnings about being late already."

"Hmh! She's just a frustrated old cow."

As the driver pulled away, Kathy saw how down Maggie was. "Stop worrying," she called out the window. "I'll be all right."

Maggie waved her out of sight. "I'll miss yer, gal." Thrusting her hands into her jacket pocket, she turned to look up at the flat, bowed her head, and walked away. "That old cow had best let me have time off," she muttered. "I need to know that Kathy's all right."

She quickened her step, the merest whisper of a smile beginning to wipe away the misery. "First, though, I've a date coming up, and a new frock to buy." With that in mind, she headed straight for the nearest shop. It was the surest thing to take her mind off her troubles.

The minute the taxi stopped, Kathy was given her first instruction. "If yer think I'm lifting that portmanteau again, you've another thought coming," the taxi driver growled. "So, if you want to catch that train, you'd best find a porter . . . and make sure he's built like a navvy, or he'll never lift the damned thing."

Giving him a hard look, Kathy ran off to see if there was a porter about. She eventually found one, but he was built more like a nanny than a navvy. "Huh! Is that the best you could do?" the taxi driver asked Kathy in a loud, insulting voice. Addressing the porter, he gave a snide little grin. "If you can lift that out of the boot, I'll not charge her a penny fare."

The porter winked knowingly at Kathy, then he glanced into the open boot at the huge portmanteau. "It's a deal," he said. Walking from side to side, he took a moment or two to mentally assess the size and weight of the article.

"Go on then!" the big man urged with a nasty chuckle. "It won't leap out the more you look at it." He thought the porter was a bad joke.

As for Kathy, her bet was on the porter. At least he *seemed* confident.

With Kathy on one side and the big man on the other, the

little porter took hold of each corner and, easing the port-manteau forward, got it to the edge of the boot. "The bet's only on if you *lift* it out!" the big man grumbled. "Dropping it off the edge onto the barrow don't count."

The porter never said a word; instead he looked up at the taxi driver with a disdainful stare. Then he spat into the palms of his hands, rubbed them together, and with one mighty heave lifted the portmanteau in the air. With immense courage he held it aloft for the slightest moment, before dropping it thankfully to the barrow.

By this time, Kathy was leaping and dancing about. "HE DID IT!" she cried. "He *lifted* it out, and I don't owe you a fare." In a mad moment of triumph she vigorously shook the porter by the hand, until she remembered how he'd spat into it. Discreetly wiping it on her skirt, she thanked him. "Even I didn't think you could do it," she apologized lamely.

"You'd be surprised at what we're asked to lift," the porter revealed proudly. Glancing at the big man, he made a suggestion. "A tenner says I can lift *you* straight off your feet!"

The other man's answer was a rude gesture, and the quickest exit from the station the porter had ever witnessed.

A moment later, after Kathy got her ticket, she and the porter headed toward the train, which had just pulled into the station. "I'd best get this on board for you," he suggested. "We don't want you doing an injury to yourself, do we?" He was also thoughtful enough to get a promise from the attendant that he would take it off at the other end.

Slipping him a generous tip, Kathy thanked him, and he wished her good day.

Once on the train, she settled into her seat. "I'm on my way," she murmured, "West Bay, here I come!" Even though she was somewhat nervous, there was still a sense of great excitement. After all, as she constantly reminded herself, she was about to start a whole new life.

The train went straight through from London to Weymouth. Throughout the long journey, she read snatches of the newspapers left by previous passengers, and occasionally struck up desultory conversations with passengers nearby. She bought two drinks from the trolley that was pushed lazily up and down by some weary woman—and had to run to the loo a couple of times for her troubles.

On the final leg of the journey, she gazed out the windows at the scenery, wondering about the house in West Bay and the woman who had shared it with her father. Several times she murmured the name "Liz," and each time she had a different image in her mind.

Finally she fell asleep, waking only when the conductor alerted her that they had arrived at Weymouth Station.

After disembarking, she secured another porter. He told her the best way to get to West Bay was by bus to Bridport and taxi, although, "I reckon you've already missed the last one." Luckily she hadn't: at the information desk she was relieved to hear, "The last bus is about to leave in ten minutes." The clerk pointed her in the right direction, and the bus conductor took charge of her trolley and portmanteau—though he had a word or two to say when lifting the portmanteau into the hold—and soon Kathy was off on the last leg of her adventure.

Dropped off in the town of Bridport, Kathy had to travel the final mile or so in a taxi. "Barden House, you say?" The driver knew the house. "Used to take a gentleman there . . . *he* was from London, too." Much to Kathy's astonishment he went on to describe her father. "Though I haven't seen him this past year or so," he said. "There was a woman—his wife, I expect—lovely lady, or so they say. I never met her myself. It seems the house is empty now . . . in need of some tender loving care." He smiled at her through his mirror. "Sorry to be going on a bit, you must be tired after your journey. I'm afraid idle gossip goes with the job."

Kathy assured him she was interested. "I'll be staying at the house," she told him.

They chatted all the way to West Bay. Kathy didn't learn

any more; except that her father would turn up every now and then, and after a while he would leave. When the taxi came to collect him, the woman would wave from the window apparently, but she never came out. "They do say as how she was a shy little thing."

Kathy did not enlighten him as to her identity. It was better that way, she thought.

By the time they got to West Bay, the sun had gone down. The first sighting she got of the house was when they turned the corner and he declared, "There she is, Barden House. Looking a bit more tired than the last time I saw her."

He drew up and got her portmanteau out of the boot. "Looks like you've got your work cut out, Miss," he said, casting his eye over the run-down garden. "Shame. It's such a lovely house an' all."

Kathy wasn't listening. Having got out of the taxi, she stood gazing at the house, through her own eyes and, inevitably, through the eyes of her father. Bathed in the soft light of a nearby street-lamp, the house gave off a warm, welcoming feel: even though, as the driver said, the paint was peeling off the window-sills and the garden resembled a jungle, the house was pretty as a picture.

In the half-light it was impossible to see the extent of disrepair, but the house seemed strong, square in structure, with wide windows and a deep porch. Myriads of climbing flowers had grown over the porch, their many tentacles drooping down either side, like two arms embracing. Kathy thought there was a peculiar enchantment about the place.

Now that she was really here, actually *here,* at the house where her father and his love had hidden away from the world, Kathy began to realize the happiness he must have found here.

Her thoughts were shattered when the taxi driver exclaimed, "How in God's name did you manage with *this!*" Puffing and panting, the driver half-carried, half-dragged the portmanteau to the front door. "It weighs a ton."

Apologizing, Kathy got the house-key from her bag and opened the front door. "Just drop it inside, if you don't mind," she asked. "I'll be fine now."

When the front door swung open, the musty smell wafted out to greet them. "You'd best get the place checked out for damp," the driver suggested. "Being close to the water an' all, you never know."

Fumbling for the light-switch, Kathy groaned when there was no response. "Maybe the bulb's gone," she said hopefully.

"I wouldn't like to say." The driver also tried the switch, to no avail. "The house has been empty a long time. They've probably cut off the electric. Water, too, I should imagine."

Going back to the car for a torch, he tried every switch downstairs and still there was nothing. "There's a guest-house back down the road a bit," he suggested. "If you ask me, you'd be better off booking in there, at least until you can get the electric back on." He shivered as the damp took a hold of him. "You can't stay here," he said, "you'll catch your death o' cold."

Kathy was torn: she wanted so much to stay in the house, yet she knew the driver was right. It *was* chilly, even in July, and the electric was definitely off. Even if she stayed the night, she wouldn't be able to sleep for the cold, and in the morning there would be no hot bath. Besides, she didn't know if there were clothes on the bed, or clean sheets anywhere; if there were, would they be damp and moldy? "I should have traveled overnight," she muttered. "At least I could have got things sorted out in daylight."

Checking in at a guest-house was the only solution as far as she could see, but it was not what she wanted; anyway, she didn't have money to throw away on such luxuries. It was a dilemma and, the more she thought about it, the more she was tempted to stay in the house, however cold and uncomfortable.

Suddenly, Maggie's remark came into her mind. "It's the seaside, ain't it? There's bound to be caravans."

Excited, she asked the driver, "Is there a caravan site around here?"

He nodded. "As a matter of fact, yes, there is . . ." He realized her line of thinking and approved. "I'll take you there. It's just the other side of the harbor."

He was about to trundle the portmanteau back to the car when Kathy had an idea. "If you'll lend me your torch for a minute, I'll take only what I need for tonight."

So, while he went to turn the car round, Kathy opened the portmanteau. She took out a clean set of undies, which she thrust into her bag, and grabbed the toiletries bag. Then she shut the portmanteau and was hurrying down the path in no time.

Passing the harbor, with the boats shifting about and the water making patterns in the moonlight, Kathy thought how beautiful it all was. "I can see why you were happy here, Dad," she murmured.

"What did you say?" The driver strained his ears.

"Nothing," Kathy answered. "I was just thinking out loud."

"First sign of madness," he said, making her smile.

Turning into the caravan park, he asked if she wanted him to wait. "If they've got nothing for you, I can take you on to the guest-house?" Thinking it was a sensible idea, Kathy readily agreed.

As it happened, the clerk at the desk was most helpful. "We've a canceled booking," she told Kathy, "but I'm not sure if the manager will let the van out for just one night . . . in case we have a last-minute request for a long booking." All the same, she went away to find him, and when she returned a few minutes later her quick smile and easy manner told Kathy she was in luck. "He says we're not likely to get any other customers tonight, so he'll take your booking."

While the clerk got the necessary information together, Kathy went out to the driver and paid him. "You've been a great help, thank you."

He wished her well. "I know a few useful blokes," he told her. "Painters, plumbers and such." He scribbled down his name and address. "Jack of all trades, that's me," he said, before he drove off into the night.

The clerk gave her the keys, a long form to sign and a small cardboard box, sealed over with a length of sticky tape. "You'll find everything you need in there," she advised. "One night . . . leaving tomorrow at ten a.m." She laboriously scribbled it all into her ledger. "You'll have to pay in advance, I'm afraid," she said apologetically.

Kathy handed over the money, thanked her.

"I'll take you down there," the girl said, "seeing as it's dark." Grabbing a torch, she led Kathy out of the office, along a lamp-lit, meandering path, through rows of cara- vans. There, right at the top, stood number eighteen; the number clearly highlighted by the two gas lamps either side of the door.

Once inside the caravan, the girl bustled around, lighting the gas mantels. Staring around at what she could see, Kathy was delighted. In front of her was a tiny kitchen with cooker, and to her left there was a comfortable living area, with seats all around the bay window, and a little table jutting out from the wall. The curtains were bright and cheerful; candy stripes on white in the kitchen; and splashes of flowers against a yellow background elsewhere. To the right a door led into a cozy bedroom. In here, too, the curtains were of a bright, colorful fabric, the same, exactly, as the corner of the eiderdown peeping out. "Oh, it's lovely!" Kathy exclaimed. "Thank you," she said to the clerk.

"My pleasure," the girl replied. "I'll leave you to it, then." She hurried out, back into the night.

Kathy gazed around once more, thrilled with her good fortune. Suddenly realizing she'd had little to eat since early morning, she felt her stomach turning somersaults. Drop- ping her toiletries and undies onto the bed, she went out, clicking shut the door behind her. "There *must* be a chip shop," she mused. "It can't be proper seaside without a fish- and-chip shop." After all, there were all those fishing-boats in the harbor.

The clerk put her mind at rest. "Go down this road—" she pointed to the road on the right—"you'll find a chip shop on your left." As Kathy walked out the door, she called out, "Or you can get a roll at the bar here."

Kathy declined with thanks. "I really fancy fish and chips." With mushy peas and a few bits of pork crackling, she thought, licking her lips in anticipation.

As she rounded the corner, she saw a telephone box. "I

wonder if Maggie's back from the Palais?" That was where she planned to spend this evening, Kathy recalled.

One by one, she dropped the coins into the box. The operator took the number, but eventually told her there was no answer. "She's probably still on the town with her new fella," Kathy mused, disappointed, as she pressed button "B" to get her coins back.

The farther she got down the street, the more Kathy could smell the fish and chips. "That'll do for me," she muttered, quickening her steps. At that minute, for many reasons, she wished with all her heart that Maggie was here.

There was a queue in the shop. "It's a ten-minute wait if you want cod," the woman told her as she came in the door. "Dabs and fish-cakes are quicker."

Kathy assured her she was willing to wait. "I'm in no rush."

From some way behind in the queue, Tom studied her for a minute. With her face turned slightly away it was difficult to see her features clearly, but he suspected she was very pretty, with that handsome profile and thick, shoulder-length hair. In the short time he'd been in West Bay, Jasper had managed to introduce him to quite a number of people, despite his efforts to keep himself to himself, but he could not recall this particular young woman. His suspicion that she was a new arrival was confirmed when the woman in front of her asked, "You're visiting West Bay, are you? Only, I saw you getting out of the taxi earlier."

Kathy told her that, yes, she *was* a stranger in West Bay. "But I hope I'll be staying for a while." In fact, once she was settled, it was Kathy's intention to seek work. It was the only way she would be able to pay for the many repairs the house obviously needed.

The queue moved swiftly on. Kathy got her fish and chips and walked away. Dipping into the bag, she wolfed down a chip, which was so hot it nearly burned her mouth out. "Be careful," Tom warned her with a disarming smile. "The chips are always straight out of the fat and scalding hot."

Kathy laughed, a wonderful free laugh that made others turn round. "Serves me right," she answered. "It'll teach me not to be so greedy." When his dark eyes smiled down on her, she felt a rush of embarrassment. *Lord, he's handsome,* she thought. *Maggie would be chatting him up if she was here.*

As she walked on by, Tom was shocked to his roots. "My God!" Swinging around to watch her leave, he realized he had seen her twice before. This was the same woman who had risked life and limb when she ran out in the street to hail a taxi. The second time he had seen her had been in the churchyard. He could hardly believe it. "It can't be!" It was inconceivable. And yet here she was again, passing so close to him he could have touched her.

It was unnerving, to say the least.

Deciding to take a walk along the harbor, Kathy was unaware that she had caused such chaos in Tom's mind, though she was inevitably curious about him. Once or twice she glanced back, smiling. "What's wrong with you, Kathy Wilson?" she chided herself. "Anyone would think you'd never seen a good-looking bloke before."

Munching on her chips, she sauntered over the bridge and on toward the house, where she sat on the garden wall, legs dangling, her quiet eyes taking note of everything: the peeling window-sills, the beautiful solid wood door with its deep-etched panels, and the garden in the foreground with its cavalcade of weeds and giant thistles. "So much work!" she groaned. "So much money!"

She must decide how to tackle it, what was urgent, and what could wait until she could afford to get it done.

For a long time she sat there, thinking and calculating and trying desperately to draw a picture in her mind of her father and the woman, Liz. "A shy little thing," the taxi driver said, ". . . waved him goodbye from the door."

Kathy was glad her father had found love and contentment, even if it was only from time to time. "I don't blame you, Dad, for wanting to get away from Mother," she whispered. "I'm glad you found someone who treated you right . . . somebody who loved you the way you deserved to be loved."

A sense of peace took hold of her and for a long minute

she was quiet, contemplating her own future. "I know why you gave me this house," she murmured. "You wanted me to be happy here . . . and maybe, just maybe, to find love." She smiled. "Already, London seems a long way off. That day, when I took flowers to the churchyard, I had no idea what was in store. I knew nothing about what you'd done . . . this house, and the fact that you had left it to me in your will."

She chuckled. "You should have seen Mother's face when she handed the deeds over . . . I think she'd rather have been handing me a poisoned chalice. And Samantha! What a terrible fuss *she* made. In the end she got what she wanted— they both have. Mother's getting wed, secretly hoping he'll pop his clogs and leave her a rich widow, and Samantha's been promised the house, and all Mother's jewelry. What do you think to *that,* eh?"

A quietness came over her, a kind of resignation. "I might be divorced and nearly broke, and you've left me a house that needs money spent on it, but I'm richer than either of those two will ever be." Kathy truly believed that. "Thank you for this lovely house, Daddy," she murmured. "I'll look after it, I promise. I'll get it done up and make it my home." With a sense of abandonment, she threw out her arms. "I'll probably stay here for the rest of my life."

Overwhelmed, she gave vent to her emotions, the tears rolling down her face. "I feel close to you here, but, oh, I do miss you so. I don't suppose you'll ever know how much."

From a distance, Tom heard the tail end of her words. Listening to her emotional, one-way conversation he recognized a kindred spirit. "She's just a lost soul . . . much like yourself," he muttered.

Quietly, not wishing to be seen, he went away, back to his cottage and his own company.

That was the way he preferred it.

Not yet ready to return to the caravan, Kathy took a leisurely stroll around the harbor. Leaning on the railings, she finished off her fish and chips and watched the boats in the water. There was something incredibly soothing about watching the water, and here it was like she had never seen before. Where the harbor outlet tapered down to a narrow funnel, the trapped water thrashed against the high walls, moaning and fighting as if trying to escape.

Just now, one of the late fishermen started his boat's engine and headed it toward this turbulent funnel of water. As it traveled the short distance before it came out into open sea at the other end, the little boat was swayed and pushed dangerously close to the high walls. In the end, though, the fisherman skillfully negotiated the waters, and a few minutes later he was headed for the fishing sites, his lights low and his engine running softly.

Having a fear of deep water, Kathy was filled with admiration.

When the boat was out of sight she screwed up her fish-and-chip paper and tossed it into the nearest bin. After a long, lingering glance at the house, she returned, slightly reluctantly, to the caravan.

Less than an hour later, after a quick wash, she was undressed and in her newly made bed. Moments later, she was fast asleep, wearied by the long journey, and the emotional turmoil of seeing the house, in what she believed was a private moment. If she had realized someone had overheard, albeit innocently, she would have been mortified.

Not far away, in his cottage on the hilltop, Tom was pacing the floor. He couldn't sleep. His mind was too full of thoughts, too active. Kathy had somehow brought back memories of his wife, and now he could not rid himself of everything else that went with it: the guilt, the belief that he should have tried harder to save them, the agony of knowing he would never see them again. Yet even while he tortured himself, he knew he had done everything humanly possible on that day. Thinking about it now merely hardened the rage inside him. He wanted revenge. He could taste it.

But he wasn't ready yet. Now, just when he thought he was almost on top of it, when he was beginning to feel the time was almost right, his thinking had been thrown into turmoil. By this troubled woman, a pretty stranger who had intruded in his life as though for a purpose.

This evening, after he had inadvertently caught the end of her heartfelt outpourings, he had known her presence here had nothing to do with him. He felt foolish for ever having thought it might be.

All the same, she had unearthed something deep inside him, something he had tried hard not to acknowledge. Feelings of loneliness and need. The normal, manly feelings that were stirred by the sight of a warm, beautiful woman. For a long time now he had felt like half a man. Kathy's touching words, her open, infectious laughter had only made him realize how lonely he really was.

But what a strange coincidence, he thought, to have seen her three times; twice in his native London, and now here, in this quiet, tucked-away place where he had sought refuge.

Beyond sleep for the moment, he put on his jacket and went out into the night. Up here, out on the cliffs, there were no lamps to light the way, only the moonlight, which hung low in the clearest of skies, shining down like some kindly beacon to guide his footsteps.

Picking his way through the low bracken, he went softly along the well-trodden path toward the cliff-edge, and down, side-stepping, half-climbing, half-sliding, to the bottom. Once he was down on the promenade, he cut around by the wall and onto the beach, almost all of which was now swallowed by the incoming tide. The sound of surging water sang in his ears, and the familiar tang of salt air stung his nostrils.

For a time he walked the beach as he had paced his room: frantic; driven by the same demons that had brought him here. With the sea lapping at his feet, he pushed onward, to where the ground slipped away into the sea and there was barely enough room for a man to walk.

Once there, where he could go no farther, he flattened his back against the rocks, a man alone with his troubles, his eyes raised to the heavens, and his heart breaking.

After a while, as always these days, his heart was calmed, his mind quieter. He began his way back, to the widest part of the beach, where he sat listening to the rush of breaking waves and the many comforting sounds of night: nesting seagulls ruffling their feathers; creatures of the water shuffling a path through the sand.

In the dark, where no one could see, the world was breathing all around him. It was *his* now, this part of night when others slept and dreamed. In the semi-darkness, this place, this world, this precious time was *his,* and he cherished every minute.

Content now, oblivious to the minutes and hours that ticked by, he stayed; satisfied just to look and listen.

After a time, when night began to merge with daylight, he made his way back.

As he wended his way along the clifftop, he thought of his wife again, he thought of Kathy and that quiet conversation while she sat on the wall eating her fish and chips.

He heard her laughter in his mind and smiled. "She's like a ray of sunshine," he mused.

From what he had heard of her intimate murmurings to her late father, he suspected things had not been easy for her.

In those few brief moments when she laughed at her mistake with the hot chip, then again when she was sitting on the house wall, he had seen a woman who had that rare talent of being able to laugh at herself, a woman of compassion and heart. A woman who had the ability to take the world by the horns and shake it into submission.

He wished her well.

Then he shut her out of his mind, for there were other things he must consider. Things of the past; things of the future.

The present was less important.

# *Five*

---

KATHY WAS AWAKE BRIGHT AND EARLY. SHE WASHED and dressed, tidied around and, taking her small cache of belongings, made her way down to the reception desk.

The clerk was still half-asleep, yawning and rubbing her hair until it looked as if it belonged to some scarecrow in a field. "Was everything all right?" she asked wearily. For one irritating minute she thought Kathy was there to complain.

Placing the caravan keys on the desk, Kathy smiled. "Everything was just fine," she said, and it was, because now that she'd had a good night's sleep she was ready for anything. "Where can I get breakfast?"

The clerk groaned with disgust. "Oh, however can you eat so early in the morning?"

"It must be the sea air," Kathy answered, "it seems to have given me an appetite." She laughed. "My friend Maggie swears I could eat anyone under the table."

The young clerk observed Kathy's slim figure. "Don't you ever get fat?" she asked enviously.

Kathy shook her head. "Not yet, I haven't. But I'll probably spread out like a balloon once I hit forty." She laughed at the girl's wide-eyed disbelief. "To tell the truth, I seem to be able to eat whatever I like and it makes no difference. Maggie hates me. She has to watch every mouthful she eats, or she piles on the pounds in no time."

"I'm the same. Lucky you," the clerk grumbled. "And you'll find the dining room is just opening." Pointing to a side door, she suggested helpfully, "To avoid you going back out and in through the main doors, you can go that way. You'll see the dining room straight ahead of you."

Heeding the directions, Kathy followed her nose, the aroma of hot food taking her through the entrance hall and into a small dining room. Observing the military rows of square laminated tables, she marched through to where the food was only now being set out. There was a basket of toast, and several other hot dishes each containing a good helping of porridge, tomatoes and sausages. There was also a box of cereal.

At the end of the table, there was a fat man frying a couple of eggs on the hotplate. "Just one, please." Taking up a plate, Kathy held it out. "Turned over and well done."

Sour-faced, the man scooped up a juicy egg and dropped it onto her plate; dripping in fat, it almost slid straight off the other side, save for a nifty backstep by Kathy. "Sorry, luv." He looked wretched, as though he'd been out all night on the tiles.

Reassuring him that no harm was done, Kathy took her plate along the buffet to collect a sausage, a wrinkled tomato and a piece of toast. She poured herself a cup of tea from the urn to finish.

By the time she got back to a table by the window, both toast and tea were cold, but that didn't bother her too much. It was the fat man at the end of the table that drew her attention. As she ate heartily, Kathy couldn't keep her eyes off him. Apart from the arm that turned the eggs, he never moved. "Like a robot!" Kathy chuckled. Then suddenly he reached around to collect a clutch of eggs from the basket behind. Just that one, swift, rigid movement and he was back again, still as a statue, one arm hanging by his side, the other turning the eggs. For a while, Kathy was mesmerized.

The sound of children outside made her glance through the window. There was a whole family of them: mum, dad, grandparents and six healthy, boisterous youngsters. "Oh, my God!" Kathy exclaimed. "Looks like they've got their hands full."

Suddenly all hell was let loose.

As that particular family burst in through the doors, an-

other followed, and soon the whole place was filled with excited, screeching children running amok among the tables.

One pretty little girl sauntered up to Kathy and stood by
her table, big saucer eyes following every forkful of food
Kathy put into her mouth. Embarrassed at the way the child
was staring at her, Kathy cut off a piece of sausage and offered it to her. "Hungry are you, sweetheart?"

With frightening speed, a woman resembling an all-in
wrestler swept the child up, with a stern warning for Kathy.
"Don't you mess with me!"

Nervously swallowing her food, Kathy watched as the
woman carried the kicking child to the buffet, where she set
about terrifying the fat man.

Seeing the humor of the situation, Kathy chuckled to herself. "I can assure you, lady . . . I've no intention of messing
with you!"

A few minutes later, having finished her breakfast and
been deafened by the growing uproar in the dining room,
she made good her escape.

Excited and a little apprehensive, she made her way to the
house. Stopping at the telephone box which was halfway,
she took out two coins and, dropping them into the slot,
asked the operator to dial Maggie's number. "Be in, Maggie!" she urged. "Come on, pick up the phone." She knew it
was an extravagance, but she had to talk to her friend.

Another few rings and the voice at the other end of the
line sounded grumpy. "Who is it?"

Kathy gave a sigh of relief. "It's *me,* who d'you think it
is?"

"KATHY!" At once the voice came alive. "Why didn't
yer phone me yesterday, you wretch? I waited in as long as
I could."

Kathy explained, "It was late when I got here. I rang you
as soon as I sorted myself out, but you weren't home." She
lowered her voice. "You were out with that bloke, weren't
you? The one I told you to be careful about?"

Maggie was on the defensive. "So! What if I were?"

Kathy knew it. "And . . . ?"

"And what?"

"You know . . . was he just after one thing, like I said?"

"No. He was *not* just after one thing."

"So, nothing happened then?"

"I didn't say *that!*"

"So, what *are* you saying?" Kathy knew the answer already.

"All right, something happened, yes. But he wasn't the one who made the running." There was a chuckle. "I were. He just went along."

Kathy groaned. "There's me traveling all day, worn out when I get here and not even able to stay in the house. And there's *you* . . . dancing the night away, doing Lord knows what! And lying in bed half the next day." A thought struck her. She whispered, "He's not still there, is he?"

"No. He went home about two this morning . . . said he had to be up early for work. But I'm seeing him again tonight . . . and don't you dare say *anything!* Or I'll put the phone down."

"I'm saying nothing," Kathy replied, "but I still think he's wrong for you. I reckon you might be heading for trouble falling for him hook, line and sinker, without even knowing him."

"I *do* know him!" Maggie decided against putting the phone down. "I spent the bleedin' night with him, didn't I?"

"Right then. Where does he live?"

There was an awkward pause. "I'm not really sure . . . somewhere the other side of Ilford, I think." Her voice rose in anger. "It's not important. He'll tell me when he's good and ready."

"And did he say where he worked . . . when he had to rush off like that?"

"I mean it, Kathy! I'll put the phone down if yer keep quizzing me." Another pause, before she said lamely, "If I'd asked him where he worked, I'm sure he'd have told me."

"All right, Mags . . . I'm sorry. It's just that I don't want you to get hurt, and . . . well, there was just something about him that made me suspicious, that's all."

"Hmh! That's because you've got a suspicious mind."

"Promise me you'll take it slow with this one?" Her every

instinct told her that this bloke was a chancer. Maggie had been through it all before and never seemed to learn. Sometimes she couldn't see beyond all the attention and flattery. In the end she always got hurt.

Now that the well-meaning "inquisition" was over, Maggie's questions came fast and furious. "What's the house like? Why couldn't you stay there? And if you couldn't stay there, where *did* you spend the night?"

Kathy explained about the caravan, which had turned out to be cozy and comfortable. "The site is just a short walk from the house," she said. "It so happened they'd had a cancellation and I was able to take the caravan for a night."

Maggie was exhilarated. "See! I told you there'd be a caravan site." She went on enthusiastically, "Happen I'll stay there with my bloke, seeing as you don't like him." She continued, in a worried voice, "Will you be able to get the house right? I mean . . . it's bound to cost you for getting the lights and the water on."

Kathy sighed. "That's not all. There's paint peeling off everywhere, and it looks to me like the window-sills are rotten."

"I can't believe yer dad let it get that bad."

Kathy had wondered about that herself. "Maybe he was in love and didn't notice, or maybe he was tight for cash since he was keeping two homes going. But it's been empty for over a year . . . maybe longer for all we know. It's stood right through the winter at least, and I'm sure the sea air can do a lot of damage."

"So, how will you afford to get it done up?"

Kathy confided her plan. "I intend getting a little job. I could buy paint and brushes, rub the wood down and do the work myself at weekends."

"Hmh! Rather you than me."

The conversation inevitably came onto men. "Go on then!" Maggie urged excitedly. "Have yer come across any good-looking blokes yet?"

Kathy laughed. "Give over, Mags, I've only been here five minutes!" Kathy's mind went back to Tom. "There was *one* man though . . . in the chippie . . . aged about thirty-five or -six,

I reckon." She recalled him clearly. "Nicest-looking chap I've seen in ages, only . . ." She paused, trying to put her feelings into words.

"Only . . . *what?*" Maggie was not the most patient of people.

"Well . . ." Kathy couldn't quite put her finger on it. "He seemed, I don't know, kind of sad. I nearly choked on a hot chip and he told me to be careful." She could see him now, in her mind's eye. "He had the loveliest smile."

Maggie laughed. "Sounds to me like *you're* the one who needs to be careful. Some bloke smiles at you in the chippie . . . and you're gone."

Kathy hotly denied it. "Don't be daft! I'm *not* 'gone,' as you call it. I don't know him from Adam and I don't want to. Besides, I reckon I've got enough on my plate without worrying about men!"

Maggie was incorrigible. "All right, all right!" she chuckled mischievously. "If you say so."

"I *do.* So you behave yourself." As her money ran out, Kathy promised to write very soon. She knew the chances of Maggie putting pen to paper were slim.

On her way to the house, she paused to look at the boats in the harbor. Everything was beginning to come alive: it was still early but the boats were being fitted out and taken to sea; down on the slipway a man and a woman were launching their boat.

Some way along the harbor, two sleepy-eyed children walked along, holding their mother's hand and looking as if they would still rather be in bed. Others were running and leaping about, excited by being at the seaside and impatient to get down on the beach with their buckets and spades. Kathy loved it all. After London, it was like another world.

Eager to get back to the house, she turned away. It was then that she saw the man from the chip shop emerging from the shop, his newspaper rolled up in his hand and his head bowed as if deep in thought.

She recalled what Maggie had said. "One smile and yer 'gone.' " That was not true, but there was something about this man that seemed to cling to her. It wasn't just that he was handsome, or that, as he strode across the road, the sun shone down on his hair and streaked it with gold; nor was it just the pleasing sight of his long, lean figure in flannels and white shirt, with short sleeves revealing strong, bronzed arms. It was more than that.

There was something else. Something the eye couldn't see. Something she had sensed last night when she saw him for the first time. There was a natural "goodness" about him . . . a warmth that reached out, yet kept you at bay somehow. She had seen it in his eyes last night. Even when he smiled at her, she had seen how his dark eyes were full of sadness.

Intrigued, she watched him walk away, over the bridge and on, past the caravan site and up the hill, until she could no longer see him. "A man with troubles," she deduced quietly. But, she shook herself, she was not here to get involved with another man.

Continuing onto the house, she realized for the first time how wonderfully sited it was. There was a well-kept public green in front and a high wall at the back, with shrubberies and lawns either side, though, like the front garden, they were badly overgrown.

As she stood with her back to the door, she had clear, uninterrupted views of the harbor on one side—a hive of activity—and the river on the other, with boats and ducks, and a restaurant whose terrace spanned the water on wooden stilts. "You chose well, Dad," she murmured, and a great sense of quietness flooded her heart. "I *know* I'll be happy here."

The extent of disrepair was more than she had realized. Apart from the peeling windows and overgrown gardens, the path itself was pitted with holes and the gate was hanging on one hinge. There was a shed at the side of the house that was already halfway collapsed, and a broken window upstairs at the back. "Blimey, Kathy!" She took a deep breath. "You've got your work cut out and no mistake."

For one nerve-racking minute she wondered if she was up to it . . . or even whether she could ever afford to do it. But the longer she stood there, the more the doubts melted. One way or another, she was determined to restore this lovely house to its former beauty.

Delaying the moment when she would open the door and go inside, she sat on the front step, gathering strength and mentally preparing herself. "It was *your* house, Dad," she whispered, "yours and hers. And now it's mine." She caught her breath in wonder and blew it out in relief. "I need a while to take it all in," she thought.

Having been to the shop for his ration of pipe-baccy and his daily paper, Jasper saw her sitting there, a small, solitary figure deep in thought. "Well, I never!" He was surprised to see the house had a visitor. "Wonder who she is?"

As always, his curiosity got the better of him.

Strolling over, he called out from the gate, "You look like a little lost fairy sat there."

Jolted from her thoughts, Kathy called back, "I'm not lost, I'm here to stay." As soon as the words were out she took a great deal of comfort from them . . . "I'm here to stay." It sounded wonderful to her ears.

Taking it on himself to come up the garden path, Jasper stretched out his hand in welcome. "I'm Jasper." He introduced himself with the most disarming grin. "And if yer haven't already guessed, I'm the number one nosey parker hereabouts."

Kathy took to him straight off. "I'm Kathy Wilson," she said, shaking his hand, "the new owner of Barden House." She said it with pride and the widest smile he had ever seen.

"Well now, Kathy Wilson, welcome to West Bay." He sat down on the steps beside her. "Did yer know yer can get piles from sitting about on cold, damp steps?"

Kathy laughed out loud. "No, I didn't," she confessed, "but I do now." She thought he was the loveliest, most natural, most odd-looking creature she had ever met. And she was delighted that he'd stopped to chat.

As was his nature, Jasper got straight to the point. "What's brought you to West Bay?" He had a particular reason for asking.

Kathy gestured to the house, shook her head. "I had to come here," she said. "The house was left me by my father."

Jasper was visibly taken aback. "Oh! I'm sorry, lass. I didn't realize your father had passed on." He had wondered whether that might be the case, but now that it was confirmed he felt deeply sorry. Her daddy had been a fine man, and a good friend. "I'm glad yer daddy had the good foresight to leave this house to you, his daughter. It's a grand old place." Full of wonderful memories, he thought sadly. "A house like this should not be left to rot away."

Kathy had been curious as to his earlier remark. "Did you know my father?"

"What meks yer say that, lass?" He hadn't meant to give away too much, but there were times when his tongue had a mind of its own.

Kathy persisted. "Just now you seemed shocked. You said . . . you 'didn't realize' my father had passed on. To me, that sounds as if you knew him."

Jasper nodded. "Aye, lass," he admitted, "I knew him right enough. He was a good man . . . the best in my books."

Momentarily unable to speak for the rush of emotion this produced, Kathy took a while to compose herself. "Tell me about him," she asked softly, "and Liz. Tell me about *her*." Each time she spoke her name, Kathy grew more curious.

"Mmm." Nodding affirmatively to himself, Jasper laid down his newspaper, lit up his pipe and, taking a deep drag of it, he blew the smoke into rivers of curls that dipped and dived in the cool summer breeze. "Well, now, let me see," he murmured. "What would yer like to know, lass?"

"Everything."

"By! That's a huge responsibility, lass."

"I know." Jasper's kindly voice and calming manner put Kathy at ease. "But, you see, I didn't know anything about her until my mother told me. And *she* only found out after my father . . ." Kathy gulped hard; it was still painful, even now. "Mother made a terrible song and dance about it, though the way she treated him, I sometimes wonder why he stayed with her."

Jasper was philosophical as always. "No relationship is easy," he pondered. "Them as says different are out-and-out liars."

Kathy knew the reason for her mother's anger and found herself confiding in Jasper. "She hated him even more when she found out he'd chosen another woman over her and, to make matters worse, Dad left their love-nest to *me*. Mother kept it to herself all this time . . . no doubt meaning to sell it and pocket the money. But when she came to have a look at it, she hated the house . . . said it smelled of fish. She wanted nothing to do with any of it. She thought the house was worthless . . . 'derelict' was what she said, and that it was . . . 'filled with cheap, rubbishy furniture.' Then she found out the deeds were in my name. Even if she could have sold it, she probably wouldn't have done. Firstly she's about to marry a wealthy old man, so she didn't need the money, and secondly, she had another, more devious plan up her sleeve."

Jasper was intrigued. "What kind of plan?"

"She intended giving my sister all her jewelry and the family home. I reckon she thought that, if she handed me this house at the same time, I couldn't possibly object. That was her thinking, I'm sure of it."

Jasper leaned forward, his voice low and intimate. "Your daddy never spoke about his life in London, but in a moment o' confidence he did tell me that he 'ad only one great regret in his life. Now I think I know what he meant." Jasper thought this delightful young woman had been hard done by, and said so. "Tell me summat, lass."

"If I can."

"Yer said one o' the reasons yer mother told yer about this place was so she could give summat more valuable to yer sister, is that right?"

"That's what I think, yes."

"And if yer hadn't been given this house . . . *would* you have 'objected' . . . about yer sister being given all these expensive things?"

Kathy managed a smile. "No. All my life my mother has given me nothing—not material things, and certainly not her love. And I never asked for anything. I had my dad's love and, in the end, I made my own way, in spite of her."

"I understand." Jasper saw the determined set of her jaw and thought how like her father she was. "It's a pity your mother saw this house as 'derelict.' " He gave a hearty chuckle. "I reckon Liz would be deeply hurt to hear her carefully chosen furniture described as being 'rubbish.' "

Kathy explained. "Mother was bound to say that, because she thought my father and Liz had probably chosen it together. In fact, I'm sure she only came to see the house out of curiosity. My mother would never have dirtied her hands on Father's love-nest . . . unless, of course, it was filled with priceless things."

"Ah, but it *was* filled with priceless things, lass." Jasper glanced up at the house. "It was filled with happiness and love. For your father and his sweetheart, every day was a new adventure." As he spoke his eyes shone. "They were so much in love . . . it was a joy to see."

Kathy felt that joy now. She felt her father's love all around her. "Did you know my father well?"

Jasper nodded. He had spoken with Kathy's father many times during his stay here. "I knew them both," he confided. "I was here the day they bought this house, and I watched them blossom and grow the more they were together."

He sighed. "In this life you only ever get one chance at true happiness; if you let it go, it may never come again. Liz and your father knew that. They lived every minute together as though it was their last." His voice broke. "I'm sorry it ended the way it did."

Kathy was anxious. "*How* did it end?" She needed to know. "Please, Jasper . . . I'd like to know."

Jasper wasn't altogether sure. "It's not my way, lass . . . to betray a confidence." It went against all his principles.

Kathy gave the answer he needed. "Daddy wouldn't mind," she said softly. "I think he *wants* me to know, or he wouldn't have left me this house."

"Mebbe yer right," Jasper conceded. "I'm a great believer in Fate. Happen you were sent here for a purpose."

Before he began, Jasper took hold of her hand and squeezed it gently. He nodded in agreement, and what he told her was a love story, of two lonely people, brought together by chance, and parted by a cruel twist of Fate.

There on the steps, in the warmth of the early morning,

they sat together, the old man and the young woman. In a quiet voice he unfolded the mystery, and she listened, hanging on his every word. Neither of them noticed the people who passed by, occasionally glancing at them. Instead, he revealed the truth of how it was. As he spoke in his soft voice, Kathy had neither eyes nor ears for anyone but him.

"It all began one winter's night, some nine years ago," Jasper confided. "Yer father were on his way to close a business deal in Dorchester. Anyway, the weather took a turn for the worse, so he came off the main road and into West Bay. He stayed at the guest-house back along the road there . . ." Pointing in the direction from which Kathy had entered West Bay, he went on. "For three days the storms raged on, the roaring seas threw up waves some twenty feet high. I'm tellin' yer, lass, it were like all hell let loose." As he related it to Kathy, he grew excited. "By! I've never seen anything like it in all me born days."

"I remember!" she exclaimed. "He told us all about the storm when he got back, but he didn't say anything about West Bay. He just said he'd found a place to stay until it died down." She chuckled. "Mother was none too pleased. She thought he should have got the train home and not been so selfish by staying out a week longer than was necessary."

The old man shook his head. "He couldn't have left . . . there were no trains running. All the roads were blocked for miles round. And there was fork-lightning, too—struck several houses an' set 'em afire. Telegraph poles were down and the harbor overflowed onto the walkways. It were a livin' nightmare!"

Kathy was enthralled. "So he stayed in the guest-house the whole time?"

Jasper recalled every detail. "Aye, lass. He were here for the whole of that week. That's how he met Liz. She were a widow: her husband was killed afore the war."

He smiled fondly. "They told me many a time afterward that the minute they met it were like they'd known each other all their lives. Sometimes they talked right through the night . . . getting to know each other—" he gave a slow, knowing wink—"falling more in love with every day that passed."

Kathy had mixed feelings. "He never told me," she murmured. "He never told anyone. Except you."

"It's easier to talk man to man. Sometimes, when Liz was off doing things, we'd sit on this very step and confide in each other. There are things you can tell a stranger that you could never tell them as are close to yer." He knew that from experience. "Anyway, I'd best not jump the gun. After the storm subsided and some o' the roads were cleared, he knew he had to get back to close that deal. When they parted the very first time, with yer dad still driven by his work, they each promised that they would meet in a few weeks. Yer dad turned up at every opportunity. He just couldn't keep away. They were becoming inseparable. Afore too long, it got so's neither of 'em wanted to go back."

Kathy gasped. "That was when he began staying away for longer periods at a time. 'I won't leave you for longer than I have to,' that's what he used to say to me, and I counted the minutes until he came home."

Jasper astonished her with his next remark. "After the war, your father bought a small cruiser . . . it's gone now, Liz sold it." He laughed out loud. "By! We 'ad some fun with that boat, I can tell yer. Y'see, a long time back, when I were young an' foolish, I joined the Navy. I had a hankering for the sea, so I got to know a bit about boats and such. Yer dad didn't know nothing at all!" He chuckled. "Matter o' fact I told him many a time that he were a danger to hissel."

Shaking his head, he laughed out loud at the memory. "I helped yer dad to manage that boat, and I don't mind tellin' yer, he soon got to grips with it . . . seemed born to it, 'e did. But there were times in the beginning when I thought the three of us would be drowned for sure! Like the first time yer dad negotiated that narrer channel out to sea. By! We crashed into the walls so many times it were a wonder we didn't end up as matchwood. Liz were screaming; I were trying to bale out the water that were splashing in; and Gawd 'elp us, yer dad were up front, fighting at the wheel."

He had to stop a minute, so helpless with laughter that he couldn't go on. "Anyroad . . . somehow or other we got out to open waters. We were safer there, y'see. Yer dad hadn't got anything to crash into, and the waters were smoother out there."

He could see the whole thing in his mind, like a film turning over. "Oh, but he soon got the 'ang of it. After a time, he and Liz would go out on their own . . . over to Lyme Regis, or into some little cove along the coast, where they'd swim to their hearts' content. Afterward they'd lie in the sun, happy in each other's company."

Kathy heard what he was saying, but could hardly believe it.

The old man saw the questions in her pretty eyes, and he realized how all of this must be a shock to her. "All right, are yer, lass?" he asked.

Lost in thought, Kathy didn't answer for a minute. "I never knew!" she said. "I had no idea. My dad was always in a suit . . . dressed for work. He bought and sold goods— anything from a fleet of lorries to a block of houses; whatever he could make a profit on. When he wasn't in his office, he was trading, buying and selling, criss-crossing the country looking for the next big deal. Especially during the war: he was away a lot then." She was amazed. "I didn't even know he could swim. And I can't *imagine* him taking a boat out to sea."

She was beginning to see another side to her father, a side she had not known existed. "It's as though you're talking about a different man."

"But that's just it," Jasper answered. "When he took off that suit, when he left the office and all his responsibilities behind, he came *alive!*" He heaved a great invigorating sigh. "Don't yer see, lass? When he was 'ere, with her . . . away from all that . . . he *was* a different man. He weren't the man fashioned and haunted by work and burden. He were a man at peace with himself."

While Kathy reflected on the old man's words, he went on. "To start with he allus stayed in the guest-house. Then one day, when they were walking along the harbor, they saw the 'FOR SALE' sign hanging right there . . ." He gestured toward the gate. "They made an appointment for the agent to meet them 'ere, an' right from the minute they went inside, your father fell in love with it. He bought it there and then. She kept her house as well, but, oh, they spent many a joyous time in this house, lass . . . until one day it all went wrong."

Sensing his hesitation, Kathy asked, "What happened?"

"He just never came back."

"I don't understand."

Shrugging his shoulders, he confided, "There was no explanation. He just upped and away, early one morning. He kissed her goodbye, went out of the house and just . . . never came back." He recalled how frantic Liz was. "She couldn't understand it. She blamed herself, then she blamed him, and soon after she grew quiet, like. Wouldn't speak to anybody. Oh, she were devastated, lass."

"But why would he just leave like that," Kathy mused, "without any explanation?"

"Who knows, lass? But, whatever the reason, as far as I know, she never saw him again. She waited for a whole month, and there was never a sign of him. She were like a lost soul. Sometimes, I'd see her walking the cliff tops, other times she'd be leaning on the rails over the harbor, or sitting on the wall by the slipway, where they laughed and played while trying to launch the boat. Most times she'd be watching out the window, willing him to turn that corner. After a time, she began to believe he'd changed his mind and wanted an end to it. So she closed the house up, and went away." He pursed his mouth, the way he did when thoughtful. "Broken-hearted, she were."

Kathy was saddened. "So she didn't know . . . about my father . . . how ill he was?"

The old man shook his head. "No, lass. Though she did ask me once if I thought he'd caught a chill out on the boat . . . said she'd noticed how pale and quiet he seemed; but when she gently tackled him, he bucked up and everything seemed all right again."

He shook his head slowly from side to side, his eyes downcast. "O' course, she didn't realize, and neither did I. Even if yer father knew he was ill, he never would have said. He wouldn't 'ave wanted to worry her. Happen he wanted it to end the way it had all started: sudden-like, without any kind o' plan."

"But if she'd *known* he was ill, she would have cared for him, I'm sure." Kathy's heart went out to this woman who had given her father so much happiness, only to have it all cruelly snatched away.

"Oh! She'd have nursed him like a good 'un, so she would!" Jasper didn't doubt it for one minute. "But now I can see that weren't how he wanted it . . . With the way it had been with the two of them, he didn't want her to see him getting more poorly day by day. I can understand his thinking, not to let on how ill he were. I'd 'ave done the very same."

"She could have called him! If she didn't want to call him at home, she could have rung his office."

"It weren't possible, lass. We neither of us had any point o' contact with him. That was the way yer father wanted it, and we respected that."

There was a moment of silence before Kathy asked, "Did she ever come back?"

The old man nodded. "For a time, aye, she did. She stayed on for a while. She waited, allus hoping he might come back to 'er. But o' course he never did, and now, thanks to you, lass, I know why."

Kathy wondered aloud. "Can I ask you something?"

"Ask away."

"Do you think my dad bought this house in my name, so I could come back and tell Liz what happened to him?"

The old man was mortified. "Never!" He tapped his pipe out on the step. "He gave you this 'ouse 'cause he wanted you to find the same happiness he knew with Liz. *That's* the only reason he wanted this house to go to you, lass, and don't yer ever think otherwise." On reflection he added: "Anyroad, he bought it long before he was ill. I've no doubt at the back of his mind he thought you might be happy here. I'd bet my life on it, lass."

Kathy felt sad, but said, "To tell you the truth, I wouldn't mind if he *had* meant for me to come here so I could tell her how it had been with him. She deserves to know why he went away like that."

The old man nodded. "Happen one o' these fine days she'll turn up 'ere and yer can tell her what happened." He smiled on her. "Yer a kind-hearted little soul," he said. "Yer dad were a lucky man, to 'ave such a lovely lass for a daughter."

Embarrassed, Kathy asked another question. "You said she came back?"

"Aye, so she did, lass."

"So, if she was living here, why are the house and garden in such a terrible mess? From what you've told me, I wouldn't have thought she was a slovenly person."

"Far from it, lass. She were forever polishing an' cleaning, and oh, but she an' your daddy loved to potter about in the garden . . . 'ad it looking a treat, they did. Never a hair outta place."

"But she let it all go when she came back, is that it?"

"Ah, well now, she didn't stay 'ere, did she? An' though I offered to keep the house tidy in and out, she didn't want that neither. She kept it closed . . . shutting the daylight out and the memories in, or so she thought. 'Leave it the way Robert left it,' she told me. 'It's his house.' So that's what I did." He glanced at the tangled grass and the wildly overgrown shrubberies. "It's been a while now, since the place were left empty. I've done as she wanted. I've not set fork nor spade anywhere near it." He groaned. "It's a pity though," he mumbled. "I do so hate a garden looking untended."

"It's up to *me* now, though," she said hesitantly, "isn't it?"

The old man chuckled. "Aye, that's right. Yer a householder now. Yer can do whatever yer like with the property. So, what 'ave yer got in mind, lass?"

"I'm not sure yet, but if I wanted you to help, what would you say?" Before he answered, she shyly added, "I can't *pay* you, at least not until I get a job. But I can keep you going with a cup of tea, and I can help, if you'll let me."

"A cup of tea it is," he agreed readily. "An' if you've a mind to find work, yer needn't concern yersel' about me, 'cause I'm perfectly able to look after mesel'!" He had a mischievous twinkle in his eye. "An' yer don't need to help me neither, unless yer really want to . . . 'cause the truth is, I work better when there's no woman under me feet."

They shook hands and the deal was done.

Kathy had yet another question. "When she came back, did she stay in the guest-house? I mean, if she closed this house up, she obviously didn't stay here."

"No, lass, she didn't stay in the guest-house."

"Where *did* she stay then?"

"That don't matter," he said wisely, "but once she left this house she never again went back inside . . . never walked up that path, nor opened that door. It were like she had to preserve what they had, for all time."

Kathy felt like an intruder. "And now I'm about to disturb all that . . . aren't I?" She needed to know. "What would Liz say if she knew?"

He shook his head. "I'm not sure, lass, but I do know one thing. She would respect yer father's wishes." He smiled at Kathy. "An' I know she would love *you,* without a shadow of doubt."

Kathy felt reassured. "Will you tell her . . . what's happened?"

"I don't know if I'll get the chance. Y'see, lass, she only stayed a few months before she went away again in the middle of the night and I haven't seen nor heard from her since. She left me a note, with a few instructions, but never a mention of yer father, or where she were going, or even when I might hear from her again, if ever."

Kathy sat quietly for a moment. She was shocked to her roots when Jasper said quietly, "There were a child, y'-know." He turned to regard her. "Has a look o' you."

Momentarily speechless, Kathy stared at him as though he had lost his mind. "A *child!*" She could hardly believe what he was saying. "Are you telling me . . . my father and Liz had a *child?*"

The old man nodded. "It were a lad . . . friendly little chap. He'd be about what—seven year old now. They named him Robert, after his daddy. But they called him Robbie."

"A *brother?*" Kathy's voice broke with emotion. "And I never knew! Why didn't he tell me? I belonged here, with them. I could have shared their happiness. Why did he shut me out like that?"

The old man didn't say anything. He knew none of this could have been easy for her, and had worried about giving her the last piece of news. It was too much to cope with. So he gently closed his arms around her shoulders and, drawing her to him, let her cry it out.

With her head against his chest, Kathy sobbed helplessly for a time, trying to come to terms with it all, and filled with all manner of emotions: regret at never knowing she had a brother; anger because her father had not told her, and through it all a great, abiding love that she could never again share with him.

After a time, when she was quiet inside herself, she looked up at the old man with scarred eyes. "He *should* have trusted me," she remarked softly.

"No, lass. He couldn't do that."

"But why not?" She drew away, her gaze curious on him. "I don't understand." She had tried so hard to forgive him, but even now, deep down somewhere inside, she was resentful of the fact that he couldn't trust her enough to confide in her.

"Happen 'e were afraid, lass." He paused, wondering how he might explain in words she could appreciate. "Happen 'e couldn't be certain how you'd handle it . . . yer might have been angry with him for deceiving your mother. Yer might have thought bad of him and turned away. Then again, in some misguided way, 'e might have been trying to protect you."

He sighed from his boots. "Oh, lass! There could be all manner o' reasons why he didn't tell yer. I can't say. But I can say one thing . . ." He held her at arm's length, his voice gentle, his bright old eyes smiling. "Yer father loved you all the more for not being able to share his secret with yer."

Wiping her eyes on the cuff of her sleeve, Kathy gave a small laugh. "That's a strange thing to say."

He winked. "I'm a strange man, or so they tell me."

Impetuously kissing him on the cheek, Kathy thanked him. What he said just now had helped her, more than he had realized. "Tell me about his son . . . my brother."

With a rush of pleasure, the old man brought the boy's image to mind. "He's a grand lad. He loves to be on the boat. Swims like a fish, and built strong-like. Curious nature . . . allus wanting to know . . . 'what's this do?' an' 'what's that for?' " He chuckled. "Drives a fella crazy, he does, with his never-ending questions."

Reaching out, he took up a length of her hair. "He's got brown hair like you . . . a bit lighter, mebbe, being in the sun whenever he could. Dark eyes like his daddy, and the gentle ways of his mother."

Kathy had a picture in her mind now. "I hope I'll get to meet him." The picture was still not complete. "What was she like . . . Liz?"

The old man thought a while before giving a brief description. "Long fair hair tied back; slender figure; pretty gray eyes—an', oh yes, she couldn't go out in the sun without getting smothered in freckles."

Following his description, Kathy could see her clearly in her mind's eye. "She sounds lovely."

"She's a darling woman," the old man concluded. "Any man would be proud to walk down the street with her."

Kathy wondered about this good woman, and the boy who was her brother. "I hope she comes back," she said quietly. "I hope I get to meet them."

The old man didn't answer. He knew from experience that hoping and wishing didn't mean it would happen.

Standing up, he stretched his aching back. "By! I've sat that long I'm all bent and twisted," he groaned.

Kathy looked at his thick strong figure and the short sturdy legs. "No, you're not," she told him with a mischievous grin. "But I expect you've got piles now, from sitting on a cold step . . . that's what you told me, isn't it?"

He laughed out loud. "By! Yer a cheeky little madam!" He pointed to the front door. "Come on, lass . . . see what needs doing inside."

"Jasper . . . I wonder . . . ?" She was loath to say it.

Now, as Kathy looked up with troubled eyes, the old man knew what was on her mind. "Yer want to go in yersel'," he remarked. "That's it, isn't it, lass?"

She nodded.

He stretched again, and tweaked his flat cap, and told her softly, "I'll leave yer to it, then. But I'll not be far away . . ." He pointed to the harbor where some of the fishing boats were returning. "There's fish to be sorted for market." He chuckled. "Just follow yer nose."

For a long time after he'd gone, Kathy remained on the steps, aching to go inside the house, but not yet ready to face what she might find.

Down at the harbor, Tom waited for the boat to return. A few days ago, in a freak wind, he had been leaning over the rails, watching the boats return, when one of the small cruisers broke free. Thrown into the path of the fishing boats, it might have caused havoc if Tom hadn't managed to catch the mooring line and draw it away.

Appreciating Tom's help, Jack Plummer, the skipper of the *Mary Lou,* called him on board and proudly showed him his catch of the day. At Jack's urging, Tom turned his hand to sorting the fish. Since then, at the same time every day, he would walk to the harbor, where he would board the *Mary Lou* to lend a hand. Having never set foot on a fishing boat before that particular day, he had come to enjoy the experience.

Today he had waited for Jasper as usual, surprised when he hadn't turned up, but knowing how the old fellow could get waylaid by any one of the inhabitants of West Bay, who all knew and loved him. They also valued his practical knowledge, and it wasn't unknown for them to recruit his help, which he gave at the drop of a hat.

Tom was already on board, sorting the fish, when he spied Jasper making his way down. "He's here." Pausing in his work, he stretched his limbs and gave a welcoming wave.

In a good mood after a sizeable catch, Jack yelled for the old man to get a move on. "I told you he wouldn't miss out on his daily treat!" he told Tom with a hearty chuckle.

Jasper was soon on board, helping the other three men to

sort the fish into crates; every now and then, up would go the cry from Jasper, "By! You must 'ave emptied the oceans with this catch!"

"Never mind changing the subject!" the skipper joked. "If you're late again, I'll have to give you your cards!"

Tom got in on the act. "If he goes, then so do I!"

"Oh, all right then," the skipper said with a wink at Jasper. "If you put it *that* way, I've nothing else to say on the matter."

They had a laugh and got on with their work. It was always like that—well-meaning banter and good-natured taunts. It was their way.

When the decks were cleared and the fish piled high into the crates, each man took a swig from the bottle of whiskey strapped under Jack's seat. They laughed and chatted and talked of the day's adventure, and afterward they loaded the crates onto the skipper's old red truck, ready for market. "When are you coming out fishing with us?" Jack asked Tom.

Tom was evasive. "We'll see," he answered, and Jack knew he wasn't yet ready. Like everyone in West Bay, he knew Tom valued his privacy. Helping sort the fish was one thing, but being closeted with others in a small boat in the middle of the ocean was quite another.

From her front door, Kathy watched the old man walk to the harbor, where the skipper and another man greeted him. She heard the bursts of laughter and saw the old man wagging a finger at the skipper, then further laughter, before they got out the whiskey and downed a well-earned drop or two.

Kathy couldn't hear what sparked the laughter, but suspected it might be the old man's doing. "What a character!" Already she really liked him.

She realized with a flush of interest that the other man was the bloke from the chip shop. He cut a fine figure in his boots and oils. He and Jasper seemed to know each other. Curious, she observed them for a time, watching as the man leapt from the boat to clamber up the wall to the top. There he swung himself over athletically. She thought him too handsome for his own good. "Better not let Maggie loose around him," she muttered light-heartedly. Brusquely, she turned toward the house. "Right, Kathy! The sooner you're inside, the sooner you can start settling down," she declared nervously. "It's *your* house now. It's up to you." All the same, the ordeal of entering what had been her father's love-nest was not something she was looking forward to.

Taking the key from her pocket, she opened the front door. As it swung gently open, she remained where she stood, peering inside, her heart bumping nineteen to the dozen, until she could hardly breathe.

Another minute, a deep breath, and she walked anxiously over the threshold.

The smell of damp invaded her nostrils; the feeling of having trespassed was strong in her. She moved further in. Without lights and with the curtains closed, it was semi-dark, with only the open door and the sunlight against the curtains giving her enough light to guide her way. "I'll need to see about the electricity," she reminded herself.

Going to the first window, she threw open the curtains; the effect was amazing. The sun burst in and lit the room with a warmth and glory that took Kathy by surprise. It was a large room, open and spacious, with high ceilings and the prettiest fireplace, surrounded by dark blue tiles with splashes of tiny white roses, so realistic they might have been picked fresh from a garden.

Gazing around the room, she was reminded of what her mother had said about the house. Kathy smiled. "Oh, Mother! How could you be so wrong?"

Certainly it wasn't the expensive, ornate furniture her mother coveted. Instead it was fine and simple. By the far wall stood a sideboard in light-colored wood, with long legs and a shelf underneath. Four beautiful blue meat-plates rested atop it, standing proud against the wall. There was a unit of shelves beside the fireplace, each displaying three small porcelain figures, all of which were of children. Some were playing, others lying on their tummies reading, and one, which Kathy thought was the most beautiful she had ever seen, was of a small girl holding an array of brightly colored balloons, her face uplifted and full of ab-solute joy. It made Kathy smile.

There were two paintings on the wall: one of the harbor,

with boats and the fishermen; another of a garden filled with bloom and color. It was not too difficult to imagine it could be the garden to this house.

In front of the fireplace was a thick, cream-colored rug, now slightly discolored by dust and neglect. Either side of the fireplace stood two deep, comfortable armchairs, one with a high back. Upholstered in plain dark blue, they complemented everything in that room.

Opening both windows wide, Kathy let the sunlight momentarily bathe her face. She didn't feel so much like an intruder now. Instead she was already relaxing, beginning to settle.

She went into the kitchen, where again she opened the window, pleasantly surprised when she saw how spacious it was. There was a white enameled cooker on the wall opposite the window, with a pine dresser one side and a wooden kitchenette the other. The sink had shelves underneath, with a pretty curtain skirting the lip of the sink. There were white and blue frilly curtains at the window, and a pine table and four spindle-chairs in the center of the room, the table being spread with a cloth of the same fabric as the curtains. A cornflower-blue vase stood on the window-sill, its once vibrant roses long ago faded.

Plucking out the flowers with her fingertips, Kathy laid them on the drainer. It felt strange, removing flowers that had been lovingly put there by the woman called Liz.

Suddenly she gave a cry when a hidden thorn tore at her skin, making it bleed. Licking away the blood, she thought it strange that the flowers had withered, while the thorns were as hard and sharp as ever.

Going upstairs, Kathy walked from room to room. She found a good-sized bathroom with two very large windows. The room itself seemed far too large and oddly shaped for the meager contents. Because only the newer houses were built with a bathroom of sorts, Kathy guessed this one might be a converted bedroom. It contained a small sink, toilet, and a bath with cast-iron legs. Here again she opened the window, and at once the room was transformed with the inrush of sunlight.

There were three bedrooms, each with a bed, wardrobe

and dressing table. All the beds were covered in eiderdowns of varying colors; all the colors were warm and gentle: much like the woman herself, Kathy suspected.

The main room overlooked the harbor. Square and spacious, it had a good feel to it, Kathy thought.

Leaning out of the window, she took a great gulp of air, drinking in the magnificent views at the same time. It was only when she turned that she saw the small photograph on the bedside cabinet. With hesitant footsteps she went over to it and, taking the photograph into her hands, she stared at it for what seemed an age, her heart turning somersaults and the tears never far away.

There were three people in the photograph: a woman of the same description the old man had given and who she knew must be Liz; a boy, taller than she'd imagined, his laughing face looking up at her and the sunlight making him squint. Standing between them, the man had his arms around the other two. She ran a sensitive finger over his features. "Why did you have to leave me?"

As the tears began to spill, Kathy sat on the bed, her gaze intent on her beloved father's face, her mind in turmoil with questions, and her heart like a lead weight inside her. "You look so different," she murmured. "Jasper was right," she conceded, "you *are* different." In a casual, short-sleeved shirt, his hair gently blown by the breeze and with a look of contentment in his dark eyes, her father seemed years younger than she remembered.

She sat there for a long time, the photograph clutched tightly against her chest and the sobs echoing in that long-deserted room. In his free, bright smile, she could see with her own eyes how happy he had been here, with that other family he had protected so fiercely.

The sobs were bitter, yet not condemning. The emotions she had pent up, the resentment and anger, all of that poured away, until all that was left were memories, and a great well of gratitude, because he had found contentment.

In Cliff Cottage the two men played their last game of cards for the evening. "Time I were off to me bed." The old man yawned. "One more hand, then I'm away. What d'yer say, Tom?"

"You're right, it's late." Getting up from the table, Tom stretched his arms almost to the ceiling, his body aching in every bone. "I think my back's broken from lifting all those crates!" All the walking he did had kept him fit, but lately he had come to realize he needed work of some kind, to keep him sane as well as supple. "I've been thinking . . . I might take Jack up on his offer to go out fishing with him," he confided. "I need to do something . . . at least until I get my life sorted out." Which meant hunting down the monster who killed his family.

"I'm glad to hear it." The old man paused before asking in a softer voice, "That other business you've been brooding about, is it done with?"

Tom was taken aback. "What business is that?" Though he feigned ignorance, he knew well enough what the old man was on about.

"Don't get me wrong, son." The old man was growing to love and respect Tom like a son. "I've known all along that summat bad drove yer to West Bay. I've seen that same look on blokes during the war—brooding, keeping it all locked up inside till it drives a man crazy."

When Tom made as if to reply, Jasper put up his hand. "No, son. Whatever it is, you'll deal with it, I'm sure. Like I said, it's none o' my business. You've never said, and I never asked," he explained. "If a man wants to keep his business to hisself, that's fine by me."

Tom neither denied nor confirmed it.

The old man persisted. "So? Is it over . . . whatever's driven yer to haunt the cliff tops in the middle of the night . . . Oh, aye!" He nodded assuredly. "I've seen yer, wandering about like a lost soul, an' I've seen yer during the day . . . with yer eyes all swollen from lack o' sleep."

He looked Tom in the eye. "So, is it over? Is that why yer all of a sudden coming outta yer shell and tekking up the skipper's offer to go fishing?"

For what seemed an age Tom didn't answer. Instead he walked slowly to the window, where he stared into the night. In his mind's eye he could see the carnage on that day when he lost them all. "No!" His voice was like a whiplash in the quietness of the room. "It's *not* over! Not yet." But soon, he thought . . . very soon!

Sensing the rage inside him, the old man sidled up to Tom. Laying a tender hand on his arm, he warned, "Easy, son. I know what it's like to be haunted by things yer can't control." He had an idea what Tom was going through, though not the reason for it. "Whatever it is yer need to do in order to regain peace of mind, I want you to remember one thing."

Turning to look down on him, Tom asked the question without uttering one word. "Tek yer time, son," the old man advised. "Don't let rage and bitterness cloud yer judgment. Sometimes a man can't see the wood for the trees. Be sure to remember that."

Tom nodded appreciatively. He knew this man was his friend, and he was grateful for that. Yet he still couldn't bring himself to talk about what happened. He squared his shoulders and, smiling, stood back. "How about if you put the cards away, while I get my jacket? I'll see you home."

Glancing out of the window, he was intrigued to see that all the houses were in darkness but for one. "We seem to be the last ones awake right now," he commented, "except for that old house down by the green." From where he stood, the light flickering in the front room was clearly visible.

Concerned, Jasper looked out of the window. "By! The lass is up late, and no mistake. I hope she's all right."

Tom was surprised. "Why shouldn't she be?"

"Because there's no electricity nor water, and yer know how long it teks 'em to turn it all back on. Quick enough to tek yer money though, the buggers!"

"Her name's Kathy." Unaware that Tom had seen Kathy as she sat on the wall eating her chips that night, the old man chatted on. "Her father left her the house, so she's decided to come and live here." Jasper thought that was about as much as he had a right to tell anyone, even Tom, except,

"Soonever she's got the house up to scratch, she'll be looking for work. Now then . . . are yer walking back with me, or what?"

Kathy had just closed the curtains and made her way up to bed, taking the lamp with her, when she heard a tap on the door. A little nervous, she looked out of the window. "Who's there?"

"It's only me, lass." The old man looked up. "I saw the light and wondered if yer were all right?"

Relieved, Kathy told him to wait and she would come down.

A moment later she was at the door. "I'm fine," she told him, "but the sooner I get the electricity switched back on, the better."

The old man was still anxious. "Yer should have booked into the guest-house, like I said," he replied. "Yer should not be sleeping in that damp bed . . . and the sheets must need a good boil, if they are still in one piece, that is."

Kathy laughed. "You're a real worrier! Look, I washed the sheets by hand and dried them on a line outside. I went across to the shop with two hot-water bottles I found, and the lady very kindly filled them with hot water, so I could air the mattress. I've had Ovaltine and toast for my supper, and a crisp, rosy apple to finish." She was grateful, though, for his concern. "I'm all right, Jasper, really I am." In fact, she was already feeling very attached to the house.

The old man was content. "It seems yer can look after yersel'," he remarked, ". . . an' I'm just wastin' me time." He had reservations, though. "I'm still not sure about the bed. Are yer sure it's fit to sleep on, lass?"

"Absolutely! Like I said . . . the sheets are washed, the mattress aired, and I'm not about to die of pneumonia, so will you stop worrying?" She gave him a smile. "Still, it is *nice* to have somebody worrying about me."

"Right then, lass. I'd best leave yer to get some sleep," he said. "Seems to me you've had a busy old day."

Satisfied that she was coming to no harm, he went back down the path. "By! She's not only bonny," he told Tom, who had waited by the gate, "she's capable, too."

As the two of them walked away, Kathy caught sight of Tom. "Goodnight!" she called. Tom returned the greeting with a wave and a smile that Kathy found appealing.

Tom was curious. "Does she really mean to stay in that house all on her own?"

"As far as I know, yes. But, like I said, she seems capable enough."

Five minutes later, having walked the old man home and chatted about this and that, Tom returned by way of Barden House. He hadn't taken too much notice of it before, but even in the lamplight he could see how anyone might fall in love with the place.

At the corner he paused, his glance traveling upward to the window where she was when Jasper first spoke to her. "Brave girl," he murmured. "She's got her work cut out keeping that place up to scratch." He smiled to himself. "She seems an independent sort; I don't suppose she'd welcome the offer of help."

His heart leapt when suddenly the curtain was drawn back and the window flung open and there was Kathy looking down on him. She didn't speak, and neither did he. Instead they looked at each other for a long, mesmerizing moment, before he hurried away, embarrassed at having been caught loitering outside her house.

Kathy watched him stride away. "I don't know who was more embarrassed . . . me or him." She thought she might relate the incident in her next letter to Maggie. But, on second thoughts, it seemed such a private moment she decided not to.

They were both so deeply disturbed by the encounter that it was a long time before either of them could sleep.

Kathy lay snuggled up in her bed, absentmindedly watching the shifting skies through her window; while Tom paced the floor awhile, before picking up the photograph of his family. He stared at their familiar faces, and as always was filled with regret, and a sense of blind rage that even now he had not brought under control.

With Kathy's face creeping into his mind, he felt the need to explain to his lost wife. "She's like you, sweetheart . . . strong-minded and independent." It tore at his heart to realize he had addressed her as though she was present.

Replacing the photograph, he strolled to the window, his gaze drawn back to Barden House. He stayed there for an age, looking and thinking . . . with Kathy's face strong in his mind.

Soon, those other, horrifying images swept away all else. Knowing what he must do before he could ever have a life again, he closed the curtains.

The next morning, back in London, a young woman rushed into a florist's shop. "Mrs. Taylor! It's happened again!"

The manageress dropped the half-finished bouquet onto the counter. "What are you talking about?" Since sending Gloria out on her deliveries, she'd been rushed off her feet, and was not now in the sweetest of moods. "Have you delivered all the flowers?"

"Yes, but . . ."

"Go on! Spit it out." She could see something had upset the girl, and now she was curious. "What's happened?"

Gloria almost ran to the counter where, red-faced and flustered, she told her boss, "You know that order, to take flowers to the churchyard every fortnight . . . that poor family that got killed? Well, it's happened again . . . The flowers I put there week before last . . . those beautiful roses and gypsophila . . . they were strewn all over the place. Somebody's filled the vase with *new* flowers! I didn't know what to do, so I squeezed ours in."

She was close to tears. "That's three times now, when somebody's deliberately vandalized our flowers. Should we let Mr. Marcus know, d'you think, Mrs. Taylor?"

The manageress considered it for a swift moment before coming to the conclusion, "It can't be children. They might take it into their nasty little heads to destroy the flowers, but they're not likely to spend a fortune on replacing them with their own, are they?"

"So, who is it then?"

"I wish I knew!" She had given it some thought before but she had not come up with any answers. "Who would do such a thing?" she asked angrily. "Anyway, I don't think we should worry Mr. Marcus about it. We'll just have to keep an eye on the situation."

"Well, *I* think it's weird!"

"That's because you've got too vivid an imagination."

Resuming her work, Margaret Taylor gave the order, "Move yourself, young lady. There's work to be done."

# *Six*

LILIAN WAS IN A BAD MOOD. WITH TOM GONE, SHE FELT lonely and irritable. Even her bright new colleague, Alice, with her bubbly manner and quick smile, couldn't cheer her up.

"Whatever's the matter with you?" Alice was at the end of her tether with Lilian's misery. "You've been so bad-tempered . . . downright rude sometimes! Are you ill, is that it?"

All day long, Lilian had been snapping and snarling, and now with only five minutes to go before finishing for the day, she was seated at her desk, head in hands, seemingly oblivious to everything that was going on around her.

On hearing Alice's remarks, she sat up to stare at the other young woman, her face unhappy. For a moment it seemed she might angrily rebuke Alice, but the moment was gone when Dougie walked in through the door. "All right, are you, girls?"

Delighted at having just concluded a new deal, he was full of himself. "So, who wants to kiss the man of the day?" Holding out his arms, he turned from one to the other, pretending to swoon when Alice planted a smacker on his cheek. "Well?" Leaning across her desk so he could look Lilian in the eye, he teased, "Too good to kiss an old mate, is that it?"

"Some other time, eh?" Lilian was in no mood for Dougie's high spirits.

"Oh, dear, caught you in a bad temper, have I?" Catching Alice's warning glance, he backed off. "Right then, I'd best get back to my desk . . . I've a few phone calls to make before I can get off home."

As he went, he warned them, "It's raining cats and dogs out there, so mind how you go, eh?" Alice thanked him. Lilian allowed a curt nod, and the merest of smiles.

Ten minutes later, after tying up a few loose ends, she had her coat on and was ready to leave.

"See you tomorrow," she told Alice.

"I hope you're in a better mood by then!" Alice muttered as the door closed behind her fretful colleague.

Giving Alice the fright of her life, the door opened again, and Lilian's eyes sought her out; for a minute Alice thought she'd overheard her mutterings.

"Look, Alice . . . I'm sorry I've been in a foul mood all day."

Relieved she wasn't about to be hung, drawn and quartered after all, Alice told her not to worry, because she knew what it was like to have a bad day.

One by one the other offices emptied, until ten minutes later Alice and Dougie were the last to leave. "What's wrong with Lilian?" Pausing in the foyer to prepare for the pouring rain, he remarked on how he'd never known her to be in such a bad mood.

Alice didn't know for sure. "Maybe she's not well," she suggested. "I think she pushes herself too hard. She does *twice* the amount of work I do." It was an odd thing. "Some days she seems tormented. It's like she has to keep herself occupied every minute. Me . . . I like to go down the street to the coffee shop for my lunch. It breaks the day up, if you know what I mean. But Lilian doesn't leave the office from the minute she comes in to the minute she goes home. She has her tea and sandwich at her desk, and if she goes to the ladies' room, the first thing she wants to know when she gets back is whether there've been any calls for her."

Dougie was beginning to understand. "And have there?"

"What?"

"Been any calls?"

Alice pondered on that. "It's usually one or other of the

architects, asking for her to go in when she gets back . . . or the boss sometimes calls down. Why?"

"I just wondered, that's all." Turning his collar up, he asked her if she needed a lift. "You'll get soaked to the skin in this lot." By now the rain was bouncing off the pavements, and leaving puddles in its wake.

Alice graciously declined. "Mum and Dad have got friends for dinner, so Ron's taking me back to his place. I'm cooking us a meal." She glanced down the road. "He should be here any minute."

Dougie gave her a playful nudge. "Sounds to me like there's *marriage* on the cards."

Blushing all shades of pink, she told him shyly, "You sound like my mum!" She laughingly mimicked her: " 'You're coming up to twenty-five, Alice my girl! It's time you settled down with some nice young man!' Honest to God, she goes on all the time."

He winked. "Well? *Is* there or isn't there?"

She shook her head, and he got the idea that the discussion was over.

"Right then. I'd best make a run for it."

Taking his life in his hands, he bid her good night and went out into the rain. Looking this way and that, he ran across the street, splashing through puddles and trying to dodge the deluge that rained down on his back. "Bloody weather!" he grumbled, scrambling into his car. "Brilliant sunshine one minute and all hell let loose the next! It's enough to give you pneumonia!"

Fumbling with his keys, he took a minute to open the car, during which he got soaked through to his shirt. "Brr!" Falling into the seat, he let out a long, withering sigh. "Straight into a hot bath when I get in—" he gave a little chuckle—"after I've had a sizeable tot of brandy to warm me up." He began to look forward to it.

As he pulled out, he saw Lilian huddled in a doorway near the bus stop. "Hey!" Winding down the window, he called out to her, "Get in the car, I'll take you home."

She waved him on. "It's all right, thanks. The bus will be along any minute now."

He wouldn't take no for an answer. "Come on, get in! I can take you right to your doorstep." Flinging open the door, he urged, "Hurry up. Make a run for it!"

With the nose of his car jutting out in the road and traffic having to swerve around him, Lilian could hardly carry on arguing the point, so she pulled her coat over her head and ran for it.

Once she was safely inside, she gave him instructions to her house. He pushed the car into gear and was on his way.

"Sensible woman," he said as he drew out onto the road. "If you'd waited for me back at the office I could have saved you getting all wet."

"I'll soon dry out, don't worry." She glanced around the interior of the car. "This is new, isn't it?"

He grinned like a boy with a new toy. "My new Ford," he answered proudly. "I thought you'd never notice."

"When did you get it?"

"Picked it up this morning. I reckon I deserved it."

Lilian's hitherto bad mood was beginning to mellow. "Some of us can't afford a car at all, never mind a new one."

"Huh! You wouldn't think so. I had a hell of a job trying to park this morning. It wasn't so long back that I could pick and choose where I parked. Lately it seems to me like every man and his dog is buying a car . . . and here's me thinking it was the privilege of the rich and famous."

"Oh!" she teased him back. "So you're rich and famous now, are you?"

"I can't complain!" Like his brother Tom, he had amassed a healthy bank balance since he had returned from the war, though he wouldn't call himself rich. "I dare say me and Tom are well off by most standards," he admitted. "But it didn't fall into our laps, far from it! We've worked hard for it." He lapsed into silence for a time, then added, half to himself, "We've both paid the price, though . . . Instead of Tom spending more time with his kids and wife, he was always on the move. I've no doubt but that he regrets every second lost with them." He shook his head. "Jesus Christ! What does money mean when compared to happiness?"

Lilian asked the same question everyone had asked at

some time or another since the tragedy. "Do you think they'll ever catch the man who ran them off the road?"

"Well, they haven't caught him yet," Dougie answered angrily. "If you ask me, the trail's gone cold." He wondered about it all. "Strange that . . ." He finished thoughtfully, ". . . Why would anybody want to kill an entire family?"

Lilian agreed, though she added, "Maybe it really *was* an accident after all—even the police thought that at one point."

Dougie shook his head. "Tom swears he was rammed by that other car, and I for one believe him. Besides, even if it *was* an accident, they should have been able to trace the other car! Instead they've let him get clean away."

Now, as he felt the anger rising in him, he changed the subject. "You never got married, did you?"

Taken by surprise at his abrupt change of direction, Lilian answered warily, "I don't see what *that's* got to do with anything."

He felt the barriers go up and inwardly swore at himself for being so unfeeling. "I'm sorry. I didn't mean to pry."

She took a moment, then said, "No, I never did get married."

He was curious. "Any particular reason?"

"No." She felt uncomfortable. "I just never met the right man, that's all. And with the war, and everything—there weren't that many to choose from . . ." Her voice trailed off.

"Well, take it from me," he warned, "romance isn't all it's cracked up to be." He sounded bitter about the way things had turned out; Lilian knew there was talk of a broken engagement in his past.

They were near her house now. "Turn right here and straight on, then first left, Camden Street. I'm halfway down."

For the next few minutes they continued to chat about work, and about his latest deal. "I've been after that shopping-arcade job for months," he admitted. "It's my biggest yet." He chuckled. "I don't mind telling you, the boss was over the moon."

"He would be," Lilian remarked. "Making money is what makes him smile."

"Ah well, if *he* makes money, so do we," Dougie answered. "It's what makes the world go round, or so they say."

Following her instructions, he drew up outside a terrace of small houses. "There you go." Lilian lived in the end one. "Safely home in one piece."

Thanking him, Lilian apologized for her behavior earlier. "I'm sorry I wasn't too sociable before."

He nodded, seeming to understand. "It's Tom, isn't it?" He knew how she felt about him. "You expected him to be in touch. That's it, isn't it?"

She gave a nervous little laugh. "You know, don't you?"

He wasn't sure how she might take the truth, but he told her anyway. "If that means do I know you worship the ground he walks on, the answer is yes." He studied her face for a reaction. "I knew about three weeks after you started working with him."

Shocked that he had guessed her secret, Lilian was slow to reply. "I suppose you think badly of me, since he was a married man and all."

"Not my business," he answered carefully.

"I never told him, though!" She thought it was important he should know that. "I never told *anyone!*"

"Best thing," he agreed. "You know how Tom doted on his wife and kids."

"I know. But surely, now . . . with him being on his own . . . I mean with his wife and everything . . ." Realizing she had strayed onto a tricky subject without meaning to, she paused, a little nervous. "I'm sorry . . . I didn't mean." She grew angry with herself for ever having mentioned it, but now it was out in the open she voiced the question, "Why *didn't* they ever catch the driver who ran them off the road?"

Dougie took a long, noisy breath. "God only knows they tried hard enough," he answered. "The heavy downpour soon after managed to wash away any tire tracks. There were no witnesses, and all they had was Tom's account of what happened. He was in no fit state to give too much of a description. The driver was wearing a hat and dark glasses, that was all he could see. The few clues they had didn't lead anywhere." He shook his head. "I don't believe their theory that it might have been an accident."

Lilian was interested. "So *you* think it was deliberate?"

"I think whoever did it must have planned it carefully, otherwise, as you say, why haven't they been caught?"

"But why would anyone want to kill Tom's family?"

"God knows, but you said 'Tom's *family*.' If they rammed his car with the intention of sending it over the cliff, the murderer must have wanted Tom dead as well, don't you think?"

Lilian shrugged. "Of course. I didn't mean it like that."

Dougie reassured her. "But you're right. Whatever the intention, it was a terrible tragedy. Thank God Tom's here to tell the tale, though."

There was a long silence while they reflected on his words. "It was a terrible thing," she agreed. "I was just wondering if Tom is feeling lonely, that's all." She grew braver. Unsure about whether she was saying the right thing, she suggested, "I was wondering if I should tell him how I feel."

"Sorry. I'm not the one to advise you about that." Dougie thought it was a tricky situation. He didn't really want to get involved. "I'd say that was up to you."

Now that she had gone this far, Lilian told him what was on her mind. "I was thinking of going to see him . . . He sent his address and everything—in case of emergencies, he said. What do you think, Dougie?"

Dougie wasn't sure. "He sent *me* his address as well," he remarked. "I must admit, it did cross my mind to go and see him once I'd caught up with work, but, to tell you the truth, I think he'd let us know if he needed company. He's been through a lot. He's pushed himself hard this past year, driven by what happened and not allowing himself to come to terms with it all. Now he's come to his senses and decided to take the time off, maybe we should give him the space he so desperately needs."

He had given it a good deal of thought recently. "If you *really* want my opinion, I think we should wait for him to get in touch."

"So you don't think he'd be pleased to see me?"

He thought about it for a minute. "I didn't say that," he cautioned. "I can only speak how I find. You'll have to make your own mind up."

Lilian's dark mood was creeping up on her again. "Don't you think he must be lonely?"

He had to concede that point. "I'm sure he is. But maybe that's what he needs for a while." He gave her the hint of a smile. "On the other hand, who am I to say? He might be grateful if you pay him a visit . . . I wouldn't know."

As she got out of the car, he called her back. "How about you and me going out one night?" he suggested with a mischievous grin. "We could cry on each other's shoulder."

Her answer did not surprise him. "As friends . . . nothing else?" Tom was the only man she wanted, he knew that.

He nodded. "Okay," he agreed. "As friends."

"All right then. We'll talk about it tomorrow."

Slamming shut the door, she made a run for it.

Excited with his new toy, and thrilled to have a date in the bag, Dougie roared off, water spraying from under his wheels.

Having let herself into the house, Lilian leaned against the closed door, her face etched with anger. "Damn him. I don't need *him* to tell me what to do!"

She walked down the passageway muttering to herself and softly crying. "Tom wants to see me. I *know* he does!"

*Since the accident, all she had dreamed about was getting together with Tom.*

The following Friday, Lilian kept a promise. She and Dougie were actually meeting up on a date.

At half past seven on the dot, he arrived at her door. "My! You look stunning!"

"Thanks." Having shed her bad mood, Lilian was now ready for a night out. Her long auburn curls were brushed to a shine, and her make-up, as usual, was discreet. She had chosen to wear a black pencil skirt with red shoes and a jacket of the same color, and had a polka-dot scarf at her neck.

"Your hair is lovely," he said, reaching out toward her. "Pity you don't wear it down in the office." Lilian stepped away from his touch. "Remember what you promised," she reminded him. "Just friends." He was all right, but he wasn't Tom. She told herself to keep that firmly in mind.

Though disappointed at her reminder, Dougie reassured her nevertheless. "Don't worry. I haven't forgotten." Cupping his hand beneath her elbow, he walked her to the car.

"I've booked us a table at a lovely little Italian restaurant I know," he said. "I hope you like it."

Spruced up in his best suit and looking as debonair as he could manage, Dougie was actually nervous. This was his first real date in a long time.

Grinning broadly, he opened the car door for Lilian to climb in and make herself comfortable. His precious new car was polished and shining, much like Dougie himself, Lilian thought.

As they drew up outside the restaurant, another taxi drew up in front of them and out stepped a pretty woman in a black dress. Looking uncomfortable in what was clearly his best suit, the man with her was slightly older.

"You're in for a wonderful evening, my dear," he promised his companion as he offered his arm to her.

The woman laughed with excitement. "It's a good job I put my best frock on."

"Nothing but the best for my little girl." Tucking her hand into his arm, he escorted her inside, like the gentleman he was.

Dougie smiled at the woman's excitement. "It looks like he means to make it a night for her to remember." He helped Lilian out of the car. "I remember when I used to get excited like that . . . when every penny I earned had to be counted."

Lilian began to see a more ordinary side to him that she had not seen before. "So, you don't count your pennies *now*, is that what you mean?"

He laughed. "That's *exactly* what I mean," he replied. "*Now* I let the accountants do it for me."

The restaurant was lovely, with plush red carpets and starched white tablecloths. Lilian's eyes traveled the room and took it all in. With crystal chandeliers hanging from the ceiling and long slender mirrors on the wood-paneled walls, she was overwhelmed by such opulence.

Dougie and Lilian were seated at an intimate corner table. "She seems a bundle of fun," Dougie commented as the couple from the taxi sat down nearby. He observed her companion. "Too old for a boyfriend, and too young to be her father," he remarked.

Lilian looked across to where the woman was now talking softly to her companion, while he smiled back with stars in his eyes. "I should think she's hooked herself a nice little earner," Lilian concluded with a smile.

Dougie tended to agree. "Well, I hope the poor bloke knows what he's in for."

On ordering the food and a bottle of wine, Dougie chose the best that money could buy. They ate and drank and, as the evening wore on, the two of them began to delight in each other's company. "You really do look beautiful," Dougie charmed her time and again. "I hadn't realized just how lovely you are."

A fool to flattery, Lilian drank another glass of wine, then another. She was enjoying herself.

Lilian dabbed at her mouth with the napkin and placed it on the table. "That was the nicest meal I've had in a long time," she confessed. "I don't bother too much about elaborate meals . . . living on my own and all that."

Appreciating the compliment, Dougie laid down his knife and fork. Leaning forward he murmured suggestively, "You don't *have* to be on your own . . ."

"Now, now!" She wagged a finger. "Remember what we agreed?"

Sitting back in his chair, he gave a disappointed grunt. "As if I could forget." But, after the wine she'd consumed and the teasing little smile she gave him just now, he lived in hope.

A helping of fruit pie and another sip of wine, and she could hold out no longer. "I need the little girl's room," she confided softly, and, taking her bag, went off in search of it. "I won't be long."

While Lilian was away, Dougie couldn't help but overhear every word being spoken at the next table. At one point, on hearing the woman laugh, he looked up and caught her eye. When she surprised him with a wink, he looked away. "Cheeky little devil," he muttered, but he was smiling, and so was she.

As he waited for Lilian, Dougie thought about his brother Tom. He reflected on a letter that he'd received that very morning from him, letting him know he'd settled in and describing West Bay. The mention, in passing, of Kathy had not gone unnoticed by Dougie. "It seems to me that Tom might be taking an interest in women again." He smiled, raised his glass and took a sip. "Welcome back, Tom," he said, replacing his glass when he saw Lilian approach.

He wondered whether to tell her. "Trouble is, she'd probably be there on the next train," he muttered worriedly, "and Tom would lay the blame squarely at my door." He decided it was best not to tell her, for all their sakes. "If she suspected he was making a play for another woman, it would only upset her."

"I'm ready to go now." Lilian had surprised herself by enjoying the evening. "It's been wonderful," she told Dougie as he waited for the bill. "I really didn't think I'd enjoy it so much, but it was exactly what I needed. Thank you, Dougie."

"Don't thank me," he replied, "I've had just as good a time. I'm only sorry it's over so quickly." Chancing his luck, he asked, "Do you think we could do it again some time?"

Not for the first time that evening, Lilian smiled brightly. "We'll see," she promised. "But if I *do* agree—and I'm not promising anything—it will be on the grounds of friendship, just like tonight."

He went along with that, albeit reluctantly. "I'd rather it was more than that," he confessed, "but if it means we can enjoy a night out occasionally, then I'm ready to abide by the rules."

"Right then." Once the bill was paid and the waiter gone, she put her bag over her arm and stood up, slightly off-balance because of the wine. "Whoops!" Stumbling against the table, she laughed at her own clumsiness. "I think I've had too much wine."

In the car on the way back to her place, she seemed to have been affected by the rush of fresh air as they came out of the restaurant, because now she was giggling and teasing, saying things she might well regret in the cold light of day.

"You devil! You got me drunk so's you could have your wicked way with me!" In fits of laughter, she poked him in the ribs. "I've never been drunk in my life before." Every corner they turned she threatened to throw up. "I feel sick!" she wailed. "Stop the car."

Dougie had an idea. "Look, we're much nearer my place than yours," he told her. "Why don't you come back with me . . . just until you feel better able to travel. A cup of strong coffee should do the trick."

"If I do come back with you, I'm not staying long." Feeling the way she did, Lilian couldn't help but accept. It was either that, or throw up all over his nice new car. "And you can forget any ideas of any funny business." Throwing herself back into the seat she warned, "Besides, I don't even fancy you . . . never have."

"Really?" He glanced at her with mock horror. "And here's me thinking you fancied me rotten."

"Hmh!" She gave him a playful dig. "Then you thought wrong, didn't you?" Launching into another fit of laughter, she cried, "So, you see, you got me tiddly for nothing."

Amazed that she seemed completely out of control, he took a sideways glance. "I would never have believed you could behave like this." Her antics made him smile, though. "I always thought you were ice-cool and untouchable." In fact it was that which made her attractive.

"I *am!* And don't you forget it." She fell back into the seat. "Oh, I do feel queasy."

"Hold onto it." Willing her not to be sick all over his seats, he pressed his foot down on the accelerator. "We're nearly there."

They soon arrived at his house, a respectable place with three bedrooms. It was more than adequate for his needs, though a little empty for a man alone.

He parked outside the front door. "Right then, my girl, let's get you inside."

By the time he'd rounded the car with the intention of helping her out, she was fast asleep. "Would you believe it?" He could appreciate the humor of the situation. "I've never had a girl pass out on me before."

Leaning heavily on his shoulder, Lilian knew nothing of how she got inside the house.

Negotiating his way into the sitting room, he laid her gently on the settee and covered her with a blanket that he fetched from his own bed. "Sleep tight," he said, lifting her legs over the edge of the settee. "See you tomorrow."

It was half past three in the morning when Lilian found herself lying on the carpet. In the night she must have turned over and slipped off the settee onto the floor. Now, still half-asleep, in these strange surroundings, it took her a full minute to realize what had happened. She recalled Dougie asking if she wanted to come back to his place for a sobering cup of coffee; after that, she recalled little else.

"Oh, Lord!" Dragging herself up by the settee, she stood for a while, holding her temples and gently swaying. Suddenly she was chuckling. "He got you drunk!" Even now, she could still feel the effects of drink, dulling her senses, making her feel somewhat disoriented. She wasn't used to wine at all.

Worried, she looked around. In the half-light she could see the shape and size of the room in which she stood, but it wouldn't keep still. "Stop moving!" she hissed. "I can't think straight!"

Suddenly she caught sight of Dougie, sprawled in a nearby armchair, fast asleep. "Dougie!" She called his name, but he didn't wake.

Crossing the room, she tugged at his arm. "I want to go home," she whispered. "Wake up and take me home, you devil." Tripping over the blanket covering his legs, she fell heavily over the arm of the chair. "See what you've done?"

Throwing out her arms, she caught him hard on the face. "I'm absolutely gone and it's all your fault!"

"For God's sake, what the devil . . . ?" Shocked awake, he sat bolt upright. "Lilian! What's wrong? Are you all right?"

Suddenly she had gone from the arm of the chair and was lying on the carpet, looking up at him with sleepy eyes. "I want to go home now."

Sliding down in the chair, he knelt beside her. "Are you sure?"

"What?"

Reaching down, he ran his hands through her tumbled auburn curls. "Do you *really* want to go home?"

She didn't answer. Instead she looked at him with tearful eyes, her gaze searching his face. In the dreamy half-light she saw that familiar lean face and the quiet smile, and she imagined it was the man she so desperately missed. *"Tom . . ."* Her voice trembled, her arms reached up to him. "Hold me."

Collecting her into his arms, he kissed her, softly at first, then when she made no objection, he went a little further. Soon they were on the floor, discarding their clothes and weaving around each other half-naked; touching, feeling. It was a fast and furious coupling, with no words of affection spoken, or even a warm glance between them.

When it was over, they lay for a moment, spent and exhausted on the floor.

Dougie was the first to speak. "I'll make us a drink," he suggested, "then I'll run you home, if that's what you want." Sensing her regret, he clambered up and quickly dressed. Going across the room, he turned on the light. It seemed a hard, cruel invasion into their private moment.

"Turn it off!" She looked away. "I don't like it." Pulling on her clothes, she seemed highly embarrassed.

Dougie understood. "I've got whiskey, beer or plain water," he told her as he went to the drinks cabinet. "Or, if you prefer, tea?"

When she didn't answer he glanced across to see her already dressed and seated in the chair, her hair still partly disheveled and her face flushed, much like his own. He tried to make light of it all. "Well, which is it to be?"

Her voice was small and reluctant. "Tea," she answered. "I don't want any more to drink."

Taking in a deep breath, he blew it out in a rush. He hoped she wouldn't blame him too much for what had happened. "Okay. Tea it is, then."

"Afterward . . . I want you to take me home." She lapsed into a sullen mood.

He nodded. "Whatever you say." He wondered if he had destroyed what slim chance they'd had of getting to know each other better. It would be such a pity, he thought sadly.

When he brought the tea, she cupped the mug in her hands and slowly sipped the hot, soothing liquid. She didn't speak, and neither did he, though the atmosphere was thick and uncomfortable in that softly lit room.

While she fidgeted in the armchair, he sat opposite, occasionally glancing up to see if she might be more settled. "I'm sorry," he blurted out, "about what happened."

"So am I." She didn't even look up.

He nodded. "We had a good evening, though . . . the restaurant, I mean." He gave a small nervous laugh. "I don't suppose you'll want to do it again, though . . . will you?"

Putting her cup down on the small table beside her, she gave him a shriveling glance. "Never!" Her voice was flat and hostile, like the look she was giving him now. "I'd like to go home now."

Not wanting to leave it like this, he warned, "You'll only waste your life, hankering after my brother. If he'd been at all interested in you . . . in *that* way, don't you think he would have shown it by now?"

Her features hardened. "Not your business!"

"It's just that . . . I don't want to see you get hurt."

"LIAR!" Leaping out of the chair, she fixed him with an accusing glare. "You're just out for what you can get! I should have seen all along what you were up to." When she darted forward he thought for a minute she was about to launch herself at him. "You took me out tonight with the intention of getting me drunk and then into bed. You bastard!" All of a sudden she was lashing out, clenched fists at his head and shoulders, and shouting obscenities that shocked him to the core.

Grabbing her fists he held her off. "No, I didn't. Okay, maybe I do find you very attractive. But it might not have happened at all if you hadn't disturbed me from my sleep!"

"GET OFF ME!" Kicking and screaming, she only fell silent when he slapped her hard around the face. "Listen to me, Lilian. Do yourself a favor and think about what I said." Lowering his voice, he entreated, "Don't make things hard for yourself. Tom isn't interested in you, not as a lover. If he felt anything for you in that way, he'd have been in touch, wouldn't he?"

Relaxing his hold on her, he was caught off guard when she lashed out yet again, this time scoring him on the face with the edge of her nails. Almost instantly the blood burst through the broken skin to trickle down his cheekbone. "How could *you* know how Tom feels?" She smiled at him, a wicked, triumphant smile.

Angry at being attacked for no good reason, he blurted out what he had learned from Tom's letter. "Tom *is* moving back into the real world . . . he's thinking about love at long last. But it isn't *you* he's turning to. It's a *stranger.* A woman he's met in West Bay. So you see, Lilian, that's how it is, so you might as well save yourself a lot of grief and accept it. Tom is starting a new life and you're not in it. It's as simple as that."

In the wake of his angry outburst, the silence fell like a blanket, silencing them both before Lilian spoke again, her voice pained and trembling. "YOU'RE A LIAR!" She looked at him through tear-filled eyes, yet when he went to take her in his arms she tore into him, again and again, until he staggered backward, horrified at the look of murder in her eyes.

Suddenly she was across the room and out the front door.

By the time he got there, she was already running down the street, her arm raised to a cruising taxi. The taxi stopped and she climbed in.

A moment later, as she drove by, the look on her face was terrible to see.

Going back inside, Dougie poured himself a drink, mentally reflecting on the colorful events of the evening. "Christ,

Tom!" He gulped down his drink and poured another. "She is one dangerous woman!"

Pouring himself another drink, he took it to the chair where he sat, drinking and thinking, the twisted humor of the situation beginning to overtake his astonishment. "I should have let her find out for herself."

He gulped down another mouthful of drink. "Whoo!" When he recalled how she'd gone for him, he couldn't help but chuckle, his fingers tracing the weal down his face. "You'd better watch out for that one, Tom," he laughed. "She's a wildcat and no mistake."

# *Seven*

AFTER NUMEROUS ATTEMPTS TO FIND WORK WITHIN A five-mile radius of West Bay, Kathy had at long last secured an interview to work at the holiday site, right on her doorstep. Wanting to look her best for the interview, she had gone into the nearby town of Bridport, where already the market was in full swing, to find something to wear.

Cool against the sweltering August heat, Kathy wore her lemon dress with its swingy skirt and wide belt. On her feet she wore the white stringy sandals that she had bought from the bric-a-brac shop in Lyme Regis only the day before. Her brown hair, a little longer now, and lightened by the sun, was hanging loose about her shoulders. In her pretty eyes there was a spark of happiness, and a deep-down feeling of contentment inside her. These days the bright lights and fast pace of London life seemed a world away.

Wandering among the stalls, searching for something that would make an impact and carry her through the interview, she felt good. She needed to look her best, she thought. She needed to be cool and casual, yet formal enough to show them she was serious and capable.

In the letter she had received two days ago, Kathy was informed that because the manager was away on holiday, the owner himself—a Mr. Charles Bradford—would be conducting the interview. That prospect only made Kathy all the more nervous.

"Morning, m'dear." Spying a likely customer, the little woman peered over her stall. Short and round with a giant of a smile, she had seen Kathy looking through the rail of dresses.

"If you tell me what you're after, I might be able to help." With astonishing speed she scurried around the stall. "Let me see . . ." She sized up Kathy's slim figure, making a mental note that if the nicely shaped legs were just a bit slimmer, the figure would be perfect. Nevertheless, she had met Kathy before, and considered her to be lovely both in appearance and nature.

Tapping her finger against her teeth, the little woman came to the conclusion, "Size ten, am I right?"

Kathy smiled. "Sometimes ten, sometimes twelve," she revealed, "depending on how tempting the cakes in the baker's shop are."

The little woman chuckled. "Same with me," she confessed. "I've a shocking sweet tooth . . . could never resist a lemon meringue, not even if my life depended on it. Not that we get many treats like that these days . . ."

While she talked she swung the dresses aside, one after the other. "There's nothing here that would suit you," she told a disappointed Kathy, "but if you come round, I've a few specials at the back." Giving Kathy a wink, she led the way to the back of the stall, where she undid a few boxes from underneath. "I haven't had time to put these out yet," she explained, "but I've an idea there's something in here that would suit you a treat."

Intrigued and full of hope, Kathy watched the little woman take the items out of the boxes. So far, as the woman shook them out and hung them up, there was a pretty pink twinset, three long skirts, two dresses, and a few summer blouses, none of which Kathy fancied.

She shook her head. "No, sorry. They're not what I'm after," she told the woman, as she unfolded one garment after the other.

"Hang on a minute, m'dear!" the woman replied with a disarming grin, "there's a couple more yet." Digging deep into the last oversized box, she pulled out two more items. This is the lot," she explained, shaking out the first. "By! You'll look pretty as a picture in this." The item in question turned out to be a green dress with a button-front and wide fancy belt.

While the woman held the dress first this way then that, pressing it to herself and then against Kathy, it seemed for a minute that Kathy might be tempted. But when she finally decided against it and turned away, thanking the woman for her help, Kathy's roving eyes caught sight of a snippet of pale blue material peeping out from beneath a selection of blouses hanging from the stall support. "Is that a blouse or a dress?" she asked curiously.

Puzzled, the little woman followed Kathy's gaze, her eyes opening wide when she spied the garment. "Oh, I'd forgotten that!" she cried excitedly. "It's a dress . . . I *think*." Reaching up, she managed—with some grunting and groaning, and a little help from Kathy—to take down the entire collection. "There!"

Dropping all but the one item onto the stall, she held it aloft. "I remember now!" she declared. "Some woman bought it, then fetched it back the next day . . . 'too tight around the waist,' she said. I'm not surprised," the woman added with a chuckle, "because if my memory serves me right, she was twice around the gasworks." Holding out her arms as wide as she could, presumably to encircle the poor creature, she smiled a sad little smile. "Shame, though . . . she had such a pretty face."

Sneaking a glance at Kathy's small waist, she observed, "I don't reckon *you'd* have that sort of a problem . . ." She peered at the label. "It's a bit grubby around the collar . . . but all it needs is a good wash." She handed the dress to Kathy for inspection. "You can go behind the stall and try it on if you want."

Kathy didn't need persuading. The dress was exactly what she had in mind. Cornflower-blue, with a pretty white collar, it was perfect. The waist was fitted, the skirt was straight, and it was her size. She need look no further. "How much is it?"

"Er, let me see . . ." The little woman peered at the label again. "It says two pounds ten shillings here, but, seeing as it needs a bit of a wash, give us two pounds. It's good material, and it'll look wonderful on you. This is the kind of frock you'll wear again and again." She gabbled on, eager to make a sale, and reducing the price a bit at a time, until the deal was finally done. "All right . . . give us one pound ten shillings," she decided. "It's daylight robbery, but I'll settle for that."

Ten minutes later, armed with her dress, and a new pair of blue, small-heeled sandals, Kathy called into the corner café for a well-earned break. "Tea and toast, please," she told the friendly waitress. That morning she had rushed out to catch the bus, with no time for breakfast, and now her stomach was turning somersaults.

"There you are, Miss." The waitress was in her mid to late fifties, already burdened with age and weariness, yet with the brightest of smiles in her eyes and a way of putting folk at their ease.

While Kathy patiently waited, she lazily offloaded the tray, explaining each item as it was placed on the table. "One pot of tea . . . nice and hot, and a slice of toast and dripping." Sliding the tray away, she gave Kathy her best smile. "How's that, m'dear?"

Kathy nodded. "That's lovely." She smiled back. "Thank you."

Grateful for another satisfied customer, the woman ambled away, as if she had all the time in the world; even though she appeared to be the only waitress, and the café was already beginning to fill up.

Digging into her breakfast, Kathy felt good about life. She had her house and her health, and now she had the chance of a job. On the face of it, everything seemed to be shaping up to her expectations.

"All right are you, dear?" All too soon, the waitress was back with the bill.

"Yes, thank you."

"And did you enjoy your cuppa?"

Kathy assured her, "It was just what I needed."

She checked the bill and managed to find the exact change in her purse, together with a few coppers for the woman.

"What you got in your bag then, dear?" Straining to see inside Kathy's shopping bag, she seemed disappointed when she couldn't make out its contents. "I never get time to go shopping . . . not proper, like. I'm allus on the rush."

Kathy had got used to these kind, friendly folk. They took an interest, and that was something she had not really been used to, but she was amused at being asked what was in her bag. That was a new one on her.

"I've bought myself a frock and a new pair of shoes," Kathy replied. "I've applied for a job at the caravan site and I want to look my best for the interview."

"Oh, that's good." The woman sat herself in the chair opposite. "Let's have a look then, dear."

Seeing how the woman looked tired and was probably using her curiosity as an excuse to sit down for a minute, Kathy took out the dress and let her see. "Ooh!" Fingering the material, the woman smiled with pleasure. "That's really nice . . . though *I'd* never squeeze myself into that, I wouldn't! Never in a month o' Sundays."

She pointed to the bag. "What else you got in there, dear?"

Kathy took out the shoes and, being careful not to incur bad luck by placing them on the table, she handed them over, smiling to herself as the woman lovingly ran her hands over the shoes. This kindly woman was a complete stranger, yet here she was, handing her shoes over to be examined. Because of the woman's naturally disarming nature, it seemed as though she'd known her for years.

The woman caressed the shoes. "You might not think it *now,*" she remarked with a sigh, "but, when I were younger I used to wear shoes like this. It's a pity, but when you get older your feet get all swollen up and you've got to wear what's comfortable, not what's pretty."

When she gave a full smile, as she did now, Kathy could clearly see a number of gaps in her otherwise surprisingly white teeth. "Just look at you, dear . . . such a pretty little thing you are." Giving Kathy a smile and a nod, she gestured to the dress and shoes together. "I bet you look a treat in this little lot."

Warming to this dear soul by the minute, Kathy confided, "I was really lucky to find them, and at a reasonable price. I need to look smart if I'm to get this job. I'm really keen to stay in West Bay," she admitted. "When I came here, I wanted to make a brand new start . . . I wanted to be on my own, away from it all," she added, almost to herself.

"I see. And have you no family?"

Kathy took a moment to reply, and then it was with a bitter taste in her mouth. "No," she answered, "I've no family, not to speak of anyway."

"You're like me then, dear. I were an only child, and my parents are long gone. Oh, I'm wed o' course, but we never had children, more's the pity." Her eyes clouded over. "I would have loved a daughter." She looked down at Kathy, then glanced around the room. "I know this isn't much to show for a lifetime's work, but it's all bought and paid for. It's provided us a living. But it would have been nice to have children to hand it all down to."

She gave Kathy a wink. "Got a boyfriend, have you, dear?"

Kathy shook her head. "No."

"What!" The woman was shocked, "A good-looking girl like yourself. Oh well, never mind, dear. I expect once you're settled in you'll have more time for that sort of thing." Suddenly her face dropped and she seemed unbearably sad. "Listen, my dear," she began in a warning tone, "when you do meet somebody, take your time. Don't rush into any old relationship, because sometimes they're not what they seem, and you can get really hurt."

"I won't." Kathy suspected from her manner that the poor soul might be talking from experience.

"Make sure you love him and he loves you . . . moreover, make sure he respects you as a person. He has to allow you an opinion, otherwise you'll never feel part of a couple. Instead you'll feel left out and useless, and you don't want *that,* do you?"

She sighed, a long, deep sigh. "It's funny how you let the years go by without seeing things . . . then, when you come to realize it's all been a terrible waste, it's too late to do anything about it."

Getting up, she pushed her chair back and seemed as before, smiling and wishing Kathy well. "I hope you get the job, dear."

"Thank you." For a few minutes there, Kathy had glimpsed a deep sense of loneliness and regret.

Suddenly, startling them both, a man's voice boomed out from the far side of the room. "Mabel!" Standing behind the counter, the man was a large, red-faced, angry mound of flesh.

Both Kathy and the woman glanced back. Grimacing and pointing, the man made it plain he was none too pleased at Mabel hobnobbing with the customers. "Get a move on!" He appeared oblivious to the customers' curious stares. "I can't do *everything* myself!"

"That's my husband," the waitress told Kathy nervously. "He's a miserable old git!"

Suddenly she leaned down to confide, "I don't mind telling you, dear . . . if I were thirty years younger and had a figure like yours, I'd not be working in this dump. I'd be away, somewhere exciting." Rolling her eyes, she muttered, "Somewhere as far away from that old bugger as I could get."

"Mabel! Come on, will you!"

She grimaced. "See what I mean?" Taking out her pencil and pad, she wrote something down and handed it to Kathy. "I don't suppose you've much time, especially if you get that job . . . but I make a nice cherry cake, so if you're ever down Monk's Way, you might stop off and visit me. He's allus down the pub on Friday and Sat'day night," she added, "and he sleeps it off most of Sunday." She handed Kathy the note. "It would be nice if you could pop in and have a chat."

Kathy promised she would pop in if she was ever that way.

As the woman went off, she called out, "I never asked your name, dear?"

"It's Kathy."

Mabel laughed. "I think you know by now what *my* name is."

Just then the man called out, "I'll not tell you again, Mabel. Hurry up! We've customers waiting!"

Mabel tutted under her breath. "They'll not be waiting long if *you* keep yelling and screaming!"

She smiled at Kathy. "Good luck with the interview, dear," she said, and before Kathy could answer, Mabel was off serving another customer.

The first thing Kathy did when she got home was to wash her new dress. Hanging on the line, it danced and shivered in the summer breeze, its colors bright and refreshed, and looking prettier than when she had first seen it.

She had already cleaned the house before going into Bridport, but now she walked through every room, throwing open windows and letting the breeze wash in. The house already looked better. It had taken hours of scrubbing and washing—and there were none of the new labor-saving devices in place that her mother had in London—but it had been a labor of love for Kathy. When she got to her own bedroom, she leaned out the window, always delighted by what she saw.

Today being Saturday, there were more people around the harbor: mums and dads; children eating ices; old couples sitting on the wall chatting; fishermen with their lines and legs dangling over the edge of the pier; other people busy in their boats—speedboats, fishing boats, small cruisers. The lively scene was a feast to the eyes and a joy to the heart. Kathy loved every minute of it.

"Hey!" From the street below, Jasper's voice interrupted her daydreams. "Where've yer been, lass? I've already called around three times this morning. What 'ave yer been up to?"

"Hello, Jasper!" As always, Kathy was pleased to see him. "Wait there. I'll come down."

Running down the stairs two at a time, she soon reached the bottom and opened the front door. "Come in"—she beckoned him inside—"and I'll tell you what I've been up to."

She hadn't seen the letter lying on the mat, but the old man caught sight of it out of the corner of his eye. "Somebody loves yer," he chuckled. Sweeping the envelope up, he followed her into the kitchen, where he dropped it onto the table. "Looks like I'm playing at being postman now," he joked. "You'll want me mekkin' me own tea next."

Taking him up on the roundabout offer, Kathy answered craftily, "What a good idea! Lots of milk, one sugar. Thanks, Jasper, you're a pal." She tore open the envelope. "I think this is Maggie's writing."

"Yer cheeky little bugger!" He saw how she was intent on reading the letter and promptly forgave her. "Oh, go on then, lass, I'll mek the tea. And don't blame me if it's not to yer liking."

Putting the kettle on, he grumbled and moaned. "While I'm at it, I might as well mek us a few slices o' toast. After that, happen you'd like me to polish the furniture, or mek the beds. I could even clean the winders . . . or, I might sweep the yard and give it a wash down. An' what about the garden . . . I might as well carry on turning that over while I'm at it." Quietly chuckling to himself, he turned to look at her, but she wasn't even listening. "All right then, lass." He got busy. "Tea and toast coming up." By now he knew Kathy's kitchen well enough to have the tray ready in no time.

"Now then, young Kathy"—he made his way to the table—"don't you go telling me the toast is burnt, 'cause it ain't my fault. It's that useless grill o' yourn!" Shoving the plate of curled-up toast in front of her, he poured them each a cup of tea, and sat himself down, continuing to mutter and complain. "I turned it right down, but it still burnt the toast . . ."

He saw that she was still intently reading the letter, sometimes smiling, sometimes groaning. "By! Yer not listening to a word I'm saying," he protested.

Raising her head, Kathy's eyes shone with delight. "Oh, it's good to hear from Maggie!"

"Is this the lass you told me about?" he asked. "The one who's allus in and out o' trouble?"

"She's not *that* bad," Kathy laughed, "but she *is* unpredictable. You never know what she'll be up to next." Catching sight of Jasper about to bite off a piece of blackened toast, she was horrified. "You're not going to eat *that,* are you?"

"I certainly am," he replied, happily chewing, "every last bite."

Kathy took a bite of hers, but couldn't stomach it. "Thanks for the tea," she said. "Now then, what's wrong?"

"What d'yer mean?" He took a huge bite of his toast and could say no more, for the moment anyway.

"You said you'd been around three times already this morning," she reminded him. "So . . . what's wrong?"

He took a gulp of his tea, catching his breath when it proved to be too hot. "Oh, aye!" He bit off another piece of toast and commenced chewing, with the words coming out in between each chew. "Where've yer been?" Instead of answering her question, he had one for her.

"I caught the early bus into Bridport," she answered. "Look!" She drew his attention to the dress on the line. "I bought a new dress for the interview on Monday morning. What do you think?"

He took a peep. "I think it's right pretty."

"So, why did you want to see me?"

"Oh, it's just that, well . . . me an' Tom wondered if you'd like to come out with us this afternoon?"

Kathy was surprised. She didn't really know Tom. "I'm not sure. Except for what you've told me about him, and the odd time we've bumped into each other, I hardly know him."

The old man winked. "Mebbe not, lass, but yer *like* him, don't yer?"

"What makes you say that?" Kathy could feel the blush spreading all over her face and neck.

"Ah!" He tapped his nose. "I don't need 'telling.' I've got eyes. I've seen the two of youse, peeping at each other. It don't tek twopenn'orth of common sense to see how you're drawn to each other. And don't deny it, 'cause you'll only mek matters worse!"

"Well, we've hardly spoken, but I do like him," Kathy admitted shyly. "But I don't know about coming out."

"Go on, lass," Jasper said as he saw her hesitate. "If yer get the job at the site, you'll not 'ave time for much else. What with overtime and that, you'll be clapped out once yer get home. So, what d'yer say?" He saw she was weakening. "It'll be entertaining, if nowt else."

Kathy thought it might be fun to spend some time in Tom's company. "All right, yes."

"Good! I'll be here to pick you up at two o'clock."

"Hang on a minute." Kathy had a question. "You haven't told me where we're going."

"We're off to look at a boat." The old man couldn't conceal his excitement. "An old friend o' mine is giving up the sea . . . he's not in the best of health these days, poor devil. Anyway, he can't keep up with it all anymore, so he's getting rid of the boat, and I don't mind telling yer, it's a good 'un!"

Though he had never been able to afford one, boats were his passion. "Anyway, the boat's nobbut four year old, and hardly done any work at all."

"So, is Tom planning to use it for fishing?" She had seen how he was always helping out on one fishing boat or another, and how he seemed to love it.

"I don't know about the 'fishing,' lass. It's not that kind o' boat." Taking a slurp of his tea, the old man wiped his mustache. "Since Tom's been helping out on the boats, he's really tekken to it. He's been toying with the idea of buying his own boat for some time, and now I've found a good 'un at a reasonable price, he's keen to 'ave a look at it."

"If it's not a fishing boat, what kind is it, then?"

"It's a sailing boat . . . a little beauty of a thing. She's easy to handle, and he's had 'er adapted so you've got the best of both worlds. When there's no wind, you've got a little engine that'll carry yer along till the wind gets up agin. By, you're gonna love it!" His eyes twinkled with excitement. "It's been kept undercover most of its life and looks good as new. It goes like a good 'un, too. I've been on it, so I should know."

With all that now settled, he glanced at the letter in her hand. "So is your friend Maggie coming to see yer?"

Kathy explained, "She always promised she'd come and see me when she'd got the time. Well, now it seems she's been sacked . . . *again!*" She shook her head in disbelief. "Anyway, she's got to find another job to pay the rent before she can come down for a holiday. But she promises it'll be soon." The idea that Maggie would soon be here in her house, sitting across the table talking about old times, was wonderful. "Oh, Jasper! It'll be so good to see her. I can't wait!"

For a time, they talked about Maggie and her escapades and laughed together.

"She sounds like a real handful, an' no mistake." Having finished his toast, the old man licked his lips and wiped his face and washed down the dregs of his tea. "Man-mad an' all, by the sound of it."

He referred to the part in the letter where Maggie had given a hilarious account of a night out with her latest man. "I'm not sure I approve of what she's up to, though . . . going out with a man years older just 'cause she fancies he might give her a life o' luxury."

Kathy dismissed his fears. "If she makes a play for you, Jasper," she teased, "I'll have something to say, don't you worry."

He laughed out loud. "Aye, an' you can tell 'er, it's no use thinking I'm loaded, 'cause I've no money to speak of . . . except a little pension an' what I earn around the fishing boats and such." Grinning broadly, he began to preen himself. "Mind you, if she's looking for a 'andsome fella with a sense of adventure, she'll not go wrong wi' me."

"You old devil!" Kathy laughed with him. "I'm sure she'll love you for the rogue you are . . . just like I do." In fact, she thought Maggie and the old man would get on like a house on fire.

"Right, lass." He stretched and groaned. "I'd best be off." Making his way to the door, he reminded her again. "Two o'clock, mind. We'll pick yer up from 'ere."

In the time she had left before being collected for the outing, Kathy brought the dress in, ironed it, and hung it carefully in the wardrobe. She then washed and changed, cleaned her teeth, and brushed her hair into a springy bob.

When Tom and the old man came for her, she was sitting on the wall, watching the boats and thinking about the one Tom might buy. She was so intent on looking at the boats, she didn't see them approach. "By! She's a bonny lass if ever there were one." Jasper secretly hoped Kathy and Tom might get together; though he knew there was a long way to go yet, he had a good feeling about these two.

Following the old man's gesture, Tom's dark gaze fell on Kathy. He agreed with Jasper; she really was a "bonny lass," he thought. In fact, in spite of himself, he had been drawn to her from the first minute he set eyes on her, when she was running for the taxi in London, then again later at the churchyard. The closest he had come to her was at the chip shop, when he had seen the sparkle in her pretty toffee-colored eyes.

There was something very appealing about Kathy, he thought.

He didn't know why she stayed in his mind. Maybe it was her wonderful, free smile and that easy way she had of chatting as though she'd known you all her life. Maybe it was her joy at everything and the way she seemed to meet life head on. To his mind, being naturally a quiet, private person, such energy and warmth was a gift.

"Right then, lass." Jasper's voice shook Kathy out of her thoughts. "Ready for off, are yer?"

Leaping off the wall, Kathy hurried toward them, blushing pink when Tom smiled down on her. "Hello, there."

Returning a bright, shy smile, Kathy thanked him for asking her along, but added, "I think I should tell you . . . I don't know the first thing about boats."

"That's all right." He smiled. "I just thought it would be nice to have you along." He apologized, "I don't know if Jasper told you, but we'll be going on the bus. My car's had to go in for repairs . . . a clattering of sorts in the engine . . .

wants new pistons, or so they tell me." He grimaced. "I wouldn't mind, but I haven't had the thing all that long."

He seemed relieved when Kathy assured him she was more than happy to go on the bus.

As they walked to the bus stop, Jasper had an idea. "Why don't we go to the pub in Weymouth afterward?" he suggested. "It's a lovely day, an' they've got the prettiest garden." He licked his lips. "A pint o' the best would go down a treat."

"Sounds good to me," Tom said. And Kathy felt the same.

"Good!" The old man was content. He was with two people he was very fond of, and on top of that there was the promise of a leisurely pint in the offing. "By! This'll be the best day out ever!" He began whistling, and didn't stop until they reached the bus stop, where he happily chatted away non-stop.

When the bus came, he gave the order to Tom, "You and the lass sit together, an' I'll keep an eye on youse from behind." Behind Kathy's back he winked at Tom.

Seeing the twinkle in the old man's eye, Tom wagged a playful finger at the old chap. "Behave yourself," he chided, "or I'll have you thrown off the bus."

With that in mind, the old man sat quietly behind the two of them, minding his P's and Q's, and occasionally grinning as he thought how well Tom and Kathy seemed to be getting on.

The very same thought was racing through Tom's mind. Somehow he felt very at ease with her.

Kathy, too, felt very comfortable chatting to him, though she was keenly aware of the physical closeness between them. He was undeniably attractive. But the last thing she wanted to do was get involved with a man. She'd just got her life in order again.

By the time they got into Weymouth, the sun was at its hottest. "By! I've never known it so warm." As they walked the short distance over the bridge and down to the harbor road, Jasper loosened the neck of his shirt. "That pint seems very tempting right now," he chuckled, and Tom agreed, though, "We've got business to attend to first," he said firmly.

Walking a step or two behind him, Tom kept close to Kathy. Whenever a vehicle got too close, he would put his arm about her waist to guide her from the curb edge. Kathy loved the feel of his arm around her. She loved being with him. She was proud to walk alongside him, where everyone must have thought they were a couple. There was a surprising mixture of emotions churning inside her, and the one that surprised her most was the feeling that she might be falling in love. It was a wonderful, terrifying thought.

"Right! Let's have a look." Stopping by the quayside, the old man raked his eyes over the many boats in the water, crying out when he caught sight of his old friend waving him down. "There he is! D'y' see? Fred Lovett, me old mate."

The three of them scrambled down and climbed aboard. "Glad to see you, old-timer." Holding out his hand in greeting, the boat-owner was about Jasper's age, though more wrinkled and gray, and with a certain stoop to his back that appeared to slow his movements.

Jasper shook his hand, grinning as he retorted, "Don't you call me 'old-timer,' yer old bugger! There's still a dance or two in me yet."

They hugged and laughed, and after Tom and Kathy had been introduced, they took the boat out to sea. "I'll run her through her tricks, and then you can make up your own minds," Fred told them.

It was the most exhilarating experience, and one Kathy would never forget. Having never set foot on a boat before in her life, it was all new and exciting; a little scary at first, but then she got into the mood and enjoyed every minute.

Gathered at the stern of the boat, Fred at the helm, the three men discussed the technical attributes of the craft, while Kathy lay on the foredeck, the warmth of the sun on her face, the cool breeze in her hair, and her ears assailed by the comforting sound of rushing water as the boat sliced a way through.

It wasn't long before she began to understand why people

loved the sea so much. There was something magical about it.

When the trial run was over, they made their way back to harbor. Kathy rejoined the three men at the stern. "Well, what d'you think?" Fred addressed himself to Tom. "Is she a beauty or what?"

Tom couldn't deny it. "What's your best price?"

"You know my price. I expect Jasper here has already told you."

Behind Fred's back, Jasper gave Tom a wink, warning him to be cautious.

Tom nodded. "Yes, he told me, but I'm sure you could think again if you had to?"

"Mmm." He scratched his chin and looked at Jasper. Then he looked at Kathy; when she smiled, his eyes visibly brightened. "All right then!" He held out a hand for Tom to agree to a deal. "I'll knock off a hundred pounds, but that's my best offer."

Grabbing him by the hand, Tom closed the deal. "Done!" In a minute, out came the bottle of whiskey and glasses, which Fred had ready under the seat. "Let's drink to it!"

"Yer old bugger!" Jasper laughed out loud. "Yer meant to do a deal today, even if yer had to come down a bob or two."

Fred chuckled. "I got the price I wanted," he confided. "You always up your price so it can be knocked down—I thought you knew that?"

Tom couldn't help but laugh. "I've learned something new about you boat-owners," he said. "I can see I shall have to be on my guard in future."

Arrangements were made to bring the cruiser into West Bay, where Tom and Jasper would be waiting. "It'll take me close on a fortnight to root out the right documents, and prepare everything for the solicitor. Then he needs to go through it all, and draw up the agreement. Don't worry, though: by the time I hand her over she'll be ship-shape and serviced."

Tom nodded his approval.

With the deal concluded, the trio headed for the pub; an old place with character, it sat right alongside the railway lines. "By! I've had many a jolly time in 'ere," Jasper imparted roguishly. "I met a lovely lass by the name of Janice in this place." He scowled. "Trouble was, it turned out she were wed, with four kids and a bad-tempered old man."

For a while he enthralled them with tales of his escapades, and the laughter rang through the room. Because he wasn't too busy at that time of day, the landlord agreed to serve them ham and chips, even though the cook had already left for the day. "But don't expect nothing fancy." Though when he arrived with the meals half an hour later, they were a credit to him.

Jasper ordered the drinks. "Three pints o' yer best," he told the landlord, and that included one for Kathy.

"You're never going to drink that, are you?" Tom laughed when Kathy picked up the huge mug in her tiny fists.

"I certainly am!" she replied. "I've already done one thing today that I've never done before . . . going on that boat. Well, now I'm doing another," and she took such a gulp of the beer that it sent her into a choking fit.

"Take it easy!" Laughing, Tom patted her on the back. "We don't want you drowning yourself, at least not before you've had a chance to do all those other things you've never done before."

Appreciating his concern, Kathy finished the pint and got a round of applause. "Happen I should order yer another?" Jasper teased.

With the room already going around in her head, Kathy wisely settled for a dandelion and burdock.

Before they knew it, the time had rolled around to six o'clock. "By! That's the best day out I've had in years," the old man said. "I can't recall when I laughed so much."

Tom thought the same. "What say we take a walk along the front?" The truth was, he didn't want the day to end.

Kathy jumped at the idea. "I could use a bit of fresh air."

Like Tom, she didn't want the day to end either. "My head feels like it's been run over by a herd of elephants."

"Serves yer right for trying to be one o' the men," Jasper laughed. "Women 'ave no right drinking beer. It don't suit 'em."

Kathy laughed. "You're right there!"

Thrilled that he would be keeping Kathy's company for some time yet, Tom went to pay the bill. Meanwhile, the old man went off in the direction of the gents', while Kathy went in search of the ladies'. "I'm just going to powder my nose," she told Tom.

A few minutes later they were heading for the beach. The sands were still crowded with holidaymakers, but the promenade was not too busy. "By 'eck, this is grand!" Jasper strolled along, hands in trouser pockets and a look of contentment about him.

"There's three things in this world worth fighting for," he said. "Taking a boat out on the open seas; a stroll along the promenade in the heat of the day—" he gave one of his naughty winks—"and a woman in your arms. That'll do for me."

After a while, they stopped at the ice-cream parlor. Taking their tubs of ice-cream to a bench, they sat and watched the children at play. "Oh, but there's nowt like it!" With melted ice-cream all over his whiskers, Jasper winked at the ladies and felt like a king.

Alongside him, Kathy and Tom chatted quietly about West Bay and their new way of life. Kathy told him about Maggie and how she was coming to visit soon. "I'll have to keep her on a short rein though." She smiled at the thought. "The truth is, you never can tell what she'll do next."

Tom explained how he had come to love his life here, though there were certain things he must do before he could really settle down. He delighted her by confessing how much he had enjoyed the day and being with her, and asked a question that put a smile on her face. "Maybe we could do it again?" he wondered aloud.

"Why not?" she said, happily.

Sitting there together, with the sun on their faces and the sound of holidaymakers having fun, they talked about many things, but neither Kathy nor Tom revealed the reasons they had come to West Bay. And while they sat beside each other, looking at the sea and sky and the children playing, they thought how wonderful it all was.

Suddenly, Tom slid his hand over Kathy's and held it ever so gently. Taken by surprise, Kathy looked up to find Tom looking down on her, his quiet eyes smiling into hers. Neither of them spoke, but that moment was cherished in both their hearts.

The old man had seen it too, and couldn't help but smile to himself. Today, he hoped, had seen the beginnings of love, and his old heart was full.

All too soon, they were on board the bus, heading home. As before, Kathy sat next to Tom and, intermittently nodding off, the old man sat behind. A silence fell between Kathy and Tom, and for the first time she felt rather awkward with him, uncomfortably aware of his powerful frame next to hers. The quietness between them was overwhelming. She wanted to ask Tom many questions, and yet she sensed he wasn't ready for that kind of intimacy. He seemed distant, as though there were things preying on his mind, private things that needed all his attention. Kathy understood that, for she also had things on her mind, which only she could deal with.

When they got off the bus at West Bay, the old man begged an early night. "I've come over all tired," he said, yawning. "I reckon I'll get an early night." He yawned again before addressing Tom. "I'll see yer at the harbor-master's office in the morning. You'll need to register for a berth, an' there's all kinda forms and rigmarole to go through. Best mek it early, 'cause he's a wily old bugger . . . won't tend to nothing after ten o'clock. Once he's locked that office door and gone fishing, you'll not find him in a month o' Sundays!"

Tom agreed to meet the old chap outside the harbor-master's office at eight o'clock sharp. "See you then, Jasper, and thanks for today."

"You've got a beauty of a boat there, son," Jasper answered. "I reckon you've got years o' fun for your money."

He kissed Kathy goodnight. "Yer did us proud, lass," he told her with a grin. "I ain't never seen a woman drink a pint afore, apart from that bearded woman at the circus . . . knocked it back in seconds, so she did, *and* asked for more!"

He walked away, leaving Kathy and Tom laughing. "He's a one-off," Tom remarked. "The finest friend a man could ever have."

Kathy agreed. "No wonder everybody loves him," she said, "*I* don't know what I would have done without him."

At the front door, she asked if he would like to come in for a while. "Best not," he answered softly, "not tonight." The truth was, he needed to put a distance between them. He needed time to think through what had happened today. "It was very special having you along. Are you glad you came?"

Kathy's heart was racing. Standing here, so close to him, with the evening drawing in and the house behind them in shadow, it was too nerve-racking. "Yes, I am . . . very glad." She wanted to sound confident and strong, but her voice emerged as small and feeble.

Suddenly he took hold of her. "You're lovely." His dark eyes enveloped her. "You're so . . . different . . . from anyone I've ever met." He thought of her running out after that taxi; then in the chip shop, talking to him like she'd known him forever. And today, drinking a man's pint. She was so alive! Ready to take on the world.

She gave a shy, nervous laugh. "I'm just a bit crazy, that's all. You'd do well to steer clear of me."

He didn't answer. Instead, for the longest moment of her life, he gazed down on her. Looking up at him, she felt herself losing control. When, with great tenderness, he now tilted her face to his, touching his lips to hers, she never wanted it to end. The sensation of his warm lips against hers raced through her senses, and turned her heart upside down.

The kiss was fleeting. For a while longer, he held her close, his arms enfolding her, his face gentle against the softness of her skin. Then, holding her at arm's length, he looked down on her, the softest of smiles twinkling in those dark eyes.

She was so sure he was about to say something intense that when he let her go with the words, "I'd best be off. Goodnight, Kathy," she was stunned.

She watched him stride down the path. At the gate she

wondered if he might turn, but he didn't. Instead he went away at a quickening pace, like a man driven by demons.

"Goodnight," she murmured. A moment later, disillusioned by his sudden action, she went into the house and got herself ready for bed, where she lay, thinking of him, wondering what it was that made him so afraid to love.

# Eight

IRENE PACED THE FLOOR, A CIGARETTE IN ONE HAND AND a port and lemon in the other. "Where the devil is she?" Pausing, she took a puff of her cigarette and squashed it into the ashtray. She finished off her drink, replacing the glass on the table beside the smart black telephone, before grabbing the receiver. For the umpteenth time she asked for Samantha's number.

Yet again, there was no answer. She slammed the receiver down and began pacing again. "Wretched girl! Why is she never here when I need her?"

The sudden, invasive sound of the doorbell startled her. Rushing to the window, she peered out to see her daughter Samantha at the door, impatiently ringing the bell. Now, seeing her mother, she threw out her arms in frustration. "Let me in, for Chrissake!"

As soon as Irene opened the door, she fled past her into the living room. Irene followed. "Wherever have you been? These past few days I've tried time and again to contact you, but you're never home!" Irene was not best pleased. She was used to people being at her beck and call.

"I took a few days off. Is that so terrible?" Looking slightly disheveled and seeming somehow disturbed, Samantha rounded on her. "Anyway, I've told you before, I *won't* come running every time you call. Just because you had a new telephone installed for me doesn't mean you've a right to call me every hour of the day or night! Why don't you leave me alone?" she asked.

"Leave you alone? Just look at the state of you!" Taking a minute to observe her, Irene noted the untidy hair and the rumpled clothes. "What's the matter with you?" She was visibly shocked. It wasn't often her daughter spoke to her in that way. A closer look showed how her daughter's face was unusually flushed, and there was something unnerving about her that she couldn't quite put her finger on. "Where've you been?" she persisted.

Samantha seemed not to have heard. Instead she ranted on. "All the time . . . calling me up! Expecting me to run around here like a dog for a treat." Swinging round, she glared at her mother with a look of hatred. "I've told you before, Mother. I *have* got a life of my own, you know!"

Walking toward her, Irene grabbed her by the shoulders. "Don't you speak to me like that . . . after all I've done for you." Summoning all her formidable authority, she gave Samantha a vicious shake. "What have you been doing? Why couldn't I get hold of you?"

Suddenly, Samantha was crying. "It's all *your* fault. You got me used to having expensive things, and then, whenever you feel like it, you cut me off. Oh, it's all right when you want me around . . . leaning on me, making demands . . . do this, Samantha . . . do that! And if I don't dance to your tune, I'm cast aside like some kind of rubbish." The tears flowed and the rage subsided. In its place came the pitiful obedience that Irene had come to expect.

"I've been good to you, Samantha. I gave you a house, and jewelry worth a small fortune . . . which you couldn't wait to sell, damn you! I've warned you time and again about being so extravagant, but you take no notice. If you're not going off to these wild parties, you're entertaining undesirables at home. You spend money like it falls out of the sky, and I'm left to pick up the pieces."

Lowering her voice, she warned, "I can't go on rescuing you. I haven't got endless funds. Richard isn't a stupid man. I have to be careful."

"Don't give me that, Mother. You can twist him around your little finger. Besides, it won't be long now before you get the lot!"

Choosing to ignore this remark, Irene told her in a quiet, authoritative voice, "I'll ask you once more." Looking her daughter in the eye, she demanded to know, *"Where have you been?"*

"I've been away." Thrusting her mother off, Samantha strode across the room, where she leaned on the fireplace, staring defiantly. "Why? Am I not allowed to go away like normal people?" It was at times like these that the nastiness of the mother was evident in the daughter. "Am I supposed to ask you for permission, or what?"

Lighting another cigarette, Irene gave her a cool, patient look. "You still haven't answered me."

"That's because it's none of your damned business!" Looking uncomfortable, Samantha took a moment to gaze absentmindedly out the window. When she next spoke, it was not to answer her mother's question directly, but to put a question of her own. "You know I got a job as reception-ist, in that new hotel on the outskirts of town?"

"A job of which I never approved. I've told you before, there's no need for you to work if you don't want to. You know I'll always look after you. I've said so often enough. But I can't have you wasting money, left right and center."

Taking a long drag of her cigarette, she blew out the smoke in long, swirling tails that settled between them like a veiled curtain. "So, what have you been up to?"

"What the hell d'you mean?"

"Don't play the innocent with me. Come on, out with it. You always come running to me when you've done some-thing wrong. What is it now?"

"I haven't done *anything* wrong! Why do you always as-sume everything is *my* fault?"

"Because it usually is!" Scowling, she stared hard at this young woman who had turned out to be such a disappoint-ment. "They sacked you, didn't they?" She laughed, a hard, cynical laugh that showed her delight.

Samantha was defiant. "It wasn't my fault!" she claimed. "The idiots sacked me for arguing with the head reception-ist—a silly, spiteful old bitch who took a dislike to me straight away. She goaded me until I thought she should have a piece of my mind. It got a bit out of hand, and she went behind my back to the manager. I was finished on the spot. They wouldn't even *listen* to my side of the story!"

Irene shook her head. "You never learn, do you?" she commented dryly. "But I can't say I'm sorry they finished with you. I never wanted you working there in the first place."

"Please, Mother, I haven't come here to be lectured."

"All right. I can see you're worried." Squashing the second cigarette into the ashtray, she came to where Samantha had sulkily flung herself into the red leather settee. "I'll help you over this one, but you're going to have to curb your spending. I can't keep up with you. I *won't!*" She gave her daughter a prod. "You sold all my jewelry, damn you! But you should still have money left from what I gave you before . . . haven't you?"

"No." Now as Samantha glanced up, her face seemed haunted. "It's all gone."

Irene knew her daughter too well. "There's something else, isn't there?" she prompted. "Something you're afraid to tell me."

There was a moment when Samantha looked away, before she answered in a sorry little voice, "It's the house."

"What about the house?"

"I took out a loan against it, and now they want all the back payments or they'll take the house."

Taking a step backward, Irene was visibly shocked. Her icy composure vanished. "You *what?*" Taking a step forward, she slapped Samantha hard across the face. "You stupid little bitch! I told you never to do that. I warned you, it was the one thing you should never risk. And now you tell me they're about to repossess it. Well, let them! If they throw you out on the street, don't come running to me, because I've had enough! Get out of here. Go on . . . I don't want to see you anymore."

"Please, Mother!" Samantha revealed her crafty plan. "Father should never have left that house to Kathy. By rights it's half mine. I can take her to court and make her sell it."

Irene shook her head. She was adamant. "No court in the

land would make her sell it to give you half. She was given her father's house, and you were given mine. Out of the two of you, I'd say you got the best deal, wouldn't you?"

"Oh, please, Mother, you've got to help me." She always knew how to turn on the tears, but now, seeing that she had gone too far, Samantha was genuinely frightened. "Don't turn me away."

For what seemed an age, her mother stared at her. She suddenly saw how, in comparison to Kathy, this daughter was weak and useless, and in some measure she knew she must take the blame. She'd always thought Samantha was like her. She had cultivated and trained her, dreaming of only the best for her eldest child. But she had spoiled her. And Samantha had none of her own backbone.

"All right! I'll help you, but only this once. I'll clear the loan on the house, but I insist you come with me to a solicitor and ask if there can be some sort of agreement drawn up, to safeguard the house."

Though she didn't like the idea, Samantha had no option. "All right, Mother, anything you say."

Heaving a deep sigh, Irene opened her arms. "Come here, child."

Greatly relieved, Samantha went to her, and they hugged for a time until, stepping back, Samantha asked greedily, "When *he's* gone, it won't matter, will it? Because we'll be rich, won't we?"

Irene smiled. "*I'll* be rich!" she reminded her. "When Richard breathes his last I'll be worth a fortune." She rubbed her hands together in anticipation. "After I've sold the business, I intend to spend like never before." She giggled like a schoolgirl. "Who knows? I might even meet a *proper* man— one with youth and looks, who knows how to look after a lady . . ." She smiled slyly. "If you know what I mean?"

"So! I'm not a *proper* man, is that what you think?" While the two of them laughed at the prospect of Richard's demise and their good fortune, he had watched from the doorway. Having overheard everything, he was white with rage; bitter with himself for having been taken in so easily.

Shocked to the core, Irene and Samantha stared at him.

"No, Richard, you've got it all wrong!" Starting toward him, a look of innocence on her face, Irene cajoled, "I didn't mean it like *that* . . . I . . . just . . ." Now, as he put up his two hands, she stopped in her tracks. "You must know how much I love you."

He laughed. "I *thought* I did, but I was wrong. I see you now for what you really are. I've known for some time how you've been bailing her out . . . squandering my hard-earned money. Well, not anymore. I might be old, but I'm not completely senile. I've worked too long and hard to give it all away to two scheming parasites like you."

Clenching a fist, he shook it at them, his harsh words addressed to Irene. "From now on, I intend keeping a tight rein on every penny. If you want so much as a new pair of stockings, you'll have to ask me. Do you understand what I'm saying?"

He pointed to Samantha who was cowering back. "As for your bone-idle offspring . . . she can *work* for what she wants, the same as I've had to do all these years."

He gave Irene a withering stare. "For the sake of appearance, I won't see *you* on the street. You are my wife, after all." His voice shook with anger. "Though, God knows, any other man would have you out the door with only the shirt on your back!"

Ignoring her continuing pleas, he warned, "When I leave this house now, I intend going straight around to my solicitor."

Horrified, Irene grasped the implications. "No, Richard. Please! Don't do anything reckless. We need to talk. I want to explain . . ."

"The time for talking is over." Smiling, he nodded. "But don't worry, my dear. I'm not about to do anything 'reckless.' In fact, I've already done that in marrying you." His once-handsome features hardened. "But I'll tell you this much: by the time I've finished, I'll have my will so watertight that neither you nor your wasteful daughter will ever get your hands on a single penny. Not while I'm here on this earth, and not when I'm gone." His smile was withering. "That much you can count on."

As he walked out, Irene ran after him. "No, Richard . . . give me time to explain. You misunderstood . . . Richard!"

But he was already gone, and Irene was devastated.

Behind her, Samantha's thoughts were already turning to her sister, Kathy.

# Nine

KATHY LOVED HER NEW JOB. EVEN THE BOSS WAS PLEAS-
ant to work with, and though he saw himself as a bit
of a Romeo, she managed to keep him at bay.

"He fancies you, so he does!" The other woman who
worked the desk with her was a red-haired, freckle-faced
forty-year-old, an Irish lassie with an appetite for men and a
way of detailing her previous flings with the same exuber-
ance as Maggie. Her name was Rosie, and she had a laugh
that would frighten horses. "I've seen the young rogue looking at yer arse," she told Kathy with big eyes and a knowing
wink. "I'd watch him if I were you."

Putting her finger to her lips, Kathy managed to quieten
her. "He could be listening," she warned softly. "You'll get
us both the sack."

Rosie laughed. "Ah, but he'll never sack you!" she said confidently. "At least, not until he's had his wicked way with ye."

Kathy chuckled. "If that's the case, I'll be working here
till I'm old and gray."

Just then the young man in question walked by with the
area manager, the two of them deep in conversation. Tall and
lanky, he towered above his superior. "He'll be kept busy
today, so he will," Rosie imparted. "That area manager is a
right one. He wants everything just right, and woe betide
anyone who steps out of line."

Kathy observed the two men: the site manager, tall and
lanky, with slightly stooped shoulders, and his superior, a
short, stocky man with piercing eyes. "He looks like a nasty

piece of work," Kathy whispered. "I wouldn't want to get in his bad books."

Now, as they went out the door, the site manager turned to smile at Kathy, his small eyes crinkling until they almost disappeared into his head. As the cool September wind blew in through the open doorway, his flyaway, fair hair stood up on end, making him look as though he'd had a fright of sorts.

"Sure, he looks like one o' the little people." Rosie stifled the giggles until he'd gone out the door. "Ah, now, how could you be making love to a man that looks like *that?*" She fell about at the thought of it. "Sure, you'd never be able to concentrate your mind."

As always, Rosie's warped sense of humor had Kathy in stitches. "Rosie, you're a wicked woman!" Kathy chided, but when Rosie started she laughed until the tears ran down her face.

For the next two hours, they were kept busy. Being Saturday lunchtime, the holidaymakers were returning their keys and settling up before making their way back home.

The first to arrive was Ray Clitheroe, a haggard, worn-out fellow in his late forties. "Another holiday over," he groaned, "it's back to work on Monday . . . !" After paying his dues, the big, homely man leaned toward Kathy. "Thank God, that's what I say!"

"What? You mean you haven't enjoyed staying with us?" This was Kathy's first encounter with him. "If you need to make a complaint I can pass it on."

Rosie's interruption was timely. "Hello there, Ray," she said with her best smile. "Glad to be off again, are ye? Sure, it surprises me you keep coming, when you always seem glad to get away. Anybody would think we didn't look after ye, so they would."

He gave a surprisingly shy grin. "Now stop the teasing," he told her sternly. "You know very well I can only stand so much of it."

Kathy thought it a peculiar conversation, until she heard someone outside yelling at the top of her voice, "For Gawd's sake, Ray, get a move on. The kids are beginning to get restless." That was his wife, a plump and shrew-like woman.

"See you next year," he cried, rushing out through the door to six clambering children, and a torrent of abuse from his wife, who propelled him toward where the children were climbing and fighting and causing mayhem. "Sort 'em out!" Having pushed him forward, she then retired to a safe distance and lit up her fag.

"Ah, will ye look at the poor divil?" Rosie sighed. "It's no wonder he's glad to get back to work."

"I bet he was good-looking when he was younger." Kathy had observed the strong physique and those bright blue eyes that in their time must have been able to charm a woman.

"I dare say he was," Rosie agreed. "His wife must have been good-looking, too, before she went to seed." Kathy looked again at the woman, with her lank brown hair and double chin, and she could see how, even now, after having had six children, there was something about her that might be described as pretty. "I think you're right," she said thoughtfully.

"Oh, I am!" Right or wrong, Rosie always defended the female of the species. "And don't forget, it were *him* who got her with children one after the other. So don't you go wasting too much sympathy there."

The next person to return her keys was a woman of about thirty, a tarty peroxide blond, her face thick with make-up. "Sure, ye could scrape it off with a knife," Rosie remarked as the woman went out the door. Luckily the woman didn't hear, for if she had there would have been a stand-up scrap, as was her hot-tempered nature.

There followed a trail of caravanners, families and single folks, and couples on a dirty weekend, all leaving a small tip for the counter clerks and all vowing to come back next year.

"See them two?" Rosie gestured to a couple snogging in the doorway. "They're both married to somebody else . . . having a naughty weekend away, so they are."

Kathy was intrigued. "How do you know that?" It seemed unlikely they would tell anyone.

"Sure, they've been here before, when I used to clean out the caravans and chalets . . ." She preened herself. "That was before I got promoted to receptionist. Mind you, I had to do a bit of creeping, but I don't mind that. You get out what you put in . . . if you know what I mean." The look she gave spelled it out.

Blushing deep crimson, Kathy had to smile. "I can't think *what* you mean," she remarked, feigning innocence.

"Well, anyway . . . I were telling youse. I went off same as usual with my mop and bucket and all my cleaning paraphernalia. I usually started at number two and worked my way through to number eighteen, but on this particular day, number two had asked if I could leave it till later, on account of they wanted a lie-in. So, I started the other way round, and when I went merrily into number eighteen, thinking they'd already left for the day, I don't mind telling you, I got the shock o' my life, so I did!"

"Why?" Kathy was all ears. She had come to love hearing Rosie's accounts of the things that went on in the caravan park. "What happened?"

Rosie lowered her voice. "I usually start in the bedroom and work my way out. So, as cool as ye please, I opened the door with my key and went in. I'd already heard all the grunting and groaning and never thought for a minute it were *them* . . . I imagined it were dogs fighting outside. Well, like I say, I opened the door, and they were that busy they never even heard me. Bold as brass, the two of them: him with his bare arse jiggling about in the air, and her spread-eagled on the bed underneath him. It's enough to give a body the heart attack, so it is."

By now, Kathy couldn't tear herself away. "Whatever did you do?"

"At first I didn't move . . . my eyes were glued on his arse . . . up and down, it went . . . up and down, like one of them horses on a merry-go-round. Then, just as I stepped backward, the floor creaked and he swung round." She laughed out loud. "Jesus, Mary and Joseph! Sure, you've never seen a sight like it in all your life!"

Kathy had conjured up the most vivid of images in her mind. "Then what?"

"Well, he looked shocked and so did she, then he laughed and said, 'Bloody hell, woman! For a minute I thought it were the wife!' He then pointed to the woman who was wriggling to get out from under. "Worse still, it could have been her husband, and you wouldn't want to mess with *him*, I can tell you."

"And did you leave then?" Kathy's face was hot with embarrassment. She hoped she would never be put in such a predicament.

"Well, I was about to . . . I mean, I apologized and groveled and said I didn't realize, and he told me not to worry, but could I please go away and give them time to finish what they'd started."

Kathy's eyes grew big with amazement. "You're having me on!"

"I'm not! I swear to God Almighty, that's what he said. Well, I had to run outta there, because I could feel the laughter bubbling up inside me. Once outside, I laughed all the way to the stockroom. And do ye know how long it took them to surface?"

"I daren't guess."

"Two hours!" She chuckled at the memory. "They came into the storeroom and gave me a quid to keep my mouth shut. 'Don't let onto a soul what I told you,' the man said, and I never have . . . until now."

After the last of the caravanners had gone, Kathy thought how fortunate she had been to land this job, with a workmate like Rosie. She couldn't help but wonder if she would still be behind this desk next year. Or would she have moved onto pastures new? For now she was happy enough in her work; with Rosie working alongside her, making her laugh, the hours just seemed to rush by.

"Right!" Rosie gave her a nudge. "That's it for the day."

Making the last entry into the ledger, Kathy glanced up at the clock. It was pointing to midday. "My God! I didn't realize it was *that* time!" Closing the ledger, she helped Rosie hang the many keys in their rightful place on the board.

Just then, the weekend shift arrived to take over. "Fancy a drink before you get off?" At the minute, Rosie was without a man-friend and, as she had told Kathy many a time, her family was too far away for her to visit too often. "I've a thirst on me like a navvy," she said. "Will ye join me in a little drink?"

Going through the main bar, they ordered their drinks—a Bacardi for Rosie, and a long cool glass of orange for Kathy. "Look, I'm a bit short o' cash," Rosie began.

"Don't worry." Kathy was used to Rosie's excuses and, as always, she discreetly brushed it aside. "This is *my* treat." The sad truth was that Rosie liked a drink too much. She'd be paid on a Friday and, after a wild night out in Weymouth, she'd have to scrimp and save for the whole week. But Kathy didn't hold that against her. She knew all too well what it was like to be lonely, and if that was how Rosie coped, then it was nobody's business but her own.

When the drinks arrived, they carried them outside to the terrace. "It's getting chilly." Rosie took a great gulp of her drink. "Come September, there doesn't seem to be the same warmth in the sun. Don't ye think so, Kathy?"

Glancing up at the drifting clouds, Kathy agreed, though, "I hope we haven't seen the last of summer just yet," she mused.

Sitting there, lazily chatting with her new-found friend, Kathy thought she had never been happier. Now, as the clouds shifted and the sun struggled through, she looked across at the harbor and the people strolling by. An image of Tom suddenly came into her mind. She felt her face flush.

"Penny for them?" Rosie's voice interrupted her thoughts.

Kathy apologized. "Sorry, Rosie. I was miles away."

"Huh! Sure, I could see that for myself." She took a swig of her drink. "Was it your *man* ye were thinking of?"

Kathy blushed again. "*What* man?"

Rosie gave a wry little smile. "Ah, sure didn't I see him walking you home from work the other night, and didn't the stars sparkle in your eyes when you looked up at him?"

Kathy laughed. "Nonsense!" she said firmly.

"Ah well, we'll see about that," Rosie declared. "I'm just a born romantic, me." Taking another swig of her drink, she asked, "So he's not your man, then?"

Kathy was slow to answer, because she wasn't at all sure what she felt, never mind what his intentions were. "He doesn't say much about the way he feels," she said finally. "He hardly ever talks about himself, or his past. I'm not sure he views me as anything more than a friend."

"What do you feel about him?" Once Rosie had a drink inside her, there were no boundaries to what she might say. Besides, she had come to like Kathy a lot, and wanted her to be happy.

Kathy thought. "I really like him," she said, "but sometimes I wish I didn't." No sooner were the words out than she regretted them; she realized she did want to be more than his friend.

"Have ye told him?"

"No."

"Why not?"

"Because there's something about him . . . some private thing that makes me keep a distance. When we're together I feel he needs to talk, but then he suddenly clams up and that's that."

"He's got troubles of a kind . . . is that what you're saying?"

"I'm not sure. All I know is, we have been alone on a few occasions, but sometimes he seems to be somewhere else . . . miles away. Yes, he *does* seem to be troubled about something, and though I feel he wants to discuss it, he doesn't seem able to."

"Do you think he is keen on *you?*"

Kathy smiled at the prospect. "Like I say, I'm really not sure."

"Why don't ye *ask* him?"

Kathy shook her head. "I can't do that."

"Why not? You want to know where ye stand, don't ye?"

"Not if it frightens him off." Leaning forward, Kathy said quietly, "Oh, Rosie! He seems such a special man, I'm afraid to spoil it."

Not wanting to step over that line between concern and interference, Rosie backed off. She could see how deeply Kathy felt about Tom.

They both relaxed, drinking their drinks and, for a time, content to watch the world go by.

While Rosie dreamed of love won and lost, Kathy thought about Tom and how he did seem haunted by something. But she never doubted his love for her, not really, because she sensed it every time he looked at her.

Just then Rosie voiced what was on Kathy's mind. "Is he married, d'ye think?"

"I don't think so." Kathy was quick to answer. It was good to discuss it with Rosie, as long as she could be discreet. "I'm sure Jasper would have mentioned his wife if he had one."

"Have you ever seen him with a woman?"

"Never."

"Have ye been to his house?"

"No."

Rosie thought on that for a minute before stating the obvious: "He could be hiding something."

"Such as what?" Kathy didn't care much for this line of thought, but she had to admit to herself that all these things had already crossed her mind.

"I wouldn't know," Rosie answered, "but if I were you, I'd find out before ye get too deep in love it breaks your heart." She paused for a minute, her mind wandering back over the years. "I've been through all that, and I wouldn't wish it on my worst enemy."

"I know what you mean, Rosie," Kathy replied quietly. "And I appreciate you worrying about me." She had told Rosie that she was divorced, that Dan had left her, and she knew her new friend was looking out for her. She gave a whimsical smile. "But the truth is, I think about him when I go to sleep, and when I wake, and all day long he's never far from my mind."

Rosie groaned. "Dear mother of God, you're a lost cause, so ye are."

Kathy laughed. "Thanks for that!" Taking a long gulp of her drink, she then confided, "Jasper goes in Tom's house often. He'd know if Tom was hiding anything."

"Is Jasper that old fella with the beard and whiskers . . . a kind of rough-looking Father Christmas?" Rosie asked.

Kathy laughed. "He's the one. The best friend a man

could ever have, that's what Tom says, and I agree with him."

Rosie nodded. "I've passed the time of day with him myself. He's a lively old bloke . . . always ready to set the world to rights." She was curious. "How well d'you know him, then?"

"He just kind of turned up on my doorstep. He saw me there and we got talking. Apparently, he knew about my father and Liz. He helped me to get myself sorted out with the house and everything, and now he comes around often. It was Jasper who organized the outing to Weymouth the other week, you know, when Tom bought the sailing boat." She'd told Rosie all about that special day.

"Did Tom seem keen then?"

"He seemed to like talking to me on the bus. And he told me what a lovely time he'd had."

"Ah, sure, is that all?" Rosie was skeptical. "To my mind he either loves ye or he doesn't. A girl needs to know where she stands, so she does."

"So, *you'd* ask him, would you?"

Rosie thought on that. "Well, mebbe not. Y'see, if ye ask him, ye might frighten him off, then your chance is gone for good. On the other hand, if ye *don't* ask him, you may never know *where* ye stand. The two of youse could go on for years and in the end it could lead nowhere.'

"I'll have to take that chance." Kathy could not see herself asking Tom how he felt about her. It was too early. Too bold.

"There ye are then." Rosie sighed. "Like I said . . . you're a lost cause." She drained her glass. "I'd best be off. I've to get meself ready for a date. Y'see, there's this caravanner who wants to take me out for a night on the tiles, and who am I to waste an opportunity like that, eh?"

Kathy had a warning. "Be careful, Rosie. Some of these single blokes are only out for what they can get."

"Ah sure, don't I know that?" She giggled like a schoolgirl. "And I don't give a damn."

She went away down the street waving and chuckling, and Kathy waved back. "Have a nice time," she murmured with a little smile, "and don't get into mischief." Rosie was made in the same mold as Maggie, she thought, and, rain or shine, she wouldn't want either of them any different.

"D'yer want that drink, missus?" The little cockney boy had slid into Rosie's seat without Kathy seeing. " 'Cause if you don't want it, you might as well give it to *me*."

Momentarily taken aback, Kathy recognized the little chap as being one of the caravanners whose mother, with one other child, had only recently arrived at the site. The mother appeared to have little money; from what Rosie had told her, the woman's husband had paid in advance to book them all into the caravan and promptly ran off with some woman, supposedly a friend of theirs.

Angry and disillusioned, the mother had been determined to enjoy their holiday anyway. As she said to Rosie, "To hell with him . . . before too long he'll come back, wanting his warm bed and an easy meal on the table, but when he does he'll be shown the door, you can depend on that."

Without hesitation, Rosie had been in full agreement. "You do right," she told the hapless woman. "Men like that want their doofers chopped off." Though, knowing Rosie, Kathy thought that would be the last thing she wanted . . . for any man to be without his "doofer," as she called it.

"Well, missus, do I get the drink or not?"

Kathy pushed the glass of orange toward him. "I'd had enough anyway," she told him with a smile. "Go on, son. You finish it if you want."

"Cor, thanks, missus!" In minutes he had wolfed the drink down. "Mam says we can't afford luxuries," he said, his eyes filled with tears. "She says our old man's run off with his tart, and we'll have to go without."

"Without *what?*"

His little face was downcast. "Everything! Me dad promised we'd be going on the donkeys in Weymouth and we'd 'ave ice-cream. He said if we were good he might take us for a ride in one o' them boats . . . he said sometimes if you pay, they let you take them out all by yourself." He glanced up, his eyes alive with anger. "An' now we ain't gonna get nuffin." As he talked he nervously wound his tiny fists one into the other. "I hate him." His bottom lip began to tremble. *"I hate him!"*

Aware that at any minute he would burst into tears, Kathy put a comforting arm around his shoulders. "I'll tell you what," she said. "How about if I treat you to an ice-cream? A big strawberry cornet, with chocolate sauce on top."

Though he licked his lips at the prospect, he shook his head. "Naw. Me mam says she'll tan me arse if I take anything from strangers. I shouldn't have had that drink, only I were thirsty, and she ain't got no money." He thought about the ice-cream and wondered if it would be all right, but then he shook his head. "Naw. I'd best not, missus."

"What if we find your mammy and ask her?"

As it turned out, they didn't have to look far for her, because just then she could be heard calling for him, and a moment later she appeared from around the corner. "Where've you been, you little sod?" Taking him by the scruff of the neck, she told Kathy, "I'm sorry if he's been a nuisance. He keeps wandering off, and I can't keep track of him."

Kathy assured her he had been fine. "In fact, I was thinking of asking you a favor." She could see how, in spite of her bravado, the poor woman looked haggard and pale. It must be hard for her to cope, she thought.

The woman was instantly suspicious. "What kind o' favor?"

"I could take him off your hands for half an hour if you like . . . give you a break?"

"Why? What you got in mind?" God only knew she could do with a break. The girl was too young to realize what was happening, but not the boy. He was in such a rebellious mood, she didn't know how to deal with him.

Kathy understood her dilemma. "He'll be safe enough, I promise. I thought I might get him an ice-cream and take him down to see the boats . . . if that's all right with you? A friend of mine has just bought a small boat. I'm sure, if we asked him, he wouldn't mind letting your lad go aboard . . . just to have a look round."

"Oh, please, Mam!" By this time the boy was leaping up and down. "Please!"

The woman studied Kathy for a minute; it wasn't often anyone was kind to them. "You're from the reception, ain't yer?"

Kathy nodded. "I work with Rosie, yes."

The woman laughed, a roar of a laugh that stopped passers-by in their tracks. "That Rosie's a buggeroota and no mistake! If she had her way she'd cut my old man's doofer off, that's what she said, and I reckon she's right an' all!"

When she'd composed herself, the woman said, "Go on then, Frank. But only for half an hour. Keep an eye on him," she said to Kathy, " 'cause he's like slippery Jack: you never know where he'll be off to next. He might be a bag o' trouble, and there are times when I could swing for 'im."

She smiled down on the boy, who returned the smile with affection. "But I don't want him drowning."

So it was agreed.

"Where's the boat?" Frank asked for the umpteenth time.

"Just there." Kathy pointed to the small boat moored at the harbor. "The one with the furled-down sails." Amongst the fishing boats it was easy to spot.

"All right. I'll be there in half an hour to collect him." Wagging a finger at the boy, his mother told him, "You behave yourself, or there'll be a smack o' the arse waiting for you when I get back!" With that, and the other, small child in her arms, she went away, "To sit by the river and watch the ducks," she said.

Kathy had bought him an ice-cream, just as she had promised, with a river of chocolate sauce running down the sides; while he slurped at that—with ice-cream and sauce mingling to form all manner of patterns on his shirt—she led him down to the harbor. When he'd finished, she wiped his face and shirt with her handkerchief, until at length he looked near enough respectable.

"I'm not sure if my friend is on the boat," she explained. "If not, I'm sure Jasper will be there. He'll persuade one of the fishermen to let you on board."

"Who's Jasper?"

"He's another friend."

"That's a funny name."

"It suits him though."

"What does he look like?"

Kathy smiled. "Rosie says he's a rough-looking Father Christmas."

The boy laughed. "There ain't no Father Christmas."

Kathy was shocked. "Who told you that?"

"My dad."

"Well, *I* believe in Father Christmas, and I don't care what *anybody* says."

There was a minute of quiet contemplation while Frank considered Kathy's profound statement, after which he declared boldly, "*I* believe in Father Christmas too!"

Kathy squeezed his hand. "Good for you!" If she did nothing else today, she had restored a child's belief.

As they approached the harbor, Kathy could see Tom on the decking. "TOM!" Having caught his attention, she took the boy at a run over the little bridge. "We need to ask you a favor," she said breathlessly.

Tom looked pleased to see her. "Who's your little friend?"

Kathy looked down at the boy. "This is Frank."

Tom held out his hand in greeting. "Hello, Frank," he said.

The boy was wary of Tom, but not shy. "Hello, mister. Can I come on your boat?"

Laughing, Tom ushered them aboard. While the boy scouted about at the helm, Kathy gave Tom a brief resume of the boy's background. "His mother's doing the best she can, but the children are having to go without."

Tom thought it was a sad affair. "All right," he said. "We'll see what we can do to make his holiday one to remember." For a moment, he gazed at her, then smiled and nodded. Placing his hand lightly on her back, he ushered her inside to where the boy was pretending to be captain. "Will it go?" he asked.

"Will *what* go?" Tom thought of his own son, and the pain was like a fist inside his heart.

"This boat. Will it go?"

"Yes, it *will*," he said as he sat beside the boy, "but I'm not yet up to taking her out to sea."

The boy's disappointment was obvious. "Why not?"

Tom tried to explain. "I've only just got it. There's a lot to learn before I can take her right out."

Seeing the boy's despondence, he had an idea. "Look, I'll tell you what. Let me have a word with an old friend of mine. I'm sure we can wangle something for you."

"Is he called Jasper?"

"Well, yes . . ." He glanced up at Kathy, who gave him a knowing wink. "So, you already know him, do you?"

"Kathy told me about him!" His smile lit the day. "He's the one as looks like Father Christmas. My dad says there ain't no Father Christmas, but me and *her* know different, don't we?" Gesturing with his thumb, he nodded appreciatively when Kathy confirmed his assertion with a smile.

Leaving Kathy and Frank on board, Tom set off to find Jasper. He tracked him down aboard one of the fishing boats. Jasper and his mate, Jack Plummer, were sitting, pipe-smoking and enjoying a glass of cider.

Tom quickly explained the situation; both men thought the boy should have the treat of his life. "Fetch him along," Jack said. "We'll take him up to the headland and back."

When Tom told him what the plan was, Frank was beside himself with excitement. "Can I drive?"

"You'll have to ask the skipper."

Once on board, Jack handed Kathy the smallest lifejacket he could find. "Put this on the boy," he ordered. "And here's another for yourself. Nobody comes out on this boat without wearing a lifejacket."

When all four were suitably dressed, the skipper kicked the engine into life, and they were away, with the boy whooping and hollering, and Kathy being thrown from side to side. "You haven't got your sea-legs yet," Jasper told her. "You'll have to come out more often, so ye will."

While the boy sat in the wheelhouse with Jasper and the skipper, Kathy and Tom kept out of the way. There wasn't enough room for all of them in there, so they stood at the stern amid the buckets, ropes and nets, watching the water churning in the boat's wake, and feeling content in each other's company. "He's a smart little boy," Tom remarked.

"It's a pity his father's gone off and left him. A boy needs his father."

He watched the boy for a time, taking great delight in his antics at the wheel. Wearing the boatman's oversized cap, he was pretending to be skipper. "So, he thinks Jasper is Father Christmas?" Tom laughed at the idea. That's *you*, is it?"

"No, it's *Rosie's* fault." Kathy relayed the discussion she and the boy had had on the way to the harbor. "His father told him there was no Father Christmas, and I'm afraid I disputed that."

Tom condoned what Kathy had done. "That's a sad thing for a father to tell the boy," he murmured. "Kids need to believe in magic. We *all* do."

He thought of the many times when his own children's eyes had lit up when faced with the magic of Christmas trees, and presents that had "come down the chimney." He remembered them being mesmerized by tales of how the little people helped Father Christmas prepare all the toys, ready for deliveries through the night. It was tradition; it was fantasy and wonder; it gave only pleasure. He thought of all that, and was saddened by the awful knowledge that his own children had never gone beyond that innocent state of wonder, before their young lives had been cut short.

Kathy had wondered at his comment, and now she wondered at his prolonged silence. When, like now, he lapsed into that dark, secret mood, she knew he was somewhere she could not go. It was as if a barrier had gone up between them, and unless he trusted her enough to confide in her, she had no way of breaking it down.

She could hear Frank laughing and shouting in the wheelhouse, and Jasper explaining everything to him. Suddenly, they made a sharp turn; the boy could hardly contain his enthusiasm, "It's like the funfair!" As they bounced from wave to wave, he was overwhelmed with excitement.

All too soon, the short boat ride was over. When his mother came to collect him, the boy was full of it. "Cor, you should have seen me!" As they went away, he could be heard telling her all about the boat and how the water splashed up on the deck, and he even wore the skipper's cap. "I'll be good at school," he promised, "because when I grow up, I want to be a fisherman!"

Somewhere in amongst all that excitement was his proud declaration that, "Daddy was wrong. There *is* a Father Christmas! I've *seen* him." He chatted on and on, a very different little boy from the sorry, thirsty child who had sidled up to Kathy earlier.

As they turned the corner, before disappearing out of sight, his mother glanced back. When her gaze alighted on Kathy, she smiled. And Kathy understood.

"You're a natural with children," Tom remarked as they walked back to his boat.

"I love kids," she confessed. "I always said I'd have four—two of each." She laughed. "Trouble is, we can't have them to order, can we?"

When they reached the boat and Kathy prepared to carry on home, he put out a hand to keep her there. "Don't go yet, Kathy." There was a well of emotion in his quiet voice. "Please?"

Kathy gave a nervous little laugh. "I won't, not if you don't want me to."

"Come on then!" Greatly relieved, he said, "Come aboard."

Having hoped he would ask her to stay, Kathy was suddenly afraid. She thought about Rosie's warning, that he might break her heart. She was already beginning to fall in love with him. But what if he didn't have the same feelings for her? What if she was making a rod for her own back by keeping company with him? She didn't want more heartbreak. Suddenly, all the old doubts came alive in her mind.

"I make a great cup of tea." His voice was soft in her ear, his smile enticing.

She nodded. "All right." She smiled. As he helped her up the gangplank, all the doubts seemed to vanish.

While Tom busied himself in the tiny galley, she took the opportunity to have another look round. "It seems different from before, when you went to buy it." She was outside now, seated on the bench in the well of the stern. "It's lovely, Tom. Really lovely."

Emerging with the tray, he explained, "I found some ginger-nuts in the cupboard. I don't know about you, but I've always been partial to a ginger-nut." The tray also contained milk, sugar, two cups and saucers and a huge pot of tea. "I've made plenty." He grinned wickedly. "I figured, the more you have to eat and drink, the longer I might keep you here."

Placing the tray on an upturned crate, he proceeded to pour the tea. "How do you like it?"

"One sugar, plenty of milk." Kathy's heart was racing after what he had said, and she was content to let him do the pouring. "Oh, and I might as well have a ginger-nut, seeing as you've gone to the trouble of bringing them out." Reaching forward, she helped herself to one. "You love this boat, don't you?" She felt so easy with him, it was incredible.

He glanced at her. "I do, yes." He wanted to say more, but the words were locked in, and he couldn't let them out.

"You said the boat was 'different,' " he reminded her.

Kathy took a sip of her tea. "Yes, I did." Turning her head, she looked back inside. Somehow the boat seemed to have taken on a heart since she had last seen it. "You've turned it into a home," she said. "Look at that—with the sun coming out, and the portholes open to the breeze, the whole place seems larger and brighter." There's something else, too, she thought. There was an air of belonging . . . a sense of achievement. "It's got your stamp all over it," she said. "I think it's . . . lovely!"

Sitting on the curve of the seat, he looked at her for a moment, the merest suggestion of a smile in his eyes as he said softly, "I think *you're* lovely."

Kathy had never been one for blushing, but since meeting Tom she seemed to be blushing all the time. She blushed now, shrugged her shoulders; she didn't know quite what to say. "Are you happy with the boat, Tom?" she stammered. "Will you take her out soon?"

He laughed. "I'm not ready yet."

Pointing to the tunnel of water that led out to sea, he explained, "That's the thing I'm worried about . . . some days the water thrashes about like a demon. On bad days, I've seen experienced sailors get thrown about like matchwood.

No, I've got to be a better sailor than I am now before I dare attempt it. Jasper reckons I'll be good enough to take the wheel pretty soon."

"Tom?"

"Yes."

"Will you tell me something?'

He grew anxious. "Depends what it is. But ask me anyway, and we'll see." He had an idea what she was about to ask, and he had been dreading it.

"It was something Rosie said."

"Who's Rosie?"

"A woman I work with." She smiled. "Lately, she's taken it on herself to look after my interests."

He nodded. "I see. And she's told you to be careful of me, that I could be married, and trying to take advantage of you?" He sensed her dilemma, and knew the moment had come when he had to be straight with her. Kathy was special to him and he didn't want to lose her, yet neither did he feel able to confide in her . . . about what happened that day on the cliff, or what his true feelings were toward her now. How could he confide those things, when what happened was still so raw inside him?

Aware of his confusion, yet not knowing how to deal with it, Kathy apologized. "I'm sorry, Tom. I shouldn't have put you on the spot like that. Please . . . just forget I ever said anything."

"I can't!" He fought the inner struggle and was determined. "You have a right to know." He took another drink of his tea and, taking a deep breath, he turned to face her. With great difficulty, he began to describe what had happened. "In a way, I *am* married," he said quietly. "Though my wife isn't alive on this earth, she's very much a part of my life, and probably always will be until I find out why she was taken."

"No, please, Tom, don't!"

Kathy had never seen anyone in such great pain as he seemed to be now. His hands were clenched and trembling and his voice almost inaudible; his face was etched with such powerful emotion, and he was clearly finding it difficult to talk.

"It's all right," she told him again, "you don't have to tell me anything." She wished she could turn back the clock to that moment before she put the question, because now she had unleashed something that made her afraid. Why couldn't she have left things as they were? Now it was spoilt; she was putting him through all kinds of agony, and he might never forgive her.

"I *have* to tell you," he answered softly, "I *want* to."

When he reached out to take her hand, she held him tight, waiting for him to go on, but it seemed an age before he began to describe his family, and how happy they were. "I was a lucky man," he said. "We had a beautiful house, no money troubles. I had a job that took me all over the country, though there were times when I would rather have stayed home with the family. I had a wife who loved me and two adorable children." His voice broke. "They were my life!"

Pausing to remember, he went on. "It was over a year ago now. We were returning home from a visit to the seaside— Bournemouth. It was a day much like today: the sun was shining and the kids were fighting in the back, as usual . . ." He smiled, a painful, sorry smile that tore at Kathy's heart. "I remember . . . the coastal roads were clear, and we were making good time."

Like so many times before, he tried hard to remember every little detail of what happened. "I saw the car in my rear-view mirror . . . it was blue; I think it was a Hillman, or it could have been a Morris, I didn't have time to get a good look. It got closer and closer, and I suddenly realized it was *too* close . . . he was on my tail . . . I could see he meant to hit us! Dear God . . . what was he doing? I yelled, but he couldn't hear me . . . I couldn't see his face . . . he was wearing dark glasses . . . his hat was pulled down low."

He leaned back, closing his eyes, composing himself . . . reliving every minute of that terrible day.

Closing her hand over his, Kathy gave him strength.

He opened his eyes and glanced down at her upturned face. "There are times when it overwhelms me," he confessed. "I can't sleep, and I can't think straight. Then I have to walk the floor until the rage inside me begins to settle."

He told her everything, every now and then his voice breaking and his hand gripping hers so hard that she could feel the blood flow out. "They tried to say it must have been an accident, but it was no accident, I can tell you. He came at me with the intention of sending me over that cliff." In his mind's eye he could see the car bearing down on them. "Can you imagine? We were being driven over the cliff and there wasn't a damn thing I could do about it! It was all too fast and furious . . . that maniac meant to kill us all, there's no doubt in my mind about it!"

As he described the way it had been, it was as though he was there again, on that day, in the car, and the driver of the other car ramming them time and again. "I couldn't turn . . . can you imagine, we were heading over the cliff, and I couldn't turn the car. The kids were screaming . . . my wife . . . terrified. Oh, dear God!"

With a suddenness that startled Kathy, he sprang off the bench and hurried into the cabin. When Kathy found him he was slumped on the seat in the corner, his hands over his face. "I'm sorry." He looked up, his tear-stained face haggard. "I thought I could talk about it without breaking down."

"It's all right." Kathy had been shocked by his story. "Don't say any more." Sitting on the floor, she held his hands and, looking up, told him, "You don't need to go on. I understand now why you seem so lonely at times . . . I do understand, Tom, and there's no need to punish yourself."

He shook his head. "No, Kathy. I need to tell you," he murmured. "I *want* you, of all people, to know what happened."

After taking a moment, he went on. "We went over the cliff. There was this awful silence. After the revving engines and the impact of bumper on bumper . . . the children's cries and my wife shouting for them to lie down . . . it seemed eerie somehow. Then the kids started screaming again . . ." His voice broke.

"We seemed to hang in the air, and then I remember hitting the ground, the car bouncing . . . then . . . nothing. Later, when I woke up in hospital, they told me they were all gone . . . my wife, the children . . . *all gone!*"

Leaning forward, he put his hands over his face and tried to shut it out, but the memories were too vivid. "Whoever drove us over that cliff meant to kill us." He was sure of it. "For some reason I may never know, he wanted us all dead."

Shocked to her roots, Kathy asked softly, "I don't understand . . . Why would *anyone* want to kill an entire family?"

"I've no idea. I've racked my brains and I don't understand it any more than you do."

"Did they find him?"

Tom shook his head. "It wasn't for want of trying. The police did all they could, and so did I . . . as much as I was able. But neither the car nor the driver were ever found."

"And you can't rest until he's hunted down, that's it, isn't it?" Kathy felt a sense of relief, though it was mingled with fear for his safety.

"Yes." He was glad he'd told her. "I gave up my job, sold the flat, and moved here to West Bay, hoping to find some sort of peace," he confessed. "But there will never be any peace, until I find out . . . who? And *why?*" A terrible anger filled his soul. "I want him hanged for what he did."

Kathy felt his hatred. It was like a physical force. "You said you couldn't see the driver?"

"Not clearly, no." He was intrigued. "Why? What are you getting at?"

"Well, if you couldn't see the driver . . . how can you be certain it was a man?"

Startled by her comment, he looked up. "My God! You're right, it *could* have been a woman! It could have been *anyone!*" That idea had never occurred to him, but now, thanks to Kathy, it was something else to bear in mind.

"You're going back, aren't you?" Kathy could see it in his eyes. "You came here to heal, and now you're going back to try and find whoever did it?"

"I have to." His soft smile was reassuring. "But not yet. I'm not ready yet."

"When?"

"Very soon. My mind's beginning to clear. I can *almost* think it through without everything clouding over. But, if I'm to track the bastard down, I need a little more time. *I need to control the hatred.*" He shuddered with emotion. "Right now, the hatred is controlling *me.*"

Getting up onto her knees, Kathy looked him in the eye, her voice tender when she asked, "Then, will you be able to—" she hesitated to ask after what he had just told her, but the words needed to be spoken—"do you think you'll ever be able to love again?"

"Oh, my Kathy . . ." Reaching out, he cupped her face in his strong, gentle hands, and, looking down into her eyes, he whispered the words she had wanted to hear. "There's nothing I'd like more in this world than to make a life here, with you. But it has to be right . . . everything in its place."

For no reason she could imagine, Kathy began crying—soft, wonderful tears that fell down her face and wet the palms of his hands. "I love you," she murmured. "Don't go." She was so afraid for him. "There's someone out there who wants you dead. Don't go, Tom. Please . . . don't go."

He leaned forward, his face almost touching hers, his warm breath fanning her face. "I have to. You must know that." Looking at her now, seeing the love and concern she felt for him, he would have given anything to stay, but he couldn't. The time to go was almost on him.

She nodded, and now, as she began to speak again, he slid to his knees and, caressing her face, drew her closer, his arms strong about her and his mouth closing over hers; in that precious moment, the love between them blossomed.

Though it was wrong of him, he wanted to make love to her there and then, but his emotions were too stirred.

They kissed and talked, and though she wanted him with every nerve in her body, Kathy knew it wouldn't be right. But their time would come, she told herself, and when it did, God willing, they would have their whole lives together.

As he held and caressed her, Tom yearned to take her to himself; there was a minute when his hands slid down her dress and brushed her breast, and all the manhood in him cried out for her. But then he slumped back, the images of his wife and family tormenting him. "I can't." He wondered if he would ever be free. "Forgive me, Kathy. It's too soon." His one terrible fear was that the demons of that day might never leave him.

Kathy didn't speak. Instead she wound her arms about him, and there, on the floor of the boat, gently rocked by the rolling movements of the water, they sat and talked, and it was a tender, unforgettable thing. "We love each other," she murmured, gently kissing his neck, his face, and then his mouth. "We can wait."

"I'll make it up to you," he promised. "When it's all over, I swear to God, I'll make it up to you." Wrapping his strong arms about her, he drew her to him. It felt good; with her head resting on his shoulder and the warmth of their bodies mingling, he thought there could be no more heaven than this.

For a long time they lay there, content in each other's company, the silence broken only by the sound of water lapping against the harbor wall outside.

The gentle rolling movement lulled their senses, and, for now at least, anxiety fell away, and all was well with the world.

# *Ten*

---

MAGGIE WAS ON HER SECOND WARNING.

Being a cinema attendant was her third job since Kathy left and, though she loved it, she could not seem to keep out of trouble. Now, having been hauled before the manager yet again, she was defending her action. "The little sod *needed* throwing out! I told him time and again and still he wouldn't listen. How can anybody watch the bleedin' film with kids shouting and bawling all over the place?"

"Be quiet!" At the end of his tether, the manager observed her through narrowed eyes. "Just look at yourself!" He had made many mistakes in his time, but never as bad as when he gave this one a job. "You're a disgrace!"

"What do you mean?"

"I mean . . . you're too . . . too . . ." Shrugging his narrow shoulders, he couldn't quite think of the right words. "You just don't make the right impression on the customers." Seeing her now, bristling with defiance, wild black hair tumbling around her face with its crimson lips, he despaired. "For a start you're made up like a tart off the streets; you're forever arguing with your workmates; and you're always finding fault with the customers. Jesus! I've lost count of the number of people you've thrown out . . . often for something as trivial as getting out of their seats to go to the toilet!"

Maggie bristled. "That's not true. If you're talking about that man who caused a riot when he stood up in the row, he was getting ready for fisticuffs with the man behind . . . it weren't *my* fault if he kept kicking him in the backside every time the film got exciting." She let out a throaty laugh. "Besides, he were a big bloke. I'll have you know I took my life in my hands when I threw that one out."

"Enough!" The manager waved his hand. "All that aside, what about the times I've caught you in the best seats up there in the gallery, blatantly watching the film instead of tending to the people downstairs."

Leaning back in his seat, he groaned. "Give me one good reason why I shouldn't finish you here and now?"

"Because I've got you by the short and curlies, that's why!" Maggie had a way with words. "If I was to tell your wife what we get up to after everybody else has gone home, she'd string you up from the highest lamp-post."

With a nervous giggle, he called her bluff. "I know my wife, and she would never believe you."

"Fair enough." Maggie knew he was bluffing. "Let's put it to the test, shall we?"

Scrambling out of his chair, he almost ran to where she stood. "Now, now, Maggie, let's not be too hasty." Pressing himself against her, he stroked her arm. "I dare say I could forget that last complaint."

Maggie gave him a cool stare. "If you mean the old biddy who threatened me with her umbrella, I don't give a bugger. If I ever set eyes on her again, I swear, I'll knock her lights out. I don't stand for nobody questioning my authority." She squared her shoulders. "When I'm out there, this uniform counts for something. That's what you told me when you gave me the job, an' I'm not having a bleedin' old cow like that tell me what to do!"

"Well, of course you're right, Maggie." The thought of his wife finding out about his antics under the stage sent a cold shiver through the manager. "That uniform *does* mean something."

"So, I can carry on as usual then?" She knew she had him right where she wanted him.

"Absolutely!" He felt his heart sink to his boots. But at least he was thankful that Maggie wouldn't tell his wife.

"Right then!" Maggie turned to leave with a cheeky smile.

"I'd best get on. They'll be arriving any minute. Sandra's off sick as well, you know, so that only leaves me and Doreen."

As she crossed the room, he dared to run after her. "Wait, wait!"

Swinging round, she rolled her eyes to the ceiling. "What now?"

Putting his arms around her waist, he smiled, that smarmy little smile she had come to know so well. "What say you try a little harder to be nice to people?"

"*What* people?"

"You know very well what people! The people who pay good money to come and watch a film; the people who pay your wages and mine . . . the people who *you* seem to think are nothing but a nuisance. Be nice to them, that's all I'm asking. See if you can speak to them without shouting . . . and don't threaten to throw their kids out on the street for the slightest little thing." Exasperated, he pleaded, "Just let them watch the film in peace."

Looking him in the eye, she continued to chew her gum, then she considered what he'd said, and took no notice at all. "Right." Taking out her chewing gum, she slapped it in his hand, and off she went, leaving him open-mouthed, and wishing he was anywhere but there, with the incorrigible Maggie; until he recalled in the twinkle of an eye what a randy devil she was when roused. With that in mind, he went back to his work with a smile on his face.

Out in the foyer, the woman in the ticket-booth gave Maggie a bit of good advice. "You'd do well to watch your step with that one. He can be a nasty little man." Lowering her voice, she imparted a bit of gossip she'd heard from Sandra. "I'm told he tries it on with all the girls . . . aims to get his wicked way with them, that's what I've heard."

Maggie gave her a wink. "Don't you worry, gal. If he tries it on with me, he'll get what's coming to him!"

"Good girl." The woman failed to see the double meaning behind Maggie's naughty words. "I'm glad to see you can look after yourself," she said.

Maggie laughed. "Oh, I can do that all right," she said.

"I'd like a pound for every man who's tried it on with me."
*And* got his wicked way, she thought.

Suddenly the outer doors opened and in came a rush of
people, all jostling to be first to the ticket-booth. "One at a
time, if you please!" The woman never did like being under
siege. "You'll not get served any quicker by pushing and
shoving."

Smiling to herself, Maggie was off. "I'd best go and check
inside."

While the older woman settled herself in the ticket-booth,
Maggie went to the cloakroom, where she repainted her lips
and brushed her hair. When that was done, she took a look
at herself in the long mirror. "It's no wonder the men fancy
you," she muttered with a wide grin. "You're such a good-
looking gal."

Another few minutes to straighten her usherette's hat and
tweak at her red uniform, with its smart little jacket and
straight skirt. Then, off she went to meet the army that
would soon be pouring in for the Saturday matinee. "And
don't forget what he said," she warned herself. "Be nice to
the people." Though it wasn't easy when some little horror
was being allowed to paint the seats with ice-cream or run
about yelling and screaming when other people were trying
to watch the film. "Stay calm, gal," she told herself. "Don't
let the buggers get to you."

Going through the big double doors, she collected her
torch from the cubby-hole and began making her way back
to the door. Before opening the doors she looked around her;
at the row upon row of red seats; plastic fold-up seats at the
back and plush red at the front where they cost three-pence
more. Bursting with pride, she thought, "Oh, if only Kathy
could see me now."

She turned her eyes upward to the little circles that jutted
out like eyelids, and the long red curtains at the exit doors,
and finally at the big, wide screen that sat like a king on its
own stage. "One day, I'll be up there," she murmured, "when
some talent scout spots me and sees what I'm worth." Sadly,
Maggie's unfulfilled dreams were many and varied. With that
she threw open the doors, where already the customers

waited to be let in. With as much pleasure as she could muster she led them two by two along the aisle to their seats.

She shone her torch for them to see their way through the dimly lit cinema, seating them and smiling sweetly before making her way back to the doors. "So far so good," she muttered through gritted teeth.

It was only when a rather large woman arrived with two children that the smile faded; it was the very same woman who had complained to the manager. Now, on seeing Maggie, she warned in a shrill voice, "Don't you start on me!" Thrusting her two children behind her, she waited for Maggie to retaliate.

When, instead, Maggie smiled at her, the poor woman was flustered and confused. Grabbing the children, she hurried to their seats, where she sat silent, occasionally peeping at Maggie and thinking she must have had a telling-off, or why would she be so nice? Whatever the reason, it was unnerving.

For the first half of the new horror film, *The Ghost Ship*, everything went well. There were a few screams from the front when the young couple began hearing strange noises, but that was only to be expected; even Maggie had a scary moment. It wasn't long before half the people in the cinema were yelling for the heroes to "Get out of there!"

Otherwise it seemed quiet enough; until a particularly creepy moment caused a young girl to scream in terror. That set off everybody else, and somewhere at the front a child started crying. Then an argument broke out; Maggie, with torch at the ready, set off to investigate.

When she got there, it wasn't the children causing the trouble. It was a frail old woman and a burly hunk of a man, who by the time she got there were already in the throes of a heated argument. "She attacked me with her stick!" The big man was leaning threateningly over the woman's seat in front. "I'm not taking that from nobody, least of all a senile old busybody!"

The words were hardly out of his mouth when the woman upped with her stick and cracked him neatly on the head. All hell broke loose.

To her credit, Maggie did manage to calm them down, while from the adjoining rows there were shouts of "Shut up!" and "Sit down!" There was even a call to "Fetch the manager!"

While the big man was willing to forget the aggravation, the elderly woman was not. "I want him thrown out," she demanded. "He's been kicking me in the back of my chair. I warned him time and again to sit still, but he wouldn't. Every time something happened in the film, he kicked me again." In spite of Maggie's surprisingly calm attempts, she would not settle. In fact, while Maggie was pleading with the man, the old biddy raised her stick and gave him another sound smack. When he snatched the stick and threw it aside, she calmly reached into her pocket and, taking out a small snuff tin, she opened it up and threw the contents all over him.

The poor man was half blinded, and so were most of the people sitting alongside. The chaos was widespread, with everybody coughing and sneezing, and somewhere near the aisle a fight broke out; stalwart as ever, Maggie tried desperately to separate the warring pair.

Suddenly the film was stopped, and the manager rushed into the fray, the ticket lady and another usherette bringing up the rear. "What the devil's going on here?" he demanded to know.

Somehow, amidst all the booing and screams of "Get the picture back on!," they managed to separate the injured and led them up the aisle to the first-aid room.

Right behind them, Maggie marched the offending couple to the door. "I shan't be coming here again!" The old lady was adamant. "And neither will I!" The man was equally adamant. And, after a stream of abuse, all aimed at Maggie, they went off down the street chatting to each other like two old friends.

Inside, with the film now back on, the people were happily screaming, while Maggie stood at the back, brushing the brown snuff from her lovely uniform, and rubbing her sore eyes.

She almost leapt out of her skin when the manager

seemed to creep up behind her. "See me in the office afterward," he said, before shuffling away. Her heart sank.

When the picture was over and everyone filed out, Maggie closed the door behind them. "I'd best get this lot totted up," the ticket woman said, and got out her adding machine.

Leaving her there, Maggie made her way to the office, where the manager was pacing up and down. "It's no good," he told Maggie as she came through the door, "this is the last straw."

"What's that supposed to mean?"

"Huh! I'm surprised you need to ask. It was bloody mayhem in there! We had to give fourteen people their money back, and I've no doubt that, come tomorrow, the complaints will be pouring in." He observed her uniform, stained with snuff, and her eyes all red and sore where she'd been rubbing them. "Look at you, woman! You're a mess . . ."

Maggie was up in arms. "It wasn't my fault."

"Oh no!" He threw up his hands in frustration. "It never is, but somehow when Sandra's away and you're up front, the world goes mad! I'm sorry, Maggie, I'll have to let you go. You seem to forget I don't own this place. I'm just the manager. I work for a wage the same as the rest of you." Though he was fearful of her reaction, he would rather *she* got the sack than him. "You stay here while I collect the takings. I'll have to pay you out of that, and rectify it later. I'll give you two weeks' severance, and a fortnight's holiday pay. That's more than generous if you ask me." In fact part of it was a bribe to keep her mouth shut about his indiscretions. He would have to make the difference up out of his own pocket, but that would be a small price to pay for getting rid of her.

By the time he got to the ticket-booth, Edith had already bagged the money. "We're well short," she said, handing it over with the ledger. "Having to pay back on fourteen tickets left a big hole in the takings."

"Don't worry, I'll deal with it." He bade her and the other usherette goodnight. "See you tomorrow, Mr. Ellis," they chorused. And they went away laughing about the night's events. "You never can tell *what* might happen in this place when Maggie's about," said the usherette as their laughter echoed through the darkened street.

While the manager was gone, Maggie waited. She was fed up: she'd liked the job. "I suppose it's time I moved on," she mused. "With a few weeks' pay, I can go and see Kathy. I might even be able to get a job with her at that holiday site." Her eyes twinkled. "I might even find myself a proper bloke."

Just then the telephone rang. Intrigued, Maggie picked it up. "Hello, this is the Rialto. Can I help you?" She liked to answer the telephone; it gave her a feeling of authority.

The caller was the manager's wife. "Could you please bring my husband to the phone?"

Maggie had an idea. "Oh, Mrs. Ellis, I'm glad you called, I was just looking for your number . . . y'see, your husband's not very well. Oh, no, he's not bad enough to send for an ambulance. He seems to think it's something he ate. The trouble is, he's been sick and he feels really queasy. He needs a lift home, and I can't help. I only wish I could."

"Get him a taxi."

"I've tried, but I can't seem to find one. So, do you think you could come and fetch him?"

The voice at the other end shook with anger. "I suppose I'll have to, won't I?" And the receiver was slammed down.

A moment later the manager returned. "Now then, let's get this over with." Throwing himself into his seat, he reached into the desk and got out his adding machine, which he proceeded to tap, while at the same time telling her, "I don't have to pay you a month's wages, but I think we know each other well enough to realize this situation can't go on." Bagging her wages, he slid them across the desk and sat back, eyes closed and his hand soothing his brow. "It's all there. Now get out!"

When she didn't answer, he glanced up and was rooted to the spot: while he had been tapping away, Maggie had been undoing her jacket. Now she stood before him with her breasts in all their naked glory. "Jesus!" His face went a purple shade of red and the sweat broke out in torrents down his back. "Put your clothes on, woman, before somebody comes in!" His eyeballs swiveled to the door then back to Maggie, and with his mouth open he gaped at her, positively dribbling. "You little vixen." He tried hard to hold the smile down but, like a certain other part of his body, it popped up, out of control. "Maggie, behave!" In truth, Maggie behaving was the last thing he wanted.

Maggie smiled seductively. "They've all gone home, my love," she teased, "we're on our own now." Sidling up to the desk, she leaned over, her rather ample breasts almost touching his face as she purred invitingly, "I thought we might say our goodbyes properly. After all, we have been very *close,* haven't we?"

Realizing what she meant, he gulped so hard that his Adam's apple bobbed up, getting stuck for a minute, before it bobbed down again. "Oooh, whatever will I do with you?"

It was all she could do not to laugh out loud. "Whatever takes your fancy," she said and, grabbing him by the collar, drew him forward, planting the longest, wettest kiss of his entire life on his open mouth; by which time he was putty in her hands.

A few minutes later, with Maggie in his arms, the door opened and in walked his wife. It was what Maggie had been waiting for. "NO! Get off me!" Putting on the best show of her life, Maggie pretended to fight him off. As soon as he realized what she was up to, he began shouting about how it was all Maggie's fault. "She's a witch! She enticed me . . ."

Falling all over the place as he tried desperately to do up his trousers, the poor man was assailed from both sides, with Maggie thrashing him with her shoe, and his wife tugging at his arm until he was sure it had come off at the socket. "You're a beast!" she cried. "You've *always* been a beast. This is the third time I've caught you at it, but it won't happen again because I'm off."

She landed such a slap on his face that it echoed around the room, and even Maggie took a step back. "I won't forgive you this time!" she cried. "By the time you get home, I'll have packed my bags and be long gone!"

Ducking and diving between the two, Maggie grabbed her wages and, buttoning up her jacket, she headed for the door.

"I don't blame you," she cried. "The man's off his head. He just went for me. He pinned me down and tore my clothes off. I'm going to the police. I'll make him pay for this! He's a maniac. He should be locked up!" Turning on the tears, she looked bereft.

"No, please." Being a respectable woman, his wife didn't want to become the target of such gossip. "Don't do that." Taking some notes from her handbag, she thrust them into Maggie's hands. "Here, take this." A horrid thought occurred to her. "My God! He didn't . . ." She glared at her husband, "You didn't . . . ?"

Seeming demure, Maggie looked down, "No, he didn't. But he would have if you hadn't come in." Clutching the money in one hand, she dabbed at her eyes with the other and pretended to cry. "You don't know how glad I was to see you." Out of the corner of her eye she saw the accused cowering by the door, muttering to himself and glaring at her with such malice she had to catch her breath. "I was so frightened."

"All right, dear." The woman helped fasten her blouse. "Look, you go away and don't say anything. I'll deal with *him!*"

With several weeks' wages in her pocket, the notes in her hands and a smile on her face, Maggie took her leave.

Outside she could hear the shouting and arguing, and laughed out loud. "That'll teach you to sack me, you old bugger!"

She flagged down a taxi. "Take me to Sooty's club," she told the driver, "I'm celebrating." And why not? she thought. She had more money than she'd had for ages, and plenty of time on her hands. What's more, she had *cause* to celebrate.

The taxi-driver laughed. "Come into money, 'ave yer?"

Maggie trusted nobody. "No, not really," she answered cagily, "I've just finished work."

"I can see that." He had picked her up outside the picture-house and seen her uniform. "That's an usherette's uniform you're wearing, ain't it?"

"Yes."

"Like your job, do yer?"

"It's all right," Maggie chuckled, "but I should have been an actress."

As they drove on, she thought of Kathy. "Watch out, gal!" she muttered. "I'm on my way."

◈

Samantha was hopping mad. "Don't you understand? I've got nothing! My house has gone and I've no job."

"I'm sorry, Mrs. Martin, but, as I see it, you have no call on your sister's house. According to the will, and what you've already told me, the house was bought in her name and passes to your sister without condition. On your mother's marriage to Mr. Lennox, *you* were given the family home, also without condition. This house was debt-free and, as you yourself said, in excellent condition. The fact that you lost it does not in the eyes of the law give you the right to a share of your sister's property."

"What kind of solicitor are you?" Samantha was vitriolic in defeat. "It was my *mother* who gave me the house. My *father* left me nothing. I'm destitute. I'm having to live in rented property again. I have debts that need paying, and there are no decent jobs to be had. My mother's got herself in a situation where she can't help, and the only way out is for me to take back from Kathy what should have been mine in the first place. After all, I *am* the eldest. *I* should have been left the house, not her."

"Not necessarily. Being the eldest does not automatically make you the heir. In any case, your father bought the house in your sister's name. I'm afraid I can see no way around it."

"You must be able to do *something!* Bring her to court. Make her sell the house and give me half the proceeds. Christ Almighty, I would have thought it was simple enough!" Springing out of her chair, she banged her fist on the desk. "If you won't do it, I'll find someone who will."

Getting slowly out of his seat, the solicitor stood up, his face twitching with anger as he told her calmly, "That's entirely up to you. But, as far as I'm concerned, you have no case." He thought she was the most selfish, spiteful and bone-idle creature that ever crossed his threshold. "But you do have choices . . . *three,* in fact."

Samantha's eyes lit up. "Well, now we're talking. And what are they, might I ask?"

"Well, you could get another job and work your way out of trouble. You might think about getting married . . . to someone who can satisfy your taste for expensive things." Her exquisitely tailored clothes and the diamond ring on her right hand had not gone unnoticed. "Or, you could go to your sister and beg her to help . . . if, of course, she is in a position to do so, and *if* she has a mind to help someone who is so obviously out to ruin her."

While the unpalatable "choices" were spelled out for her, Samantha's hands clenched and unclenched. Now, as she spoke, her voice shook with rage. "How dare you? I could report you for speaking to me like that."

Quite unconcerned, he smiled. "I don't think so," he said. "I am merely expressing the choices you have, as I see them."

Straightening up, she took a long, noisy breath through her nostrils. Staring at him with murder in her eyes, she threatened, "My stepfather is a powerful, influential man. I shall tell him how you treated me, and you may be sure he will be in touch! Moreover, I shall make certain my friends are warned about you."

Unmoved, he returned the copy of her father's will. "I'm sorry I wasn't able to help," he said, then showed her the door. Head high, she marched out, threatening hell and damnation as she went.

Shaking his head, he closed the door and returned to his work.

He'd had them all in this office at some time or another: the evil and the gullible, and those who were really in need of help. But this one was unique. A woman who was able enough to work but chose not to, who had squandered her own inheritance and who, without compunction, was prepared to rob her sister of her home, had to be amongst the worst.

Going to the window, he flung it open, as though needing to rid the room of her presence.

🐚

In Bridport, Kathy made straight for the café and Mabel.

Seeing the older woman at the far end of the room, Kathy gave a quick wave and, smiling, Mabel hurried down to be with her. "It's good to see you," she said. "I'll be finished in a minute or two, then you can walk me home and stay for a cup of tea. We've not been so busy today, and I've had very little company."

Patting Kathy's arm affectionately, she added, "Besides, we hardly ever get time to talk properly, do we, dear?" Kathy had to agree.

🐚

A short time later, arm in arm, the two of them strolled down the street, Mabel setting the pace, and Kathy content to chat as they walked. "Will your husband be in?" She had visions of that ugly lout waiting for them as they entered the house.

Mabel shook her head. "He's off down the pub with his cronies," she answered. "Come Friday, he can't wait to pack up and get away."

Sensing the sadness underlying Mabel's words, Kathy merely nodded. And no more was said on the matter.

🐚

The cottage was spotless; every nook and cranny scrubbed and shining, and each ornament polished until you could see your face in it. "This is such a pretty place, Mabel!" Kathy thought it enchanting.

Peeking out the back window, she observed the same loving care and attention to detail: the tin bath hanging neatly on its hook, the flagstones washed clean, and the pegs on the line all lined up like little wooden soldiers. Even the brick walls were washed white.

Mabel was flattered. "I like to potter about," she answered. "If I had more spare time, I'd have it looking even nicer." Going into the scullery, she put the kettle on to boil. "And how are you, my dear?" she called out. "Settling in all right now, are you?"

"I'm doing fine," Kathy answered, but did not sound very convincing.

Returning with the tray, Mabel set it down on the table. "What's wrong?" Pouring them each a cup of tea, she handed Kathy hers and sat opposite on the big armchair. "Family, is it?" she asked. In her experience it was always family that caused the worries.

"I just can't understand," Kathy began, knowing she could confide in this dear soul. "My sister Samantha is beautiful, spoiled, selfish, and greedy. She has little compassion for those around her, she treats Mother like dirt, and yet, in Mother's eyes, she can do no wrong."

"I see." Mabel had heard it all before. "And why do you think that is?"

"I'm not sure, but I imagine it's to do with Mother's personal disappointments." Kathy had often thought about it and this was the only answer she had come up with. "I reckon Mother only wanted one child, a beautiful creature much like herself . . . someone people would pause in the streets to look at, and gasp with admiration."

"I see. And that was Samantha, was it?"

Kathy nodded. "Then I came along . . . an accident, no doubt; plain and noisy with chubby legs and unruly hair. I spoiled all her ideas of being special, and having that one very cherished, magnificent child."

Mabel was having none of it. "You're certainly not 'plain,' or 'noisy.' You're a very pretty young woman with a beautiful nature."

Kathy smiled naughtily. "And chubby legs."

Mabel returned her smile. "We can't all be perfect, but there are worse things than a sturdy pair of legs, my dear!"

Kathy satisfied Mabel's curiosity about Samantha, and in the telling, Kathy began to feel less disillusioned about the situation between herself, her mother and Samantha, though she knew things would never change. "It's too late for all that," she told Mabel. "Mother gets worse as she gets older. She's one of those people who are never satisfied with what life gives them. She yearns for glamour and excitement . . . all the things she never quite seemed to acquire. You see, she married my father, a quiet, hard-working man who worked long hours to provide her with a lovely house and expensive clothes and other luxuries she may never have enjoyed. When Father was lost to us, she seemed to grow more arrogant and domineering. There was no living with her."

Mabel could see the regret in Kathy's troubled eyes. "You loved your father very much, didn't you, my dear?"

Kathy nodded. "He was a very special man . . . he loved me for what I am, not for what I might have been. As for Mother, I can't remember a time when she put her arms around me with affection, or told me she loved me, or held my hand as we crossed the road." Her voice broke. "Do you know, Mabel, there were times when I thought she'd be happier if I'd never been born."

"Oh, I'm sure that's not true, my dear. No mother could ever wish that."

It did Kathy's heart good to talk with this sweet, kind old dear, who was more of a mother to her than her own had ever been.

When it was time to leave, she wrapped her arms around Mabel and held on to her for what seemed an age. "You're a lovely lady, Mabel," she told her, and Mabel's heart went out to her.

"I'm here whenever you want me," she reminded Kathy. "Don't ever forget that, my dear."

On the bus home, Kathy recalled the old woman's words. She was more content now than she had been in a long time. After all the niggling doubts, she was really happy with her new life.

"I'm sorry, my dear, but you know how things are." Irene had her own troubles. "I'd like to help you, but it's not possible." Pouring herself another drink, she poured one for Samantha, too. "He puts only the tiniest amount into my account; just enough for basic necessities. I have to ask him for every little thing, and even then he wants receipts." Gulping down her drink, she was close to tears. "He's moved into the spare room . . . though I don't mind that, but he treats me like a stranger. It's just awful!

"I haven't finished yet, though." She grinned—a wonky, half-drunken gesture that distorted her face. "I've been thinking. If you were to help me, I could be rid of him." Her secretive expression told it all.

Samantha couldn't believe her ears. "You're drunk!"

"Oh no I'm not." Sidling up to her, Irene lowered her voice to a harsh whisper, at the same time glancing at the door to make sure he wasn't hiding there like last time. "I've thought of a way to finish him off." She giggled. "Then we can *both* enjoy his money."

Samantha thought her mother was losing her mind. "I might have been persuaded," she confessed, "but you seem to have forgotten one thing."

"What's that?"

"He's cut you out of his will, hasn't he?"

Irene was taken aback. Unsteady on her feet, she fell into the nearest chair, eyes glazed over after hours of steadily knocking back the booze. "The bastard! You're right, I forgot about that." She forgot most things these days.

Samantha stared at her with loathing. "Look at you! What good are you? I came here for help and find you drunk!" She began to shout. "You're *always* bloody drunk lately."

Irene laughed. "You should try it, dear. It helps to pass the time of day."

Samantha was in no mood for this. "You disgust me!"

"Don't be like that, my dear." Sitting up in the chair, she focused her gaze on this wayward, beloved daughter of hers. "Look, dear. You do what the solicitor said . . . go to your sister and tell her how things are. You know how soft she is . . . I'm sure she wouldn't turn you away."

She giggled. "You might even find yourself a rich old man down at the seaside . . . that's where they usually retire to, isn't it?" Throwing her arms about, she laughed insanely. "Perhaps I should come with you."

"Who would want *you?* You're becoming an old slag," Samantha warned. "If you're not careful, *you'll* be the next one out on the street!"

Slamming out of the house, she left her mother in tears. Yet, as she walked down the street to the bus stop, she thought on what her mother had said. Her sulky mouth turned up in a devious little smile. "You could be right, Mother," she murmured. "Maybe it's time I paid my little sister a visit."

But that would take money. "I need a whole new wardrobe, and money in my pocket," she mused. "I might have to think of a way to earn some money fast." Just then a man walked by and winked, obviously making a play for her.

Though she rebuffed him, it triggered an idea in her mind.

She smiled to herself. "Hmh! If the end justifies the means, I'm sure it wouldn't be too much of a hardship."

# *Eleven*

---

JUST AS THE POSTMAN WAS ABOUT TO DROP THE MAIL through the letterbox, Jasper opened the door and saved him the trouble. "Morning, Ted," he yawned. "What you got for me then?"

Thinking Jasper looked a right sketch in his old, worn pajamas with his hair stood up on end, the postman turned the letter over in his hand. Squinting at the postmark, he told Jasper, "It's from Buckinghamshire."

"Can't be for *me* then," Jasper remarked. "I don't know anybody who lives in Buckinghamshire."

"Well, it's addressed to you." The postman checked the address. "There you are, it's for you all right." He handed the letter over. "Looks like a woman's writing." He laughed. "A woman from your past who's tracked you down."

Jasper shoved the letter in his pocket. "If they're after me money, they'll be disappointed 'cause I ain't got none." He collected his milk and stepped back into the passage. "Come in, Ted. I've just this minute put the kettle on."

"Can't." Heaving his heavy sack onto his shoulders, Ted apologized. "Any other time I'd be glad to, but not today. There's a union meeting at twelve. I daren't be late for that."

Jasper knew all about these union meetings. "I suppose yer all planning to go on strike. An' never mind the poor folks as won't get their mail for weeks on end. What's it all about now?"

"I never said we were going on strike, Jasper, and I'll thank you not to spread that about. It could cause all manner of trouble."

Jasper grinned. "What meks yer think I'd spread it about?"

The postman shook his head, his smile as wide as Jasper's. " 'Cause you're a mischievous bugger, that's why!" Knowing how Jasper could always get the better of anyone in an argument, he bade him good morning and went on his way.

"Good job yer know when to quit!" Jasper called after him in light-hearted humor. "I've a reputation for making mincemeat outta troublemakers like you."

With his milk under one arm and his paper under the other, he made his way to the kitchen. Throwing the letter on the table, he ignored it while he tucked into his bowl of porridge, helped down with two mugs of tea. "I don't know anybody in Buckinghamshire," he grumbled on. "It *can't* be for me!"

He finished his porridge and read his paper, and every now and then cast an eye on that small white envelope, but he made no move to open it. "It'll be some damned silly company, trying to sell me summat."

A few minutes later, as he cleared the table, his curiosity got the better of him. Leaning down to examine the letter more closely, he was shocked. "My God!" Recognizing the handwriting, he snatched up the letter and tore it open. "It is!" he murmured. "It's *her!*"

As he read the letter his old face creased into a smile. "Well, I never." He gave a delighted chuckle. "It's from *Liz!* After all this time." He read the letter again just to be sure.

*Dear Jasper,*

*I'm sorry I haven't written before, but I knew how you would be taking care of everything, so I didn't feel there was any urgency. Besides, as I'm sure you can understand, I had a great deal to think about, and young Robbie was so upset about his daddy not coming back. It's been so hard, trying to understand why he abandoned us like he did, but then I don't really know the circumstances behind it all.*

*I took Robbie away for a long holiday, and when he
seemed so happy in Scotland, I decided to stay there
for a time. I rented a house and Robbie went to school,
and for a time it seemed as though we might make it a
permanent home. But then, Robbie got homesick, and
we decided to come back south. Since we've been back,
he's smiled a lot more, and slowly but surely he's coming to terms with not having his daddy close by.*

*Did Robert ever come back, Jasper? Have you
heard from him? I miss your old face, with its whiskers
and that mischievous grin. The truth is, I would very
much like to see you, though I'm not ready to return to
West Bay; it would be too painful . . . I know I would
see him everywhere I went.*

*Thank you for looking after the cottage, Jasper. I
see from the bank statements that you have a tenant. Is
it a man or a woman, or maybe a family? And what
about Barden House? Is it falling to rack and ruin? I
know I asked you to leave it the way it was, and I still
feel that way about it. But I've begun to feel that
maybe I didn't have the right. It wasn't my house. It
was his. But, you see, Jasper, it was our home . . . the
happiest place on God's earth. To clean it, or to re-
arrange the garden, would be to change the memories,
and I couldn't bear that.*

*Maybe he'll come back and decide what to do with
the house. Maybe he'll look for me and his son, and
explain his reason for abandoning us. We do miss him
so much.*

*I have many questions, Jasper.*

*You'll find a train ticket to Bletchley in the envelope,
together with instructions from there and my address.*

*Robbie and I would love to have you come and stay
for a while . . . if you can bear to leave your beloved
West Bay.*

*Please say you will.*

*All our love,
Liz and Robbie*

Slumping into the chair, Jasper held the letter in his hand. "How can I tell her?" he wondered. "It might be kinder to let her go on thinking he abandoned them."

It was a terrible decision for him to make, but after a while he knew what he must do. "She'll *have* to be told, but not in a letter."

Now that his mind was made up, he didn't hesitate. Getting out of the chair, he went to the dresser, where he found a writing pad and pack of envelopes. "I'll go and see them." In fact, now that he'd decided to go, he began to look forward to it.

Jasper was not a man of letters, so his reply was short and to the point.

> *Dear Liz,*
>
> *It was wonderful to hear from you. I knew you would get in touch eventually.*
> *Thank you for the ticket. I shall be up to see you . . .*

He glanced again at the date on the ticket.

> *. . . Thursday 25 September.*
> *Meanwhile take care of yourself.*
>
> *Love to you both,*<br>*Jasper*

Closing the letter into an envelope, he sealed it with the tip of his tongue. Then he copied down the address she'd given him, and laid it on the table beside the train ticket and travel instructions.

"I'm sorry, lass," he muttered, "but you'll happen not be so glad to see me as you think." Imparting the sad news to that lovely lady was not something he looked forward to.

That night, over a drink in the privacy of the cottage garden, Jasper confided in Tom. "I'm going away," he explained. "There's summat I have to do."

Tom had seen how the old man had been unusually quiet, and was concerned. "Is it serious?" he asked now. "I mean . . . you're not *ill,* are you, Jasper?" That would be a shocking blow, for he had come to love the old man like a father. In fact, he seemed *more* of a father than his own had been, since he had deserted him and Dougie when they were small. When they lost their mother soon after, Tom put it down to a broken heart. After that they were shifted from relative to relative. It had been a harsh and unsettled upbringing.

Jasper put his mind at rest. "No, lad, I'm not ill. But I've a terrible duty to perform, and it's playing on my mind."

"Would it help to talk about it?" Tom could see how it was worrying the old man.

It took a moment for Jasper to answer, but when he did, it was with a deep-down sigh. "Happen it would," he agreed. "Aye, happen it would."

Before commencing, he took a fortifying sip of his tea, and there in that pretty garden on that pleasant autumn evening, he told Tom the whole sorry, beautiful tale of Kathy's father, Robert, and the woman he loved.

"Liz and her husband Gordon lived here in this very cottage for many years," he began. "He had a thriving ironmongery business in Bridport and another in Dorchester, so they weren't short of brass. But 'brass' doesn't always make for contentment, and they were far from content. From what Liz told me, it wasn't an ideal match. He was a bit of a bully and she, being the gentle, compassionate soul she is, suffered his temper tantrums with dignity."

He gave a tender smile. "She was trained as a nurse, so I expect she was used to handling every situation, but, because of Gordon's nasty ways, over the years he lost her respect, and in the end he lost her love."

He described how it all ended. "Gordon took to womanizing. One dark night just before the war he'd been into Bridport . . . seeing this woman he'd taken a fancy to. It turned out later that the pair of them had drunk enough booze to sink a battleship. Anyway, he'd missed the last bus, so he decided to walk back to West Bay. Coming across the junction he must have stumbled; he was run down by a lorry . . . the driver said he just seemed to come out of nowhere. A car driver coming the other way witnessed it, too. He said the lorry driver couldn't have done a thing to stop what happened."

The old man threw out his hands in a gesture of helplessness. "Gordon were killed instantly, and Liz was left on her own, though after a time she came out of her shell and seemed a far happier person than she'd been with him. But she was that lonely. Sometimes you'd see her walking the beach, deep in thought, and other times she'd call me in for a cup of tea and she'd tell me about when she were a girl and how she'd allus longed for a brother or sister. Then, like now, she felt terrible lonely."

Tom nodded. He knew how that felt. "She's fortunate to have you for a friend. We *both* are."

The old man thanked him for the compliment, and added, "She were a lovely-looking lady, still young . . ." He chuckled. "I can never tell a woman's age."

Tom was curious. "Did she ever marry again? Is that why she moved away from here?"

"No. It weren't like that. Y'see, one day in early spring some nine years ago, a man came to stay in West Bay." His memories took him back, and made him smile. "Oh, but he did love this place. He once told me how he left all his troubles behind when he stayed here."

He explained how Liz and Robert became good friends, and then how friendship blossomed into love. "I introduced them," he said proudly. "Liz and I were collecting shells for her garden, when we bumped into him. I asked if he'd like to join us for a drink at the café, and before yer knew it, he and Liz were like old buddies."

Leaning back in his chair, he went on, "They saw each other most every day; when he went away, she watched at the window for him to come back. By! I've never seen two people so much in love . . . it were a pleasure to watch. It weren't long afore Barden House was on the market, and he bought it. He were a businessman . . . worked hard and traveled far in his work. He bought the house, and spent time here, whenever his work allowed. They lived there together, and then they had a son."

He took a moment before going on, in a quiet, reverent voice. "Folks round here turned a blind eye to them not being married . . . we all reckoned Liz deserved same happiness. Then, one day last year, he went away and never came back. Poor Liz were broken-hearted. She spent weeks watching and waiting, but he never did return. Soon after that, she closed up Barden House, put this cottage up for rent, and left. She said she were headed for Scotland or Ireland or somewhere. Me and the agent were given joint responsibility for the cottage, and I've done my best by her. Yet, it's a strange thing, working for someone you can't contact."

Tom wondered aloud, "Why would he do that . . . just leave and never come back? Especially if he was so happy with her."

The old man explained how Robert had discovered he was very ill. "He didn't want her to know; he were trying to protect her," he said. "But I wonder if that was the right thing to do? It caused her so much pain . . . mebbe even more pain than if he'd let her know the reason for his going."

"It does seem harsh." Tom thought it was the saddest, most noble thing he had ever heard. "I suppose he thought he was doing the right thing for her. But he was making a tremendous sacrifice, when he must have wanted her close, more than anything in the world."

"She certainly suffered, I can tell yer," Jasper told him. "And, like you say, I'm sure it was a hard thing for him to do, poor devil!" Jasper had thought long and hard about it since Kathy told him. "While Liz was thinking he'd left because he didn't want her or the child anymore, the poor man was fighting for his life; probably aching to let her know, but not wanting to hurt her."

He now revealed what Tom had begun to suspect. "He were wed, d'yer see? Got children from his marriage an' all. It couldn't have been easy either way."

Finally, he told Tom of Liz's letter and of how she wanted him to go and see her. "So there yer 'ave it, son. I've a sorry duty to perform, but she has to know. It would be wicked not to tell her the truth."

Tom was intrigued. "If he went away and just never came back, how did you find out what happened? Did he write and ask you not to tell her?"

"No. It were a *lass* who told me." He gave a little secret smile. "A lass that you know very well." While Tom searched his mind, Jasper revealed, "It were *Kathy* as told me."

Now Tom was confused. "But . . . how would *she* know?"

"Because the man Liz fell in love with were Kathy's own father."

"My God! Did she know . . . about Liz, I mean?"

The old man shook his head. "The poor lass knew nothing of his life here in West Bay until after he were gone. He bought Barden House in her name, before his son were born. When she found out about her father and his secret life, she were terrible upset. Oh, not because of that, but because he hadn't trusted her enough to confide in her. Y'see, from what I can gather, she and her father were very close. She were distraught at losing him. I reckon that's why she's settled so well in the house, because that's where he found the happiness he never found with her mother."

He went on. "We talked, y'see . . . me an' Kathy. That's when she told me who she was, and how she came to be here." He pursed his lips when deep in thought, as he was now. "She's had a hard time all told," he said. "I'm glad you've taken her to heart."

Tom was astonished. So it seemed he wasn't the only one with secrets. "I never knew. And does she know . . . about Liz and her father?"

The old man nodded. "She does now, because I told her. She wanted to learn everything about her father and his life here. I told her all I knew . . . about how much in love they were, and how she's got a baby brother she's never seen. It were a terrible shock, I can tell yer."

Tom thought about Kathy, and his feelings for her, and it

seemed to him that her father had loved this woman, Liz, with the same passion and commitment with which he loved Kathy. He thought it a strange and wonderful thing; but then, Fate had a habit of weaving her web in a way that surprised them all.

"Will Kathy be going with you . . . to see Liz and the boy?"

The old man shook his head. "No. Like I say, I've only just found out myself where Liz is staying. I haven't told Kathy, and I don't intend to. Y'see, Tom, it ain't my business to do that . . . It's for Liz herself to do."

His mind was made up. "Soonever she gets over the shock of what happened to Robert, I mean to ask her to come and meet his daughter."

"Do you think she will?"

"I don't know. But it has to be *her* choice."

"So, you don't want me to mention any of this to Kathy?"

"I'd be grateful for that."

"Then I'll forget we even talked about it."

"Can I ask you summat else?"

"Ask away."

"I think it might be best if I don't see Kathy before I go, in case she asks where I'm going. I've never been one for telling a lie, and I don't want to start now. Especially when it's Kathy."

Tom anticipated his question. "So, you want me to tell her you're away, is that it?"

"That's it, son." Jasper was relieved. "If yer could just say I've gone to see an old friend, you'll not be lying, and hopefully that should satisfy her curiosity."

"Consider it done." It was little enough, Tom thought.

"I appreciate that." The old man explained, "If I can persuade Liz to come and see her, or even write to her, it'll all be worth it, I reckon."

"I hope she agrees." Tom also thought it would be a good thing. "From what you've told me, I think it would benefit them both."

Before leaving, the old man shook Tom by the hand, telling him in a half-whisper: "It would do my old heart good to see you and Kathy as happy and content as they were."

Tom understood. For didn't he want the very same, with all his heart?

The following morning at early light, the old man left his house and made his way down George Street. Not a soul was awake, and only the cats were about. "Hello, you." Pausing to stroke the tabby cat, he tickled its ear and gave a word of warning. "You'd best take yersel' in outta the cold, afore yer tail drops off."

Chilled by the early mist that rolled in off the sea, he pulled up the collar of his coat and, quickening his steps, made off toward the main road.

There were only two passengers on the bus besides himself: a sleepy-eyed young lad who, judging by his worn black Wellingtons and the cut of his clothes, was a farmhand on his way to work; and a businessman in trilby and long coat, carrying a battered briefcase. From his confident smile and chirpy manner, Jasper assumed he was some sort of salesman.

"Morning." Returning the man's bright greeting, Jasper set his small case down beside his feet, shuffling uncomfortably in his best coat and hat. He didn't look at the man again, because he wasn't in the mood for conversation. He needed to plan how he would tell Liz why her beloved Robert had not come back.

After being deposited a short distance from the railway station, he quickly made his way there. He boarded the train and showed his ticket, and was no sooner settled in his seat than the train was off. With a great whoosh of steam and a tug on the whistle, it was soon chugging away, its noisy, rhythmic motion lulling him to sleep.

On the same morning, Kathy was coming out of the shop when she almost collided with the postman. "I've a letter for you, Miss." A jolly-faced man with a head like a billiard ball, he knew every man, woman and child within a ten-mile radius of West Bay. "I really should deliver it through your letterbox myself," he said dryly, "but, well, seeing as I've bumped into you like this, I don't suppose it would do any harm, just this once." He glanced down at the letter. "From somebody important is it, d'you think?"

"I won't know till I look inside." Holding out her hand, Kathy thought she had better take it from him before he opened it himself. "I don't know who could be writing to me," she remarked, quickly taking possession of the letter. "Hardly anyone knows my address."

"Really?" He liked a bit of gossip, and being a postman offered unique opportunities in that direction. "Is that from neglect or choice?" he wanted to know.

"Choice," Kathy declared. "The fewer people who know where I am, the more peace and quiet I'll get."

"Peace and quiet!" He was amazed. "I should have thought a young woman like yourself would welcome company?"

Kathy gave him one of her sweeter smiles. "Well, you'd be wrong then, wouldn't you?" Itching to see who the letter was from, she hurried away.

She could hear him moaning as she went. "Well, I never," he complained to the old shopkeeper. "There's a young madam if ever I saw one!"

If he thought to get support from Jasper's old pal, he was mistaken, for as Kathy turned the corner she could hear the old woman's curt reply. "Serves you right for being such a nosey old so-and-so!" And off she went back inside to take a well-earned pinch of snuff.

Closing the front door behind her, Kathy threw off her coat. Going to the table, she sat herself down. The handwriting was childish, but she knew whose it was.

Ripping open the envelope, she read the first line. It was enough to tell her that the letter really was from Maggie.

As she read she began to smile, then she tittered, then she was laughing out loud. In full color and with her incorrigible sense of humor, Maggie had written a lengthy account of her recent exploits. It began:

*Hello Kathy, old gal,*

*What yer been up to then, eh? Whatever it is, I bet yer ain't been having as much fun as your old friend, Maggie.*

    *What have I been up to now, you may well ask. Well, I'll tell you. First of all, that asshole of a manager at the pictures gave me the bleeding sack! Would you believe it, eh? Bloody cheek! And me the best usherette he's ever had . . . no, not in that way, gal . . . I mean, I'm the best usherette he's ever had . . . under the table, and on it. In between the rows of seats after everybody's gone home, and anywhere else that took our fancy.*

    *Only I had this unholy row with this old woman, and her snotty-nosed ratbag of a kid! I'd like to have wrung both their bleedin' necks, only I never got the chance. Anyway, the upshot of it all is this; me and the old cow got into another fight, and there was this other old bugger who went berserk with an umbrella, and all hell were let loose. Everybody walked out and the manager had to pay money back, and I got the blame . . . as usual!*

    *So then I got the sack, but he paid me well, though I bet he wished to God he hadn't, 'cause I phoned his wife and said he were sick. Then I teased the old bugger like there was no tomorrow. When his wife walked in, I started crying an' screaming about how he'd taken advantage of me, poor girl that I am. She offered me money to keep my mouth shut—all to do with pride and shame I expect. Truth is, gal, I don't give a bugger what it's to do with, so long as it's me as comes off best in the end, which this time I did!*

    *Anyway, that's all my news, except to say I ain't forgot where yer are, gal, don't think that. Now I got some money, I'm hoping to have a little holiday. One o' these fine days, I'll turn up on your doorstep like a bad penny, you see if I don't.*

    *Till then, take care of yourself, gal.*

*Luv yer till the cows come home,*
*Maggie.*

There was spilt ink and coffee stains all over the pages. "You'll never change, will you, Mags, and thank God for that." Kathy had laughed so hard her sides ached. She longed to see her friend.

She turned her attention to the chores of the day.

The laundry was her first task. Being used to taking her clothes to the laundry in Acton, and washing out her smalls in the sink, she had found it hard to get used to the copper-boiler that sat in the corner of the outhouse. She still washed her smalls in the bath, but for sheets and towels and anything heavy she had learned to use the boiler; though she had seen an advertisement for a twin-tub washing machine that she meant to buy when she had enough money. For now, though, it was sleeves rolled up and get on with it.

When the water was boiling she dropped the clothes in one by one, submerging them with the help of a long wooden stick which stood beside the boiler. When the clothes were rising and steeping, she went back inside the house.

Taking a newspaper and handbrush, she went to the fire-grate, where she dropped to her knees. It wasn't a hard job, but it was dirty and dusty. So, she went slowly . . . shoveling the ashes out from underneath and placing them ever so gently into the laid-out newspaper.

When the ashes were all out, and the cinders piled onto the grating ready for the next fire, she folded the newspaper to make a little bag. She then carried the bag out to the bin, and returned to the kitchen.

Taking a floorcloth from the cupboard, she wet it through, wrung it out, and, going into the sitting room, wiped the hearth over until it shone. Next, she made a fan of the left-over newspapers, and set it in the hearth.

She then dusted the furniture and plumped the sofa cushions. All that remained was for her to go into the stair-cupboard and take out the carpet-sweeper.

This was a job she hated, because the stiff bristles on the carpet-sweeper soon got clogged up and needed cleaning every five minutes or so. Still, she told herself, it did a good job and that was all that mattered. "I need one of those vacuum cleaners," she muttered as she worked. That was another thing she meant to buy when she could afford it. There were a few things she needed, but they weren't yet priorities on her list.

When the carpet was cleaned, she put away the sweeper and checked the washing; it was ready. Filling the deep pot sink with cold water, she took up the stick; teasing the clothes out one by one, she slid them into the sink, her face bright pink as the warm steam rose like a cloud to envelop her.

She gave the clothes a thorough rinsing, before wringing them out and folding them into her laundry-basket. Next, the boiler was emptied and the job done. "Thank goodness for that!" It was the worst chore of all, she thought.

It didn't take long to peg them out. Ten minutes later, they were hanging on the line, limp and dripping; until she sent the line sky-high with her wooden prop. Then the clothes caught the breeze and came alive, dancing and leaping about like crazy things.

Stooping to collect the stray pegs from the ground, Kathy was astonished to hear a voice calling her name. "Yoo-hoo! Where are ye, gal?"

Kathy couldn't believe her ears. "MAGGIE!" Dropping the pegs, she ran to the side gate, and there was Maggie, peering over the top and grinning from ear to ear, asking to be let in. "If this is the way you treat yer visitors, I might not come 'ere again!" she said with feigned disgust.

Throwing open the gate, Kathy grabbed her in a fast embrace. "What are you doing here? Why didn't you let me know?" The questions came thick and fast, with Maggie claiming she was "gasping for a cuppa" and that she would answer all her questions when she'd been "fed and watered."

Once inside, Maggie asked to be shown around the house, examining every nook and cranny, and making comments as she went. With wide, wondering eyes, she went from room to room upstairs and down. "Cor! Some place *this* is, gal," she remarked proudly. "Whatever will yer do with all this space?"

Kathy sighed. "Oh, I expect I'll have to manage somehow," she answered with a chuckle.

"What! Ye could get three o' my flats in 'ere an' no mistake!" Maggie couldn't believe that Kathy had been fortunate enough to be left such a beautiful place. "An' you've got it so pretty, gal," she said admiringly, "but then you were allus good at that kinda thing."

Kathy was glad Maggie had given her approval. It meant a lot for her friend to appreciate her home. "You're staying with me for a long time, aren't you?" she asked hopefully.

Maggie was cagey with her answer. "Head for the kitchen," she suggested, "make us a brew and see if ye can't find a piece o' cake or summat, an' I'll tell you me plans."

First settling Maggie in the sitting room with a piece of fruit cake, Kathy set about making a pot of tea, which she then carried into the sitting room along with two cups and saucers, and another helping of cake, just in case Maggie was still hungry. "I can make you some cheese on toast if you like?" she offered. "Or there's two eggs in the cupboard . . . I can fry them or poach, whichever way you like."

Maggie was satisfied. "The cake will do fine, gal," she replied, "but thanks all the same."

Thrilled to see her friend, Kathy let herself get carried away. "How long will you stay . . . a week . . . two? Oh, Maggie! It's so good to have you here."

Maggie dashed all her hopes. "Sorry, gal," she said with a grimace, "but it's only a flying visit. I'll be starting a new job in a couple of days' time, and I need to get back. I just grabbed the opportunity to come and see you, but I can only stay the one night. Still, now that I know where you are, I'll make it my business to get back just as soon as I can. Then, maybe I can stay a while longer, eh?"

Kathy was disappointed and it showed, but she did her best to make Maggie feel comfortable. "Never mind," she said, "as long as you're here now, and yes, maybe next time we can enjoy a week or so together. Oh, Maggie! I've got so much to tell you."

They sat and talked for a time, about how Kathy was settling in, and how she thought she would be happy here in West Bay, and the two of them were so obviously delighted to be in each other's company again, even if it was for such a short time.

"And are you going to show me what this place is like then?" Maggie asked pointedly. "I'll tell yer what I really fancy . . . a piping hot bag o' fish and chips."

"Then you'll not be disappointed," Kathy promised her.

It was mid-afternoon by the time Jasper arrived in Bletchley. Then he had a short bus-ride to Woburn, before he found himself in the prettiest village. "By! She certainly chose an interesting place to live." Impressed by the main street, which was a hive of little craft shops, tall Georgian houses all in a row, and a smattering of cafés and quaint old pubs, he took a minute to glance at the directions that Liz had sent him.

There was a little hand-drawn map. He studied it, mumbling as he read, "Straight up the High Street, past the Bull Inn; keep going, with the market square on your right. Then you pass the Town Hall. Cross the road to a terrace of cottages. You'll find us at number eight . . . third along."

Folding the letter into his pocket, he could see the Bull Inn from where he stood. "By! I could do with summat to wet me whistle," he muttered. But then he decided the pint of good stuff could wait. Right now, he had other priorities.

Following Liz's directions to the letter, he eventually came to the row of cottages, as she'd described. Number eight had a pretty red door and a black lion's-head knocker. He was about to raise the knocker when there came a shout from some way behind him. "JASPER!" As he turned he was almost knocked over by a brown-haired lad, who wrapped himself around Jasper so hard that the old man could hardly breathe. "Oh, Jasper, you came to see us!" Looking up, the boy was in tears. "I never thought you'd come. I never thought I'd see you again!" Laughing now, he held onto Jasper as though he would never let go.

Taking the lad by the shoulders, the old man smiled down on him. "By! Look at you . . . all growed up and handsome as ever." Cradling his hands around the boy's face, his voice shook with emotion. He hadn't realized until now just how much he'd missed him. "What med yer think I'd not come to see you, eh? Yer shoulda known better."

The boy looked round. "Have you brought my daddy?"

"No, son, I haven't seen your daddy." Now, as the boy dropped his gaze to the ground, the old man thought how like Robert he looked, and how much of a shock it would be for Kathy if ever she saw him. "Where's yer mam?"

"There!" Quickly hiding his disappointment, the boy pointed. Jasper turned and there she was, almost on them now. Waving and smiling, she began running, with the old man's fond gaze following her every move. Lovely as ever, with her hair plaited back, and her figure slim and elegant as before, he felt a pang of sorrow at the way she and Robert had been torn apart in such a cruel way.

Dropping her basket to the ground, she threw herself at him, holding onto him as fiercely as the boy had done, as though she was afraid he might suddenly disappear.

After a moment, she drew away. "You can't know how good it is to see you," she murmured, and Jasper felt the same.

Holding the boy's hand, he followed her inside. "You look well," he remarked. "You've not changed, either of yer." Yet they had, he thought. They seemed older, mellowed somehow, and the light of joy had gone from their eyes. He supposed that was because of Robert, and the circumstances which drove them from West Bay, a place they loved as much as he did. At his words, Liz turned, her whimsical smile betraying what was in her heart.

The cottage was warm and welcoming—like Liz herself, the old man thought. The living room was surprisingly open, with light wood furniture and a pretty Victorian fireplace, and at the far end, beyond the french doors, the garden seemed to stretch away forever. Still alive with late-blooming plants, it was a feast for the eyes. "You've got a lovely place here," he told Liz, and she agreed, but, "It's not home, Jasper," she murmured. "It never could be."

"Come and see your bedroom." The boy grabbed his hand. "I've made you a present."

Liz laughed. "He spent all week making it," she explained, and Jasper said he couldn't wait. "Take your case up," Liz suggested. "You might as well unpack."

"Lead on," he told the boy, who took him at a run across the room and up the stairs. When they got to the far end of the landing, he paused at one door and pointed to another. "That's the bathroom," he said, "and this is your bedroom."

Taking stock, the old man dropped his case to the floor and looked around. It was a pleasant room by any standards. There was a double bed with a cabinet alongside, a wardrobe and a chest of drawers, and on top a vase of yellow chrysanthemums. The curtains were of plain blue fabric, as was the bedspread. On the walls were pictures of boats and seascapes, and when the sun poured in through the window as it did now, the whole room was bathed in light, bringing the seascapes to life.

The boy ran to the dresser. "Look, Jasper! Here's your present."

Jasper was amazed; it was a sailing ship, all decked out, its sails unrolled to the wind, its smooth hull brightly painted. "By!" He looked at the boy with admiration, and the smallest tinge of doubt. "Did *you* make that?"

He nodded. "Mum bought me a model. At first I couldn't understand the instructions and I got a few things wrong, then Mum showed me and I was all right after that." He was quick to assure Jasper. "I made it all by myself. Honest!"

"Well, you've done a grand job, son. Thank you." He took the ship into his hands and examined its every feature. "I'll tell yer what." Replacing it, he gave the boy a hug. "When yer grow up, I reckon you'll mek a fine craftsman. I expect you'll make beautiful objects and travel the world. And I for one will be very proud."

The boy shook his head. "No, Jasper! I want to be a sailor, like you."

Jasper laughed. "You can be whatever yer like, son, as long as yer happy."

From the doorway, Liz watched them together. She recalled how Robert used to speak to his son in much the same way. Thinking on it now almost broke her heart. How could he have deserted them like that? Time and again she was forced to remind herself of it. Robert deserted her and the boy. How could she ever forgive him?

Coming across the room, she walked into Jasper's embrace. "You look well," she said.

He chuckled. "You know me," he answered, "I haven't got time to be owt else."

"The journey wasn't too tiring, was it?"

"Not so I noticed."

"Did you manage to get anything to eat on the way?"

"No. I made straight here, lass."

"Good! So you must be hungry. I've got ham salad. And lemon meringue pie for afterward. I've been saving my coupons specially."

The old man's stomach grumbled at the thought. "And have yer a suitable drink for an old man who's traveled miles at yer slightest whim?" He winked at the boy. "I bet yer mam's forgot what me tipple is."

She hadn't forgotten, because when they all trooped downstairs, she poured him a glass of good ale. "You enjoy that while I set about getting the meal."

Raising the glass, Jasper drank her health and that of the boy. "I reckon me and the lad will sit in the sunshine awhile, if that's all right with you?" he asked.

She nodded. "That's a good idea." Her glance was meaningful. "We'll talk later, when you can catch me up with all the news."

"Aye, lass." He had not forgotten why he was here. "I dare say we've a lot to talk about." At the back of his mind was the knowledge that he was obliged to tell her how Robert was gone for good. It was an unsettling prospect. For the moment, though, he would indulge the boy and do a bit of exploring.

For the next half-hour the two of them roamed the garden. Robbie showed him his favorite tree, complete with treehouse. "It was here when we came," he explained, "but it was falling apart, so I tidied it all up and made a door. When you're inside, you can shut it and pretend you're in the middle of the ocean, all on your own."

"And is that what you'd like . . . to be in the middle of the ocean, all on your own?" The old man had noticed how the boy's voice trembled, and could only imagine what was going on in his young mind.

The boy looked up at him, his eyes welling up with threatened tears. "Why didn't my daddy come back for me?" Suddenly the tears fell, and he could say no more.

"Come here to me, son." The old man opened his arms. When the boy clung to him, he spoke softly. "Sometimes things happen that we don't understand. But your daddy loved you, that I do know."

For a while the boy cried softly, but when Jasper deliberately brought his attention to a pigeon that had settled on the tree-house, he was momentarily diverted. "I reckon he's after some of our breakfast, what do *you* think?"

The boy was instantly concerned. "I've got an apple in the tree-house."

"How long's it been there?"

"Only a week." Already his tears were gone, but not the ache in his heart. That was hidden like before.

"Will it still be crispy, d'yer think?"

"It might be."

"Look, I'll tell you what," the old man suggested. "*I'm* partial to a crispy apple. How about yer fetch it down and we'll share it?"

"All right!" He liked that idea. "Why don't we eat it in the tree-house?"

Jasper gave a cry of horror. "What? Yer mean yer want *me* to climb up there?"

The boy tugged at his sleeve. "Come on! It'll be fun. You can be captain if you like."

"Gerraway with yer!" The old man laughed out loud. "If I were *half* the size, I'd never fit in that little house. Not in a month o' Sundays, I wouldn't." He made a suggestion. "How about if yer show me the rest of the garden?"

Content in the old man's company, Robbie showed him some old birds' nests, now deserted, that he had discovered. "I like this garden," the boy confided as they sat together on the old rustic bench, "but I want to come home. I miss the sea." A sadness touched his voice. "Mummy says we might go back one day, but not yet."

The old man's heart was sore. "I'm sure yer mammy means to take yer back," he promised. "Else why would she keep the cottage, eh?"

The boy looked up, his eyes moist with tears but a smile on his face. "Yes, that's right. Mummy told me we still have the cottage. Oh, Jasper, will she take me back? Will she?"

"That's summat for your mammy to decide, son." He had more sense than to raise the boy's hopes too high.

Suddenly his heart lurched when the boy asked in all innocence, "Then, will *Daddy* come back?"

Liz's call that the food was ready spared him from giving an answer. He clambered off the seat. "We'd best go," he said, feigning excitement. "We don't want to miss that lovely lemon meringue pie, do we, eh?" He was thankful when the boy readily agreed, seeming to forget for the minute that Jasper had not answered his question.

Liz had decided to set the table in the garden. "I thought you'd rather be outside," she said. She knew Jasper from old.

"I don't mind admitting that I'd rather be outside than in," he confessed. "I expect it comes of being an old sailor."

The next few hours were some of the best in the old man's life.

Liz had prepared a wonderful meal, all set out on a pink tablecloth. There were jugs of cold drinks, plates of crusty bread, and a delicious salad of ham, laid inside large lettuce leaves and surrounded by sliced tomatoes, thin rounds of apple and cucumber.

"By, lass! This is grand." Tucking in, the old man enjoyed every mouth-watering morsel, and when later the lemon meringue pie arrived, it went down a treat. "Is that one o' yer specialities?" he asked, wiping the last crumb from his beard; she, proud of her cooking, promptly gave him another large helping.

After the meal was cleared away, they went for a walk in the park. "Me and Robbie stroll through here often," Liz explained. "The park belongs to the Duke of Bedford, but you're allowed to go through, as long as you don't stray too far from the path."

The park was huge: a vast, impressive expanse of lake and shrubberies, overhung with huge, ancient rhododendrons that reached into the skies and filled the world with color. On either side the parkland stretched away for miles, dotted here and there with herds of grazing deer, and in the far distance another shimmering lake danced in the evening sunlight.

"This place can't be all that different from heaven," Jasper declared with awe. "I ain't never seen anything so lovely." Unless it was a boat in full sail across the ocean, he thought fondly.

"LOOK AT THAT!" Pointing to the large stag coming toward them, the boy was wide-eyed with wonder. "If we keep ever so still, it might come near, so we can touch it!"

The stag was magnificent: broad of chest, with large dark eyes and thick, strong antlers that could maim or kill in a fight. He kept his distance, wary, menacing. Then, while the three of them looked on in admiration, he turned gracefully, and ambled back to his herd. "Well, I never!" The old man was entranced.

On leaving the park, Robbie had a suggestion. "Why don't we go to the pub for a drink?"

Jasper laughed, but Liz explained. "There's a pretty garden behind the Bull Inn. Sometimes me and Robbie go in for a leisurely drink before going home. If you're thirsty, we could call in now?"

With a thirst on him like a sponge in the desert, Jasper didn't need asking twice. "You've said the magic words," he chuckled. "Lead on."

Woburn being a very old village, there were many little nooks and crannies, and old stone arches through which, once upon a time, carriages would make their way to the stables at the back. Now, though, it was people who sat beneath the arches, and the cobbled stableyards were pretty gardens, with tables and chairs and pinafored waitresses to fetch and carry for the thirsty visitors.

"Two lemonades and a pint of beer, please." Liz gave the

order, and when it arrived they sat back and enjoyed the moment, chatting and laughing and simply enjoying each other's company.

Inevitably, and much to the old man's concern, Liz and her son had many questions. The boy was mainly interested in the harbor and the boats and what Jasper himself had been up to, while Liz asked about the cottage, and its tenant.

"He's called Tom," Jasper imparted with a knowing smile. "A nice fella. Keeps himself to himself mostly, but we've become good friends." He laughed. "I even persuaded him into buying a sailing boat—smart little thing, it is—got many years o' work in her yet, I shouldn't wonder."

"D'you think he'll let *me* go on it?" Robbie was so excited he could hardly sit still.

"We'll have to see, won't we, eh?"

Liz was curious. "Is he married?"

The old man shook his head. "He's come to West Bay, like so many of us, to escape whatever it is that haunts him." Beyond that he couldn't say. "But I know you'd like him. He's a fine, good man."

"And there's no problem with the cottage or anything?"

"Not that I can think of, no. I look after the maintenance, as always. He pays the rent and the money goes straight into the bank. The cottage is kept nice, just as you like it."

"So, everything is the same as when we left, is that what you're saying?"

The old man swallowed hard. Though she had worded her question carefully for the boy's sake, he had seen the beseeching look in her eyes. He knew what she was asking, and his old heart lurched.

Again, for the sake of the boy, and for Liz herself, he worded his answer equally carefully. "It's more or less the same, lass."

She gave him a curious glance, and for a minute he was afraid she had more probing questions. But the moment passed when the waitress arrived to ask if there was anything else they would like.

Liz shook her head and thanked her.

The old man insisted on paying the bill, and they were

soon making their way back to the house. "It's been a lovely day," Jasper told her. "I can understand why yer chose to settle in this beautiful place."

Opening the door, Liz let them in. "We're not 'settled,' as you call it. We're much like yourself, Jasper: in transit, always looking for the next port of call."

"I understand." He looked into her sorry face and read her thoughts. Knowing the time had come for her to learn the truth, he took her aside. "Later, when the boy's in bed, we'll need to talk, lass." There was no more hedging, no more wishing he didn't have to tell her, because now there was no option. In fact, there never had been.

It was nine o'clock when the boy finally tumbled into bed. Weary and worn out by the day's events, he threw his arms around the old man's neck. "I love you, Jasper," he said, and Jasper was deeply moved. "I love you too, lad."

Even before he got to the door, the boy was soundly sleeping. "Goodnight, son." Quietly closing the door, he went down the stairs and into the kitchen. Liz was waiting at the table, with two mugs of cocoa and a look on her face that betrayed her anxiety. "Come and sit down." Gesturing to the chair opposite, she reminded him, "Like you say . . . we need to talk."

"Aye, lass." Seating himself, he sighed heavily, his old heart pained by what he must tell her.

Sensing his dilemma, she anticipated his news. "It's Robert, isn't it?"

"Yes, lass. It's Robert." He had to swallow the hard lump in his throat or it would have choked him.

Her eyes lit up. "Oh, Jasper! Is he back?"

Again, he had to swallow hard. "No, lass. He's not back. But there is summat yer should know."

A look of apprehension crossed her kindly features. "What is it, Jasper? Have you heard from him, is that it?"

He shook his head. He had to get it over with, however painful it might be. "I'm sorry, lass, but I'm afraid Robert is dead."

Liz blanched, and tears filled her eyes. "How do you know?" she asked shakily.

The old man took a deep breath before going on. "A young lady turned up, and what she told me is what I've come to tell you now."

"*What* young lady? Who is she?"

"Her name's Kathy." He paused a moment, not wanting to shock her further, but seeing no other way. *"She's Robert's daughter."*

Pressing her hand to her mouth, Liz stared at him for a minute, her eyes wide with astonishment. "I never knew he had a daughter." She looked him in the eye. "He never talked to me about his life outside of West Bay and I never asked. I was always afraid that, if I pushed him too far, he'd leave and I would never see him again." Her regrets were many, but meeting Robert and sharing part of his life was not one of them. "Please tell me. What happened to Robert?" Though filled with a sense of dread, she urged in a small voice, "It's all right, Jasper. Say what you've come to say."

Reaching out to cover her hand with his own, the old man related in the gentlest manner he could what Kathy had told him: about how her father had passed on, and how Barden House belonged to her. He explained how she had come there to see where she imagined her father had spent some of the happiest times of his life. And, oh, how she had loved him, and how desperately she missed him still.

And as he talked, Liz quietly wept, looking up now and then with scarred eyes and an aching heart, urging him on.

He described what a delightful young woman Robert's daughter was, and how he had told her about Liz and her father, and how wonderfully happy they had been. Jasper told Liz that he had explained to Kathy that, when Robert didn't come back, Liz had begun to believe he didn't care for her or his son anymore, and it was a burden she could no longer carry. So she had moved away.

When finally the old man was silent, he felt her hand in his, holding on as if she would drown if he were to let go. His heart went out to her. "I'm sorry, lass," he murmured. "I'd have given anything not to be the bearer of such terrible news."

Through eyes swimming with tears she looked up. "I

didn't know," she whispered. "I thought he didn't want us anymore." Her voice broke. "I should have known better! Oh, Jasper, *I should have known better!*"

When at last her composure broke and she dropped her head to her hands, sobbing as if her heart would break, the old man went to her. Folding his arms around her, he let her cry, much as he had let Kathy cry that day when she talked of her father. And, when the crying was done, he made them each a cup of tea and they sat together, talking about Robert, and how his son would take the news. "It'll be a terrible blow to the lad."

Liz promised that Robbie would cope. "He's like his father. He has a way of dealing with things," she said. "And what about you, Jasper? This can't have been easy . . . having to bring me such news."

"You had to know," he answered. "And who better to tell you than me?"

She gave a tiny smile. "You know, Jasper, in a peculiar, roundabout way it's a blessing. You see, I know now that he *did* love us, more than ever." She bowed her head. "I only wish he'd told me, so I could have looked after him."

Jasper chided her for punishing herself like that. "It was his wish that you should not see him the way he was. I can imagine he didn't want to put you through all that pain."

She nodded. "Yes, I can see how he would do something like that," she agreed. "All the same, I wish I could have been there to comfort him."

They talked a while longer, and when the mantelpiece clock struck midnight, they went their separate ways. "Goodnight, Jasper, and thank you." At the top of the landing she gave him a hug. "It's Robbie we have to think about now."

Weary of heart but glad it was over, the old man threw off his clothes and, putting on his striped pajamas, climbed into bed. Within minutes he was sound asleep, though his dreams were disturbing.

He couldn't have been asleep for more than an hour or two when he was woken by a strange sound which at first he couldn't quite make out.

Then he realized. The sounds were coming from an adjoining bedroom. He recognized the muffled "thump thump" of pacing feet, and the quiet, heart-wrenching sobs. "Oh, dearie me!" He knew it was Liz, and he blamed himself. "What have I done?"

Getting out of bed, he sat by the window, listening and hurting, and helpless to do anything that might ease her sorrow.

After what seemed an age the sounds died away—first the pacing, then the sobbing. When silence fell over the house, the old man wasn't sure whether the sound of her grief wasn't preferable to that awful, crippling quiet. After a minute or two, he was tempted to knock on her door to see if she was all right. But then he heard the soft patter of her feet against the lino floor, then the window being thrust up on its pulley. And now the same quiet patter of feet as she returned to her bed.

Not long after Maggie's arrival, Kathy had taken her friend out and headed straight for the fish and chip shop. Afterward, they sat by the harbor and enjoyed what Maggie described as "the best bleedin' fish an' chips I've ever tasted, gal!"

They walked along the shoreline and sat in the sand, talking and reminiscing, and wanting the day to go on forever. When it began to grow dusk, they made their way to the bar at the caravan site, and Maggie said she "wouldn't mind one day getting a job here."

Taking their drinks outside to a table, they watched the sun go down, and Maggie eyed every young man that passed. "I could go for that one!" she whispered, or, "Oh, no! I couldn't fancy *that* one in a million years!" and Kathy thought it was just wonderful to have Maggie here by her side, though, with her high heels, wild hair and outlandish clothes, Maggie stood out a mile. But that didn't matter. It was Maggie, and Maggie was a one-off, something special.

They were sitting companionably together enjoying a

second drink when suddenly Tom turned up to join them. From the start, and with a twinkle in her eye, Maggie obviously approved.

The three of them sat and chatted and Maggie made them all laugh, and later, when Maggie said she was ready for her bed, Tom gave her a peck on the cheek and for a while she was unusually quiet.

Kathy and Maggie made their way back to the house, and once or twice Maggie saw Kathy turn to smile at Tom as he strode away, and he, too, had eyes only for her.

"You've found a good 'un there, gal!" she told Kathy as they entered the house. "Hang onto him. Men like him are few and far between."

Kathy understood. "I will," she said, and meant it.

"Cor! It's been an 'ell of a day!" Maggie said, falling into the nearest chair. "I don't mind tellin' yer, gal, I'm whacked!" Looking sheepish, she asked, "Would you think me a selfish bugger if I went off to bed?"

Kathy assured her she would think no such thing, and Maggie followed her up the stairs to her bed. "Thanks, gal," she said, giving her a crushing bear hug. "I'm glad I came."

"So am I," Kathy told her, and quietly closed the door.

Not long after, Kathy went to bed. For a while she lay there, thinking of Maggie and the fun they'd had. And Tom too. Never a night went by when she didn't go to sleep thinking of him.

Finally she dropped off, content and happy.

Lying there, wondering how the boy would cope when he was told about his father, Jasper closed his eyes time and again, but there was no sleep in him. He heard the downstairs mantel-clock strike every hour between two and five, before he finally sank into the pillow and succumbed to the weariness which suddenly lapped over him.

When morning came and the watery sun filtered in through his window, he woke with a start. A glance at the bedside clock told him it was already eight o'clock.

"Good God! I've never slept so late in all me life!" Springing out of bed with as much enthusiasm as his old bones would allow, he quickly washed and dressed and made his way downstairs.

Liz and the boy were already in the kitchen. "Sit yourself down, Jasper," Liz told him. "I'm cooking porridge . . . how does that sound?" Turning from the gas-stove, she smiled on him.

"Aye, lass, that sounds like a right treat." He was shocked to see the dark hollows beneath her eyes, and the pale, pinched features, suggesting that—like him—she had spent most of the night lying awake.

Blissfully oblivious to the tension in that tiny room, young Robbie chatted away, excited about an idea he'd dreamt up to entertain the old man before he set off back to West Bay. "We can go and see the barges if you like?"

Just then, Liz brought their breakfasts to the table. "Not today, Robbie," she said cautiously. "I think Jasper would prefer to stay around the cottage for today." Recruiting the old man's support, she asked with a smile, "That's right, isn't it, Jasper? You'd rather stay around the cottage, at least for a while?"

"Aye, lass, that's right enough." Addressing the boy, he said with a cheeky grin, "I bet you that pigeon's out there, looking for a bite o' that juicy apple."

The boy's eyes shone. "Will it?"

"I'm sure of it, lad. We'd best have us breakfast, then we'll sit outside, shall we, and keep a lookout?"

They ate their breakfast and while Liz and the old man sat quiet and thoughtful, the boy chattered on.

When breakfast was over, Liz suggested the boy should go and see if the pigeon was there, while she and Jasper had a little chat.

As the boy sped out the door, she turned to Jasper. "I don't know how to tell him." Dropping into the nearest chair, she rubbed the palm of her hand over her eyes. "Never a day goes by without him asking after his father. He's been so good, asking so many questions, and never getting any real answers, and now . . . oh, Jasper! How do I tell him his father is never coming back?"

The old man knew how hard she must be finding it all. "Look, would yer like *me* to tell the lad?"

She shook her head. "Oh, no! I couldn't ask you to do that. It's my place. I can't shirk that responsibility." Getting out of her chair, she kissed him on the cheek. "Thanks all the same." Looking out of the window, she saw the boy climbing out of his play-house to shin down the tree-trunk. "He's a treasure," she murmured. "I don't know what I would have done without him." She looked appealingly at the old man, her voice quivering. "Will he ever forgive me, do you think?"

"Oh, he'll forgive you all right." The old man had few doubts about that. "The lad loves yer, and besides, he'll know it weren't your fault, any more than it were his." Jasper paused. "Do folks around here ask . . . about his father?"

Liz looked down at her left hand, which was bare. She touched her finger and looked back at the old man. "I did worry, after we left West Bay. People there were kind to us, tolerant. They never mentioned the fact that Robert and I weren't married—and it never seemed to matter." She sighed. "But I knew that in the real world it would be harder. I tell people I'm separated. But now I suppose I should say I'm widowed." Her eyes filled with tears.

Jasper awkwardly rose to his feet and patted her shoulder. "There, there."

"I suppose a part of me always knew, deep down, that Robert was married. All he ever said to me was that he wished he could marry me. But I didn't care. And neither did anyone else at the time. As long as it isn't hard for Robbie."

"You just tell them whatever you like, lass, whatever makes life better for the pair of yer."

Liz straightened her shoulders. "Will you be there when I tell him . . . please?"

"Whatever yer want, lass."

"Then let's get it over with."

Liz led the way into the garden. While the old man made

for the seat, Liz called her son across. "Robbie . . . sweetheart! Can you come here a minute? I've got something to tell you."

Bounding across the garden, Robbie arrived breathless before them. "What?"

Patting the seat beside her, she slid an arm around his shoulders. "It's about your daddy."

"Oh!" He began leaping about. "He's coming home! Is he, Mummy?"

When it seemed Liz might lose her composure, the old man's sober voice cut through the boy's excitement. "Sit down, son. Let your mammy finish."

Astonished, Robbie looked from one to the other, realization dawning. "No!" Backing up, he stared at his mother. "He's not coming back, is he? That's what you want to tell me, isn't it?" His voice rose to a crescendo. "DADDY DOESN'T WANT US! AND NOW HE'S NEVER COMING BACK!" Taking to his heels, he ran for the tree-house. "I hate him. I HATE HIM!"

Going after him at a run, Liz called up to where he'd hidden himself in the farthest corner of the tree-house. "Please, Robbie, come down. It isn't like that."

"Tell me the truth. Is he coming back?"

"No, sweetheart. I'm sorry . . ."

"GO AWAY!" In a sudden rage he ran across the floor. Flinging the hatch cover over the opening, he threw himself on top of it; the sounds of his crying tore at both their hearts.

"Come away, lass." When Liz too began softly crying, the old man tenderly moved her aside. "Let me talk to him, eh?"

Unable to speak, Liz nodded.

"Robbie, lad." Going steadily up the ladder that rested precariously against the tree-trunk, Jasper made his way up. "Oh, be careful!" Liz was fearful that the ladder might fall and he would be injured.

"Don't you worry, lass," he called back. "I've climbed too many masts in my time to be worried about a rickety old ladder." All the same, when he heard the trap-door shift back an inch or so, he smiled to himself. It told him the boy was concerned about his safety, too.

Almost to the top, he decided to try the old trick of distracting the boy's attention. But first he winked at Liz, so she would know he was up to some trick or other. "Oh!" In a loud voice he called out, as if to Liz, "I nearly went there, lass. By! If I fall off this ladder, I'm likely to break me back!"

"You get off my ladder!" Robbie's voice sailed down to him. "I don't want you up here. GET DOWN!"

The old man secretly chuckled. "You invited me to your play-house, and now I'm tekkin' you up on it."

There followed a banter between the two of them, with the boy urging him to get off his ladder, and the old man insisting that he had every right to be there, and, "What's more I'm coming inside, so you'd best open that trap-door, else I probably *will* fall and break me neck!" And for effect he yelled out, "Oh, my God! I nearly went then. Watch out, lass . . . stay back in case I tumble."

Suddenly the trap-door opened and there was Robbie peering out, his face stained with tears and his eyes red-raw. "You can't get inside here," he warned. "You're too fat."

"FAT!" Feigning indignation, the old man edged his way up toward the opening. "Move aside, lad. I'll show yer whether I'm 'fat' or not, yer cheeky young rascal!"

Much to his own surprise, and not without trepidation, the old man managed to squeeze his bulk in through the opening. "There y'are!" Reaching his gaze into the farthest corner where the boy was sitting, he softly chuckled. "You'd best not call me 'fat' again, 'cause I got through the door, and now I'm coming over there."

Seeming little more than a shadow, the boy began to cry. "Leave me alone, Jasper."

"I can't do that, son." Carefully, on all fours, he made his way across the floor. "I can't have you crying and not do owt about it."

When he reached the boy he took him into his arms. There they sat—the two of them—an odd sight in that tiny, cramped corner. With the boy's head on his shoulder, the old man told him in as kind a way as possible why his father had left them. "It weren't his fault. Y'see, son, he never wanted to leave you, only he got poorly, and went away so you and yer mammy wouldn't see him hurting. Then, he just never got better."

With big, wet eyes and the sob still in his voice, the boy looked up. "*I* was poorly once, when I had chickenpox."

The old man nodded. "I remember."

"Daddy looked after me too. He told me stories and made me laugh, and he never sent *me* away, did he?"

"No, son, he didn't."

"So, why did *he* go away? Why didn't he stay and let us look after him, like he looked after me?"

"Because sometimes it's hard to know what to do for the best. Y'see, when a man gets ill, he begins to wonder about all manner o' things. And when it comes down to it, the only thing he's worried about is his family . . . them that he loves."

"Do you think he loved me and Mummy?"

"Oh, son!" He pressed his arm tight about the boy. "He loved you more than anything in this whole wide world. He told me that once . . . he said as how if he hadn't got you and your mammy, life wouldn't be worth living. You made him very happy, lad. You and yer mammy were very precious to him. Whatever else yer believe, yer must *allus* believe that."

"When somebody doesn't get better, they go to heaven, don't they?"

"Aye, lad, if they've been good, that's where they go all right."

"Daddy was 'good,' wasn't he?"

"I'd say so, yes, lad."

"Jasper?"

"Yes, lad?"

"What does heaven look like?"

The old man couldn't help but chuckle. "I can't say as I've ever been there, and I reckon I'm not ready to go yet, but, well, I'd say as it looks summat like this pretty garden . . . with flowers and birds, and all kinda lovely smells an' colors."

The boy was quiet for a time; the sobs subsided and he drew away. "I want my mummy now."

Tears welled up in the old man's eyes. " 'Course yer do, lad."

Sighing to his boots, he shifted around to let the boy go first. "Can't say as I'll be sorry to get down," he confessed. "You were right, lad, I *am* too fat to be up here!" In truth the bones of his backside were aching and his back felt like it had been twisted off its axle. "Go on, lad, I'm right behind yer."

Getting out proved more arduous than getting in.

Again, not being able to stand up in there, the old man carefully backed up toward the trap-door. Once there, he put his legs through, then his backside, and bit by bit, with great difficulty, he managed to emerge; then it was a trial negotiating the ladder, as it wobbled and creaked with his every step. "I can see next time I come and visit I shall 'ave to mek you a stronger ladder!"

Afraid Jasper might get hurt, Robbie watched until he was safely down.

With a great sigh of relief, the old man dropped to the ground. "By! Never again!" He was all hot and bothered, his face as red as a beetroot and every bone in his old body shrieking out.

He watched the boy run to his mother, who had been anxiously waiting. As he ran into her arms, she closed her love about him, and together they walked into the house.

Realizing their need to be alone, the old man didn't follow for a while. Instead he sat on the bench, recovering from his own ordeal.

From behind him, the sound of the boy sobbing, and Liz's gentle reassurance, even though her own heart was breaking, was something the old man would remember for the rest of his life.

Some time later, Liz came out to bring him inside. "Thank you, Jasper," she said. "You've been a real friend to both of us."

When they came into the kitchen, Jasper asked after the boy. "Will he be all right, d'yer think?"

She led him into the sitting room. "He's more settled now, thanks to you."

The old man was choked to see how the boy was fast asleep on the sofa. "It were a hard thing for him to find out," he said as Liz quietly closed the door. "Look, lass, I'm sorry I had to bring such awful news."

"In a way, I'm glad you did," she said quietly. "You've answered so many of my questions. Robbie's, too, though it's all a bit too much for him right now."

He understood what she meant. When he first set foot in this pretty place, there was an air of confusion and doubt, and a sense of deep unhappiness. Now it was as if the curtain of doubt and confusion had lifted. And yes, there was still unhappiness, but it would pass in the fullness of time; he knew that from experience.

"Will you stay a few more days, Jasper?"

"If you want me to, lass."

"We *both* want you to."

"Aye, well"—he gave her a wink—"it'll give me time to build a new ladder. That one's falling apart at the seams."

She threw her arms around him. "Thank you."

That was all she said.

But it was enough.

# Twelve

IT HAD BEEN LATE WHEN KATHY WENT TO BED, HAVING waved goodbye to Maggie earlier in the day, and since then she had hardly slept a full hour.

Now, at four o'clock in the morning, she was wide awake.

For a time she lay there, her head in the pillows and her arms flung out across the sheet. Pent-up and restless, she closed her eyes and tried to relax, but it was no use.

"Damn it!" Throwing off the bedclothes, she clambered out of bed and went to the window. Whenever she found it difficult to sleep, Kathy always went to look out of the window: there was something calming about seeing what was going on in the outside world; it seemed to focus the mind.

"I wonder if Dad used to stand by this window and look out?" she murmured, her eyes shifting to the photograph on her bedside cabinet. "I wonder if he ever got so churned up and worried that he couldn't sleep?"

She thought about his double life, and imagined there must have been many a time when he was worried he might be found out, and that it would all cave in on him.

Suddenly, out of the corner of her eye, she thought she detected a movement down on the beach. A closer look and she recognized the shadowy figure. "Tom!" She glanced at the clock: it showed the time as ten past four. She wondered what he was doing down there at this time of morning, yet she wasn't overly concerned, for hadn't she seen him, time and again, strolling the beach, pausing every now and then to pick up a pebble or a shell? The old baccy jar on his mantelpiece was filled to the brim with them; he'd shown them to her one day when Jasper and she were visiting.

She watched him for a while, then shivered when the chill of early morning began to penetrate her bones. Returning to the bed, she collected her robe and threw it over her shoulders. By the time she got back to the window, he was gone. Saddened, she turned away. When a moment later she climbed into bed, Tom was strong in her mind.

Holding her father's photograph, she opened her heart to him. "I know how you used to say that one day I'd find the right man. Well, now I think I have, but isn't it strange how I had to come all this way to find him?"

She wagged a finger at him. "You knew, didn't you?" she chided. "You bought this house for me, because you knew I would come here and there he would be."

A sense of regret washed through her. "He's going away, though. I don't know when, but I do know it will be very soon." In the circumstances she couldn't blame him. "Maybe when he finds the person who murdered his family, he'll be able to put it behind him, and there'll be a chance for us."

She smiled wistfully. "If you have any influence up there, see what you can do, will you?"

Growing serious, she confessed her innermost thoughts. "I love him, Dad. He's the kindest, most wonderful man I've ever met."

Replacing the photograph, she slid down in the bed, but there was no sleep in her. For a while, she was half tempted to go and find him, but common sense prevailed. She told herself that he might not thank her, that walking the beach in the dead of night when the world was sleeping was his way of clearing his mind. From what Tom had already confided, he needed to gather the strength and purpose to deal with what was potentially an explosive situation.

Fearful about the outcome of it all, she went downstairs, where she made herself a cup of cocoa and sat at the table, rolling the warm cup around in her hands and lazily sipping at the hot, frothy liquid.

After a time, when the warmth of the liquid dulled her

senses and the sleep crept up on her, she climbed the stairs back to bed. Within an hour she was sound asleep.

It was Tom who woke her.

His persistent rat-tatting on the front door startled her.

In two minutes she was at the front door. "Who is it?"

"It's me . . . Tom."

Inching the door open, she was embarrassed to let him in, what with her hair uncombed and the sleep still in her eyes.

Tom thought she looked lovely. He liked the way her hair tumbled over her forehead, and that sleepy, childish look that made her seem vulnerable. "I wondered if you'd like to come out on the boat later?"

Kathy shook herself awake. "Is he back then . . . Jasper?"

"Not yet."

Kathy was impressed. "What? You mean you're taking the boat out by yourself?"

"That was the idea." He shrugged. "Jasper reckons I'm about ready to take over the helm." He feigned disappointment. "But if you don't trust me?"

"No! I mean . . . 'course I do, and yes, I'd love to come out on the boat with you." She thought it was a wonderful idea. "What time?"

"Half past ten all right?"

"I'll be there."

"And don't forget to wear something sensible . . . you'll need plimsolls and a warm jumper. There's a bite in the breeze this morning."

He gave her a slow, lazy smile, then he was gone. "Don't be late!" His voice carried back from the path.

After he'd gone, Kathy rushed around like a crazy thing. First she had a quick soak in the bath, then rummaged through her wardrobe, before she located a warm jumper. With that secure, she quickly found what she thought was a "sensible" skirt: straight and knee-length, it was a smart navy-blue in color. The white plimsolls were no problem—she had already bought them some weeks back on Jasper's instructions.

By half past ten she was ready. She tied her hair back with a pretty red ribbon, dusted only the slightest hint of powder on her face, and touched her lips with the merest suggestion of dusky-pink lipstick.

As she ran downstairs, her heart leapt at the prospect of a day out alone with Tom on his boat. "Your dad must have heard you, after all!" It was a comforting if fanciful thought.

Tom was waiting as she ran toward the harbor. "Well, at least you *look* like a sailor," he teased. "Let's see if you have the *makings* of one."

"I'm out to surprise you," she promised.

He gave her the same wise instructions Jasper had given him when first going out. "Don't stand too near the edge. The waters are rough through the channel. Once we're out in the open water it won't be so bad."

He was right. With the breeze gently lifting the sails, they went softly toward the narrow tunnel of water, but once they were inside and between the high walls, the wind heightened. It whipped up through the sails and swept them along, buffeting the boat from side to side, and hurling them about. "Hold on tight, Kathy!" While Tom fought to keep the vessel straight, Kathy hung onto the rails. The last thing she wanted right now was to be a heroine.

It was only minutes—but it seemed like forever—before they broke out into open seas. "Jasper was right!" Easing the boat into the breeze, Tom laughed at the sheer joy of it all. "Once you get the hang of it, there's nothing to it!"

It was a day Kathy would never forget. For two hours or more, with the sails billowing and the sea churning beneath them, they rode the wind, until, breathless and exhausted, Tom steered the boat into a tiny, sheltered inlet along the coast. Becalmed and private, Tom suggested Kathy might like to go for a swim. "I can't." She flushed with embarrassment. "I never learned to swim."

He smiled at that. "I can see I'll have to take you in hand."

He took a moment to observe her, and his heart was full. As she leaned against the rail, her hair loosened by the wind, he saw the seductive yet innocent way her blouse was open to show the rise of her breasts, and those wonderful light-brown eyes looking up at him with a sense of curiosity. He thought she was the most beautiful creature on God's earth.

As always, whenever his emotions ran riot, the guilt enveloped him. His wife had been beautiful, he reminded himself. And, suddenly, the magic of the moment was gone.

His mood was instantly changed. "Let's have some lunch."

"Yes, I'm ravenous." Kathy had seen the swift change of mood in him and she knew why. Yet she daren't open that particular conversation, for fear it might drive him further away. Instead she answered in light-hearted vein, "The sea air seems to have given me an appetite."

"So, what do you fancy?"

"Let's see . . . As you're doing the cooking, I'll have roast beef, Yorkshire pudding—oh, and an apple pie." She felt full up just saying it.

He laughed. "I've got a bag of sandwiches, and some lemonade." He grimaced. "Sorry. It's not much of a choice, is it?"

Kathy smiled brightly. "That sounds wonderful to me."

In fact, Kathy thought everything was wonderful. Lazing here in this pretty bay, with the late summer sun shining down, and the sea sparkling all around them, was wonderful. More than that, just being here with him was the most wonderful thing of all.

Watching her, Tom was torn. He longed to take her in his arms and ask her to be his wife, but always the same crippling memories held him back.

He wanted Kathy, more than anything in this world, and yet too much of him was still back there . . . going over the cliff-edge, with the sound of his family screaming in terror. And, though he tried hard to put it behind him, it continued to haunt him day and night.

Suddenly, Kathy was standing before him. He had been so steeped in those vivid, crippling images that he hadn't even noticed her approaching. "Do you want to go back?" Her voice was soft, gently soothing.

Ashamed, he apologized. "I'm sorry."

Kathy wished with all her heart she could do something,

but it wasn't in her power. "Don't be sorry," she urged. "I understand."

He wondered how *anyone* could understand, yet she really *did* seem to. It was the amazing way she lifted his spirits, and her genuine, heartfelt compassion, that made him love her all the more.

Coming closer, he looked into her face and saw the anguish there. "I know how difficult it must be for you as well. But I meant what I said before," he promised. "I *do* love you. And our time *will* come."

She slid her hand into his. "I know."

His smile was tenderly intimate, yet teasing. "So, are you hungry?"

"Starving . . . I told you! But I'll get the sandwiches."

"Absolutely not!" With a stern expression, he playfully demanded, "Who's the captain on this ship . . . you or me?"

"You, sir!" She snapped her heels and saluted smartly.

"Exactly," he laughed. "So sit yourself down and enjoy the view, while I get on with my duties."

Smiling happily, Kathy obeyed the order. It was all a game, and she was content to play along. She was with Tom, and nothing else mattered. But in the back of her mind, the questions never went away. Would he ever be free of those nightmares? Was there a future for them? Or would it all end in tears?

After lunch they made their way further along the coast to the village of Lyme Regis. Here, they came ashore, and, hand-in-hand, they went off to explore the narrow streets. They walked along the Cobb and up to the cliff-tops, from where they could see the coastline stretching away in both directions. They held hands and ran and laughed like children; when he kissed her, she melted into his arms. Now, more than ever, she knew that was where she belonged.

The hours passed and soon the daylight was fading. When evening began to draw in, he suggested reluctantly, "I think it's time we went back."

Equally reluctant, Kathy agreed, pulling on her jumper as the air grew chillier. "Will you teach me to swim?" she asked him on the way back, and Tom said he would.

As they threaded their way along the coast, it started to rain. Tom fell silent. Kathy sensed his dark mood, but wisely said nothing. If he wanted to confide in her, he would, she thought.

And to her relief, he did. The minute the boat was safely anchored in the harbor, he asked her to stay a while. "Wait till the rain stops," he said. "I'll walk you home later."

"What is it, Tom?" She always knew when he was troubled, but this time it was different somehow. "What's wrong?"

He shook his head from side to side as he fondly observed her. "You know me too well."

"So, there *is* something wrong?" Afraid now, her stomach lurched. Was this where he told her he wanted it all to end?

Her heart sank when he admitted, "There's something I need to tell you."

Trying to put on a brave face, she urged, "You don't want to see me anymore. That's it, isn't it?"

His dark eyes grew wide with amazement. "Oh no!" Gripping her by the shoulders, he told her reassuringly, "I would *never* want that! If you believe anything, you must believe that I want to spend the rest of my life with you. Oh, Kathy! I can't tell you how much I want to be with you." His voice shook with emotion. "You're *everything* to me!"

Relieved, she clung to him, and for a time they took comfort in each other. Presently, he held her at arm's length. "You knew I would have to go away sooner or later, didn't you?"

She nodded resignedly. "Is that what you have to tell me . . . that you're ready to leave me?"

He nodded, a look of reluctance on his face. "I've already made arrangements to see Inspector Lawson, the man who handled the case from the outset. He's based in London now. I want us to go through everything again, with a fine-tooth comb. Dorset police say they've exhausted all lines of enquiry, but there *has* to be a way of tracking that car, and the person who sent my family to their deaths."

His fists clenched and unclenched as he thought about it. "The police have missed something, I'm sure of it. A car and its driver can't just vanish into thin air!"

Seeing how, in spite of him saying his rage was under control, Tom was growing agitated, Kathy wrapped her warm, gentle hands over his fist; it was clenched so tight his knuckles had bled white. "Tom?"

"Yes, darling?" Calmer now, his dark eyes smiled down on her.

"Are you sure you're ready to deal with all that?"

Again, for a brief second, he seemed miles away. "If we're to have any future, yes. I need to see it through." He readily admitted, "There are still times when the anger takes a hold, but now, at long last, I really *can* think clearly about what happened. And there's another thing . . ." He hesitated. "I'm convinced my wife Sheila knew who it was that drove us over the cliff."

He let his mind go back to that moment when he first sensed it. "Just before we went over the cliff, she glanced back. I saw the look in her eyes, Kathy! I saw the flicker of recognition, then it was too late and all hell was let loose." Running his hands through his hair, he closed his eyes in torment. "She *knew*. I swear to God she knew who it was!"

Realizing how it was troubling him, Kathy tried to rationalize his suspicions. "Did she call out a name?"

"No," he recalled, "there was no name."

"Did she *say* anything at all that caused you to think she knew who it was?"

Again he shook his head. "It wasn't anything Sheila said . . . there was no time for that. It was just that instant when I glanced at her . . . an instinctive thing. It was there in her eyes . . . the way she looked back . . . the way her face fell in astonishment."

He banged his fist on the hull. "There was no time! Later, I forgot all about it for a while. I was too sick with hatred . . . I couldn't think of anything else . . . But, now, I'm certain of it. She *did* know who it was. There's no doubt in my mind about it."

"And have you thought who it could be?"

"Endlessly!"

"And?"

He shrugged. "And I've come up with nothing."

"Surely it couldn't have been a friend?"

"Maybe. Maybe not." His answer was hesitant.

"Do you *know* all her friends?"

He nodded. "You could count her friends on the fingers of one hand. They met once in a while, went shopping, and did all the things that women do. They were women just like her, married with children. I shouldn't think any one of those would want her hurt."

He described her. "Sheila was well liked, had lots of interests, always going to some class or other." He gave a small wry laugh. "I could never keep up with her!"

Something he said made Kathy wonder. "You said she went to classes?"

"That's right." He cast his mind back. "The children were growing up, and she decided she wanted to learn a new language . . . She started French classes. She went twice a week, and loved it. She was getting very good, too."

Kathy considered that for a minute, then said, "What about the people she went to class with? Did you know any of *them?*"

Her question hit hard. "My God! I never thought of that." It was possible, he thought. "She will have made friends there, but she never mentioned anyone in particular." He grew frantic. "There's something else too—something really strange!"

Digging into his trouser pocket, he took out an envelope, which he handed to her. "Read this, Kathy. The letter is from the florist I appointed to deliver a regular supply of flowers to the churchyard. Read it . . . tell me what you think."

Curious, Kathy opened the envelope. Taking out the letter, she proceeded to read it aloud:

*Dear Mr. Marcus,*

*I know you asked me not to contact you, except in the event of any hiccup with the regular payments for the fortnightly delivery of flowers. This is not the reason for my contacting you. The flowers are delivered as we agreed, and the payments are paid into my bank account on time. There is no problem there.*

*The trouble is, someone appears to be deliberately
destroying the flowers by throwing them out of the
container and strewing them about. They then replace
your flowers with their own.*

*I can imagine how distressing it will be for you to
read this letter, and I'm very sorry to have to be writing it. I haven't written before, because at first I
thought it might have been an accident, or someone
playing a prank. But then it happened again and
again, and it began to look like a deliberate and calculated act of wanton destruction.*

*Of course I quickly replaced the flowers, and kept
an eye on them as far as I could. But it's happened
again. This time they were torn into shreds, and were
almost unrecognizable as the roses and gypsophila we
delivered. Some attempt appears to have been made to
burn them on the path close by; the church-warden
came to the shop and told me about it. He was most
upset, and so was I. It beggars belief that someone
could do such a thing.*

*In all my years as a florist, I have never known any-
thing quite like it. The church-warden has confirmed
that no other flowers in the churchyard have been in-
terfered with, so I'm afraid it appears to be a personal
attack on either you or your family. I'm sorry, Mr.
Marcus, but I really am out of my depth here. Please
advise as to what you would like me to do.*

*Yours respectfully,
Margaret Taylor*

"But that's terrible!" Kathy was shocked to the core. "Who
in their right mind would want to destroy flowers in a
churchyard? And why only the flowers sent to *your* family?"
Knowing the history of his family's tragic circumstances,
Kathy couldn't help but be afraid for Tom himself.

Tom had been stunned by the letter, and it showed in his
voice now as he confessed, "The letter came yesterday. I
couldn't bring myself to discuss it with anyone, not even

you. Oh, I wanted to! But I thought it was unfair to burden you with it."

Now she could see why he had been out there walking the beach at such an ungodly hour. "That's why you couldn't sleep, isn't it?" she remarked. "That's why you were pacing the beach when everybody else was tucked up in their beds?"

He smiled. "Not you, it seems."

She admitted it. "No. For some reason, I couldn't sleep either."

"But you're right," he murmured. "What's happened is shocking and awful, and whoever is doing it must be sick in the mind!"

Kathy found it hard to believe. "I just don't understand why anybody would destroy your flowers."

Tom had thought long and hard about it. "Someone must really hate me."

"Or someone hated your *family?*"

Tom had already considered that, but it was inconceivable. "It doesn't make sense. It's me they want to hurt . . . they can't hurt my family anymore. It's me who sends the flowers. Besides, if it was my family they resented, why would they replace my flowers with fresh ones? It must be me they have a grudge against."

His explanation only served to make Kathy even more fearful for him. "Can you think of anybody who would hate you enough to do this?"

He smiled sardonically. "I've beaten many a rival company to a lucrative contract."

"Do you really believe a business rival would do such a thing?"

Serious now, he shook his head. "No. That's not the way it works. We all have to make a living. You win some, you lose some. That's the way it is in business."

Talking with Kathy had helped his mind to focus, because now something else occurred to him.

"I'm beginning to think that whoever drove us off that cliff was after me and not my family. They just happened to be there when the opportunity presented itself. I've thought and thought, and I reckon that's why the flowers are being left . . . as a kind of twisted apology. Don't you see, Kathy . . . whoever did this is getting at *me*. It's *my* flowers they're destroying. It's *me* they want dead!"

Though Kathy followed his reasoning, she daren't think about it too deeply, or she would never have another night's sleep. "I'm not so sure." Like a dog with a bone, she was loath to let it go. "I can't believe anybody would kill an entire family just to get at you. Maybe you were just unlucky enough to meet some mad killer that day; someone who started out with murder in mind, and you and your family just happened to be there."

Tom had to admit, "All right, it's possible." But it wasn't enough to satisfy him. "It still doesn't explain why somebody is destroying my flowers and putting fresh ones in their place. To me, that seems like a personal thing."

Kathy relented. "You're right. It's a strange business. It's best you go and try to resolve it one way or another; I can see that now."

"I want rid of it, Kathy." His mind was made up. "Whoever it was that robbed my wife and children of their lives must be made to pay for it." His voice fell to a hush. "I need to know *why!* And if it was me they were after, I also need to make sure they don't get another chance to finish the job."

He took her in his embrace, his face against the softness of her hair and his voice low in her ear. "It's coming between us, and I don't want that. It will always be there. Unless I can put it to rest once and for all."

She knew that. "When are you going?"

"Not until after the weekend," he promised. "Inspector Lawson is away on a course until Wednesday morning; his secretary's put me in first thing. So, I'll be leaving on Tuesday, staying overnight in London." Turning her face to his, he kissed her tenderly. "Besides, I'm hoping that Jasper will be back by then."

"Why? Are you missing him as much as I am?"

"There is that, yes." He smiled mischievously. "But I need somebody to keep an eye on you . . . protect you from all those handsome chaps who come in and out of the site office. I don't want you running off with any of them."

"Oh, you needn't worry." She had an urge to tease him. "Mind you, there was a man last week though . . . big, handsome chap . . . he had a brand-new car. Now, if *he* were to ask, I might just be tempted."

"Would you now?" Swinging her round, he kissed her long and passionately.

When he let go, she still had her eyes closed. "All right, you win," she muttered. "He can keep his car. I prefer your kisses any day."

They kissed again, and talked some more; the rain fell all about them and the skies grew black with the onset of night. "Time to go," he murmured, and she didn't argue; though she longed for the day when the kisses wouldn't stop there.

Arm-in-arm, oblivious to the rain, they walked back to Barden House, talking of their future, and contemplating the outcome of Tom's visit to London. "We've got three full days before I leave," Tom reminded her. "Let's make the most of it."

That night, alone in the house, Kathy lay on the rug in front of the fire, her wistful gaze uplifted to the photograph of her father and the woman he had loved. "I wonder if I'll ever know the same kind of happiness as you found," she whispered. "I know I'll never want anyone else but Tom, but I'm so afraid I might lose him."

The clock ticked on the mantelpiece and the minutes sped by. The heat from the cheery fire and the rhythmic sound of rain pattering on the window-panes made her sleepy. She thought how cozy it all was.

Yet it felt empty and cold without Tom. "Dear Lord, bring him safely home again." Believing we make our own mistakes and have to find our own solutions, Kathy rarely asked the Lord for anything, but at this moment she felt in need of comfort and reassurance.

After a while she fell asleep, her head resting on her arms and her heart heavy with love.

One way or another, it had been a long day.

# Thirteen

WITH THE HOUSEWORK FINISHED, KATHY GOT READY to go into Bridport, where she would get her weekly shop, and hopefully a few bargains from the market. "I'll even have time to pop in and see Mabel," she told herself in the hallway mirror. She had come to look forward to their intimate little chats; though it was a furtive affair as her husband was always lurking in the background, ready to pounce.

Before leaving, she glanced at the mantel-clock. "Half past ten . . . plenty of time before I see Tom." They'd arranged to meet at six thirty, when he'd planned to take her into Dorchester for a quiet restaurant meal. It would be a real treat; they could sit and talk, and enjoy every possible minute before he took off for London on Tuesday.

Another glance in the mirror ensured she hadn't forgotten anything: hair brushed, lipstick on; yes, that was all right. "Got my purse and bag . . . yes."

At last, she was ready for off. Yet when she opened the door and saw the rain-clouds gathering, she decided, "Best take a coat, just in case!"

Going back to the peg in the hallway, she unhooked her macintosh. Throwing it over her arm, she secured the front door, then made her way down the path, her gaze reaching toward the harbor, where she hoped she might see Tom.

He wasn't there. "He's probably getting ready for Tuesday," she muttered. The thought of him going away laid a dark cloud over her mood.

Unusually, the bus was on time. "Morning, Miss." The conductor was a funny chap, with the jerky manners and appearance of a bird.

Small and quick, he had a slightly bent head and pointed features, the most prominent of which was his long, narrow nose. "Morning," she replied brightly. "How are you today?" Rain or shine, he always seemed to have one thing or another wrong with him: either it was too hot for him to breathe, or it was so wet it got into his bones. Today was no different.

He gave a strangled groan. "It's my back," he answered painfully. "I got out of bed this morning and could hardly walk."

Kathy always sympathized, which was fatal because now he made a beeline for her every time. "You'll have to see a doctor," she advised, handing him her fare.

"Seen him already . . . that many times I might as well set up house in the surgery." Turning the rachet on his ticket-machine, he expelled her ticket and handed it to her. "I'm a martyr to pain, that's what I am," he moaned, before moving on, at surprising speed, to another passenger, where exactly the same conversation ensued.

A while later, the bus turned into the stop and Kathy got off. "See you later," the conductor told her.

Kathy smiled and waved. "Poor devil!" On this particular journey he had even found time to sit beside her, regaling her with stories of his bad leg and his poor heart, and the awkward way he had to lie in bed because of his back pain.

Though she would rather have spent the journey sitting on her own, thinking about her and Tom, Kathy didn't begrudge the conductor a few minutes of her time.

Quickly covering the few hundred yards along Bridport High Street, she breezed into the market. This was a place she loved; with its many stalls and colorful stallholders, it had a cheery, happy atmosphere. "Got some lovely red apples . . . tanner a bag," one chap called; being fond of a good apple, Kathy promptly bought a bag.

For the next hour or so she went from stall to stall. She chose some chintz fabric to make a set of curtains for the bathroom, and for fourpence-halfpenny she purchased a small, pretty picture of a sailing boat to hang on the hallway wall. She was slowly adding her own touches to Barden House. She bought fresh bread from the baker's stall, some vegetables from the greengrocer, and a scrubbing-brush for the back step, where the gutter dripped and made a mess.

When her bag was full and her feet were beginning to ache, she made her way to the café.

Pleased to see that the window-table was empty, Kathy went inside. Dropping her heavy bag to the floor, she sat herself down. "Morning, madam, what would you like?" The waitress was a sloppy young thing, with a face that said, "I couldn't care less what you want, just order it and let me get back to my wireless."

Her off-hand manner didn't bother Kathy one iota. "Dandelion and burdock, please."

Without a word the waitress moved off to fetch her drink.

Meanwhile, Kathy was expecting Mabel to appear any minute. But there was no sign of her. When the waitress returned with her order, Kathy asked, "Is Mabel in today?"

"Not today, no."

"Is she all right?"

"Who knows?" Shrugging her shoulders, she hurried away. Nat King Cole was in the middle of his song, "Unforgettable." Being a great fan of his, she didn't want to miss it.

Kathy was worried. It wasn't like Mabel to miss work. Kathy thought her to be of an age when most people retired, but Mabel just kept going. Whether it was from choice or necessity wasn't clear, but she hardly stopped, at least from what Kathy had seen on a busy day. And in this café, most days were busy.

While she sipped her drink, Kathy was acutely aware of Mabel's husband peering at her from behind the serving hatch. She didn't care much for him, so she averted her eyes as much as possible.

When she went up to the counter to pay, he was standing by the till. She counted out the coins and placed them on the counter. "Is your wife all right?" she asked.

"Gone to see her brother!" he grunted. He then slapped

her change onto the counter, and took himself off at great speed into the kitchen.

Kathy neither liked nor believed him. Never mind that his manner was highly suspicious, when he told her that Mabel was with her brother, Kathy knew he was lying.

Mabel herself had told her how she had not spoken to her brother in years because of something that happened before the war. Looking back, it had been something and nothing, Mabel had told her, but they had lost touch. Now Mabel did not know where her brother was; it was a great sadness to her.

Now, as Kathy put the change into her purse, she was aware of someone watching her. When she looked up, it was to see Mabel's husband disappearing behind the kitchen door. "He's hiding something," she muttered as she went down the street. "Why is he lying about Mabel?"

At the bus stop she took out her handbag and, rummaging through it, found the piece of paper with Mabel's address.

"I wonder . . ." She remembered it wasn't too far away, but did she have enough time?

By the time the bus pulled in, Kathy's mind was made up. "Sorry," she apologized to the conductor, who was urging her on board, "I'll catch the next one."

She went down the High Street and, finding the street where Mabel lived, she hurried past the cottages until she found the right one. She thought it strange though that all the curtains were drawn.

Apprehensive now, Kathy tapped on the front door. When there was no answer, she lifted the knocker and let it drop. When there was still no answer she dropped her bag to the ground, opened the letter-flap and, putting her mouth close so as not to disturb the neighbors, she called out, "MABEL! It's me, Kathy. MABEL, are you in there?" The silence was deafening. "Answer me, Mabel. Are you all right?"

Squinting through the letter-flap, she cou    t make out a dark shape, right there on the floor at the foot of the stairs. "MABEL!" She believed it must be Mabel, lying unconscious, unmoving, arms spreadeagled and her legs twisted in a peculiar fashion. "Oh, my God . . . MABEL!" Still there was no answer, and not a flicker of movement.

With her heart in her mouth, Kathy realized there was no time to be lost.

Running to the nearest neighbor, she banged her two fists on the door. Startled by all the noise, the man flung open the door. "What the devil's going on?"

"It's Mabel! I think she's fallen down the stairs . . . she's not moving. We need to get an ambulance . . . quickly!"

Flinging on his shirt, he told her, "The nearest phone box is at the end of the street. You run and phone the ambulance, while I see if I can find something to get me inside the house."

With that he hurried back inside his house, while Kathy went at a run down the street, leaving her shopping bag where it had fallen.

Once inside the phone box, she quickly got through to the emergency services. After giving Mabel's address, she was instructed to "Get inside the house if you can, and stay with the injured woman. Keep her calm and still. The ambulance will be there in ten minutes."

Relieved, Kathy ran back to where the man had given up trying to break the door with a crowbar, and was now running at it with the weight of his own body. Once, twice, he put his shoulder to it, before the door splintered and sprang open. "We're in!"

Mabel couldn't be woken. "Do you think she fell down the stairs?" Distraught with worry, Kathy sat on the floor, not daring to lift or hold Mabel for fear of hurting her. "It's all right, Mabel," she whispered softly. "I've got you now. You're going to be all right."

The man ran his concerned gaze over Mabel's obvious injuries. He noted the gashes on her forehead and the large, torn areas of skin on her neck. "If you ask me, *he* did this!"

Kathy knew who he meant. "What? You think her husband pushed her down the stairs, is that what you're saying?"

"I heard them," the man revealed. "I work night-shift at one of the hotels in Lyme Regis. I got home about seven o'clock this morning . . . I heard them arguing." He shook his head in disbelief. "I never thought he'd hurt her this badly. He's a nasty bugger, though . . . a right bully. How she's put up with him all these years, I don't know."

Suddenly the clanging bells of the ambulance could be heard. In minutes they were drawing up, and the ambulance men were gently tending Mabel. "Easy as you go." The two of them stretchered her into the ambulance.

"I'm coming with her." Kathy clambered in behind the stretcher. "She's got nobody else."

"Here, Miss . . . don't forget your bag!" The kindly neighbor handed it up to her.

The ambulance ride was a nightmare. Mabel lay apparently lifeless on the stretcher, while the ambulance man tended to her, trying to get some response. Kathy was deeply worried.

At the hospital, Kathy waited nervously while the doctors assessed Mabel.

It was over an hour later that the doctor sought Kathy out. "She has no broken limbs, but apparently she's taken a bad tumble. She has some nasty wounds, which will need treatment, and she's suffering from shock and bad concussion. But she'll be all right." Curious as to how Mabel received such injuries, he asked, "Have you any idea how it happened?"

"Not really. It looked as if she might have fallen down the stairs, but I can't be sure." It was on the tip of her tongue to say how she suspected Mabel's husband of hurting her, but then thought it wise to say nothing until she was able to speak with Mabel. "Can I see her?"

He nodded. "Matron will take you. But don't stay long." Gesturing to the matron who had been waiting close by, he turned on his heel and went.

As she walked Kathy to the ward, Matron had a few questions of her own, such as, "Were you with her when it happened?" and "Do you know of anyone we should contact?"

Kathy was wary. "I think you might ask Mabel that," she suggested.

"Oh, we have, but of course she is still concussed . . . not quite thinking straight just yet."

Matron threw open the door to the ward. "Perhaps you

could have a word with her? Oh, and no more than a few minutes. She's very weak."

It was a small ward with only four beds in it; besides Mabel's, only one other was occupied, by a young woman who looked very ill.

As Kathy went in, the nurse came out. "You mustn't stay long," she warned, adding with a smile, "Give her a week or so, and she'll be fine."

Mabel appeared to be asleep, but when Kathy softly called her name she opened her eyes. Covered in bruises, they seemed swollen to twice their size. She looked at Kathy, and for a minute didn't seem to recognize her. "It's me . . . Kathy." It was painful to see her friend like this.

Slowly, agonizingly, Mabel reached out her hand. Quickly, Kathy took it in her own. "They tell me you've got no broken bones or anything like that," she imparted fondly, "but you'll need to be here about a week."

Mabel continued to look at her through those sorry eyes. Suddenly, the eyes moistened and the tears ran away down to the pillow. "Don't . . . don't . . ."

Her voice was so small, Kathy had to bend close. "What is it you're trying to say?"

It seemed as though Mabel had exhausted what little strength she had, because now she closed her eyes and fell silent. Close to tears herself, Kathy spoke to her, and in a minute Mabel was looking up again. "Don't . . ."

"What is it, Mabel?" Leaning forward, Kathy asked in a whisper, "Don't tell them it was your husband? Is that what you're trying to say?"

When Mabel gave a feeble squeeze of the hand, and what appeared to be a nod, Kathy knew she had guessed right. "Did he do this to you, Mabel?" she asked. "Was it him that threw you down the stairs?"

Again that slight nod.

"And you don't want me to say anything . . . to anyone? Not even the doctors?"

Again, the nod.

Kathy's voice dropped a tone. "Not even to *him?*" He was the lowest of the low, to hurt his wife like this.

Now, at her suggestion, Mabel's eyes flickered with fear. "It's all right!" Kathy promised. "I won't say a word to anyone . . . not even to him." She smiled. "But I'd really like to throw *him* down the stairs, if only you'd let me."

At Kathy's vehemence, Mabel's eyes crinkled into a twisted smile. Her hand squeezed Kathy's; it was a sign that, despite her injuries, the old spirit was still there. Kathy almost read her mind. "I know," she chuckled, "you want to throw him down the stairs yourself, is that it?"

Mabel's eyes sparkled and her mouth opened, as if trying to smile. Then the eyes closed and she appeared to have fallen asleep.

Just then the matron returned. "I want you to leave now," she told Kathy. "The doctors need to tend her."

Kathy voiced her concern at Mabel falling asleep like that. "Is she all right?"

Checking her patient, the matron put Kathy's mind at rest. "Your friend was concussed in the fall," she explained, then, with a hint of suspicion, she asked, "She *did* fall, didn't she?"

"Down the stairs as far as I can make out." Kathy had answered the question wisely, without giving anything away.

"Mmm." Matron explained how Mabel had muttered something about falling down. "And of course the injuries are consistent with that. Poor thing." She had another question. "Are there any relatives that you know of?"

Kathy merely shook her head. "I haven't known her all that long." Again, she had answered the question without actually lying. "I'd best go now . . . let her rest."

She gave Mabel a kiss, and promised she would be back to see her in the morning.

On the way back to West Bay, she said a little prayer of thanks for the promise of Mabel's quick recovery. "And maybe you could give that big bully what he deserves!"

By the time Tom arrived to collect her, Kathy was ready. It had been a terrible rush, but she made a special effort, and now, as she glanced in the hallway mirror before going out to him, she mimicked Maggie to a tee. "For Gawd's sake, stop fretting! You'll pass, gal." The thought of Maggie made her smile.

When she opened the door, Tom thought she looked especially lovely. She had on a smart little brown two-piece, and the cream-colored blouse wonderfully complemented her light-brown shining hair, which tonight was brushed into an attractive bounce. "My! There won't be a man in the room able to keep his eyes off you." Flinging his arms about her waist, he swung her round. "Your chariot awaits."

Now, as he gestured to the curb-edge, Kathy was surprised to see a taxi. "Such extravagance!" she chided light-heartedly. "I suppose now I shall have to pay for your dinner as well as my own?"

"Hmh! You'd best mind I don't take you up on that, my girl!"

Laughing, they got into the taxi and set off for Dorchester. On the way, Tom noticed her quiet mood. "Penny for them?" Sliding his arm around her shoulders, he drew her face around so that he could see her eyes. "You've gone quiet all of a sudden. What's wrong?"

"It's Mabel."

"What . . . the old lady who works in the Bridport café?" He smiled. "The one you've adopted as your own?" She had spoken often about Mabel, and he had come to know all about her. "Don't tell me she's been rowing with her husband again?"

Not wanting to spoil their evening, Kathy tried to close the subject. "I'll tell you later. Not now, eh? You'll be leaving on Tuesday, so let's not spoil tonight."

"If you're sure?"

"Yes." There would be time later to talk about Mabel. "I'm sure."

As they drew up outside the restaurant, Kathy gave a gasp of delight. "Oh, but it's so pretty!" In mock-Tudor style, with oak beams and lovely old lanterns at the porch, it was like something out of a fairytale.

Inside was breathtaking: rose-chintz curtains at the lead-lighted windows; thick burgundy carpets on the floor; pink tablecloths on the intimate round tables, and a vase holding a single red rose in the center. There were old-fashioned lanterns hanging from the ceiling and walls, and soft music playing in the background. "Oh, Tom, it's just lovely!" Kathy was thrilled.

That evening was the best of her life. They ate and drank and toasted the future, and when the meal was finished they danced until the early hours.

At two o'clock in the morning, Kathy and Tom finally left to climb into their waiting taxi, and the waiters breathed a sigh of relief.

The journey back to West Bay was a quiet one.

Leaning back with Tom's strong arms around her, Kathy thought she would never be happier. At the back of her mind, Mabel's predicament threatened to throw a shadow over her joy, but she refused to let it. Mabel would be all right, that's what they had told her, and this was her special night—hers and Tom's. "I love you." Shy of the taxi-driver, she whispered in Tom's ear. "I'm going to love you forever."

Her face uplifted, she observed his strong, chiseled features and that soft, full mouth. Intrigued, she traced her finger along it. "Kiss me."

Smiling, he bent his head to hers, his dark eyes searching Kathy's. In that precious moment, his love for her was like a raging storm inside him.

When he bent to kiss her, she felt her heart soar. The kiss went on and on, hearts merging, their love like a shield around them; as though nothing could ever come between them. It was a magical experience.

In the mirror, the taxi-driver saw their love and it made him think about his own youth, and the many loves he had found and lost. "Cherish what you've got," he murmured quietly. "Don't ever let anything spoil it."

He had never married. Long ago, through his own stupidity, he had lost the only woman he had ever really loved. Even now, after all this time, that loss was a heavy cross to carry.

When they arrived at Barden House, Tom walked Kathy

to her front door. Neither of them said a word. Instead they held each other, and kissed again . . . and again, holding onto each other a moment longer before Tom walked away.

At the gate he turned to gaze on her one more time before climbing into the taxi.

Kathy watched the car drive away. She saw him looking out of the window at her, and knew exactly what he was feeling. "I love you too," she said.

She watched until the taxi had gone out of sight, then she went inside, ran straight upstairs and undressed for bed.

Lying in her bed, she thought of Tom; her love for him was like an unbearable ache inside her. "Please, God, don't let me lose him, not now," she whispered.

She said a prayer for Mabel, and in minutes she was fast asleep; a contented sleep that augured well for the future.

The following morning, bright and early, she went to see Mabel. "She's had a good night," the nurse told her. "You can help feed her if you like."

Kathy said she would like that. When the broth arrived, she actually persuaded Mabel to take a sip or two—but that was all, before Mabel pushed it away. "Never mind." The nurse had seen it all before. "We'll try again later."

Though Mabel could not hold a conversation, Kathy kept her interested by telling her all about her night out with Tom, and how he was going away on Tuesday and she didn't know how long he would be gone.

Mabel listened awhile, then she slept awhile, then she squeezed Kathy's hand and looked sad when Kathy said she had to leave, but, "I'll be back to see you soon as I can," she promised, and Mabel's eyes lit up.

She gave her a kiss and a hug; even before she got across the room, Mabel was sound asleep again.

On the way home, Kathy sat on the bus thinking about everything. It was good talking to Mabel. She was like a mother to her. Sadly, neither she nor Mabel had another woman to confide in. But they had formed a bond now, and

Kathy knew without a shadow of doubt that the friendship she and old Mabel had found would remain strong throughout their lives. It was a warm, comforting thought.

On arriving in West Bay, she didn't go straight home. Instead, with everything churning in her troubled mind, she felt the need to walk the clifftop, much as Tom did whenever he was troubled.

The wind in her face was uniquely refreshing, and the salty tang of the sea air was cool and invigorating on her skin.

More content now, she sat for a time on the edge of the cliff. "It's like sitting on the edge of the world!" she whispered. "I can see why you love to walk these beaches," she murmured, with Tom in mind. "They have a way of calming the soul."

From here she could see the harbor. The many boats within it were jangling together, heaving up and down with the waves. Tom wasn't there. "I expect he's got more important things on his mind for the minute."

After a while, when the wind picked up strength, and when her toes and nose grew cold, she started back. "Best get some milk," she muttered, coming into the harbor. "I used the last of it on that stray cat this morning." The cat was a skinny little gray. For some reason it had taken root in her shed and, though she had tried to entice it inside, it refused. Sometimes it went away, and after a few days it was back again.

It was a bit strange. Who did it belong to? And why was it hanging around the house? And, if it really was lost, why did it go away at intervals and come back again, as if it had a plan? Kathy had given up wondering. All she could do was feed it when it came back, and forget about it when it went away. Like her own life, she had little control over it.

Amy Tatler, the little shopkeeper, smiled to see Kathy come through the door. "Don't tell me," she said. "You're out of milk because you've been feeding that cat again!"

Kathy laughed. "Is there *anything* you don't know?" Like Jasper, she had grown fond of Amy.

"Ah! There's one thing I know that you don't," came the crafty reply.

Kathy was intrigued. "Oh, and what's that then?"

"You've got a visitor!"

Taken aback, Kathy asked, "*What* visitor?"

"A woman."

"How do you know?"

"Because I told her where to find you." She was enjoying herself. " 'Go to Barden House across the way,' I said. 'I saw young Kathy go out earlier, but I dare say she'll be back any minute.' "

Kathy was racking her brains as to who it might be. "And she's there now?"

"Well, she headed off in that direction. I watched her through the window. Whether she's still there or not, I can't say."

"You said it was a woman?" Kathy was hesitant to go and see, because the thought that it might be her mother had just flashed across her mind. "What was she like?"

The old shopkeeper gave it a bit of thought. "She was youngish . . . bold as brass."

Thrilled, Kathy gave a whoop: it had to be Maggie. "Was she small and dark, with a way of making you smile almost before she spoke?"

The older woman shook her head. "Nothing like that. As a matter of fact, if you don't mind me saying, she was a sour-looking creature, who forgot to say thank you. What's more, she took a newspaper without paying."

Kathy was shocked. "Did she say who she was?"

"No. She didn't say anything much, except that she was looking for a Miss Kathy Wilson, and would I point her in the right direction."

"All right, thank you. I suppose I'd best go and see." First though, there was a debt to settle. "How much was the newspaper?"

"Threepence, but it isn't your responsibility. I've no doubt, from the size of the suitcase she was carrying, she intends staying a while. I can ask her for the money next time she comes in." Though kind-hearted and amiable, Amy was particular about good manners. "I shall give her a piece of my mind into the bargain an' all!"

Kathy laid the threepence on the counter. "Please let me pay," she said. "If only to save any bad feeling."

"Well, if you're sure . . ." Taking the threepence, she gave Kathy a receipt. "I was surprised to hear her ask for you, my dear. She's not the kind I would associate with a well-mannered young thing like yourself."

Curious, though a little apprehensive, Kathy walked toward her house at a quickening pace.

At first Kathy didn't recognize the figure sitting on the wall, but then, as she drew level, she realized who it was. "My God . . . SAMANTHA!"

The woman turned, confirming Kathy's suspicion. "Hello, Kathy." Getting off the wall, Samantha came to kiss her on the cheek. "I'm glad you're back." She sounded sorry for herself, Kathy thought. "I've been waiting for ages. My backside's numb, and I'm starving hungry." She was not altogether pleased to see how lean and pretty Kathy was, nor how her face glowed with health. Her hair, which was longer now, shone with a deep gloss, and her light-brown eyes had a definite sparkle. "Hmh!" She looked her up and down. "Looks like the sea air suits you."

Kathy hardly noticed what Samantha was saying. Instead she was open-mouthed at seeing her sister here in West Bay. "What are you doing here?"

Samantha laughed. "I've come to see you. Why? Can't a sister visit without being quizzed as to her intentions? Anybody would think I was after something!" Though she said it teasingly, there was a hardness underlying the words that warned Kathy to exercise caution.

"Why didn't you write and tell me you were coming?" Forgetting all her manners, Kathy was concerned as to what might have brought Samantha to her doorstep. "Roughing it" at the seaside had never been her idea of fun. "Is it Mother? Is she ill?"

Samantha greeted her question with gales of laughter. "Mother . . . ill? I don't think so. She's positively bursting with health; though she might not be as rich or content as she was."

"What's that supposed to mean?"

Samantha refused to reply until she was inside. "Are we going to stand out here all night, or am I being invited in?"

Kathy felt ashamed. "Sorry. You'd best come in. I'll get you something to eat."

"I'm gasping for a drink." That was Samantha's first thought. "I wouldn't mind a gin and tonic." Collecting her suitcase, she followed Kathy up the path.

"If you want a gin and tonic you'll have to go to the pub." Kathy stepped aside to let her in. "You know I'm not a gin and tonic person." She hated herself for it, but she couldn't help the jibe. "I never got the taste for it. I've never moved in the same exclusive circles as you and Mother."

"Hmh! I should have thought you'd keep some by for your guests, though of course I don't suppose you get many of those, out here in the back of beyond."

"Sorry"—the biting comment rolled off Kathy's back— "no gin and tonic." Closing the door behind her, she led Samantha into the sitting room. "I've got half a bottle of whiskey, which I keep for an old friend. You're welcome to a tot of that or I've tea or soft drinks . . ."

Dropping her case on the carpet, Samantha ignored her offer. She made a face. "You don't seem too pleased to see me!"

"I'm not!" Kathy saw no point in beating about the bush. "I've not heard a word from you or Mother since I left, and this is the last place on earth you would want to visit." She took note of Samantha's meticulously groomed long, dark hair, the brown high-heeled shoes and that shockingly expensive suit that clung to her like a second skin. "So, tell me . . . why are you really here?"

Samantha's green eyes narrowed in a sly little smile. "I could be missing you, have you thought of that?"

"Oh, please. Credit me with some sense! You haven't just turned up here because you're 'missing' me," Kathy pointed out with brutal honesty. "There's something going on. What are you up to?"

"My! My!" Dropping into the armchair, Samantha lolled back, looking for all the world as if she was here to stay. "What a suspicious mind you've got."

Kathy's back was up now. She knew her sister too well,

and she knew something was not right. "I've had reason too many times to be suspicious," she replied curtly. "Or have you forgotten how deceitful and mean you and Mother have been . . . or how you shut me out of your lives whenever you felt like it?"

"Ah, well, that was Mother's fault. Not mine."

"Really?"

Realizing she had better not be too arrogant, or her plan wouldn't work, Samantha smiled sweetly. "I don't want to put you to any trouble, but my stomach's rumbling hungry."

"I'll see what I can rustle up." Kathy went into the kitchen and peered into the cupboard. "I've got ham and tomatoes, or beans on toast."

"What!" Samantha came running in, her face wreathed in disgust. "Is that *all* you've got?"

"I wasn't expecting visitors." Kathy paused. "I think you'd better settle for fish and chips," she said finally.

"Hmh!" Samantha gave a shiver of disapproval. "If you ask me, the place is uncivilized!"

Kathy laughed. "Not your usual scene, is it?"

"I dare say I'll get used to it." Samantha was determined to get what she came for, however grim it was here. "If you'll just show me my room, I'll unpack while you go for the fish and chips . . . a large cod for me, and just a small portion of chips." She patted her thighs. "I don't want to lose my figure."

"They're not open until six."

Kathy wished her sister could be the genuine article. It would have been so nice to have someone she could sit and talk with. And she did so want it all to be pleasant. "Look, Samantha, get your case and I'll show you where you'll be sleeping. Then we'll have a cup of tea and a proper chat. If you're that hungry, I can make you some toast if you like, while we're waiting for the chip shop to open."

Throwing out her arms in frustration, Samantha refused the offer. "I don't fancy any of your bloody toast." She had seen the primitive kitchen, and wasn't even sure it was hygienic. "Don't bother. A cup of tea will keep me going until the fish shop opens."

Leading the way into the sitting room, she left Kathy shaking her head and muttering, "Keep on like that, and you'll be leaving sooner than you think!"

In the sitting room, Samantha took closer note of the furnishings: the newly made curtains and the plain, well-worn furniture, which she wouldn't have accepted if it was given to her. As Kathy came back in, Samantha gave a grunt of disapproval. "Don't tell me this is the same furniture *he* had?"

"The very same." Kathy's back was beginning to bristle. "Why?"

Again, that haughty look of disapproval. "Well, look at it! It's absolutely disgusting . . . I'd have thrown it out by now and got myself something decent."

"Well, I like it. But then, I'm not you, am I?"

"But it belonged to *them!*"

"If you mean Father and the woman he loved—yes, it did. Father left it to me, and that makes it mine now. So, it really doesn't matter whether you like it or not."

"Hmh!" Samantha was amazed at Kathy's new-found self-confidence. There was a time, not so long back, when she could intimidate her sister and get away with it. There's no need to get on your high horse."

"And there's no need for you to be so insulting."

Kathy was taken aback when Samantha put a very personal question. "You've found yourself a man-friend, haven't you?"

"What makes you think that?" Kathy didn't know whether to be pleased or wary.

"Well, just look at you!" Samantha had never seen her sister so attractive. "You're positively blooming. Your eyes have that secret little sparkle and you appear to have lost weight. There must be a man involved!"

"Maybe there is, maybe there isn't." Still cautious, Kathy gave nothing away.

"Well, if there *is,* you want to be careful."

"What d'you mean?"

"Well, for a start . . . have you been stupid enough to tell him that you own this house lock, stock and barrel? Is he after you for your charms? Or is he after moving in here?

Perhaps he doesn't think anything of you at all. Perhaps he's just looking for a cushy number?"

"I doubt if he's after this house." Tom had told her all about his work, and the fact that while he had more money than he knew what to do with, he would give it all away in exchange for peace of mind. "I think I can safely say that Tom and I have something very special. And, in spite of what you might think, he isn't looking for a 'cushy' number, as you so colorfully put it, because he's already a wealthy man."

At that, Samantha's eyebrows went up and her mouth fell open. "Well, I never! My little sister's hooked herself a big fish, eh? Good for you."

Kathy's anger was evident as she retaliated. "It's not like that! I love Tom, and he loves me. I know you might find it hard to believe, but money doesn't even come into it!"

Smiling maliciously, Samantha tutted. "Really? But you're right. I *do* find it hard to believe."

Kathy needed no reminding of her sister's opinion of her. "Whether you believe it or not, I haven't had an easy ride these past few years. But I've got my life together now, and I'm more content than I've been in ages. I won't let you spoil that, Samantha," she told her quietly. "So, if you intend staying with me for a few days, you had better get used to the idea that this is not the Ritz or the Savoy. *This is my home.*"

Stunned into silence by her sister's quiet self-confidence, Samantha wondered if her task was going to be as easy as she had first thought. She realized she was dealing with a woman who had thrown a protective barrier around herself and what was hers, and it was a sobering thing to see. On the face of it, she could not envisage how she might get Kathy to sell this house and give her half the proceeds.

The solicitor was right after all. It would not be easy, she could see that now. But it didn't put her off, not for one minute. In fact, if a fight was what Kathy wanted, then a fight she would get!

For what seemed like an age, the two sisters stood facing each other: one with hatred in her heart; the other with a deep-down need for the company of family, and peace of mind.

For the moment, though, the atmosphere in that room was electrifying. In the background the clock ticked, and somewhere outside a dog could be heard barking.

A sudden knock on the door broke the brooding silence. "Seems you've got another visitor." Samantha soon recovered her arrogance. "You'd better go and see who it is."

It was Tom.

"I just thought, if you weren't doing anything, that we could go into Weymouth. Maybe have a meal on the seafront; sit and watch the sun go down. What do you say?"

Before Kathy could answer, Samantha appeared. "It sounds good to me," she told Tom, astonishing him with her boldness. "I haven't strolled on the sea-front in ages."

When Tom looked questioningly at Kathy, she introduced one to the other. "This is my sister, Samantha." Kathy felt a surge of anger that she was in this position. "And this is Tom Marcus."

She felt no obligation to explain Tom's very special role in her life. Instead she was quietly seething. How dare Samantha interfere like that? But then, she reminded herself, it was Samantha's way. Unfortunately, she knew no other.

Tom held out his hand in greeting. "What a lovely surprise. Glad to meet you, Samantha."

Samantha positively glowed. "Glad to meet you too," she purred. "I don't suppose Kathy even told you about me?"

Sensing Samantha was out for trouble, Kathy intervened. "Look, Tom. Samantha's only just arrived, so if it's all right with you I think I'll have to forget about Weymouth." More's the pity, she thought angrily. "But we're having fish and chips later." Her face brightened. "Why don't you join us?"

She hoped he would, yet she was worried about him being too close to Samantha, who had an unenviable reputation for stealing other women's men.

"Well, thank you, darling. I'd love to!" he said, though he would have preferred to take Kathy to Weymouth, where they could be alone. The truth was, they had so much to talk about, and in a few days he would be gone from here, for who knows how long. But he understood how Kathy could not desert her sister who, judging by the look of her suit and attire, had only recently arrived. "What time do you want me?"

"Why don't you come in *now?*" Samantha had a soft spot for a good-looking man, and this one was all the more desirable because he was her sister's. "I'm sure we could while away the time until the fish shop opens," she suggested blatantly.

"Samantha!" Kathy addressed her sharply. "I think it might be a good idea if you used the time to unpack and change." She tried hard to keep the annoyance out of her voice, but Samantha had a way of riling her that sent all common sense out of the window.

"Fine," Tom said quickly. Realizing there was some sort of deep-rooted friction here, and not particularly having taken to Samantha, Tom addressed himself to Kathy. "What say I come down about ten past six? I could call in to the chip shop on the way and pick up the order."

Samantha hid her disappointment. "What a good idea!"

Wanting to slap her, but restraining herself, Kathy told her, "You can take your case upstairs if you like, Samantha." She gave her directions to the guest room. "You'll find everything you need in there."

"Okay, sis." Smiling at Tom, Samantha sighed. "Kathy was always the bully." She gave him one of her loveliest smiles. "I'd best go, before she loses her temper with me." Rolling her eyes like a frightened little girl, she hurried away.

When she had gone upstairs, Tom looked at Kathy with raised eyebrows. "She's nothing like you!"

Already upset and disillusioned, Kathy retorted, "You mean she's sophisticated and well groomed, while I'm more suited to plimsolls and a sloppy top?"

Seeing he had innocently touched a raw spot, Tom slid his arm around her shoulders; drawing her forward, he kissed her full on the mouth. "I love you in your plimsolls and sloppy top," he said mischievously. "Besides, you're 'suited' to *me*," he told her softly, "and I'm 'suited' to you."

When he looked down she was smiling up at him. "That's better," he chuckled. "Now then . . . walk me to the gate, and I'll tell you how much I love you."

When he put it like that, Kathy thought, how could she refuse?—and anyway, in spite of Samantha, he had put back the heart in her. "You're an old charmer," she said, laughing.

"Hey! Not so much of the 'old'!"

From Kathy's bedroom window, Samantha watched the two of them. She saw how wonderful they were together. She heard their laughter; she cringed when Tom kissed Kathy, and her hatred grew tenfold. *"I'm not finished yet!"* she hissed. "This house and everything in it should have been given to me. I came here to get what's rightfully mine, and I'm not leaving without it."

She thought Tom was a real man: handsome, rich, and attentive. "You're a great catch," she said, ogling him from afar. "*She* doesn't know how to handle a man like you. But I do. By the time I've finished, I'll have you *and* the house." The idea of marrying a man with money was too appealing to brush aside.

# *Fourteen*

KEEPING A CAREFUL WATCH FOR ANYONE WHO MIGHT recognize her, Lilian got off the bus and quickly made her way to the churchyard. The gift of flowers was cradled in her arms, as a child might be.

She knew exactly where to find Tom's family. After all, she had attended the service after the tragedy, and since then had been many times to visit alone.

Coming in through the tall iron gates, she headed for the far side of the churchyard, where Tom's family were laid to their rest. For a time she looked down at the headstone and the beautiful words written there, and she felt a pang of guilt at loving the husband of this kind-hearted woman. Yet there was a feeling of envy too; a feeling that he should have been married to *her*, and not to this woman lying here. If he had been, this awful tragedy might never have happened!

Her feelings were all mixed up: envy, regret, love and hate; they were all there, etched in her aching heart for all time. "I'm so sorry." Whenever she came here, she always felt the need to apologize. "I know you were a friend to me, and I was always grateful for that, but it isn't my fault if I love him, you need to understand that."

Undoing the wrapping, she took out the flowers: twelve beautiful yellow roses. With tender loving care she set them in the pot at the foot of the headstone, her heart leaping with fear when a voice at her shoulder said, "I'm glad to see you're putting them in the vase and not throwing them all over the place!"

The caretaker was an old fellow with a bent back and a sour face, and he was fed up with forever clearing up behind other people.

"Go away!" Lilian had no time for him. "Clear off. Leave me alone."

"Huh! No need to be so downright bloody rude! All I'm saying is, I'm not paid to sweep up after you lot, so just make sure you leave the place tidy when you go."

He ambled off, mumbling to himself. "Got no respect, that's the trouble. Damned visitors . . . no thought for nobody but theirselves."

Lilian watched him for a minute before getting back to the task in hand.

When she was satisfied the flowers were arranged to her liking, she went to the tap, found the small jug which was there for the purpose and, filling it with water, returned to the headstone, where she topped up the vase.

That done, she looked down on the headstone, her voice trembling with emotion as she whispered, "I love him, you know that, don't you? I've *always* loved him. You were my friend, though. When you came to the office and we talked, and you bought me presents for my birthday . . . and that Christmas, when I was on my own and you asked me to your house . . . I loved you, too, in a way . . ."

Emotions overwhelmed her. "It was so awful . . . the accident and everything. I'm so sorry. It was my fault, you see. You don't know how often I'd dreamed of getting you and the children out of the way, so me and Tom could be together. While you and the children were there, I didn't stand a chance, don't you see that? I wanted him, and I know he wanted me . . . but you got in the way!"

She gave a nervous little giggle. "We've got a chance now, though . . . with you gone. I know it's a terrible thing to say, but it seems to me it was meant to happen this way." She outlined her plans. "He's gone away for a while, you see. He said he wanted to be on his own, to think about everything— which is understandable in the circumstances."

She stood up tall and proud as she declared, "I've decided to go and see him tomorrow. I know he's ready to talk about us. He won't turn me away, not now. Not with you out of the way for good. You see, he's been feeling guilty about wanting me, that's what it is. But it'll be all right now, you'll see."

Suddenly she heard a sound behind her. Swinging round, she saw a young woman approaching from the bushes. "What are you doing hiding there?" A kind of madness took hold of her. "What are you up to?" Lilian was afraid the stranger might have heard what she'd been saying.

"I'm not 'up to' *anything!*" Gloria laughed with embarrassment. "I was just delivering flowers," she said. "I took the wrong turn and had to cut through the bushes." Feeling threatened by the striking woman with her long auburn curls, she told Lilian, "I'm sorry to interrupt."

Spying the pretty bouquet of flowers in her arms, Lilian asked, "Are they for here?"

"Yes."

"But there's no room in the vase now."

"Oh, it's all right. Look!" Shifting the flowers, she revealed how they were contained in a vase of their own. "The boss decided this was the best way of going on. You're right. That vase is far too small. We've got a regular order, you see, and sometimes, if there's flowers in the vase, I have to take mine back . . . it's such a shame."

Lilian wondered what was the matter with the young woman. Her voice was quaking, and she seemed in a hurry to get away. "You'd best do what you came for then." Lilian stepped aside. "I'm just going, anyway," she said. "I'll leave you to get on with it."

Gloria nodded her appreciation. "Like I say . . . I'm sorry to have interrupted."

"It's all right." Lilian glanced at the headstone. "She was a friend of mine. It was a terrible thing that happened."

"Yes, I know . . . Mr. Marcus told us. Terrible business!"

Lilian had a question. "Are the flowers from him?"

"Yes."

"They're lovely."

She ran her gaze over the mix of dahlias, carnations and roses, all bright and dazzling. "I should think they were expensive."

"Yes. Very."

"I'd better go." It hurt her to realize that Tom was still sending flowers to his late wife. "Be careful not to hide mine." Another lingering glance, before she hurried away.

Behind her, Gloria shivered. "God. She may be a looker, but she's a strange one!" Setting the flowers beside the ones Lilian had brought, she tweaked them until they were to her satisfaction, then she stood up. She glanced around her nervously. Delivering flowers to the church-yard was not her favorite pastime, especially when they were meant for this particular place, and she thought she'd heard a noise.

It was probably nothing, she reasoned, turning and heading back to the car park, and her waiting van. She had an-other few deliveries to make in the churchyard, and then she'd be on her way.

She had finished the last of the jobs here, when she heard hurried steps behind her. "Oi, you!" The old caretaker was out of breath as he waddled to catch up with her. "Where the devil d'you think you're going?"

"What do you mean?" She recognized him straight off. He was the one who had alerted her last time, when the flowers had been destroyed.

"What do I *mean?*" Grabbing her by the arm, he urged her to get out of the van. "I'll *show* you what I mean!"

Leading her back to the far side of the big churchyard, he pointed to where she had recently set the flowers beside Lil-ian's. "I suppose you were going off without clearing that little lot up, were you?"

"Oh, my God!" She could hardly believe her eyes. The vase, the flowers she had brought, were all smashed and strewn about the churchyard. It seemed whoever did it must have been driven by a terrible hatred, for not only was every head removed from each flower, but the stems were torn to tiny pieces.

"See what I have to put up with?" The old caretaker was beside himself. "It's bad enough clearing up the usual rub-bish, without being made to clear up deliberate vandalism!"

"They were all right when I left—what—quarter of an

hour ago," she muttered. "There was this woman . . . she was talking to . . ." A thought occurred to her. "Oh, my God!"

The old man's voice pierced her thoughts. "You'd best clean it all up, 'cause *I'm* not going to!"

Before she could protest he had stomped off, and Gloria had no choice but to clear up the mess, retrieving the widely strewn pieces and carrying them to the nearest bin.

When she returned to the shop, it was to an icy reception. "Where on earth have you been?" Mrs. Taylor was hopping mad. "I've had to manage all on my own this past hour."

"I've been at the churchyard."

"What . . . all this time?"

"I think I know who's been tearing up the flowers."

"How?" Now she was paying attention.

"Well, there was this woman . . . about thirty-four . . . thirty-five. Attractive, well dressed."

"What are you saying . . . that this woman is the one who's been vandalizing the flowers?"

"I might be wrong, but, well . . . you judge for yourself."

In an excited voice, she began outlining the events at the churchyard. "I was coming along the main path when I saw her there. She was bent right down, staring at the headstone and talking to herself . . . well, either that or she were talking to somebody else, and there was nobody else that I could see."

"So . . . what did you do?" The manageress hoped they had spotted the vandal, because Mr. Marcus was coming to see them soon. It would be good if they had something positive to report.

Her colleague continued. "I didn't like the look of her, so I turned off the main path and crept up around the back. I could hear her murmuring and whispering, and at one point she even wagged a finger at the headstone. I don't mind telling you, I was scared. I tried to press back so she wouldn't catch sight of me. Then I must have trodden on a twig or something. Anyway, she heard me, so I had to come out."

She shivered from top to bottom. "She were a strange one. She had these staring eyes." To make her point she stared at the older woman, who promptly told her to stop being silly and "get on with it."

"Well, then she asked me what I was up to, and when I said I'd lost my way, I could see she didn't believe me. But she wasn't nasty or anything. Just a bit . . . 'far-off,' if you know what I mean."

"No! I *don't* know what you mean. So tell me."

"Well, when I was talking to her, she kept looking back at the headstone. She hardly ever looked at me. She just kept staring at the flowers."

"What did she say?"

"She asked if they were expensive. Then she said it was a tragedy what had happened."

"Is that all?"

"She asked if the flowers were from *him*."

"I see. And did you tell her?"

"Well, o' course I did. I couldn't very well say I didn't know, being as I was delivering them and all."

"All right. So, she asked about the flowers. There's nothing untoward about that. She was probably just making conversation."

The young woman shook her head. You wouldn't have said that if you'd been there!" She told her boss about the way in which the woman in the churchyard had quizzed her, "About Mr. Marcus, and the flowers, and when she left she told me not to hide her flowers. I got the feeling she meant to watch me."

"For heaven's sakes! What an imagination you've got. I expect the poor woman thought you were just as strange as you thought she was . . . emerging from the bushes with a large bunch of flowers, how strange is *that?*"

"I told you. I was watching her."

"Did she threaten you?"

"No."

"Then what on earth are you making such a fuss about?"

"I haven't told you about what happened afterward, have I?"

The older woman groaned. "No, but I'm sure you will, and you'd better make it quick. We've got customers." Just then the two men who had been looking through the window made their way into the shop.

The young assistant lowered her voice. "I was just getting into the van, when that old caretaker came running after me. He took me back, and you'll never believe what had happened."

When the older woman appeared to be intently listening, she went on. "The flowers were all ruined . . . every one, only this time it was worse than before. The flower-heads had been ripped off, and the stems were torn up and hurled away."

The manageress was suddenly very attentive. "And where was the woman?"

"Gone! Vanished like a will-o'-the-wisp."

She imparted one last piece of information. "Every single flower was destroyed. *All except hers!* They were still in the vase, just as she had left them."

"No, Mr. Martin." Lilian's colleague, Alice, was having to explain to an irate boss why the papers he had asked for were not already on his desk. "Lilian isn't in again today." After taking almost an hour to locate the files in question, she scrabbled together the documents and handed them to him. "We're really missing her down here. Y'see, she knows where everything is. You've only got to ask her, and it's there straight away."

John Martin was a patient man, but today he seemed to be two steps behind with everything, and that was not his way. "This blessed influenza has knocked out four of my staff," he groaned, "and now it seems it's worked its way down here. Get onto the Labour Exchange. Tell them the situation. They might be able to help."

Alice thought this was her big chance and took it. "Er . . . excuse me, Mr. Martin, only my friend who works in Woolworth's has told me about this new office that's just opened next to them in the High Street."

Drawing in a labored breath, Martin blew it out in a loud whoosh. "What does that have to do with me, young lady?"

"Well, it's a woman who's just started up. She calls herself the 'Good Temper.' "

"Come on, child, spit it out. I haven't got all day!"

"She sends clerks and typists and all that to offices where there's people off sick, or they're short-staffed for whatever reason. They're just temporary, until the person comes back, or the job is filled permanently." She was well pleased with herself for mentioning it. "Do you want me to ask her if she can help?"

"No, I do not!"

Angrily waving his papers at her, he ridiculed her idea. "No doubt she expects me to pay the earth for this 'temporary' person, and how do I know she's not sending a spy to root out information on my business?"

"But sir . . . I think it's a brilliant idea. It could get you out of trouble, and my friend says she's already got two companies interested."

"More fool them! I've never heard of anything so ridiculous. Paying for temporary staff who you don't know from Adam, when you can get people who've been properly vetted from the Labour Exchange."

He gave another of his long, noisy sighs. "It'll never catch on. Give it a few weeks and she'll go under, you mark my words."

"Yes, sir." Alice knew better than to argue with the boss. "I'll get onto the Labour Exchange right away."

"How long will Lilian be off?"

"I'm not sure, sir. When she rang yesterday morning she said the doctor told her she was to stay in bed for at least a week."

"Good God!" The news did not please him.

Storming off, he yelled back at her, "How am I supposed to cope, with Tom gone and Dougie and John away overseeing the Leeds job? On top of that, I've got my secretary and three typists off, and now Lilian! In my day, when you had a snivelling cold, you didn't call it influenza, nor did you laze about in bed for weeks on end. You got on with the job, that's what you did!"

That said, he strode off, muttering and moaning about the

world and its people in general, and his staff in particular. "And you get on with your work."

"Yes, sir!"

Wagging her head from side to side, the beleaguered Alice dropped her voice to a whisper. "Yes, sir; no, sir; three bags full, sir!" She was up to her neck in work because of the staff shortage, and she wasn't in the mood to be bellowed at, especially when she was only trying to help . . .

"OH, AND GET ME A TEA, WILL YOU?" His booming voice startled her.

"COMING UP, SIR!" She chuckled. "Laced with rat poison and a dollop of witches' brew!"

As she made her way to the corner cabinet where the tea and kettle were stored, her desk phone rang. "Oh, blast!" She gritted her teeth. "I hope it's not him again."

It was Lilian. "Oh, Lilian!" Relief flooded her voice. "Has the doctor said you can come back yet?"

On hearing Lilian's answer, relief turned to disappointment. "Oh, that's a real shame. No! Well, of course I want you to get well . . . you sound awful! Only, it's Mr. Martin. He's being a right pig. With Tom gone and both Dougie and John not due back until next week, and another four people off with the 'flu . . . he's going mad. And he's got me running around like a headless chicken. Honest to God, Lilian . . . if somebody doesn't turn up soon, I'll throw myself off the bleedin' roof!"

There was a minute while Lilian told her in nasal tones how she was feeling like death warmed over, and that she would be back as soon as she got the okay. The doctor's coming out again on Thursday," she said. "I really hope I feel better by then."

"So do I." Alice regretted taking it out on poor Lilian. "Look, I'm sorry if I sound miserable. Get yourself well and hurry back, eh?"

Just then, the boss's voice rang out from the stairway. "It's a good job my bloody life doesn't depend on that tea!"

"On my way, sir!" She listened while Lilian spoke, then said, "You're right. He's like a bear with a sore head, and no, I won't tell him you called, or he'll say that if you're well enough to get out to a phone box to call, you're well enough to come in."

She listened a moment longer, then promised, "All right, I'll do my best to keep things going, and yes, I'm keeping the files in order." She crossed her fingers. "I *am*! Honestly." She almost leapt out of her skin when the boss's voice sailed down from the heights. "HAVE I TO COME AND MAKE THAT DAMNED TEA MYSELF!"

"Sorry, Lilian . . . got to go."

Dropping the receiver into its cradle, she rushed about like her life depended on it. A few minutes later she swanned into the boss's office. "Tea, sir . . . oh, and I've brought you a piece of fruit cake to go with it."

It was the fruit cake that did the trick. "Well, thank you, Alice." His smile enveloped her. "What would I do without you?"

Back home, and lolling in a chair, Lilian congratulated herself on a job well done. "Oh, Alice . . . I feel so ill." Mimicking the nasal tones she had employed in the telephone box only minutes ago, she laughed out loud. "Truth is, I've never felt better. Besides, it'll do them good to manage without me."

She rested for a minute to think through her plan. "I wonder if he'll be glad to see me?" Telling no one, she had carefully planned this day for weeks; now that it was here, she could hardly contain herself. The thought of seeing Tom again made her dizzy with excitement.

"Come on, Lilian. You've got a train to catch." A glance at the hallway clock told her it was already half past ten. Standing by the door, her smart new suitcase was already packed; she had her mackintosh at the ready. All she needed to do now was to change into her best dress, put on her make-up, and it would be time for the taxi to arrive.

With that in mind, she went back upstairs, and stripped off her everyday skirt and blouse. Taking out the flimsy underwear bought only yesterday, she slipped her slim form into it; admiring herself in the wardrobe mirror, she ran her hands over every seductive curve of her body. "He won't be able to resist you."

Next she put on her favorite dress: a burgundy, straight-skirted creation with belted waist and drop neckline. The final touch was the sheer nylons she had also bought yesterday. She slid them voluptuously over her long, slim legs, straightened the dark seams, slipped her manicured feet into her new, high-heeled, dark burgundy shoes.

A few minutes to brush her long auburn curls, a healthy layer of face-powder, a smarm of crimson lipstick, a touch of rouge to her cheekbones, and she was ready. Taking a final glance at herself, Lilian smiled with pleasure.

"I hope you like what you see, Tom," she murmured, her heart leaping at the thought of coming face to face with him. It had been such a long time.

Going downstairs, she put on her mackintosh and checked that the house was secure. When the taxi arrived five minutes later, she was already at the door waiting. "I'm on my way, Tom," she whispered, climbing into the back of the cab. "We'll be good together, you and me. You've had plenty of time to get over what happened," she chided. "There's no need for either of us to be lonely anymore."

Convinced he would be thrilled to see her, she settled back in the seat and smiled a little smile. "It's time for us to start planning a future together."

Looking in his mirror, the driver thought Lilian was a real knockout. It was a shame she was mad as a hatter: he could hear her muttering to herself.

Now, as she looked up and saw him eyeing her, he asked tentatively, "All right, are you, Miss?"

"Never better!" she answered.

"That's good."

He put his foot down and sped along. Usually he would chat to his customers on the journey. But this one seemed to be doing all right talking to herself, he thought.

# *Fifteen*

---

KATHY WAS DUE TO FINISH WORK AT LUNCHTIME TODAY; afterward she was planning to go and see Mabel. "It's a crying shame, so it is." Rosie at work had been horrified to hear of Mabel's sorry plight. "Sure, the poor woman should get rid of him, and buy a cat or a dog!"

Chuckling at Rosie's straightforward, no-nonsense nature, Kathy told her she would pass on the suggestion.

When she stopped in at home, her sister had a few different ideas. "If you ask me, she deserved what she got!" Kathy had told her where she was going, and that she wouldn't be long. "You tell her from me: any woman who lets a man boss her around is a damned fool!"

Ignoring her sister's spiteful remarks, Kathy informed her she would have to root about in the cupboard and get her own lunch. "I had a sandwich at work. That should keep me going while I'm out."

Samantha had not planned on getting her own meals. "I hoped we could go out for a meal—you, me and Tom?"

"Did you now?" Because of the blatant way she was flirting with Tom, Kathy wanted her gone, but was too polite to say so.

Insensitive at every point, Samantha retaliated. "You seem very insecure these days," she said harshly. "Anybody would think I was trying to steal him from you."

Kathy picked up on that. "And are you?" It wouldn't be the first time Samantha had stolen a boyfriend of hers.

Instead of giving a straightforward answer, Samantha

simply smiled. "He might even prefer me to you. Have you thought of that? Oh, but don't worry. If he makes advances on me, I'll put him in his place, I promise."

"Like you did with other men I've liked?" In her heart Kathy had never forgiven Samantha for her behavior. "You just lured them away, and when you'd had your fun, you dropped them. It was all just a game for you, wasn't it?" Kathy was annoyed with herself for rising to the bait, but Samantha's taunts had brought the memories flooding back.

"It wasn't *my* fault! They came on to me!"

"Maybe they did, and maybe I ought to thank you for showing me what swine some of them were, but I can promise you that Tom is a different kettle of fish altogether."

"Are you sure about that?"

"As sure as I am about anything, yes."

"Really? Well, if you're so sure, why are you afraid of inviting me along this evening?"

Kathy was losing her patience. "You know very well he'll be leaving for London tonight. He's busy tying up a few loose ends, but I want to see him on my own later." Her voice hardened. "You're welcome to stay here, but occasionally Tom and I would like some time to ourselves. And another thing, while we're at it. I'll thank you not to keep inviting yourself everywhere we go. Or including yourself in every conversation we have."

Samantha had been painting her nails, but now she looked up with a feigned expression of horror on her face. "Do I do that? Oh, I am sorry."

Not wanting to get into one of Samantha's one-sided arguments, Kathy walked away. "I'd best get ready."

"Yes, I should if I were you." She blew on her nails. "If Tom pops in, I'll look after him, don't you worry."

After the conversation they'd just had, that remark cut deep.

Kathy asked her outright. "You still haven't told me why you're here."

"I've come to see you. I would have thought that was plain enough."

"I don't know why you should." Kathy had learned not to

mince words where Samantha was concerned. "You've never bothered about me before. Why start now?" She was no fool. "You're after something. What is it?"

Taking Kathy by surprise, Samantha suddenly became tearful. "You don't want to know," she said, wiping her eyes.

Kathy was adamant; she would not be taken in by her sister's show of emotion. "Try me."

"It's Mother."

"What about her?"

"She's been such a fool. I've been trying to comfort her, you see. And now she's cost me my job. I've lost my home and everything."

Kathy could see now that Samantha was here for a purpose. "Go on. I'm listening." If they really were in trouble, she could not turn her back on them.

"Well, she got really depressed. He's not the easiest man in the world to live with. In fact, I think he's hit her now and again, only she's too proud to say so."

Samantha congratulated herself on the ease and skill of her lies. "Anyway, I went to see her the other week. She was all worked up. She began telling me that she had been wrong to marry just for money, and that now she wanted to find herself someone kinder. She didn't care how rich he was, she just wanted someone who would take care of her."

Kathy was amazed. "Are you sure we're talking about the same woman?"

Samantha snivelled. "She's changed, Kathy. *He's* changed her. Anyway, while she was saying all these things about him . . . like how she would make a new life and all that, she had no idea he was there, listening at the door. Now he's stopped her allowance and won't give her a single penny. I'm really worried about her." In fact, the only person she was worried about was herself.

For one foolish minute, Kathy was tempted to believe her. Concerned, she sat down.

"Are you telling me the truth?" she asked pointedly. "I know you can spin a good story when it suits you, but I would hate to think of Mother being knocked about."

Images of her mother flashed through her mind: the jewels, the family home, the callous way she had treated Father. And all those many times she had made Kathy feel worthless. "I couldn't stand back and see her being ill treated," she told Samantha now. "Though if she *has* messed up her life, she's got no one to blame but herself."

"Of course I'm telling you the truth!" Samantha could put on a good act when needs be. "She's not only ruined *her* life. She's ruined mine as well. Why do you think I'm here?"

Kathy's suspicions were never far away. "Why *are* you here, Samantha?" Kathy still couldn't quite believe what Samantha was telling her. Irene was a strong, arrogant woman who could look after herself in any circumstances, and who would certainly find life without a wealthy husband very hard to bear.

Samantha reiterated what she'd already said. "I'm here because I needed to see you. Like I say, I've lost my job, and I've nowhere to live."

"What about the jewels Mother gave you?"

"She took them back. After he stopped her allowance, she couldn't pay her bills. She was suicidal. I had to help! You would have done the same."

"But the house!" Kathy was saddened about that. "How in God's name could you lose that? It was worth a small fortune!"

"It just went. She kept draining me of money and I kept borrowing on the house."

A picture was beginning to build up in Kathy's mind and it was frightening. "You're lying as usual!" Clambering out of the chair, she faced her down. "I know why you're here!"

Suddenly it was all too clear. "Mother had nothing to do with it. You've squandered everything, like you always do, and now you're after taking this place from me, aren't you?" Her voice shook with rage. "Have the decency to admit it!"

Samantha gave another sniff; she even had real tears in her eyes as she pleaded, "All right! I admit it! But you have to help me, Kathy . . . And anyway, Father should have left this place to me. It was my right as the eldest. You could sell it and split the money, and you'd still have enough to put down a deposit on a smaller place."

"You really are a cunning, selfish creature." Kathy stared down at her sister. Deep down she thought she had known all along that Samantha was not here for the love of it. She had lost her own inheritance, and now she was after Barden House.

The idea was unthinkable. "If you think I would sell this place, you had better think again. Father left me Barden House, and now it's my home. You had ten times more than I ever had. It's not my fault if you've squandered it."

Seeing her one, easy chance slip away, Samantha came back at her, this time with anger. "You owe it to me! I really am in trouble. I'm not lying about that. And it's true that he's stopped Mother's allowance: he overheard her planning how she would spend his money after he'd gone. He heard her say she would have the time of her life; and maybe she'd find herself a younger man. What the hell is wrong with that?"

"Not a lot as far as I can see; except the poor old fool who married her might have wanted her to be just a bit more loyal, instead of waiting for him to drop dead so that she could get a younger man to fill his shoes."

"Hmh! All she did was to say how she felt. It was just a shame he overheard her."

Kathy could only smile. "At least we're getting to the real truth of the matter. All right! So Mother may well have spoiled her chances of going through that poor man's money like a house on fire, and now he's put a stop to her extravagant ways . . . what man wouldn't in the circumstances? But I don't suppose for one minute he's thrown her out, has he?"

"No."

"So she's still living in luxury, with everything at hand?"

"It's not the same as having your own account and being able to buy what you want when you want it!"

"I'm sure she'll wheedle her way around him somehow. She usually does."

"Don't you care that she's unhappy?"

"Well, of course I do. But, when you think about it, the whole thing might be a blessing in disguise. Maybe she'll begin to understand what it's like to make a pair of shoes last a bit longer, or wear the same dress twice. So what if she has to stretch every penny to make it go farther? We all have to do that. It won't kill her. I'm sure he would never throw her out. As I recall, he thinks the world of her. Like I say, it's only a matter of time before she has him wrapped around her little finger again."

Samantha was on her feet now, thinking about herself as usual. "And what about *me?* What do I do? I've got nothing."

"You *work!* That's what you do. Like the rest of us. Get a job and rent a flat. Learn to look after your money, the same way we all have to do."

She had never in her life met anyone else like Samantha, who thought the world owed them a living. Even Maggie worked and, if she got the sack—which was more often than Kathy cared to remember—she found another job, and so it went on. She didn't laze at home all day feeling sorry for herself. "Knowing you, Samantha, sooner or later you'll meet some rich fool who'll lay the world at your feet."

"Right! I've asked you in a civilized manner and you won't listen." She was in no mood for a lecture. "I'll see a solicitor, that's what I'll do!" Though she knew it would be of little use. Her only chance was to frighten Kathy into doing what she wanted. "You'll be made to sell this house, or take a loan against it, so I can get what I'm entitled to. I warn you, Kathy. I mean to fight for what's rightfully mine, and I *will* win. You can be sure of it."     •

Shaken to her roots, all of Kathy's fears were suddenly confirmed. There was absolutely no doubting the real reason for her sister's visit.

In a quiet, controlled voice Kathy told her, "I'm going to see a friend. I want you packed and gone by the time I get back."

Going to the mantelpiece, she took down a small vase. Reaching inside, she drew out the folded ten-shilling notes and handed them to her. "This is money for paying bills and keeping the wolf from the door," she said. "But you're the biggest wolf of all. Here! Take it. I dare say it doesn't seem much compared to what you're used to. But it's all I've got.

If you're careful, it should be enough to tide you over until you get yourself a job."

"This is peanuts!" Samantha held the money at arm's length, as if it was tainted.

"Take it or leave it, I don't care which." Kathy just wanted her out of there. "Just remember what I said: by the time I get back, I want you gone. And I never want to see your face again."

Samantha had never seen such resolve in her younger sister's face before. Usually she was able to cajole or bully her into doing whatever she wanted. Only now, Kathy had grown stronger, more confident. It was a real setback to her plans.

But she would not give in. "I intend to get this house, or part of it," she warned again. "I always get what I want, you should know that."

Kathy tried to ignore the fear that bubbled up inside her. Looking her straight in the eye, she smiled. "Do your worst," she said and, turning away, she went out of the room and up the stairs.

In the privacy of her own bedroom, she sat on the bed, head in hands, her heart aching. It was true. Samantha had a way of always getting what she wanted.

Out of the corner of her eye she saw her father's photograph, his smiling, happy face looking up at her. "Did you hear all that?" she asked wryly. "Your eldest daughter wants this house, and to tell the truth I'm not sure if she has a claim or not."

The harsh exchange with Samantha had only made her all the more determined, though. This house was too special. It had been her father's place of contentment and now it was hers. And Tom would help her, she knew he would. "She won't get it!" she whispered. "I'll burn it to the ground first!"

Pushing it all to the back of her mind for now, she began getting herself ready to visit Mabel at the hospital.

Twenty minutes later, as she passed the sitting room, she could see Samantha pacing the floor. "That's it!" she muttered. "Work out what you're going to do, now that I'm onto you." She didn't doubt for one minute that Samantha was already cooking up some mischief or other.

All the same, now that she was armed with the facts, she was ready for her.

But for now, she had a friend to see.

A brisk walk down the street, a ten-minute bus ride, and she was at the hospital.

She could see the change in Mabel already. Though the bruises were still evident—mellowed to yellow and purple now—they were on the way out; that dear woman was recovering fast from her ordeal. She wasn't yet able to eat by herself but, thank God, her strength was returning.

Mabel's ready smile greeted Kathy as she came in the door. "I've something to tell you," she said.

Kathy gave her a kiss. "Something exciting, is it?"

Mabel revealed her little secret. "I told you I had a brother I hadn't seen in years, and I had no idea where he was anymore," she said animatedly.

"Yes, I remember." Kathy settled herself into the chair beside the bed. "So, have you heard from him?"

Mabel's eyes shone. "It seems that eventually he found out where I lived, and went there. The next-door neighbor heard him knocking and told him what had happened . . . how he didn't believe that I'd fallen down the stairs, and that my husband had beaten me twice before, that he knew of."

She paused to take a breath, before going on. "Well, my dear, Eric, that's my brother, he went to the café and gave that bully a real roasting. He warned him that, if he had his way, I wouldn't be going back there to be his skivvy."

Exhausted now, she had to stop for a moment.

Kathy waited for her to recover before asking softly, "And did he?"

"What?"

"Did he get his own way . . . about you not going back there to be his skivvy?"

Mabel chuckled. "Oh, Kathy, I'm that excited. When I get out of here—in a few days, they say—Eric will have a car to take me away from here. Apparently he never married. He tried many a time to find me, but never could."

Taking a moment to calm herself, she smiled. "I'm not sure I believe that," she said wisely, "but at least he's found me now, and that's all as matters. He's done well for himself. After he got demobbed he set up a taxi business. He's got a nice house and he's not short of money, or so he tells me." Again that wide, happy smile that gladdened Kathy's heart. "He wants me to go and live with him, and I've said yes."

She giggled like a naughty schoolgirl. "I'll be shot of the café and I'll be shot of that big bully! Oh, Kathy! I can't believe my good fortune."

Kathy was delighted for her. "You deserve it," she said warmly, but added, "You'll have to tell me where you're going, Mabel. I don't want us to lose touch."

"That won't happen," Mabel promised. "Look in that drawer." Pointing to the bedside cabinet, she waited for Kathy to open the drawer. "There! That piece of paper."

Kathy found it.

"Read it, my dear," Mabel urged. "It's my new address."

Kathy read it aloud. "The Grange, Pleasington, Blackburn, Lancashire."

"That's where you'll find me," Mabel told her.

"But that's North—inland, isn't it, Mabel? Won't you miss the seaside?"

"No." Softly, Mabel slid her hand into Kathy's, her eyes swimming with tears and her voice quivering with emotion. "I'm going *home*, lass," she told her. "Me and Eric were born in Blackburn. It turns out he went back there after the war, and I wish to God I'd done the same. But, oh, you don't know how glad my old heart is that, after all this time, I'm going back where I belong."

The next half-hour was filled with talk of Mabel's new-found family, and of her great excitement at going home to Blackburn.

Kathy made no mention of her own troubles. She was glad for Mabel, and wished her well, but was sad for herself. She had grown extremely fond of Mabel, an older woman whom she could trust and admire in a way she never could her own mother.

Just before she left, Kathy met Mabel's brother, who had

come to tell her of his plans. They hugged and held onto each other and Kathy thought it was a joy to see.

A small, stocky man with a kindly face and a warm, pleasant manner, Eric thanked Kathy for befriending his sister. "My Mabel has talked a lot about you," he said. "Thank you for being such a good friend to her."

Kathy told him how much she thought of Mabel and that she was happy for her now. "Take care of her, won't you?" she said, and he promised he would.

When she left it was with tears in her eyes and a great lump in her throat. At least that dear woman would never again have to put up with being beaten to within an inch of her life.

It was late afternoon when she climbed onto the bus. Troubled about her own affairs, she turned her thoughts to Samantha. She hoped she might have gone but, knowing Samantha from old, she somehow suspected that she would still be there. If that was the case, then she would have to be firmer. She felt a sudden desperate desire to be with Tom. He would understand; he would know what to do. But with a lurch of her heart she remembered that he might not be around to help her fight this battle. He was leaving for London tonight. Well, Kathy decided, she would have to manage by herself. Samantha had come here to rob her of her home, and she was not going to allow her to get away with it!

Five minutes later, as the bus made its way down the road that led to West Bay, it passed the boarding house. Deep in thought, Kathy didn't see the taxi draw up, or notice as it dropped off a young woman in a burgundy dress, burgundy shoes and a black coat, and carrying a smart leather case.

As the bus came to a halt, Kathy stepped off and hurried through the streets, along by the harbor, and toward Barden House.

Tom would be here soon; more than ever she was looking forward to seeing him. He was leaving for London on the early evening train. Who knew when she would see him again?

It was with a sinking heart that she saw a light burning in the house.

Coming into the sitting room, she found Samantha still there. Lolling in the chair, with her bare feet propped up on the fender, she was happily warming her toes.

On Kathy's arrival, she said casually, "The kettle's on if you want a drink. Oh, and if you're making a brew, I'll have a cup as well." Bold as brass, and with the slyest of grins, she added, "Oh, by the way, Tom came here looking for you this afternoon."

Kathy was instantly on the alert. "Did he come in?"

"I asked him to, but he said he'd come back." Softly chuckling, she wiggled her toes. "Shame, that. We could have spent a pleasant hour together." She gave Kathy a curious glance. "Still, there'll be another time, I expect."

She had worked out that if she couldn't have the house, she might have to settle for Tom instead. After all, he was good-looking, rich enough to keep her happy, and he had a boat. What more could a girl want?

"Did he say why he'd come down earlier than we'd planned?"

"No, why?"

Kathy murmured her answer. "That's funny. I told him I might not be back from the hospital until about tea-time."

Again, that sly little glance. "He's a man, isn't he? A woman never knows what's on their devious minds."

Wisely ignoring Samantha's jibes, Kathy pointed out, "I asked you to be gone when I got back. What's keeping you?"

Getting out of her chair, Samantha sauntered to where Kathy stood. "I told you before," she said, "I'm not leaving until I get what I came for."

"I can see I'll have to get you *thrown* out!"

Samantha thought that amusing. "Hmh! I don't think so. I'm my father's daughter, too . . . the eldest one, don't forget. So, if I were you, sis, I'd be very careful what you say to people around here. They might begin to wonder whether it was fair that you alone should get our father's house."

She stared at Kathy for a full half-minute before laughing

in her face. "I'm going out tonight—oh, and don't try locking me out, or I'll have to break a window, and what would the neighbors say then?" She yawned. "I'm just going for a lie-down. Then I'll have a bath . . . I hope there's hot water in this dump. After that, I'm off to the pub to get drunk."

Realizing she was being goaded, Kathy didn't say anything. Instead she stepped aside to let Samantha through.

When she was gone, Kathy wondered how it would all end. There were times with Samantha when she felt out of her depth. *This was one of those times.*

She desperately needed someone to confide in. She really wanted to talk to Tom, but was it fair to burden him with all this, especially when he was leaving for London tonight? Maggie was in London. There was only one other person who would understand.

"Hurry back, Jasper," she muttered. "I need your help!"

After asking the taxi-driver to wait for her, Lilian climbed the steps to the front door of the boarding house.

One push on the big heavy door and she was inside a small vestibule. Another door led to the hallway, where she found the reception desk set into the recess under the stairs. None of it was what she was used to, but apparently there were only two boarding houses in the area, and no hotel as such. This one was nearest to the harbor, or so she had been told.

There was a brass bell on the desk, which she thumped a couple of times before a small woman with an angular face appeared. "Yes, can I help you?" In spite of her sharp appearance, she was extremely pleasant.

"Lilian Scott," she introduced herself. "I have a booking; I rang a few days ago."

The woman located her name in the ledger. "Oh, yes. And how long will you be staying?"

"Just the one night." Lilian had high hopes. "I'm here to locate a friend; I expect to be staying with him from tomorrow."

She would have gone straight to Tom's with her suitcase,

but felt it might be best to see him first. She could always come back for her case.

"How did you find out about us, my dear?" The landlady always asked her guests that question: it helped to place the adverts in the right places.

"One of the salesmen from my company knew the area. He had stopped here a few times on his travels. He gave me your address some time back." And she had kept it safe until she thought the time was right to pay Tom a visit.

Showing a double row of small, brilliant white teeth, the woman grinned. "That's good," she said. "Word of mouth is by far the best way to build up a business."

A moment later, Lilian had signed the necessary form, paid her deposit and, following the woman up a long narrow flight of stairs, was taken to her room.

It was a poky place, with a tiny window overlooking the main road, and a bed that looked as if it was out of the ark. "I pride myself on my cleanliness." Flinging the eiderdown back, the woman displayed the stark-white sheets underneath. "If the bed is clean, you can be sure everything else is too, that's my motto."

She showed Lilian where the bathroom was, and told her what time breakfast would be, and which room to go to. "You can get food at the pub, or there's the fish and chip shop," she told her. Then she bade her goodnight and went back down to her half-read newspaper.

Left on her own, Lilian unpacked only what she needed, afterward laying the case on the armchair in the corner. She paid a visit to the bathroom, where she splashed her face and neck with cold water to freshen up.

Ten minutes after arriving, she was on her way out, to where the taxi-driver had been taking a well-earned nap. "Sorry, Miss!" Her tapping on the window had woken him. Leaping out, he let her into the car, before clambering back into the driving seat, shivering when the chilly evening air got into his bones. "The harbor is it, Miss?" She had mentioned it before.

Lilian gave him the full address and, filled with excitement at the thought of seeing Tom, she anxiously settled back. She had to think what she would say, because he didn't even know she was coming. "I hope he'll be pleased to see me."

The driver cocked an ear. "What was that, Miss?"

"Nothing." Lilian grew agitated. "I was just thinking out loud."

Curious, he sneaked a look at her in his mirror; to see her softly talking to herself, and sometimes smiling. "God! I hope I haven't picked up some bloody crackpot." There had been a case in Dorchester where a driver was attacked by his passenger. It was the first time anyone had heard of such a thing. In the end it turned out to be some drunk who'd had an argument with his girlfriend. Right now, he was languishing in prison where he belonged.

By the time they came up the hill toward Tom's house, Lilian's heart was beating nineteen to the dozen. "Be in, Tom," she muttered, increasingly anxious. *"Please be in!"*

She was disappointed. When they arrived, the house was in darkness; however many times she banged on the door, there was no answer.

"What the devil d'you think you're doing . . . trying to knock the damned door down, from the sound of it!" The man from next door had been alerted by her continuous banging. "He's not in—can't you tell that . . . I mean, look! The house is in darkness. If he were in, you'd expect there to be a light on."

An old misery, he kept himself to himself, though he quietly relished the gossip in the village shop, and liked to watch the goings-on from his window. What he *didn't* like was being disturbed by some stranger pounding on next door.

He shook his fist at her. "Clear off! And give an old man some peace, why don't you?"

Lilian was desperate. "Do you know where I can find him?"

The man continued chewing on his baccy, his avaricious old eyes noting the slim figure and the pretty face, and he smiled knowingly. "Who are *you* then?"

Now that she was here, Lilian's fantasy had become reality. "I'm his sweetheart."

"I see." He chewed a bit more and stared at her a bit longer before asking, "Does he know you're looking for him?" In his own youth he had often played one woman off against another. It was a man's thing.

"No. I wanted to surprise him."

He chuckled, and chewed a bit more and rolled the baccy around in his mouth, before telling her with great glee, "Oh, you'll do that all right. He's gone to see his *other* sweetheart . . ." He pointed in the direction of Kathy's home. "You'll find him down there . . . Barden House, that's the name. That's where you'll find him . . . with his other sweetheart, name of Kathy." Muttering and chuckling, he went back inside.

Lilian was confused and upset. "Barden House," she told the driver. "Back down to the harbor. Be quick!" She must have told him that a dozen times as he drove around looking for Barden House, but in the end, impatient and edgy, she told him to stop the car.

Glad to do so, he parked by the harbor while she set off to find the house the old man had mentioned. "You needn't wait for me." Digging in her purse, she took out a handful of coins and threw them into his lap.

He watched her running across the road to the houses. "Mad as a hatter!" he muttered, driving off with his foot hard down on the accelerator.

As he went, he couldn't help but see another taxi parked at a big old house opposite. "Watch out, mate," he laughed, "you don't want to be picking that one up. If you ask me, she's straight from the funny farm!"

Having located the house, and being camouflaged by the dark, at a point where there was no street-lamp, Lilian crept up the path. From here she had a clear view in through the window. What she saw only served to infuriate her all the more.

As promised, Tom had called in before setting off to London. "I don't want to leave you," he murmured, his gaze enfolding Kathy, "but I have to, you know that, don't you?" He saw the misery in her light-brown eyes and his heart ached to be with her. "I had thought about asking you to go with me," he confessed, "but I know you can't just leave your job. And in any case, I would have to be out and about, going places, seeing people, asking questions. I need to get to the bottom of what happened. The inspector's already promised he'll work with me. He says he's as keen as I am to see this case solved."

Drawing her to him, he held her for a time. "I'll be back as soon as I can."

"I wouldn't let you go if I didn't believe that."

In his arms, Kathy felt safe from the world. She had shed her tears, and now she was resigned to the idea of Tom going away, if only because she knew it meant they could be together all the sooner.

"Look at me." Holding her at arm's length, he smiled into her troubled eyes. "I love you."

She gave a small nervous laugh. "I love you too."

"If I asked you, would you come with me?"

"No." She wanted to go with him, but it was wiser not to. "It's not my place. You go and do what you have to do," she murmured. "I've got my job to do, and I'll still be here when you get back."

He nodded, a smile lighting his face. "You'd better be!"

They talked a while longer, and kissed, and held onto each other for a while. There was so much in their hearts they wanted to say, yet each knew what the other was feeling, and it was all right.

*Outside, looking in, Lilian was beside herself with rage.*

She could not hear what they were saying, but the sight of another woman in Tom's arms was too much. "Bastard!" she kept saying. "You bastard!" In her tortured mind, she could only see that he had deceived her. He had left her alone in London, and now he was deceiving her with another woman. "BASTARD!"

"I'd better go, darling." With his arm around Kathy, Tom started toward the door.

"I'll see you to the taxi."

"No need. It's chilly out there. You stay in the warm."

Kathy would not take no for an answer. "I'll get my coat. I think I left it in the kitchen when I got back earlier."

He shook his head and smiled. "What will I do with you, eh? An obstinate woman who won't do as she's told?"

*"Marry me."* Kathy's deep-down love was alive in her eyes as she looked up at him.

For a precious moment they held each other. "That's what I've promised for us," he murmured. "There is nothing I want more in all the world."

From outside, Lilian saw Kathy go through a door at the back of the room. A moment later she returned, dressed in a long blue wool coat.

Tom put his arm around her and they walked across the sitting room; when Lilian saw them turn, almost as if they were coming right at her, she panicked.

Running away, she hid behind the wall, where they could not see her. And neither could she see them.

Panting and fearful in her hiding place, she peeped around the corner to see the two of them walking down the path, arm in arm, for all the world like lovers.

When suddenly Kathy looked back, she dived behind the wall again and kept out of sight.

Enraged, she didn't see Tom get into the taxi, and she didn't see how Kathy waved him goodbye, her sad face betraying her deeper feelings.

Instead, she stayed where she was, stiff with rage, her back pressed against the wall, her nails scraping the brickwork until the blood spurted from her fingertips. "Bastard!" She was distraught. "Bastards, the pair of them!"

Inside the house, as Kathy closed the curtains, Samantha appeared. Bathed and beautiful, she was combing her long tresses. "How do I look?"

Busying herself, Kathy didn't even turn to look.

Samantha smiled. "You might as well accept it, sis." Putting a final dab of lipstick on, she collected Kathy's blue wool coat from the arm of the chair. "You don't mind if I borrow this, do you?"

When Kathy appeared not to have heard, she threw the

coat on and buttoned it up. "There's nothing you can do," she said, preening herself in the hallway mirror. "I'm owed half of what Father left you. So you might as well sign an agreement to that effect and get it over with."

Confident that she had got Kathy on the run, she declared triumphantly, "I'll make us an appointment with a solicitor first thing in the morning." She gave a wry little chuckle. "That's if there *are* any decent solicitors in this half-baked place!"

*Not if I can help it!* Kathy thought angrily.

She had no intention of signing any such "agreement."

Jasper tumbled wearily out of the last bus of the evening. Having spent almost all day on the road, the traveling bag in his fist felt twice the weight it had when he'd started. His poor old back ached from the long hours in the train, and his feet were throbbing in his shoes.

"Goodnight, mate." The bus conductor was a jolly sort, who had chatted to his few passengers all the way. "Mind how you go."

Jasper bade him goodnight before walking the few hundred yards to his cottage, where he quickly let himself in, made a cup of tea, and fell into bed almost immediately. "By! I must be getting old," he complained. "Once upon a time I'd 'ave walked all the way to Woburn and back, wi' never a second thought."

He was looking forward to seeing Tom and Kathy tomorrow. "I wonder what they've been up to while I've been away." No sooner were the words out of his mind than he was snoring like a good 'un.

Half an hour after Jasper had gone indoors, Samantha emerged from the house.

Once outside in the cold evening air, she shivered. "This is a godforsaken place," she muttered, drawing the coat about her. "The sooner Kathy signs that paper, the sooner I can get out of here."

Needing to clear her thoughts, she headed for the pub, by way of the harbor, making her way carefully along the slippery stones of the harbor wall. There were no railings along this stretch of the walkway; the bollards were the only markers of the wall's edge. Beyond them she could see the oily, dark waters of the harbor and the looming shapes of the boats. There was no street-lamp here and only now did Samantha realize how hellishly dark it was. "Dammit!" Tripping once or twice, she began to walk more carefully. "You'd think they could at least afford to put up another street-lamp!"

She was almost at the pub when she imagined she heard footsteps behind her. Quickly, her heart leaping, she turned, and there was no one there.

She quickened her steps, almost running. And there again, seeming right behind her, was that same sound. She swung round, angry now. "Who's that? Is that you, Kathy?" Her stern, harsh warning belied the fear inside her. "If you're trying to frighten me, it won't work, so you might as well show yourself."

There was a low, throaty laugh, then the dark shadow lunged at her. She saw a raised arm, and that was all; there was no time to scream before she felt a vicious push which sent her toppling over the wall edge. As she fell, her fingers clawing aimlessly at the air, another laugh was the last thing she heard before her head crumpled against the side of a boat as she plunged into darkness.

After Samantha had gone, Kathy found it hard to settle. It was always the same when Samantha was near. She had the uncanny ability to rile her, until her emotions were in turmoil.

For a long time she sat in the chair thinking, full of regrets. Then she went to the window and looked out. The night was dark, eerily silent. "If she's not at home by midnight, I'd best go and find her." Even now, she had a kind of affection for her impossible sister.

Pacing the floor, she grew agitated, angry that she should be made to feel responsible. "No! Why should I?" she thought. Determination shaped her features. "If she wants to stay out all night, it's up to her!" With that, she went upstairs and got ready for bed. From outside, she could hear the pub turning out, then the sound of people softly talking, and a woman's laughter.

She climbed into bed, and was soon asleep, though troubled by dreams she had not experienced in an age.

The fishermen were out with the first light. "Good luck, matey!" The tall, lean fellow nodded to his colleague as they parted to go their separate ways.

Climbing down to his boat, he imagined he saw something floating in the water, half submerged, yet cradled by the broken oil spills, which shifted back and forth amongst the boats. He peered down for a closer look, taking care as he came nearer, his footsteps negotiating the narrow decks and fishing paraphernalia which littered his way.

Suddenly, he saw her. The shock momentarily silenced him. With wide, disbelieving eyes, he stared down at the still, white face and the hair, now matted and disfigured by oil and debris. "Jesus Christ!" The whisper became a shout. "Kenny! Come quick . . . there's somebody drowned!"

Quickly, the two of them pulled the body out of the water. "I reckon she's that woman staying at Barden House with her sister," Kenny remarked, "but I can't be sure . . . poor devil."

"Best alert the police."

Kenny covered her over. "Stay with her," he advised, before going at a run to raise the alarm.

# Sixteen

MOMENTARILY DISORIENTATED, TOM COULDN'T FATHOM where he was for a minute or two. Then he remembered: he was in a hotel room in the heart of Knightsbridge, and the telephone was ringing insistently.

Groaning, he picked up the receiver. A familiar voice greeted him.

"Tom," Inspector Lawson said. "Sorry to disturb you at this early hour, but I just wanted to check you were definitely coming in."

"Yes," Tom said, puzzled.

"There've been some developments up here in relation to your case, and I've decided it might be wise to check them out. Can you come in and see me at the Chestnut Walk station?"

Fifteen minutes later Tom was shaved, washed and dressed, and ready for breakfast. "Let's see . . . ground floor, past the desk, down the corridor and the breakfast room is straight ahead." The receptionist had given him directions when he had arrived very late last night.

Rather than take the lift to the ground floor, he ran down the stairs two at a time. The receptionist was still there as he hurried by the desk to his breakfast. "Good morning, Mr. Marcus," she called.

"Good morning to you," he answered. "Been here all night, have you?"

"I go off in half an hour," she told him, her blue eyes and inviting smile escaping him as he hurried away.

He was keen to see Inspector Lawson, so breakfast had to be tea and toast. It wasn't enough for a grown man, but with two large cups of tea and the toast being thick and crusty, he enjoyed it all the same.

When breakfast was over, he went straight out the main doors to hail a taxi.

The Knightsbridge streets were already humming, with people and traffic rushing in every direction. After the easy pace of life in West Bay, it seemed odd to be risking life and limb for a taxi.

The taxi carried him straight to the police station, where he ran up the steps and in through the doors. "I have an appointment with Inspector Lawson," he informed the policeman on desk duty. The name is Tom Marcus."

The young rookie ran his long, lean fingers through the day ledger. "That's right, sir. If you would like to wait over there, I'll let him know you're here."

It seemed a long wait. Twice in the next half-hour, Tom went to the desk and asked what was keeping the inspector, and each time he got the same answer. "Something important cropped up, sir. I'm sure he won't be long now."

It was quarter to eleven before the inspector finally emerged from his office to shake Tom by the hand. "Telephones and paperwork!" he apologized. "There are days when I wish the damned things had never been invented!" A big bumbling figure of a man, he had an amiable, disarming manner, but was reputed to be one of the sharpest minds in the force.

"Come through. I'm sorry to have kept you waiting, only we've recently uncovered a protection racket. It's like turning over a stone: on top it's smooth, but underneath it's crawling with all sorts of nasties."

Opening the door, he let Tom through into his office. "We're on top of it now," he concluded. "We've already got the heavies. It's only a matter of time before we've got the ringleaders under lock and key."

While Tom went inside he called to the officer at the desk, "Two teas in here, at the double, if you don't mind."

Closing the door, he walked over to seat himself behind

his desk. "Good to see you, Tom." He had spent many a long hour in Tom's company after the tragedy. "Sit yourself down."

Pushing aside all the "damned paperwork," he sat back in his chair and stared hard at Tom. He thought he looked well, and said so. "You went away then?" he said.

"I had to," Tom explained. "I did my best to carry on afterward, but you know as well as I do that I wasn't coping, not really. It was eating me up . . . it got so I couldn't sleep, couldn't think. In the end I had to get away . . . I needed to find some sort of quiet, to get a clearer mind, if you know what I mean."

The inspector nodded. "I know exactly what you mean," he answered thoughtfully. "It was a bad thing that happened. I'm only sorry we still haven't got that bastard behind bars."

Just then there was a tap on the door. "Yes?" the inspector called.

The door opened and in came the young officer, carrying a tray. "Here's your tea, sir." Pointing to the desk, the inspector instructed him to "Put it down here." Again he shifted the two piles of paper aside to make room for the tray.

When the officer had gone, with the door closed behind him, the inspector picked up the teapot and began to pour, first one cup, then the other. He dropped two spoonfuls of sugar in one, enquiring of Tom, "How do you like yours?"

"One sugar, and milk to color," Tom answered. He could contain his impatience no longer. "What are the developments that you mentioned then?" he asked Inspector Lawson.

The inspector passed him his cup of tea. "Well, this business of the flowers being destroyed for a start: seems a *strange* business, don't you think? Quite sinister."

Tom nodded. "It's weird."

"From what you told me on the phone, it's happened at least three times?"

"So the florist mentioned in her letter."

"And have you been to see her yet?"

Tom shook his head. "It was late last night when I got to London. I intend going straight there when I leave here."

"I'd best come along." The inspector was hopeful that at last they might have a breakthrough. "I was keen to see you because this could be very important. Have you any idea who would want to destroy the flowers you send?"

"I can't imagine." Tom had turned it over and over in his mind, and had come up with no answers. "It's presumably somebody who hates me, or why would they do it?"

"Hmh." The inspector took a gulp of his coffee. "Hates you . . . or hates your family."

Tom's eyes flashed with anger. "Whoever it is, they've got a lot to answer for!"

"There are some evil devils out there. We none of us know how their minds work."

Tom had a question of his own. In fact he had a hundred of them. "So, are you any nearer to catching whoever it was?"

"I'm afraid not. I can assure you, it's not for want of trying. But there is something one of my men is checking out. I'll tell you about it later."

Tom's heart sank. "What about the car?"

The inspector slowly shook his head. "Nothing yet, though we're still working on it. As you know, we tracked the make and color of the car through the paint smears we found on your bumper. That particular shade of blue is only used by Hillman. We've made exhaustive searches, but still haven't been able to trace it."

"And there were no witnesses." Tom despaired. "Surely to God somebody must know *something!*"

"I'm not sure. You said yourself there was nobody else on the road that day."

"Will you tell me something, Inspector?"

"If I can."

"Do you think whoever did it was just after me?"

The inspector sighed. "We've had this conversation before as I recall, and, no, if the killer had wanted you dead, for whatever reason, he could have chosen his moment. No, Tom. Whoever came at you that day meant to kill every one of you."

Tom knew as much in his heart of hearts. He passed his hand over his face.

The inspector got out of his chair. "Let's go," he said briskly. Grabbing his trilby and coat, he made for the door. "It's time we talked to that florist of yours. She may hold a vital key!"

With the inspector leading the way, the two of them went quickly out of the station. They climbed into his Wolsey, and away down the main street, hopping in and out of traffic, with the inspector continuing the conversation.

"At first I thought it might have been an accident . . . that his car went out of control or some such thing; or that it was deliberate, but that he was a crazy man out on the road looking for weird thrills. Who knows?"

Caught up in traffic now, he glanced across at Tom. "But now there's no doubt in my mind that it was premeditated."

Tom was shocked. For a long time he had tried to make himself believe that maybe it had been some kind of lunatic who came at them that day . . . maybe to frighten them, but not to kill. Now, though, the inspector was confirming his own worst fear that it really was a cold, calculated act. But who could have done such a terrible thing? *Who could have wanted all of his family dead?*

For the umpteenth time he relived it now. The car seemed to come out of nowhere. It didn't give him time to react in the way he might otherwise have done. Taken completely unawares, he had instinctively accelerated, desperate to get out of the way, trying to turn. But there was no time. The car was on him every second, pushing, bumping him along, driving him ever closer to the cliff-edge. It was all too fast. Too late! Oh, dear God, did he react in blind panic? Was it his fault that his entire family was killed? What could he have done? Dear God, what could he have done? All the old doubts and the guilt came back to haunt him.

"Tom!" The inspector's voice cut through his agony. "I haven't closed the case. I mean to get him, however long it takes."

"But how could he just disappear like that?"

"Who knows? There could be any number of answers. He may have hidden the car where we haven't yet been able to find it. He could have been miles away by the time you were found at the bottom of that cliff."

Time and again, like Tom, he had gone through all the possibilities. "Maybe he had the car destroyed somehow, or ran it into some deep water miles away from the scene of the crime."

"What's the next move?" Tom wanted to know.

"Well, it's not easy, I won't deny it. We've already followed up all the obvious possibilities. We don't know yet who we're dealing with . . . we can't be certain whether he's local, or if he was just passing through. The only thing I'm certain of is that it *was* a deliberate act of murder. And that's how we're treating it."

The florist told them everything she knew. "Mr. Marcus placed a regular order for flowers, and we delivered them as arranged. The first few times there was no trouble, but then it started. Every time we took flowers there, they were destroyed. Fresh flowers were always put in their place."

The inspector pre-empted Tom's question. "Did you ever see anyone hanging around?"

"No. My assistant always kept a look out, but never saw anyone. Until last time."

"Where is your assistant now?"

"She's out the back loading up the van. I'll get her for you." With that she hurried away, returning a moment or two later with Gloria.

"Tell the inspector what you saw." The manageress pushed her forward.

Seeing how nervous she was, Tom addressed her gently. "There's no need to worry," he assured her. "We just need to ask you about the person you saw at the churchyard the last time you went there."

"What do you want to know?" She looked from Tom to the inspector.

"Well," the inspector said, "for a start, what did he look like?"

Gloria's eyes opened wide with astonishment. "Oh, no! It wasn't a *man!* It was a *woman* I saw." She glanced at her boss, as if she suddenly imagined she was being accused of lying. "It *was* a woman . . . she spoke to me . . . asked me questions, she did!"

Both men were taken aback, but it was the inspector who voiced what was in both their minds. "What did she look like . . . this *woman?*"

"Auburn hair, long and curly; she was taller than me. About twenty-nine . . . maybe thirty, I suppose. Oh, and she was dressed smartly, for the office, I reckon." A look of envy crossed her homely features. "She was attractive and all."

The inspector didn't notice Tom's look of astonishment as he heard the familiar description. Instead he concentrated on the matter in hand. "You said she asked you questions?"

"She did, yes."

"What kind of questions?"

The assistant cast her mind back. "She asked me if the flowers were from Mr. Marcus." Glancing at Tom, she saw his reaction, and wondered. "She said she was a friend." Her implication was clear.

The inspector continued to question her. "What else did she say?"

"Nothing much. She was kinda weird." Shrugging her shoulders in a shiver, she added without being prompted, "I reckon it was her who's been vandalizing the flowers!"

Having listened to her account of the woman, Tom was loath to believe the suspicions that were beginning to seep into his mind. "What makes you think it was this woman who destroyed the flowers?" He needed to know.

"Well, because she was spooky . . . watching every move I made, as if she resented me even being there. She said she was going, but she hung about for a while. She'd already put some roses in the vase, so it was a good job I'd taken a vase of our own."

"*I* told her to do that," Margaret Taylor informed them with a proud smile, "in case the other vase had been broken, or maybe filled with somebody else's flowers, like before."

Nodding appreciatively, the inspector prompted Gloria,

"Go on . . . You arranged the flowers, and she hung about. Then what?"

"Well, she went off eventually, and I finished arranging the flowers. Then I went back to my van and collected a couple of other bunches that had been ordered for other graves."

"And you never saw her again?"

"No, but something awful happened. I had finished in the churchyard, and was just getting into the van when the old caretaker came running. He was in a real bad mood . . . 'Come and see!' he said, and made me go back with him." She rolled her eyes. "You should have seen the mess!"

"What? You mean the flowers were thrown about like before?" Tom asked.

"Not only thrown about," she replied, her voice growing louder with excitement. "All the heads had been broken off, and they were flung all over the place . . . ever such a long way, like somebody got mad, if you know what I mean."

While Tom was trying to take it all in, and slowly coming to realize that he had an idea who the culprit was, the inspector asked, "And what about the flowers that the woman had left?"

The assistant leaned forward, her voice dropping almost to a whisper. "*Her* flowers were still there! I reckon that proves it, don't you?"

Before they left, the inspector informed her that she would need to make a statement, and that he himself would be back.

She didn't mind. "That's all right," she said. "I'd like to see whoever could do a thing like that locked up."

Outside, the inspector looked preoccupied. "It seems to me, we'd best find this woman and bring her in for questioning," he told Tom. "If she *is* the one who's been destroying your flowers, who knows what else she's been up to?"

Tom had no choice but to agree.

He was convinced from the description that the woman in the churchyard was Lilian, but he wasn't ready to confide in the inspector. He intended speaking with her first. It could well be that the florist's assistant had got it all wrong.

Lilian had been a good friend to the family. She and Sheila had known each other well . . . spending time together, shopping and suchlike. In which case, she might just have been taking flowers as a gesture of friendship.

He needed to see her to clarify the situation. Even if she had been there, it didn't mean . . . he turned his thoughts away from the terrible idea.

With that in mind, he politely refused the offer of a lift with the inspector. "I have things to do," he told him. "But I'm staying at the White House, if you need to get hold of me. And let me know as soon as you can about the other lead, will you?"

"Of course," the inspector assured him. "The minute I have any firm news."

# *Seventeen*

ALICE WAS SHOCKED AT LILIAN'S APPEARANCE WHEN she turned up for work that morning. "Whatever's wrong with you?" she asked. "You look awful!"

"I've been ill, haven't I?" she lied. "Now leave me alone and get on with your work." Slamming the door to her office, she threw herself into the chair, leaning over the desk with her head bent forward and her hands over her face.

She was desolate. It had been the worst few days of her entire life. She had even considered ending it all, but always at the back of her mind was the notion that Tom would want her in the end. She mustn't upset herself, because he was sure to come looking for her. He loved her. He'd always loved her. He was bound to realize that now.

In the corridor, Alice was in conversation with one of her colleagues. "I'm worried about her." She discreetly gestured to the main office where Lilian was still seated at her desk, her hands nervously tapping the surface, her face wreathed in a strange smile. "She's been like that ever since she came in . . . locked in her office, talking to herself. She's ill, and I don't know what to do."

Her colleague had no qualms on that score. "Fetch Mr. Martin. Let *him* deal with it." She peeped at Lilian, who had left her desk and was now pacing the floor, drawing the concerned attention of the other women in the typing pool. "She's obviously not properly recovered from her illness. I dare say he'll send her home again."

Leaving her colleague to man her phone, Alice made her

way upstairs to the boss's office. She tapped on the door, always nervous of this important, influential man. John Martin could make or break a person.

"Come in!" his authoritative voice boomed out.

When she gingerly opened the door, it was to see Mr. Martin on the phone. Gesturing for her to sit down, he concluded his conversation. "Thanks, Harold. I'm glad you told me. No, that's perfectly fine. You're doing a grand job out there. Yes, it's all right. I'll catch up with him later."

Replacing the phone, he leaned forward on the desk and, wiping his hands over his thick, graying hair, looked up to address her. "Don't tell me you've got a problem as well?"

Nervously, Alice swallowed, before blurting out the reason for being here. "It's Lilian, sir."

Frowning, he looked her straight in the eye, unnerving the girl even more. "Lilian? She turned up all right this morning, didn't she? I was just on my way down to see her, but the blessed telephone hasn't stopped since I got in."

"I don't want you to think I'm being a snitch, or anything like that, sir, only—"

"Well, get on with it!" Exasperated, he blew out his cheeks; already this morning he'd had problem after problem. "If you've something to say, I'd best hear it now."

Alice sat up, angered by his attitude. After all, she had only come here to help. "Yes, Lilian did come in this morning, sir, only I don't think she should have come in at all."

"Why ever not?"

"She's not well, sir. She should be at home in bed. I really think she needs to see a doctor."

"But I thought she'd got over the 'flu." He couldn't understand. "When she phoned, she said she was ready to come back to work. She sounded fit enough to me."

"It's not the 'flu, sir."

"What is it then?" Falling back in his seat, he groaned. "Don't tell me she's got 'women's problems.' Honestly! That's all I need." As he spoke he thrust a fist here and there to emphasize what he was saying. "Just look at it! There's paperwork piled mountain high, filing to be done, urgent things to be dealt with . . ." He ran his hands over his temples. "Since she's been away, the whole damned place seems to have fallen apart."

Alice blushed at his mention of "women's problems." Hastily she said, "It's not that kind of a problem, sir. She's . . . she's . . ."

"For God's sake, woman . . . say what you came to say and be done with it."

"Well, sir . . . I think she's—" It was difficult for her to say, because she was fond of Lilian. "I think she's unstable, sir." There! It was said.

"Unstable!" He glared at her, eyes wide with astonishment. "What the hell is *that* supposed to mean?"

"She's not like her usual self, sir." Wanting it over with, Alice gabbled it all out in one breath. "She was really upset when she came in . . . bad-tempered . . . shouting at everybody. And now she's shut in her office, pacing the floor, talking to herself. And she won't come out, or even talk to anybody."

"I see." This wasn't like the Lilian he knew—bright, organized and efficient. "Has she done any work since she's been in?" Normally she was straight onto it.

"No, sir. She went directly to her office, and hasn't come out since."

"Has she asked you to do anything on her behalf . . . or ordered a résumé of what's been happening in her absence?"

"No, sir. Nothing like that."

"How long has she been in?"

Alice couldn't be exact. "About an hour . . . or thereabouts."

Alice hated having to run to him like this, behind Lilian's back. But she was concerned. "It's not like her, sir. She's usually so talkative and she works harder than any of us." She cautioned herself. "As hard as any of us, I mean . . ."

He seemed not to have heard her self-condemning remark. Instead he was deep in thought. "Mmm." He found it all very disconcerting. "It sounds as if she might well have come back to work a bit too soon."

"I think so, sir."

"Right then!" Picking up the telephone, he asked the operator for a number. "I need to return an important call, then I'll be right down." He eyed her with suspicion, and a hint of humor. "This isn't a ploy between the two of you to get her more time off work, is it?"

"Oh, no, sir, and I'd be very grateful if you didn't tell her I've been up here talking to you. I'm only looking out for her. She's been very good to me."

He could see she was genuine in her concern. "And you're a good friend to her. I hope she realizes that." He reassured her that she had done the right thing in coming to him.

"How will you approach Lilian, without her knowing you're checking up on her?"

He patted the side of his nose. "I wouldn't be successful in business if I didn't know a trick or two."

Downstairs, her colleague was waiting as Alice got to the bottom of the steps. "What did he say?"

"He's coming down."

"Good. She's still acting weirdly," she said. "I knocked on her door and she told me to go away . . . said she didn't want to be disturbed. She's not answering her phone either . . . it's been ringing for ages."

It was still ringing when Mr. Martin came down.

A glance through the window only confirmed what Alice had said; Lilian was seated at her desk, muttering to herself and smiling, as if amused by a private joke.

Tapping on the door, he went straight in. Having brought a sheaf of paperwork as an excuse to check out Alice's worries, he placed it on the desk before her. "Glad to see you back," he said with a bright smile. "Fit and ready for work, are you?"

Lilian nodded.

"Right then, here's the surveyor's report for that Brighton hotel. I need you to get onto it straight away . . . four copies in all, and a covering letter for each." He pointed to the papers. "I need them back on my desk within the hour."

Going out of the door, he turned with a compliment. "This whole damned place has gone to pot since you've been gone."

Lilian didn't look up. "I'll deal with it straight away, sir."

Emerging from the office, he saw Alice waiting anxiously

around the corner. "She seems fine," he told her. "In fact she's in there now working on a surveyor's report."

Alice shook her head. "No, sir, she isn't. Look!"

Curious, he turned, and was shocked to see Lilian standing over the waste-paper bin and slowly tearing up the report. Bit by bit she began dropping it into the bin. "Hey!" Going at a run, he burst back through the main office door. "What's the matter with you? Have you gone stark raving mad, or what?"

Anger turned to shame when, suddenly, Lilian dropped into her chair and began sobbing: deep sobs that shook her frame and tore the heart out of Alice, who was watching. "Hey, now!" Going to her, she slid a comforting arm round Lilian's shoulders. "It's all right . . . everything's going to be all right."

Ignoring the bewildered stares of the other staff, and stooping to look into Lilian's face, she asked gently, "Don't you think it would be better if you went home?"

Lilian didn't answer.

Having successfully retrieved the pieces of his precious report, Mr. Martin offered, "I'll arrange a car. Get her home. Call the doctor. She's obviously ill."

Instructing a secretary to organize Lilian's ride home, he went to her and softly apologized. "I should have seen straight off how ill you were." Until now, though, he hadn't noticed the pale, pinched skin, or the abject misery in her eyes. Her hands, too, were trembling uncontrollably. "You need a doctor, Lilian," he said kindly. "Alice will take you home. Let her call the doctor. She can stay with you for the rest of the day if you like."

Being the businessman he was, it crossed the back of his mind that, if Alice was away too, he would be desperately short of staff. But suddenly, in the midst of it all, he realized there were times when he wished he could just walk away from it all. Instead of working for a living, the work had taken him over.

It was a sobering thought.

Within ten minutes, Alice was escorting Lilian from the building. Now a shivering wreck, Lilian clung to her. "I didn't mean it to happen," she kept saying. "I didn't mean it to happen."

Alice helped her into the car. "It's all right," she kept saying. "Don't worry. It'll be all right."

The driver softly hummed a song as he went away. If there was one thing that unnerved him, it was a sobbing woman.

In the back, Alice was deeply concerned about Lilian, who was muttering and crying, and telling her how she was "sorry." "You don't need to be 'sorry' for anything," Alice assured her.

Yet she could not imagine why Lilian was in such a state. She wondered if it was because of what she had done to the surveyor's report. Then she wondered if it might be something in Lilian's private life that had rendered her such a shivering wreck.

Whatever it was that seemed to be eating away at her, Alice knew one thing for certain: it had sent Lilian dangerously close to a breakdown.

It was a ten-minute ride to Lilian's small house; with the streets busy, it was a stop-start journey.

When they arrived at their destination, Alice thanked the driver and told him he could go. "If I need to, I'll catch the bus," she told him.

At the door, Alice asked Lilian for the key. While Lilian fumbled in her pockets, Alice noticed the front door was partly open. Her first instinct was that Lilian had been burgled. "You stay there a minute," she told Lilian, who was still preoccupied searching for the key.

"I can't find it," she was muttering. "I don't know where it is."

Cautiously, Alice went inside. From somewhere close, she could hear a wireless playing loud music, and Alice began to feel apprehensive of what she might find inside the house. "Who's there?" Any minute now, she expected to be confronted by a burglar.

With her heart in her mouth, she came into the sitting room, and what she saw gave her a shock.

The room was littered with newspapers and empty cups. Two of them had turned over on the table, the spillage of tea now dried on the surface and on the lino, where it had at one stage dripped and had left a dark smudge.

There were other cups in the hearth, and writing paper torn into shreds and thrown across the rug. The fire-grate was piled high with ash and cinders, and the curtains of one window were still drawn. There was a crumpled pillow and blanket in the fireside chair, as if somebody had been sleeping there.

Alice couldn't understand it. This was not the work of a burglar.

She almost leapt out of her skin when Lilian's voice whispered in her ear, "I've been too busy to clean it up."

Recovering her composure, Alice took the blanket and pillow from the chair. "Here, you sit down. I'll make you a cup of tea, and don't worry about all this." Knowing how Lilian was always so particular about her appearance and the tidy manner in which she kept the office, Alice still could not believe that she had been living in such a pigsty as this. It was unthinkable, and only served to confirm how ill she was.

Once Lilian was comfortable in the chair, Alice asked her where the doctor's number was.

Lilian said she didn't want the doctor, and when she seemed to grow agitated, Alice calmed her down. "All right. Let's have a cup of tea and a chat first," she said. "Then we'll see." Though she was determined to get a doctor to her, she thought another few minutes wouldn't hurt; at least until she had tidied the place up and got a fire going in the hearth.

After a quick look round, she soon found the matches. Lighting the stove, she filled the kettle and set it on the hob, leaving it to boil while she took the pillow and blanket upstairs.

Another shock awaited her, and this time she was shaken to her roots.

In the first bedroom, where the blanket and pillow obviously belonged, there were pictures plastered everywhere:

over the wall, on the dressing-table mirror, and even on the bed-head.

Alice could hardly take it all in. "Oh, dear God!" Never in her life had she encountered anything like this.

She walked slowly around the room, looking at the pictures, unable to believe her eyes.

*They were all photographs of Tom.*

In different settings: walking from his car; sitting at his desk; climbing into a taxi; even several with his children. And here was another, of him sitting in a café, and yet another, of him with his brother, heads bent over the desk where a sheet of drawings was laid out. And another, of Tom discussing business with John Martin.

With the exception of the one with his children, which was taken from close up with Tom obviously aware it was being taken, they were all shot from a distance, Tom apparently unaware that his picture was being taken.

Horrified, Alice began to back off, when she saw other scraps of photographs at her feet. Stooping to pick them up, she pieced them together, one by one, in the palm of her hand.

*The pictures were all of Tom and his wife, smiling into the camera.*

In the background of one, Alice could see a Christmas tree, and baubles strung from the fireplace. In another, Tom had his arm around his wife, looking down with a smiling face and the look of love in his eyes. And in another, they were outside in the snow. All carefully taken pictures of a man and woman, happy and in love.

And every one torn to shreds, with the woman's head being deliberately torn off, while the man was kept intact, yet discarded, as though in anger.

Alice shivered.

From the doorway, Lilian watched her. "That's private," she said, her voice as cold and hard as her hate-filled eyes. *"You shouldn't be in here!"*

The streets were busy, with mothers pushing prams and hurrying about their chores. They didn't take too much notice of the young woman running through the streets, wild and frantic. A female in flight was not an uncommon occurrence in these winding streets.

Her mind alive with fear and suspicion, Lilian wasn't even aware of their presence. She was running away; looking for some kind of forgiveness. Driven by the ghosts that would not leave her be, she knew one person who would gladly take her in. One friend in all the world.

*For all their sakes, it was time he knew the truth.*

# *Eighteen*

JASPER WAS ON JACK'S BOAT, THE *MARY LOU*, LISTENING to the news on North Korea, where U.S. Marines had been forced to resort to using flame-throwers in an effort to rid the area of snipers. "By! It's a bad old do, an' no mistake," he muttered, sipping his mug of tea. "Thousands med homeless and soldiers being tekken home in boxes. Will it never end?"

He thought back to the terrible years of the last war, and further back to the time when he had been a sailor. He had seen the horrors of war first hand, and it was not something he would ever want to get involved in again. Yet tragically, premature death had now come to West Bay; he'd arrived back from his visit with Liz and Robbie to find that Kathy's sister had met with a terrible accident. Poor Kathy was beside herself: more so, since her mother had turned up.

He thought about Kathy's mother, Irene. She was a hard, unforgiving woman, it seemed to him. "Aye, she's a bad 'un, is that Irene!" he muttered, swilling back the dregs of his tea. "How a mother can turn agin her own child like that is a mystery to me. All right! I know she's grieving and I'm sorry it had to happen that way, but to blame that lass is a sin an' a shame, that's what it is!"

"Talking to yourself again, is it?" Jack's ruddy face peered through the cabin door. "They do say as how it's a sign of madness."

Jasper's face broke into a half-smile. "Oh hello, lad. I were just thinking aloud, that's all. It comes o' growing old,

I expect . . . I hope you don't mind me mekkin' meself at home here while I waited for you?"

"No, of course not," the skipper said, settling himself down before remarking, "Bad business, though, and now they say Kathy's mother is ranting and raving . . . blaming Kathy for what happened. She seems a right old witch; from what I'm told, they can hear her all over the place, screaming like a fishwife. I know she's had shocking things to deal with, but for the life of me I can't see the reasoning behind her attitude to Kathy."

Jasper shook his head. "Ours is not to reason why," he said. "But you're right about one thing . . . her mother has had to bear up to the most shocking news. Summat like that could affect a body real bad." Once more he shook his head slowly from side to side. "It's terrible what happened. It just don't bear thinking about."

"I couldn't help but hear what you were saying . . . just now." While he talked Jack poured himself a cup of tea from the pot. "How is Kathy? Is she coping all right?"

"She's devastated, poor lass." Jasper had only now come back from there. "I were there a few minute since, doing me best, like yer do. Trying to help where I can. Only her mother arrived, so I thought I'd best mek mesel' scarce."

Taking out his hankie, he wiped a dewdrop from the end of his nose. "I can't imagine how it must feel . . . being told that yer daughter's drowned. In one way me old heart goes out to her. But though I say it as shouldn't, that woman's a bad bugger if ever there was one."

"Why don't they get on, her and Kathy?" Jack asked.

"Goes back a long way, from what I understand. According to Kathy, she's never been like a real mother to her. It were Kathy's father who seemed closest to the lass."

Just then he peered out the porthole. "Hang on a minute! Look! Her mam's just going."

Two pairs of eyes followed Irene as she emerged from Kathy's house. Dressed in a dark suit with fur collar and black ankle boots, she was a picture of elegance, much as her elder daughter had been before her.

With her, and holding onto her arm as if to support her,

was a portly man, somewhat older and graying at the temples. "Who's that?" Jack was curious.

"It's Kathy's stepfather." Jasper switched off the radio. "I'd best go and see how she is. I'll see you later."

"Aye, you go on. I'll sit here awhile, afore I take myself off for my tea." He winked. "I reckon the missus will have a tasty hotpot bubbling away on the stove, time I get home."

"Hmh! It's all right for you. Some of us 'ave to do for usselves."

Concerned about Kathy, Jasper clambered his way out of the cabin and onto the deck; from there he shimmied up the mooring rope like a two-year-old. "You ain't lost it yet, old-timer!" Jack called from inside the cabin.

Jasper nodded appreciatively. "Yer should see me on a bad day," he chuckled.

In a minute he was wending his way across the green toward Barden House. Kathy saw him coming and ran to the door. "Oh, Jasper, I was hoping you'd come back when you saw them leave."

"What's up, lass? Yer look badly." Kathy's brown eyes were red and swollen, and her face was all puffed up; it was obvious to anyone who knew her that she was distraught.

Trying hard not to show her emotion, she said, "Tell me the truth, Jasper . . . do you think I was cruel to her? Do you think it's because of me that she's—" After the crippling confrontation with her mother, her resolve failed and she broke down.

"Now then, lass. Take a hold on yersel'." Grabbing her by the shoulders, he drew her to him. "For a start off, I don't think you could be 'cruel' if you tried. And for another thing, it weren't 'cause o' you that she went out."

"But maybe I could have stopped her."

"No, lass! From what you tell me, that sister o' yourn was a law unto hersel'. I dare say if you'd pleaded with her to stay in that night, she would still have gone out and done things the way she wanted. God only knows, what happened to her was a shocking and awful thing, but there was nothing you could have done . . . except maybe to baby her and follow her everywhere she went."

He held her at arm's length, his old heart breaking to see

what a state she was in. "You gave her nowt but kindness. You let her into your home and allowed her to stay . . . even when she let it be known that she were out to take it from you." He gave her a comforting shake. "No, lass, you weren't 'cruel.' You were a good sister. Nobody can tek that away from yer. Just remember that."

Kathy found it hard to believe him. "Mother says I've been selfish and greedy. She says I should have sold this house and given her half . . . that it wasn't much to ask, and I turned my back on her when she needed help." Taking a deep, choking breath, she went on. "Maybe if I'd promised to do what she wanted she would still be here today."

"Now then! Don't torment yersel' with them kinda foolish notions. Y'see, lass . . . we're all on us sent into this 'ere world with a number agin us. When that number is called, we're away to God Almighty, and there ain't nobody—not you, nor me, nor anybody else—as can mek the slightest difference to that."

For a time, Kathy couldn't answer him. Instead, she held onto him, her face buried in his shoulder, and the tears ran freely as she thought of Samantha and the awful way she had died: slipping and knocking her head as she fell into the harbor. "You're a good friend, Jasper," she murmured. "I don't know what I would have done without you."

"I'll tell yer what, lass."

Sniffing, she wiped away the tears. "What?" Looking up at him, she felt safe; absolved somehow.

"How about you mek us a brew, eh? An' we'll sit and decide what's to be done."

A great, heavy sob escaped her, but with it came the tiniest of smiles. "I forgot my manners, didn't I?"

He wagged a podgy finger. "So yer did. Shame on yer!"

He thought it would be good for her to busy herself and take her mind off things. While he waited, he asked about Rosie. "She's been that worried about yer."

Kathy returned with the tea. "Rosie's been wonderful . . . just like you."

Placing the tea in his outstretched hand, she sat in the other chair.

Hesitating just a little because he knew it was a thing close to her heart, he asked pointedly, "D'yer intend asking Tom if he'll come back?"

"No."

"Yer do know where he's staying, don't yer, lass? I mean . . . he did give you an address of sorts, didn't he?"

"I have the address of his hotel, yes." So many times she had been tempted to write to him or telephone, but she hadn't, and she wouldn't. "See, Jasper, if I were to phone him he'd be here straight away, and that wouldn't be fair . . . to get him back just for my sake. He has a job to do, and the last thing I want to do is interfere with that."

"He's bound to telephone *you* sooner or later."

"I know."

"And what will you say to him?"

"That I'm all right, and that I'm missing him. That I love him and can't wait for him to come home."

"Nothing about what happened, then?"

"No."

"What's the name of his hotel?"

"I'm not saying."

"I see." Jasper realized he'd been rumbled. "All right, but he'll not be best pleased when he finds out what's happened, and that you didn't contact him."

"I know that."

"Your choice, lass."

"It's the only choice I've got." She was doing the right thing in leaving Tom out of it. Only she did need him so desperately, especially now.

"I'm going to see Samantha, before she's taken away." Her voice broke, but this time she steadied herself. "I have to say my goodbyes. I have to see her one more time." She bowed her head. "There are things I need to say."

"I understand that, lass. And you do right to go and see her." Though he didn't like the idea of her going on her own, not in her state. "If yer want somebody to come with yer, I'll be on hand, lass."

Kathy thanked him. "Rosie's going with me, but thank you all the same, Jasper. It's good of you to offer."

She glanced toward the stairs. "There's something you could do, if you don't mind, that is?"

"That's what I'm here for, lass . . . to help wherever I can."

"Mother told me to get Samantha's things ready, but I haven't the heart to do it on my own."

" 'Course not, lass. I'll be glad to give a hand, whenever yer ready."

Kathy was in no hurry. "Mother said she'd be back in an hour. We've time yet."

When, an hour later to the minute, Irene and Richard returned, all of Samantha's things were ready for collection.

Fighting back the tears, Kathy had gathered the more personal items, while Jasper had folded her clothes and put them in the small case.

Irene banged on the door in her usual impatient manner. When Kathy opened it, she barged through; on seeing Jasper she demanded to know what he was doing there. "I should have thought this was a time for reflection," she said, spying the two teacups, "instead of drinking tea and behaving as if nothing had happened!"

Up until now, Richard had kept his own counsel, but with Kathy looking so upset and Irene overstepping the mark, he stepped in to chide her. "Easy now, Irene. Everyone needs a friend at times like this." Allowing Jasper a friendly nod, he gave his wife a gentle pat on the shoulder. "I think we should leave now."

Swinging round, she was about to give him a piece of her mind, when she remembered he was not the soft touch she had at first imagined him to be. He had only now reinstated her account because, being the good man he was, he thought she had suffered enough.

"All right." Since he could take her account away any time he thought fit, she needed to keep him sweet, particularly now she no longer had her elder daughter as an ally. "You're right. There's nothing to be gained by getting myself upset all over again."

Before they left she had a warning for Kathy. "I've spent the worst day of my life!" she told her. "The police have given me little peace. I'm desperate to organize for your sis-

ter to be taken home, only they won't release her, not yet."
Her voice trembled. "As for *you!*" She came forward threateningly. "You *monster!*"

When Kathy involuntarily took a step back, Jasper was
there to hold her, his face set hard as he looked at her
mother, and thinking how he was on the verge of showing
her the door.

"It should be you lying there, not Samantha! I know you
plan to see her at rest, but I don't want you anywhere near
her! It's all your fault that this has happened. You're a
wicked, selfish creature, and I wash my hands of you. As far
as I'm concerned, I have no family now . . ." She turned to
smile weakly at her husband. "Only my darling Richard,"
she added disingenuously.

When again she turned to round on Kathy, Jasper stepped
forward. "I would not normally interfere in family business," he said respectfully, "and I'm very sorry for your loss.
But I think you should listen to your husband." He smiled
sadly. "Best to leave now, I reckon."

"Really!" After staring at him for what seemed an age,
she stormed out, with Richard lingering to apologize to
Kathy before he, too, was gone.

"She can't stop you from seeing yer sister, if that's what
you want, lass." Jasper had never before encountered such a
horrid creature as Kathy's mother.

The tirade of abuse had shaken Kathy but after a minute
or two at the window, watching them depart, she quickly recovered. She felt stronger and more determined. "If they'll
let me, I *will* go and see her. I *have* to." Her mind was made
up.

Later that afternoon, she and Rosie set off. "Are you sure
you want to do this, me darling?" Rosie was nervous for her.
"Sure, it'll not be a pleasant thing, you do realize that?"

"She's my sister."

"Ah, I know. I'll be there with you, so I will."

Just as Rosie promised, seeing Samantha like that was not

a pleasant thing. In fact, it was the hardest thing Kathy had ever had to do in the whole of her life. With her father, the pain of losing him had been lessened by the fact that, for him, it was a merciful release. That was not the case with Samantha.

After being greeted at the desk, she was quickly taken downstairs; big green doors were swept open and she was led into a large, clinical-looking room. In the center of the room was a trestle, and on the trestle was Samantha's body, covered in a white cloth. "We've done our best," the policeman explained, "but you do realize she isn't as you would see her in a chapel of rest." The man was a kindly soul, with the gentlest of smiles. The police had been concerned at first, wanting to establish how Samantha had come to fall in backward: there was a nasty blow to the back of her head. But with no evidence of foul play, they were about to release her body.

Kathy nodded. With Rosie at her side, Kathy stepped forward; while Rosie turned her head, she watched him peel back the cloth. There, cold and still, was Samantha.

Catching a breath, Kathy fought back the tears. "Can I have a minute with her?" she asked brokenly.

"I understand." The policeman and Rosie stepped back, toward the far end of the room, from where they watched but could not hear. Only the soft murmurings of Kathy's voice broke the silence.

Taking a moment to gaze down on that familiar face, Kathy wondered at her sister's proud beauty. In all her life she had never seen Samantha look so calm and pure. Her head was discreetly covered with a fine, lace cloth, while her face was like cold, chiseled marble. "You're very beautiful, Samantha," she whispered, "but you shouldn't be here. You should be dancing and shopping, and wearing the fine clothes you love so much."

For a minute she couldn't go on. Unbearable emotion clogged her throat and the tears fell, regardless of her determination not to cry. "Forgive me," she murmured, "but I couldn't let you take what you wanted. If that was wrong of me, then I'm sorry. I don't know if I was right or wrong to refuse you, but oh—" her voice broke; the tears blurred her vision—"if only I could turn back the clock, we might have come to some sort of compromise. I don't know. I'll *never* know."

Reaching out, she touched her face, shocked by the coldness of her skin. "What went wrong between us? Why couldn't we get it right?"

Raising her hand, she wiped away the blinding tears. "Rest now, Samantha," she whispered. "I only wish things could have been different . . ."

She looked at her sister's quiet face for a moment longer, taking it in, preserving it in her memory. Leaning forward, she kissed her, shocked to realize that it was a long time since she had done that. "Goodbye, Samantha."

When, a few minutes later, she and Rosie emerged from that formidable building, Kathy needed a moment to lean against the wall, her face ashen, her whole body trembling.

In this moment of harsh reality, she needed Tom more than ever.

# *Nineteen*

TOM HAD CALLED IN TO HIS OLD OFFICE TO SAY HELLO. "Well, I never!" The boss was delighted to see him. "I daren't ask whether you've come back to work?"

Tom laughed. "Still running full pelt, with never enough staff to keep it covered, eh?"

John Martin laughed: Tom knew the ins and outs of this business almost as well as he did. "You've got that right."

"I just called in to see Lilian, but she wasn't there. Gone out on an errand, has she?" Occasionally, she might have to go out for emergency supplies, such as typewriter ribbons when her own stock ran out; it was unusual but had been known to happen. Or meat pies from the corner shop, when the boss hadn't had time for breakfast.

John Martin explained. "Alice came up here this morning in a panic. She had this idea that Lilian was, well . . . not her usual self—" he grimaced "—if you know what I mean?"

"Not really, no." Having already heard disturbing news which he believed had to do with Lilian, Tom felt decidedly uncomfortable. "Is she *ill?*"

"Well, yes, I suppose she is." He still didn't know what to think. "Well, anyway, I thought Alice might be acting a bit hysterical, but when I went down to take a look, she was quite right to fetch me . . ." He nodded to himself. "Sensible young thing, Alice. Yes, I can see her going places in this establishment."

Right now, Tom wasn't interested in internal politics. "You were saying?"

"Oh, yes! Lilian was acting very strangely, talking and muttering to herself. When I gave her some important papers to deal with, she immediately began tearing them up and throwing them in the bin." His face contorted with astonishment. "Lilian, of all people! Can you believe that?"

Tom grew increasingly worried. This news only heightened his suspicions that it really was Lilian in the churchyard. What was she playing at? Even now, he found it hard to believe. "Where is she now?"

"I had to send her home. What else could I do? It's obvious she needs a doctor. I laid a car on, and Alice went with her. I made sure Alice knew to call the doctor from a phone box once she'd got to Lilian's house."

Before he could say any more, Tom was out of his chair and at the door. "I have to go and see her," he said. "See how she is."

The boss nodded. "But you'll call back, I hope. We could go out for a drink. I'd like us to catch up on things."

Tom had been his right-hand man. If he could persuade him back again, it would make life that much easier. "Dougie and John have been up in Leeds. Hang about until they get back, won't you? Apparently they're having serious problems with that roof design you warned about. You were right. It's been nothing but trouble from the outset."

"Well, I hate to say it, but you should have listened." Tom was a hard taskmaster when it came to business. He knew his stuff and had no patience when others chose to bypass him.

"First and last time, I swear!" John Martin had no choice but to admit he was in the wrong. "Look, Tom, they really are getting into deep water with this one. I'm sure they'd love to talk things over with you. Spend an hour or so with them, will you do that, Tom . . . for old times' sake?"

"I'll try." Tom couldn't say no. "When are they back?"

"Any time now, I reckon . . . They'll ring in today, anyway—I'll let them know you're in London."

"Okay." With Kathy heavy on his mind, he wanted to get back as soon as possible, and that meant concentrating fully on getting to the bottom of who had caused the accident. He could do without distractions like these.

He promised to see them if he was still in London when they returned. "I don't know how long I'll be here," he admitted. Taking in a deep breath, he then blew it out in a soft whistle. "If I can, you know I will." And, knowing how Tom never gave his word unless he meant to keep it, the boss was a happier man.

Having run down the stairs two at a time, Tom was almost out the door when the receptionist called him back. "It's Mr. Martin on the telephone for you, sir." Being young and aware of Tom's admirable reputation in this establishment, she addressed him with a degree of reverence.

Thanking her, Tom took the call. "Tom here."

"Sorry, Tom, but Dougie just called. Apparently he's just got back from Leeds to find Lilian in his house. Seems she broke a window to get in. She was stretched out on his couch, her arm dripping blood all over the place, and asking after *you!* Dougie reckons she's drunk, or drugged, or some such thing, because she's not making any sense. He doesn't know what to do, so he asked me to go over, but when I told him you were here, he asked me to tell you that you're probably the only one who can do anything with her. Look, Tom, I'm sorry. But he wants you to get over there as quick as you can!"

Tom was both relieved and worried. "Right! I'm on my way. Thanks." Replacing the receiver, he hurried out to the street and hailed a taxi. When one slewed over from the main run of traffic, he climbed in and gave the address. "There's an extra five bob in it if you can put your foot down."

Five bob was the only incentive the driver needed.

In a matter of seconds, he was screeching in and out of traffic with no thought for life or limb.

At the same time a frantic Alice was arriving back at the office and trying to work out what on earth she could or should tell her boss. She could only guess at where Lilian had got to, and feared she might somehow get the blame for letting her out of her sight.

From the sitting room couch, where Dougie had thought-fully tended her arm and made her as comfortable as he knew how, Lilian stretched her neck to hear what he was saying.

She suspected he had gone into the hall to make a tele-phone call, and now she was proved right. "Who are you calling?" Struggling up, she felt dizzy and unwell, but fear proved stronger than pain. She made her way into the hall just as Dougie was replacing the receiver. "You called the doctor, didn't you?" Her eyes were wild. "I told you not to call the doctor! I said to call Tom . . . *that's* what I said."

When he reached out to calm her, she jerked away from him, her back to the front door and her arms jutting out, warding him off. "You knew I wanted to see him, but you've tricked me!"

Desperate to reassure her, Dougie spoke softly. "No, Lil-ian . . . please, listen to me. I *didn't* call the doctor; I called John Martin . . . I thought he might be able to help. Only Tom was there. He was at the office, looking for you. He's on his way now, Lilian . . . he'll be here any minute!"

"LIAR! You rang the doctor. Well, you wasted your time because I won't be here when he comes."

Before he could stop her, she had opened the front door and was on her way into the street, careering and stumbling as she went. "LILIAN, COME BACK!"

Running out of the front door, he went in pursuit, afraid for her safety as she ran across the road, with traffic coming at her from all quarters. "I WAS TELLING YOU THE TRUTH!"

The driver of Tom's taxi was well pleased with himself. "Here we are, guv. I reckon I've earned that five bob." Turn-ing into the road, he saw Lilian dodging the traffic. "Christ Almighty! What the hell does she think she's doing?" As she ran onto the pavement, he slowed down. "Look at that!" In her desperate effort to get away, Lilian skidded into a woman with a pram; the pram was overturned and the child left screaming in fright.

"Stop the cab!" Tom was amazed to see that it was Lilian.

"Stop here!" Digging into his pocket, he threw a handful of money onto the passenger seat.

Even before the wheels had stopped turning, he was out of the cab and after Lilian, who by this time was causing havoc as she swerved and stumbled, crashing into passers-by and shouting abuse when they confronted her. When one irate man gave her a shove, she laid into him; a police officer who had been patrolling the area in his car saw the fracas, screeched to a halt and, running across the road, came between them.

Pushing the man away with a caution, he began lecturing Lilian on the trouble she was causing.

Seeming to find her second wind, Lilian began kicking and fighting. While he tried hard to control her, she went for him like a wildcat, scoring his face with her nails and lashing out with fists and feet.

"Right, young lady!" Managing to take a firm hold, he promptly arrested her for being "drunk and disorderly, and causing an affray in a public place." But still she fought. It was only the sight of Tom jumping from his taxi that calmed her. Instantly, she became passive and quiet.

With both Dougie and Tom on the scene now, the police officer felt order returning. Inundated with protests, he conceded that, yes, she did need a doctor, and, no, he would not turn her loose. "She's a menace to herself and others. But she'll get a doctor once we're at the station."

As they went across to the car, Lilian kept glancing at Tom. When she was being bundled into the car, Dougie climbed in on the other side; the police officer made no protest at that. His thinking was that, if she ran off again, he would have to run after her, and he was not as slim and quick as he used to be.

"Make sure she gets a doctor," Tom advised Dougie. "I'll see you later."

He took it on himself to close the door on her; it was at that moment she looked up at him. In the softest of whispers that only he heard, she told him, "I'm sorry, Tom. I didn't mean to do it."

The door shut, and the car was soon away, Lilian looking back at him with stricken eyes.

For a long time, Tom stood there, her words echoing in his mind. *"I'm sorry . . . I didn't mean to do it."*

He couldn't believe what she had implied. That day? Surely to God, it couldn't have been Lilian. *Could it?*

His instincts were to go after her, to ask her outright what she meant just now when she said she was sorry . . . that she "didn't mean to do it."

Dejected and unsure, he made his way back to his hotel; even now he was reluctant to convey his suspicions to the inspector.

Back in his hotel room, he took a small drink to steady his nerves.

Never far from his thoughts, Kathy preyed on his mind. "Oh, Kathy, what am I supposed to think?"

Just to talk to her, to know she was there, waiting for him, might settle his mind.

With that in mind he picked up the receiver and asked the operator to put him through to the caravan site; with luck he should catch her there, he thought.

It was Rosie who answered. "No, she isn't here," she said. "She's just popped out to one of the caravans, but I'll tell her you called."

"Thank you, Rosie. Is she all right?" he asked. He was bitterly disappointed, but it wasn't the end of the world.

"She's fine," she lied.

"Oh good," Tom said. "I'll ring later. Tell her that, will you?"

"I'll tell her the minute she comes in, so I will," Rosie promised.

Putting the phone down, she made the sign of the cross over her chest. "God forgive me!" she muttered. Lying was not one of her usual traits, but she knew that, however much Kathy needed him here, she did not want him rushing back on her account.

Later, during her break, she made her way around to Barden House, not surprised to see Jasper there. "Hello, Jasper. How are you doing?"

"Not so bad, lass." He shook his head. "Terrible business, ain't it?"

Rosie nodded but made no comment. Instead she glanced at Kathy. "What you got there, me darling?"

Until Jasper came to see how she was, Kathy had been looking through old photographs of her and Samantha as children. "I keep looking at these photographs," she said, showing one to Rosie.

Rosie glanced at the tiny black-and-white photograph of the two little girls, all dressed up and sitting on a bench. Even then you could see how different they were, with Samantha neat and tidy, her hair in ribbons, and the smaller girl, hair blowing in the wind, and a huge grin on her face. "Sure, I could tell you anywhere," she said, handing back the photograph.

Sliding them back into the envelope, Kathy told them, "We were close as children, and then somehow it all went wrong." She glanced at Jasper, who for the past half-hour had sat with her, quietly listening while she opened her heart to him. "And now it's all too late."

She choked back a sigh. "I still can't believe what's happened. I can't sleep. I keep thinking about it. Why Samantha?"

"I'm sure I don't know why, me darling," Rosie answered. "I think it was just a terrible accident."

Jasper had thought about that. Since he'd learned how Samantha was wearing Kathy's coat that night, he couldn't help but wonder.

*If for whatever reason it had not been a terrible accident, it could so easily have been Kathy.*

Rosie's voice interrupted his thoughts. "Tom rang."

Kathy's eyes lit up. "What did he say? How is he? Does he knew yet when he'll be coming home?"

Rosie replied, "He didn't say anything much, except that he would call later."

"You didn't tell him, did you, Rosie . . . about Samantha?"

"Not a word passed my lips."

Kathy thanked her. "You're a good friend." She smiled at Jasper, who winked back at her. "You're *both* good friends."

Jasper was of the same mind as Rosie. "He would want you to tell him. You know that, don't yer?"

"Yes, but I won't do it." Kathy had not changed her mind on that score. "Tom's got enough to be worrying about," she said. "There'll be time enough to tell him when he comes home."

Though Rosie was all for bringing him back to be with Kathy, Jasper could see her reasoning. Tom had confided in him, and he knew how hard it had been for Tom to gather the strength of mind and purpose to tear himself away and go back to what had been his own personal nightmare. Jasper believed that Kathy was right; besides, there was nothing anyone could do to change things. He and Rosie would look after Kathy, while Tom got on with his business in London.

He got out of his chair. "Right, you two, who's for a brew?"

Ambling into the kitchen, he put the kettle on.

In his room, pacing the floor, Tom continued thinking and wondering, his mind in a whirl.

He went over everything that happened on that day, trying to imagine it might have been Lilian in that car, ramming and pushing them nearer and nearer to that cliff-edge.

Somehow he still could not bring himself to believe it was her.

Then he recalled his wife's face as she glanced back: he had seen the recognition in her eyes, and the horror of realization. *She knew whoever it was!* And yet in that split second, when she might have cried out Lilian's name, she didn't. *Why not?*

Was it because, like him, she couldn't believe it? Or didn't want to?

Was it for the same reason he had not gone after Lilian just now . . . reluctant to implicate her? Trying to delay the inevitable?

Or was it because, in the goodness of her heart and with

only moments before they went over that cliff-edge, she saw Lilian as the friend she had been. Did her instincts—the goodness in her—make her hold back?

Or was she merely silenced by the shock of it all?

These were only more questions to be added to the ones already troubling him.

"There's only one way to find out!" He would have to go and speak with her, ask her what she meant just now.

With his heart in his mouth, he made for the door, but as he was about to open it and leave, the ringing of the telephone startled him. Going back, he snatched up the receiver. "Yes?"

A moment, then, "Oh, it's you, Inspector. Any news?"

"Yes, finally," the inspector said. "We think we've had a bit of a breakthrough!" The inspector cautioned, "Nothing is certain yet; I need to see for myself . . . ask a few questions before I get too carried away. But it sounds hopeful. My sergeant had a hunch and it seems to have paid off. Look, I'm on my way to him now. Stay where you are. I'll pick you up as I go."

At the station Lilian was signed in as being drunk and disorderly on a public highway.

The doctor was sent for and she was made to wait in the cubicle. Dougie had stayed with her throughout it all.

It wasn't long before the doctor arrived. Gray-haired and gray-faced, he looked as if the world weighed heavy on his shoulders. "And what have you been up to, young lady?" He had one of those soothing voices that made a body feel calm. "Apart from the gash on your arm, is there anything else I should check out? Have you broken anything, do you think?"

"No, I don't think I've broken anything."

"Well, we had better give you a thorough check all the same. We don't want to send you away with a broken leg or a dislocated vertebra or goodness knows what else, or we'd have to answer for it afterward, wouldn't we, eh?" He frowned. "Now then, young lady. From what I've been told, you've been on quite an adventure."

First rolling up her sleeve so the doctor could get to the gash on her arm, Lilian asked Dougie, "Could you give me a minute, please, Dougie?" Calm and rational now, she smiled appreciatively. "I'm glad you're here though."

Satisfied to leave her in safe hands, Dougie agreed. "I'll see if I can scrounge a drink of sorts," he said. "But I won't be far away if you need me."

As he made his way along the corridor, he was amazed at his own feelings. "You've fallen for her, haven't you?" He gave a soft, cynical laugh. "You promised yourself you'd never get trapped again, and now here you are . . . caught, hook, line and sinker!"

Finding a friendly young officer who brought him a "nice cup of tea," he sat on the bench by the window and watched the traffic go by. "Who would have thought it?" he wondered with a smile. "Me and Lilian." He supped his tea and settled back. Life wasn't so bad after all.

Behind him, with the curtains closed and the two of them alone in the cubicle, Lilian beckoned the doctor closer. "Is everything all right?"

"What? Apart from the wound, you mean?"

"Yes."

"Everything's fine," he said. "You should be on your way home quite soon now, especially when I tell them you are *not* 'drunk,' as they claim, and that, as far as I can see, you are certainly not 'disorderly.'"

He bustled off to disclose his findings to the officer-in-charge.

Some time later, in view of the circumstances, Lilian was allowed to leave, with all charges dropped. But not without a stern warning. "You caused havoc on the street and attacked a police officer in the execution of his duty. However, on the doctor's recommendation, we'll waive any charges this time. But if ever I hear your name or see you in this station again, I'll throw the book at you. Am I making myself clear?"

Calmer of mind now, Lilian nodded acknowledgment.

She then apologized to the police officer who had been on the receiving end of her feet and fists, and hurried out of there while the going was good.

"Come on, I'll take you home." Putting an arm around her, Dougie urged her toward a waiting taxi.

Lilian paused. "I don't want to go home." Afraid of what awaited her there, she urged, "Can we go to your place instead? Just for a while?"

"I've got a better idea."

"What's that?"

"Are you hungry?"

She hadn't thought about it before but declared, "I'm starving!"

"Right! Then let's find some quiet little café."

Lilian wasn't sure. "I'm not dressed for going out. Besides, I look a mess." Lately she had not bothered about her appearance so much. Everything had been a chore. Her life had been empty and it hadn't seemed to matter, but now she was beginning to realize how wrong she had been. "Do you know a restaurant where they might not take too close a look at their customers?"

Having heard the conversation, the driver's ears pricked up. "I know a place where it won't matter *what* you look like," he interrupted. "Italian . . . best food in London, and I should know, because it's my mamma who owns it."

Unbeknown to Dougie and Lilian, this was the same driver who had recommended the place to Tom.

"You're on!" For Lilian's sake, Dougie took him at his word.

When they got there, the Italian mamma came running out. "Oh, look! Come on inside . . . we have the special pasta today . . . pizza . . . everything you want!" Small and round, her teeth flashing brilliant in her smooth dark skin, she ushered them inside. "You get away and find me the more customers!" she told her grinning son. "Hurry! Go! Go!" And, as always, he did as he was told.

As they were shown to their table, Dougie told Lilian, "I'd best ring the boss and tell him I'll be in later," and that Lilian had calmed down, he mentally added. He slid an arm around her shoulders. "There's no rush though. I want you and me to talk . . . I need to know what made you flip your lid like that."

Lilian smiled as though in agreement. But she wouldn't tell him.

*She couldn't!*

Not without telling him the truth, and she was too nervous to do that.

# *Twenty*

---

IN THE CAR WITH INSPECTOR LAWSON, TOM WAS IMPA-
tient for details. "So, what's happened? You said
you'd made a breakthrough."

"I hope so, yes, but I can't tell for certain until I get there."

"What exactly is it . . . this 'breakthrough?' "

"Well, you recall, along with everything else, we checked
every breaker's yard in the vicinity of the accident and your
home."

"So?"

"So, one of the yards up here belonged to a Jimmy
Rollinson." Overtaking a bus, he paused for a minute, continuing when he slid back into the flow of traffic.

"We turned his place upside down like all the others,
looking for a blue Hillman Minx, but at the time we were
satisfied the car had not been taken in. Well, this morning,
we had a call from Jimmy Rollinson. He said he'd found
something, and that we should go and take a look."

Arriving at the scrapyard in question, the inspector drew
the car to a halt; there, only a few feet away, was his sergeant
and with him—a long, slim beanpole of a man.

As Tom and the inspector climbed out of the car, the sergeant came rushing forward. "I think we're onto something!" he said excitedly. "Take a look at this."

Leading the way, he and Jimmy Rollinson took them to
the back of the yard, where work was underway to clear a
huge area. "I'm selling up," Rollinson informed them.
"After thirty years at this little lot, I've had enough. It's time

I put my feet up and took things a bit easier. So, as you can see, I'm clearing the whole site and putting it up for development."

He gave a click of admiration. "This yard covers upward of two acres—in a prime position, too. I've seen land go for silly money and I want some of it. Once it's cleared and made respectable, I reckon there'll be plenty of companies who'd pay a fortune for this little parcel."

The inspector was more interested in what his sergeant had found. "What's the panic then?"

"Round here, sir." Going ahead, he went around the mountainous piles of junk, deeper into the maze of crushed cars and broken metal, and there, in a deep hollow of earth up against a wall, was the blue Hillman Minx car which Jimmy Rollinson had found on scraping back the mangled wreckage.

"I had no idea," he said. "Like I told your sergeant, the damned thing was so well concealed, I'm not surprised you couldn't find it the last time you were here. I pride myself on knowing every single car that comes in here . . . it's all logged in the book. But not this time, more's the pity!"

"So, when you're not here," the inspector asked, "who keeps the ledger then?"

"Even when I *am* away, which isn't often enough, I can tell you, I make sure the foreman records everything for when I get back. He's a trusted bloke, Cyril. I've never had any reason to doubt his word, and I don't doubt it now. If he says he knew nothing whatsoever about this particular car, I believe him, all the way."

"Where is he, this foreman of yours?"

Jimmy Rollinson jerked a thumb toward the run of buildings on the other side of the yard. "The sergeant told him to wait in the office. He knew you'd want to speak with him."

The inspector nodded. "He's not likely to scarper, is he?"

Rollinson chuckled at that. "Cyril? Hardly! It takes him all his time to *waddle,* let alone 'scarper.' And he's got a gammy leg into the bargain. The poor old bugger should have been retired years since, only I've a soft spot for him, and, besides, he knows how to make a belting cup of tea.

Apart from that, he needs the money. His wife's not been well of late. He's had to get her a wheelchair, and a special bed so she can get in and out more easily. It all costs money, I'm afraid."

Proud of himself, he grinned from ear to ear. "I sent the pair of 'em on a little holiday last year, but you can't keep on helping out, can you? I reckon I'm doing more than my fair share by keeping him on here . . . he's coming up seventy if he's a day."

Aware of how quiet Tom had gone, the inspector turned toward him. "All right, are you, Tom?"

Tom's gaze was glued to the car: with its bent body and crushed bumper, the blue Hillman Minx was burnt into his brain. "I can't be sure until I see it front on, but, from here, it could be the same one."

In his mind it came alive: the big headlamps set either side of the high grille—like bared teeth. Through that broken window he could see the shape of the figure behind the wheel, but he couldn't see the face; the hat was pulled down and he couldn't see! "I can't be sure . . ." he murmured. "But it could be . . ." All his instincts cried out. "Yes, it could be."

Rollinson was chattering on. "That's yer 1947 Hillman Minx, there," he said. " 'Mediterranean Blue,' they called that color." He laughed. "Where they get these names, I can't imagine!"

"Right!" The inspector issued orders to his sergeant. "Give me what you've got so far."

The sergeant told him all he had learned. "Apparently, there used to be a young lad working here, name of William Aitken. Some weeks after we'd searched this yard, he handed in his notice and left."

Rollinson thought to interrupt here. "I didn't think nothing of it at the time. Lads come and go every week." He grimaced with disgust. "There's none of 'em can do a day's work . . . always looking for a handout, looking for that pot of gold at the end of the rainbow."

Not happy at having been interrupted in that way, the sergeant continued. "Anyway, Mr. Rollinson heard nothing of this William Aitken until another lad came here looking for work."

To the sergeant's annoyance, Rollinson butted in again. "I didn't set him on . . . too skinny by half, he was. This is heavy stuff here. You need stamina to shift these big machines and such. Besides, the young bugger stank of booze . . . full of himself, he was."

"Thank you, Mr. Rollinson, I've got it all written down, exactly as Cyril told me." Giving him a warning glance, the sergeant went on. "Anyway, sir, as I understand it, the lad had something interesting to say to the foreman. Mr. Rollinson here thought it was the drinking—that is, until the bulldozer uncovered this car. He remembered what the lad said to Cyril, and decided to call us. Perhaps it would be easier if we carried on in the office," the sergeant suggested. "Then we could hear the foreman's side of the story."

They made their way back to the buildings on the far side of the site, eventually installing themselves in the office with the foreman.

Having explained to Cyril what they knew so far, the inspector directed his next question to him. "What was it this lad said to you, then?"

"Well, you can imagine, I didn't take no notice at the time—lads will say anything when they've had a pint or two. But, well, he'd got chatting to me before the boss spoke to him—the boss was busy with a delivery. Anyway, he said as how he and another young lad, who he kept referring to as William, had been out on the town, and that he had mentioned to the other lad that he was looking for a job."

Cyril tried to recall the lad's exact words. "He said William had told him he should come and work here, because there was money to be had . . . that he'd been given a small fortune to conceal a car . . . said the boss was hardly ever there, so it was easy enough to do. He asked me if I'd ever got money for hiding a car, cheeky devil!" Cyril looked suitably indignant.

His boss gestured to the other side of the site. "It wasn't until we uncovered that car that I put two and two together."

The sergeant took up the story. "I'm afraid we've got no name or address for this young man. Mr. Rollinson sent him on his way with a flea in his ear, and he's not seen him since."

"Well, o' course I sent him on his way!" Rollinson wasn't taking the blame for anything. "You can't have people drinking and such on this job! You've got to have your wits about you, working on a site like this!"

The inspector was not a man to be beaten. "Right, then!" He instructed his sergeant to "Get that little lot cordoned off, and don't let anybody near it. I want a forensic study of that car; make sure it's gone over with a fine-tooth comb!"

Addressing Cyril and the site-owner, he said, "Right, I want a description of this young man, and anything else you can remember."

Tom sat silently, every now and then glancing over to the car, seeing it all, his heart heavy. But there was hope.

At long last, there was hope.

❧

Further questioning of Cyril produced no more information. The old foreman was adamant. "I knew nothing about that car." Sucking on his pipe, he explained. "Okay, I may have nipped down the shop for a wad o' baccy occasionally, but otherwise I was here all the time with that lad, William. And I always padlocked the gate if I went out! Mr. Rollinson will tell you the very same." His weary old gaze shifted to the boss. "Ain't that so, boss?"

Jimmy Rollinson backed up his statement. "I'd trust Cyril with my life. It was the young layabout who did it. Find him, and you'll find the culprit!"

A few minutes later, when Tom was preparing to leave them to it, he drew the inspector aside. "The old man's holding something back."

The inspector didn't agree. "What makes you say that?"

"I'm not sure." Tom gave it a moment's thought. "He seemed shifty. A bit too nervous for my liking."

Though he wasn't convinced, Inspector Lawson agreed to go and have another word with the old man. "My money's on the William lad," he said. "But look, you get off now. Leave it to us. When we find him, I'll be in touch."

Tom wanted to be sure. "You will keep me informed every step of the way, won't you?"

The older man slapped a hand on his shoulder. "Stop worrying. Now that we've got a lead, you can be sure I won't let it go until it leads us to the killer."

He pointed to the car driving toward them. "Look. Here's your taxi. I'll get back to Mr. Rollinson and see if there's anything else he can tell me about that young William Aitken."

Still unsure about the old foreman, Tom climbed into the taxi.

It was time to go and speak with Lilian. "I'm sorry," that's what she'd said. "I didn't mean to do it."

Tom couldn't get it out of his mind.

On arrival at Lilian's house, he was not wholly surprised to find she was not at home. Surely she wasn't still at the police station, though?

He made his way back to the waiting taxi, disappointed and thoughtful. I wonder if she's at Dougie's, he mused.

With that in mind he climbed back into the taxi and gave the driver Dougie's address. Later, when he got back to the hotel, he would call Kathy. God! How he was missing her.

John Martin was a patient man, but when he'd asked for his documents from a file, he didn't expect to be kept waiting. "What the devil's going on around here! I called that girl more than ten minutes ago. It can't be taking her all this time to find one set of documents!"

Alice was back in the office. He thought she'd looked rather subdued, and maybe a little pale since the incident with Lilian, but when he asked her if she was all right, she told him she was fine. Lilian, too, she'd said—sleeping soundly.

Irritated, he picked up the telephone to call again, but, deciding the best course of action would be to go down and "collect the damned documents myself!," he slammed the receiver back into its cradle. "If you want anything doing, do it yourself!"

Bouncing out of his high-backed leather chair, he marched out of the office and, running down the steps two at a time, was soon in the lower offices.

He went straight to Alice's desk. She wasn't there. "Jesus! Where the devil is she now?" Looking round, he could see she wasn't with any of the typists. He was on the verge of asking one of them where she was when, out of the corner of his eye, he saw her.

He glanced through the window of Lilian's office and there she was.

Seated at Lilian's desk, Alice was holding something in her hands and staring down at it. "What the hell is she playing at?"

Red-faced with anger, he marched across and flung open the door. "If you can't do the job anymore, you'd best tell me now!" he yelled.

Startled, Alice leapt up, her face riddled with guilt. The papers she had been staring at were now all over the floor. "I'm sorry, Mr. Martin, only I was just putting these away." Scrabbling them up, she kept glancing at him, frightened he might see. "I'll have the documents on your desk in five minutes," she promised.

Seeing the guilt and worry on her face, and seeing how her hands trembled as she quickly grabbed up the pieces of paper, he became suspicious. "What have you got there?" Leaning down, he collected one of the papers from the floor.

At first he didn't realize what he was looking at, but then he recognized Tom, smiling and content, with his family. "Where did you get this?" Reaching out, he took the pictures from her, looking through them one by one and growing more curious by the minute. "I think you'd best explain, young lady!"

Tom had only just arrived back at his hotel room, after finding his brother still out, when the phone rang. It was John

Martin. "I'm glad I've caught you," he said. "I've got Alice here. She has something to tell you—" he lowered his voice to an intimate level "—something I think you should know."

Intrigued, Tom waited while Alice was put on the phone.

In a trembling voice, she put together all the missing pieces: of how she'd taken Lilian home and stayed with her for a while; how she had been amazed to see the house "like a tip," and how she had gone upstairs to see if that was the same. "I only meant to tidy it all up," she explained in tears. "I wasn't being nosy, only I found something in her bedroom: photographs, dozens of them, all over the walls."

When she started crying, Tom urged her to take a minute and calm herself. Somehow he had known Lilian had been involved, only his affection for her had clouded his judgment. "All right, Alice, go slowly now. Tell me everything you know. Don't leave anything out."

Encouraged, Alice told him everything: about the photographs of himself and his family; about the way Lilian had seemed ready to kill her when she saw her looking at the photographs. "She was like a stranger," she sobbed. "For a minute I really thought she would hurt me. But then she ran out of the house, and down the street—like a wild thing, she was!"

Feeling like he'd been kicked in the stomach, Tom asked her quietly, "When was this?"

"This morning, about eleven or something. She just ran and ran . . . I don't know *where* she is."

In his mind's eye Tom saw the hysterical Lilian being charged by the policeman at Dougie's house; the way she'd looked at Tom, and those words . . . The long, slow sigh seemed to come up from his very soul. He thought for a minute, then in a quiet voice he thanked her. "Let me speak with Mr. Martin now."

When the boss came on the phone, Tom explained the situation. "I had a gut feeling she might be involved somehow," he explained. "But she was a good friend to Sheila . . . she came to the house, and even went away with us one weekend." He shook his head disbelievingly. "It just seems too incredible. I had no idea . . . no idea at all."

She was obviously ill; needed help—and quickly. "Look, if she comes back to the office, keep her there. If she calls in, keep track of her. Call the police now. Tell them what Alice just told me. I'll try and get hold of Inspector Lawson."

When the other man assured him he would do it, Tom rang down to reception. A moment or two later, having got the number of the breaker's yard, he quickly dialed it, relieved when Rollinson answered. "This is Tom Marcus," he told him. "Is the inspector still there?"

"There are all sorts of people here, crawling about the car. I think the inspector was talking to his sergeant. Do you want me to give him a message?"

"Is it possible you could get him to the phone?"

"I should think so. Hang on a minute." Leaving Tom waiting at the other end, he rushed outside, where he soon found the inspector. "Mr. Marcus is on the phone," he said. "He'd like a word."

"Dammit!" Though he appreciated Tom's concern, he still had a job to do. "Tell him I'll ring him back when I can."

"Sure."

But as Rollinson made his way back, the inspector had a change of heart. "No, wait!" He went after him. "It's all right."

In the office, he listened to what Tom had to say.

Afterward, he had two questions. "And you say you can't find her—either at her home, or at your brother's?"

"No, and, like I said, the last time I saw her she was being taken off to a police station."

"Okay, I'll check at the nearest one to your brother's house whether she's still there, or whether they know where she is. Also, give me her home address." He waited for Rollinson to bring him pen and paper. "Yes, I know she wasn't there when you went, but she's bound to turn up there sooner or later, and when she does, I'll have    of my officers waiting."

He wrote down Lilian's home address. "And your brother, where does he live?"

After giving him Dougie's address, Tom asked, "Do you want me to go and see if either of them are back?"

"No. I'll deal with it. You just sit tight. I might have need of you before the night is out."

Tom had some questions of his own. "The car . . . is it the one?"

"We can't be sure yet, Tom, but yes, it does seem that way."

Tom took a minute to speak, and when he did it was with another question. "What about that young man . . . the one Mr. Rollinson said came looking for a job? Have you found him yet?"

"No. But we will. I've already got two officers on the case."

"What about the other one . . . William Aitken?"

"He's being pulled in even as we speak. I'm on my way back to the station now."

When the conversation was over, Tom went down to the hotel bar, where he ordered a whiskey short. Sitting quietly at a corner table, he mulled over the events of the past few days.

After a while, when he began to grow lonely, his thoughts turned to Kathy.

He decided to give her a call.

With that in mind he went back up to his room and dialed the caravan site. This time it was the manager who answered. "You've just missed her. She and Rosie aren't working this evening—they've gone off together . . . things to do and all that. I'm sure you understand." He lowered his voice. "Rosie's been a godsend. I thought it only fair to give her a night off, since it's quiet."

"Thanks," Tom said. "I'll try her tomorrow." Replacing the phone, he mused aloud. "Rosie's been a godsend." He wondered about that. "Hmh! Strange thing to say." He knew Rosie was a good friend, and he supposed what with him being here and Kathy being there, she was feeling every bit as miserable as he was, but it sounded . . . Oh, maybe he was being over-analytical about everything at the moment. He shook himself. "I'm glad Rosie's keeping her company. But it should be me!"

He wished with all his heart that he was back there, with Kathy.

He reminded himself that he had a job to do. After it was over, he and Kathy would have all the time in the world. The rest of their lives together. Yes! That was worth waiting for.

He decided to try Dougie's number again, but there was no answer.

Disappointed, he rang the station. The officer at the desk knew him straight away. "I'm sorry, Mr. Marcus, but the inspector is busy, and he'll be busy for some time yet. Look, if you want to leave a message, I'm sure he'll ring you back when he's finished interviewing."

Tom pounced on that particular remark. "So, have they brought the young man in? William Aitken, the one who worked at the breaker's yard? Is he the one being interviewed?"

"I'm sorry, Mr. Marcus, sir, I can't give out that kind of information."

"For Chrissake, man! You know what it's all about. I've been with the inspector for most of the day. I already know they were onto Aitken. All I'm asking is for you to confirm that they've got him."

The officer's voice took on an officious tone. "Sorry, sir. I'll tell him you called."

The conversation was abruptly ended.

Frustrated, Tom paced the floor. "Jesus! I'll go crazy if I have to sit here waiting!"

In minutes he was out of the door and into a taxi, heading for the station, all the while keeping his eyes peeled for a sight of Lilian or Dougie.

Some way across town, the police were cruising the streets, searching for the woman who was to be taken in for questioning. They had her description; they knew she had been arrested once before for causing a public nuisance, and, having been given a detailed description, they would recognize her if they saw her. So far, though, they had seen neither hide nor hair of her. But they wouldn't give up. This was a murder hunt. She must be found, and taken in for questioning.

Oblivious to the fact that she was being tracked down, Lilian strolled along the street, talking to Dougie, pouring out her heart. "I'm sorry," she said. "I've been a real problem to you."

"You're not a 'problem.' " Dougie was surprised at how much she now meant to him. He smiled. "Well, maybe just a *little* 'problem.' "

She laughed.

Serious again, she confessed how it had been with Tom. "From the first minute he walked through the door of the office, I loved him. He's such a fine man . . . so caring. When my mother was taken ill, he was wonderful . . . both him and Sheila."

She paused, thinking of Sheila and the children, and of what she had done. "I hurt them . . . Sheila and the children. I shouldn't have done what I did," she whispered. "That was so wicked of me."

Dougie had heard her say that over and over, and yet she would not admit to what she'd done. "Do you want to talk about it?" If he was to help her, he would have to know.

She opened her mouth to speak, but then shook her head. "I can't. But if I tell you something else . . . you won't tell Tom, will you?"

"Not if you don't want me to." He was shocked to learn how obsessed she had been with Tom. He had seen a side to Lilian that frightened him, and yet at heart she was just like a small child, needing love and reassurance.

She went on. "I used to go and see his family. I took a lot of pictures of Tom; he didn't know I was taking them. And when I was invited to his home, I took pictures of his children, and his wife." Frowning, she momentarily lapsed into a deep, thoughtful silence. "Sheila was a really good friend to me."

"I know." That much, at least, he had been aware of.

"She was a lovely person, so kind . . . so pretty." Her face hardened. "Tom adored her."

He nodded, a hard expression shaping his homely features. "I know that, too." He smiled encouragingly. "But go on . . . you were saying . . . about the pictures?" Now that she was beginning to open her heart to him, he needed to keep her talking.

"Well, Sheila invited me over a lot, and once I even went away for the weekend with them." It gave her pleasure to explain. "I became almost part of the family. There were so many photographs, you see. I put them on my dressing table, and on the doors of my wardrobe." She gave a nervous little laugh. "I even put them all over the walls. I needed to see him all the time . . . before I went to sleep, and when I woke up, I needed him to be there!" Tears of anger clouded her vision. "I loved him so much." Quickly, impatiently, she wiped away the tears.

"Lilian?"

She turned. "Yes?"

"What did you do to Sheila and the children that was so 'wicked?' "

She shook her head. "I can't tell you."

"Do you still love him?"

"NO!" Vigorously shaking her head, she told him through gritted teeth, "He's ruined my life. I HATE HIM!"

"Do you hate him enough to kill him?"

She turned to stare at him; in the growing twilight he imagined he saw the glint of madness in her eyes. "You're trying to trick me, aren't you?"

"No." He realized he would have to tread very carefully if he was to regain her trust. "I'm sorry."

"I want to go home now."

"That's where we're headed."

"Will you stay with me?"

"If you want."

She slid her hand into his. "I think you're like Tom."

"In what way?"

"You're kind. You take the time to listen."

"But you haven't told me anything yet . . . not really."

"Only because I don't want you to feel bad toward me."

For the umpteenth time, the police car nosed its way down a side street. "Look!" The officer pointed ahead, where Lilian and Dougie were strolling away from them. "Isn't that her?"

He checked his description. "Yes, long curly auburn hair, that looks like her. Best move in before she sees us."

Deep in conversation, both Dougie and Lilian were unaware of the police car until it stopped beside them. Flinging open the doors, both officers got out. While one of them stood guard on Dougie, the other confronted Lilian.

"Are you Lilian Catherine Scott?" he asked.

Calmer now, and knowing she must be punished, Lilian made no attempt to run. Instead, she verified her name and was quietly placed in the car.

Seeing how frightened she was, Dougie declared that he was coming with her. "She's told me things you should know!"

"All right, sir," they agreed, and he, too, was bundled into the car.

Ensconced in the interview room with Inspector Lawson, William Aitken was visibly nervous. "I dunno what yer talkin' about! How many times do I 'ave to tell yer? I don't know nuthin' about no hidden car."

Inspector Lawson was in no mood to be lied to. "Don't give me that! We already know you were paid to conceal the car. What I want is a description of the driver: was he tall, short, nervous, arrogant . . . ? I want to know every word he said, every move he made. You must remember how he left . . . was it on foot or by taxi? Was the driver on his own, or was there somebody else there, and if so, what can you tell me about the other person? Have you seen him since? Or maybe it was a woman. Was it a woman, eh, Aitken?"

His questioning was relentless.

The more Aitken claimed ignorance of the event, the more nervous he got and the more Inspector Lawson knew that it would only be a matter of time before he cracked.

Having arrived in reception, Tom was told, "I'm sorry, sir, but you'll have to wait. Inspector Lawson is not to be disturbed."

Tom asked again about Aitken but was given the same runaround. "If you'll just be patient, I'm sure the inspector will be out soon."

So he waited, pacing the floor and willing the time to pass so that he could know what was happening. The big clock on the wall ticked the minutes away; with every passing second, he thought of Kathy.

Why hadn't he been able to get hold of her? Why hadn't she rung the hotel? What was she doing? His mind was alive with her, his heart overflowing with love.

It was an odd thing, he thought, that the nearer they got to finding out who had murdered his family, the more distant he seemed from it all; as though he was a stranger looking on.

The love for his family was still there, but it was moving away, to that corner of his heart where he could put down the shutters and keep it safe for all time, without allowing it to overwhelm his life.

The realization made him feel guilty, yet strangely relieved.

Suddenly his thoughts were shattered when he heard the outer doors swing open. Into the reception area came two officers. With them, and obviously in custody, was Lilian, accompanied by his brother, Dougie.

Dougie saw Tom there and nodded. Lilian, however, glanced once and afterward kept her gaze averted.

*The shame of what she had done to him was unbearable.*

Taken to the desk, she was duly charged in connection with the murder of Sheila Marcus and her children.

When she heard the charge, she was riveted with shock. "No!" Shouting and struggling, with both officers holding her still, she vehemently protested her innocence. "You've got it all wrong. I wouldn't murder them . . . they were my friends!"

Appealing to Tom, she screamed, "Tell them! Tell them I would never hurt them. I'm innocent. Tom, please . . . tell them!"

Torn by powerful emotions, Tom was out of his depth. "If you're innocent, you have nothing to fear," he said quietly.

His gentle voice and quiet manner seemed to calm her, for suddenly the fight was gone from her and she was sobbing. "I wouldn't hurt them, I wouldn't."

Dougie spoke to her. For a moment she looked at him, then, as they took her away, she told him, "You believe me, don't you, Dougie?"

He nodded.

She smiled. "You understand me, don't you?"

Again, he nodded.

Now, as the officer urged her away down the corridor, she shocked both Tom and Dougie to their roots: addressing Dougie, she revealed, "I didn't tell you before, but now I want you to know . . . *I'm having your child.*"

As they took her away, Dougie stood stock still, eyes wide with amazement and something else: a look of horror on his face that Tom had never seen before. "Dougie, are you all right?" What Lilian had said was a complete and utter shock. Not for one minute had Tom imagined anything was going on between his brother and Lilian.

And it wasn't only that, because there was something here he could not understand; some dark business he could not quite get to grips with.

Behind them, Inspector Lawson flung open the door of the interview room. "Charge him!" Having got the information he wanted, the interview was over.

"Bastard!" William Aitken had not taken kindly to being interviewed.

As he looked up at the inspector, standing there in the open doorway, his attention was caught by Tom and Dougie quietly talking beyond: one calm and reassuring, the other seeming to be upset and agitated.

Without warning, Aitken was out of his chair and running across the room. "THAT'S HIM!" Surging forward, he was swiftly intercepted by the officer, who fought hard to hold him. "THAT'S THE GEEZER WHO PAID ME TO HIDE THE CAR!" Pointing and yelling, he struggled to escape.

All eyes turned to Dougie, who by now was edging toward the door.

*To his horror, he had recognized the young man who had*

*been at the breaker's yard. The very same young man who
had taken his money and hidden the car so well that it had
never been found. Until now!*

Disbelieving, Tom looked at the young man, then he
turned his gaze to Dougie. "YOU?" Unable to comprehend
what was happening, he stared at his brother for what
seemed an age, his brain echoing with what Aitken had said.
It was too much to take in. He shook his head, a half smile
creeping over his features, now gray with shock. "No!" The
word was soft, almost gentle, then stronger as he asked,
"Was it *you* who killed my family?"

When he saw the guilt in his brother's eyes, the truth hit
him like the blow of a hammer. "Oh, God!" Lurching forward, he grabbed hold of Dougie, his voice escalating to a
scream, his eyes swimming with tears. "NO . . . o . . . o . . .
oo!" Tom's heart-wrenching scream sent a chill through
everyone there.

In that split second, everything erupted: Dougie made a
dash for the door, and Tom went after him, leaving chaos in
his wake.

Yelling for somebody to help, and taking along the only
free officer, Inspector Lawson sped after Tom and his
brother, but they had a head start, and with the smog closing
in all over London they could be lost to sight in minutes.

Outside, the fall of night mingled with the choking smog,
lying like a dark blanket over everything: a real "peasouper,"
the officer called it.

They scanned the road ahead. "THERE!" The officer
caught sight of Tom, relentlessly pursuing his brother along
the narrow streets.

"Quick! Get after them!"

Sending the younger, fitter officer to try and head them
off, Inspector Lawson stayed with Tom; through the railings
on the far side of the street, then on, across the park, and
toward the railway embankment. One minute he was there,
the next he was gone from sight, dodging in and out; hidden
where the fog was thickening, and visible again where it
wasn't quite settled. He could see Tom going like a crazy
thing. "Leave it, Tom. We're onto it!"

His heart went out to Tom and, though he wouldn't blame him if he closed his bare hands around his brother's neck and squeezed till his eyes popped out, he didn't want Tom to pay the price for what his brother had done. "TOM! LET IT GO!" And still Tom dogged his brother's footsteps, closing in on him with every second, suffocated by hatred and confusion. It had been Dougie all along, he knew that now. Yet, how could that be?

When the chase took them across waste ground, the smog had settled low and heavy; it was difficult to see a hand in front of your face, but Dougie was slowing down, stumbling and tripping, giving Tom the advantage he needed. Behind him, equally determined, the inspector kept sight of Tom.

Ahead of them, the officer cut across, trying to hem them in, but several times they veered away and he lost them again.

Tom had only one thing in mind. He had to look Dougie in the eye. He had to know the truth. Why did he do it? WHY? *WHY?*

In his frantic mind he could see Sheila's face, the way she had glanced back and recognized him. What was going through her head? Why didn't she call out his name?

As he ran, he could hardly see for the tears that ran down his face: tears of rage; tears of sorrow. As they trickled down his face, the cold night air dried them on his skin. He felt like a man broken—a man, yet not a man.

The thick burning smog clogged his throat, yet he could feel none of it. All he could see was Sheila's shocked face as she had glanced out of the back window. Then they were over the cliff and she was no more.

For a minute Dougie disappeared. Frustrated, Tom paused and looked about. Out of the corner of his eye he caught sight of Dougie. Suddenly he seemed to dip and fall, vanishing from Tom's view, before Tom, too, fell over the edge, slipping and sliding, until now the two of them were on the railway track.

As the dry, smouldering smog closed in about him, he could taste it on his tongue, feel the burning in his eyes. His vision was impaired. Negotiating the slim, hard tracks beneath his feet, he kept up, with Dougie slowing and stumbling just ahead.

What happened next was so sudden it took the breath out of Tom.

They didn't hear Inspector Lawson's warning as he called out, "FOR GOD'S SAKE, GET OUT OF THE WAY!" Nor did they see the train until it was on top of them.

Frantic, Tom threw himself forward, at the same time screaming out a desperate warning to his brother. Dougie, though, was intent on escaping, his mind filled only with the horror of what he had done to his own brother. He thought of what Lilian had told him . . . "I'm having your child." Oh, God!

Thundering forward, the train bore down on him. At the last minute he tried to leap out of the way, but it was too late. His foot caught in the track and he was mown down. Unaware, the engine-driver shoveled more coal onto the fire. He had a timetable to stick to. The train sped on.

Clambering forward, the inspector had seen it all. "Oh, Jesus!" Like Tom, he ran on, to find Dougie writhing in a river of his own blood, his leg severed at the thigh.

Distraught, Tom knelt beside him. For a minute he couldn't speak. All he could do was hold his brother, and listen.

"You had them . . . *all* . . . not fair." He gave a half smile, more sad than wicked. "I killed them . . . Sheila . . . *mine.*" Dougie's life ebbed away, and with it his confession. "She wanted . . . me." He gave a yell of pain that tore at Tom's heart. "She . . . changed her . . . mind."

The look he gave Tom was filled with hatred. "You always . . . had *everything!* I wanted her . . . so much. She did . . . love . . . *me.*" Lying back in Tom's arms, he closed his eyes. "Six years . . . together. Not . . . *your* . . . son." He looked into Tom's stricken eyes, and felt a measure of regret. "Forgive me."

His head lolled backward, that fragile, gossamer-like sigh telling Tom that Dougie was no more.

Mortified, the sobs racking his body, Tom drew him close to his chest, then, tenderly, he raised his fingers and closed his brother's eyes. But he couldn't shake off the devastating impact of Dougie's confession. He couldn't let him go. Not yet.

*Not until the hatred had subsided.*

Gently, the inspector pried him away. "It's over, Tom," he whispered. "It's over."

# PART THREE

November 1952

*Going Home*

# *Twenty-one*

"GOOD GOD, MAN!" INSPECTOR LAWSON COULD SEE how the events of the past twenty-four hours had taken their toll on Tom. "You look *terrible!*"

Tom nodded wearily. "I'm sure I do," he acknowledged. "I can't seem to sleep. I still haven't come to terms with what Dougie did."

"Sit yourself down. I'll get you some tea." Waiting until Tom was seated, he added kindly, "It's no use you punishing yourself over what happened. You're not the Lord Almighty. You couldn't have foreseen, or prevented the outcome."

Tom knew that. He also knew that, however long he lived, he would never forget Dougie's confession. Every word was engraved on his mind.

"Have you had any breakfast?" The older man's voice cut through his thoughts.

"No."

"I've got a couple of bacon sarnies. You're welcome to one of 'em."

Tom thanked him. "I wouldn't say no."

He heard the inspector go out, and he heard him come back, and it seemed to Tom as though only a minute had passed, so deep in thought was he.

"Here!" Handing Tom a paper bag containing the bacon sarnie, he explained, "The wife always gives me more than I need."

Tom gave a half smile. "You're a liar."

The older man chuckled. "Maybe, but you look as if you

need it more than I do. So get it down you. We'll talk while we munch."

He pointed to the mug of tea he'd placed in front of Tom. "That's good strong stuff," he said, adding thoughtfully, "I reckon you'll need it."

Tom was already anxious. "You've got Dougie's things, then?"

"Yup. Got 'em yesterday. There's not much in all . . . papers and business schedules, that sort of thing. More to do with work than anything else." He paused. "Eat up!"

Tom had seen how agitated he was, and he needed to know. "You've found something else, haven't you?"

The inspector nodded. "Did you know your brother kept a diary?"

Tom shook his head. "I'm beginning to think I didn't know anything about him at all. More's the pity."

Whatever it was the inspector had found in Dougie's home, Tom knew it must be incriminating or he wouldn't have called him in. "This diary. Does it throw any light on what happened?"

"It tells us all we need to know."

Tom was curious. "Can I see it?"

"Not yet. It's still being tested in the lab. But I can tell you the guts of it."

Tom waited, but he was not prepared for what the older man was about to reveal. "Your brother was jealous of everything you did . . . everything you had. Your wife, your kids, even the job you taught him." He paused, before going on in softer tones, "He envied you, Tom . . . resented the very ground you walked on."

He momentarily glanced away, then, raising his gaze, he looked Tom straight in the eye. "Look, Tom, I don't take any pleasure in telling you these things. But, at some point or another, the contents of that diary will be made known. It's better you know now exactly what was in it."

Coolly returning his gaze, Tom kept control of his emotions. "I understand that, and I appreciate you giving me forewarning. I can't pretend I'm not deeply hurt by what he thought of me, because I am. I had no idea. Can you believe that? He wanted me out of the way . . . was prepared to kill my entire family. For *what?*"

He shook his head slowly and thoughtfully from side to side, as if making himself believe it. "I spent most of last night thinking about it, and the harder I thought, the more I understood—and the *less* I understood at the same time."

"That's a strange way of putting it, Tom."

"No, not really." Leaning forward, he wiped both his hands over his face, gave a long, drawn-out sigh, took a swig of his tea and was quiet for a minute. "I can take him being jealous of me," he murmured presently. "I can take the hating . . . I even understand it a little. Older brother, first born, first to walk, first to school . . . to have a sweetheart, a wife and family. Setting standards . . . showing him the ropes at work; always one step ahead."

He gave a thoughtful nod. "I can see how Dougie might have resented that." He could see it, but not really accept it. "He was my brother. I did everything I could for him. But now I know . . . it was never enough."

"Did you not suspect anything, about the affair with your wife?"

"No. Nothing." Tom needed to know. "Did the diary confirm what he said . . . those last few words?" He had only one thing in mind, and it was more painful than anything he had ever before encountered in his life.

"I'm sorry, Tom. The answer is yes." The inspector had been dreading this moment. "He and your wife had an affair for six years. They planned to go away, but then she changed her mind and finished it. He couldn't take that."

Tom was distraught. "How could I not know? Six years she and Dougie were seeing each other, and I had no idea!" He was angry, angry with them, angry with himself. "How in God's name could I not know?"

He looked up at the older man. The question burned in the air between them. He wanted to ask . . . was desperate to know, yet didn't want to know.

The inspector read his mind. "Why don't we leave it now, Tom?" he suggested kindly. "Put it behind you. Get on with your life."

Tom wanted to, but he had to know. Otherwise how could he ever go forward. "Was it true," he asked, "what he said about my son?"

There was a moment when the inspector thought he might lie to save Tom a great deal of heartache, but somewhere down the line the truth would out and he would be the villain. "I'm sorry, Tom."

A loud, broken sob caught in Tom's throat. He stared down at the floor, the air thick with silence. *The boy he had adored was not his!* He was Dougie's son. *DOUGIE'S SON!* The cruel words echoed over and over in his mind. But then an even more terrible thought struck him. "Dougie was prepared to sacrifice his own son to destroy me."

Now, when he looked up, his eyes were blinded by tears. He didn't say anything more. It was too late. *All too late!*

He got out of the chair and, turning away, walked slowly across the room. At the door he paused, but he didn't look back. Instead he slowly turned the door-handle and, leaving the door ajar, went away, down the corridor and out of the building.

The chill struck his face as he walked out into the daylight. Reality!

Thrusting his hands into his coat-pockets, he walked along the street like a man in a trance, the stark truth leaping in and out of his mind like the stab of a dagger. "Not my son. Dougie's son."

Some time later, never really sure how he got there, he found himself standing in the churchyard looking down at her gravestone. In his mind he could see her as if it was yesterday. "How could you do that to me . . . to *us?*"

Anger had crumbled to sadness. "It won't change the way I loved him, nor will I ever forget the great times we had together. He's still my son, whatever you and Dougie did. *Peter . . . is . . . still . . . my son!*"

The words were issued through gritted teeth, deliberately spaced, quiet but forceful. Nothing and no one could change the way he felt, or wipe out what he and his son had together.

The following morning he paid his bill, called the inspector to tell him where he could be found, and left the hotel. He had done what he came to do, and now it was time to leave. It had been too long a journey. Too lonely.

Every day, every minute, Kathy had been on his mind and in his heart. Yet he had kept a clear head and worked his way through, and now, thank God, it was over.

Though he felt he didn't deserve it, he had a wonderful woman, and a life waiting.

Behind the counter at the site office, Kathy confessed to Rosie how desperate she was to phone Tom, and how she had promised herself that she wouldn't. "Even if I did call him, I wouldn't tell him about Samantha." She was still adamant on that score. "Only I would like to know how things are going with him."

"Why don't ye ring him then?" Rosie urged. She knew how, several times, Kathy had been on the verge of calling Tom. "Ah, sure, ye know where he is. He's called you umpteen times, so you know he wants to talk." Leaning one elbow on the desk, she gave Kathy a nudge. "Aw, look, me darlin'. He must be just as anxious to talk with you, or why would he call?"

Just then a weathered young man came in. "Do you have any caravans? Only I've been walking the hills hereabouts and I'm looking for a base for the winter."

Rosie was sympathetic, but replied, "I'm sorry, luv. Sure, I'd give ye a key straight off, so I would. Only we don't let caravans through the winter. Matter o' fact, we're just now closing down. But there are any number of guest-houses in the area."

Reaching under the counter, she brought out a directory. "Look through that if ye like. I'm sure you'll find something to suit."

With a snarl, he threw it back at her. "Don't talk bloody stupid, woman! I wouldn't be asking for a caravan if I'd got money for 'guest-houses.' Much use *you* are! It'll be another night on the hills, I expect. Thanks for nothing!"

With that he stormed out, with Rosie calling after him: "Good riddance to ye then, ye bad-mannered bugger. I hope yer arse freezes over, so I do!"

With everything she had on her mind, Kathy couldn't help but chuckle. "One of these days that bad temper of yours will get you in trouble," she said.

Rosie laughed out loud. "Ah, sure, it wouldn't be the first time I've been in trouble. It's what keeps me going, so it is."

She got back to the matter in hand. "Are ye going to call that man of yours, or what? Especially since he's been calling here, anxious to find out if you're all right."

Kathy nodded. "I *will* call him. Besides, I need to hear his voice. I need to know he's okay."

Now that Samantha had been taken home, she wanted Tom close, but she continued, "I know how hard it was for him to go back there, Rosie, and how long it's taken him to face up to it all. The last thing I want is to send him off track. You know as well as I do, if he thought I needed him, he'd be back here like a shot, and then where would he be?"

Rosie had seen first hand how Samantha's death had upset her, and how broken she was about her mother's blaming her for it. "Aw, look now, Kathy. I'm so sorry about your sister, and I'd give my right arm if I thought it would bring your mammy to her senses, but it won't. Sure, I can see that now. I know it's not been easy, and I know you've taken it real bad. But you've come through it with a strong heart, so ye have."

Many was the time since Samantha's death that she had taken Kathy in her arms and talked the tears away.

She took her in her arms again now. "Aw, Kathy, me darlin', I'm proud of ye, so I am!"

Kathy smiled up at her. Rosie had a way of making her smile, even when her heart was heavy. "I don't know what I would have done without you and Jasper," she said. "You've been wonderful."

"Ah, but it should have been *Tom* looking after ye! He's missing you, that's for sure."

Now, as Kathy made to protest, she put up a staying hand. "All right! I know what you're going to say, and you're right, so ye are! Tom has to concentrate on what he's about. Sure, I do understand."

All the same, Kathy thought, she wished she had the courage to call him. The truth was, she had never needed Tom more than she did now.

They both turned at the creak of the front door inching open.

It was Jasper, his hairy face and bright eyes peering through the gap he'd made. "It's midday," he reminded them. "Time for summat to eat." Like Rosie, he had Kathy's welfare at heart.

Rosie gave him a wink. "Come to take us somewhere exciting, have ye?"

He winked back. "You'll have to wait an' see, won't you?"

Rosie had her own ideas. "The foyer of a posh hotel, and a pile of cucumber sandwiches with the crust cut off," she suggested, "with a couple of tight-panted waiters obeying our every command."

"Hmh!" Jasper laughed out loud. "That's 'cause yer man-mad, you little hussy!"

Arriving from the inner office, the manager urged that they should not be gone longer than an hour. "There's a mountain of paperwork to go through—apart from the filing—right down to the last receipt." He groaned. "After that, every caravan wants cleaning and making ready for the winter."

Rosie moaned. "I thought you were taking on a couple of part-timers to do that?"

"I've changed my mind." Leaning on the counter, he grumbled, "It's all right for you two. You've got a whole month off to do as you please. I'll have to stay here, keeping an eye on the place."

"You'll be all right, so ye will." Rosie had to have the last word. "No doubt you'll be helping yourself to a tot of booze from the bar whenever the mood takes ye!" She laughed. "It wouldn't surprise me if you didn't have a woman here to keep ye company an' all."

"Hey!" Wagging a finger at her, he warned, "Unless you

want me to take a firm hand with you, you'd better watch that wicked tongue of yours."

Giving him the glad eye, Rosie winked at him. "Is that a threat or a promise?"

"I don't make promises."

"Shame!"

He blushed bright scarlet. "Go on with you. And make sure you're back within the hour."

Grabbing their coats, they went outside with Jasper. "Where are we going?" Being as they only had an hour, Kathy thought they might just have a sandwich at the bar.

"Don't be so hasty, lass," Jasper said with a grin. "Look at what I've got." Rounding the corner, he pointed down the street. "Ladies! Your chariot awaits."

At first Kathy couldn't see what he meant, but then she saw and couldn't believe her eyes. "That's not *yours,* is it, Jasper?" He had been known to play a few tricks on the odd occasion, and she thought this was one.

Rosie looked down the street and saw it too, then she looked at Jasper. She saw the mischievous twinkle in his eye and laughed out loud. "Why, ye old bugger, you!" With her high heels clattering against the pavement, she went running down the street, whooping and hollering and frightening the pigeons. "Jasper's got a car—" she wanted the whole world to know "—and a green one at that!"

Kathy was amazed. "What made you get a Morris Minor?" she asked with a chuckle.

"I just fancied going a bit mad, that's all." He grinned from ear to ear. "I allus wanted a car, and when I passed me test I could never afford one. I've saved over the years . . . not a lot, mind you, but enough to treat mesel' in me twilight years. It's not a new one but it's in good nick."

Clustered around the car, a few stragglers were taking an envious look over it. He told Kathy, "She's so sweet, I've give her a name."

Sliding her arm through his, she said softly, "Go on then . . . you can tell me."

Patting her hand affectionately, he declared with pride,

"Her name's Dorothy. After me very first girlfriend." He blushed at the memory.

Reaching up, Kathy gave him a kiss. "I think that's a lovely name," she said, "and I think *you're* lovely too."

She had never seen Jasper blush before, but today he had blushed twice. She couldn't help but wonder if he had fallen for someone.

"Come on then, lass." Propelling her forward, he opened the doors and invited them in.

It was quite a squeeze, with Rosie almost on Jasper's knee and Kathy trapped between the seats. They managed to climb aboard, much to the amusement of the onlookers.

"Right then, Dorothy, lass." Starting the engine, Jasper urged her on. "Let's see what yer med of!"

It was a stuttering take-off, and when the little car leapt over the bumps in the road, Rosie twice banged her head and wouldn't stop laughing. Kathy found herself doubled up, and Jasper accidentally put his foot on the brake, sending them forward to within an inch of the windscreen. "Will yer look at that?" he shouted. "I allus knew Dorothy was a goer!"

As they went off down the street, the sound of their laughter echoed from the walls. And though she had not intended it, Kathy found herself laughing until the tears fell. It was the first time she had laughed like that since before Tom left.

Arriving in Bridport, Jasper had three goes at trying to park. The first was when his front tire went up the curb and they all fell to one side and couldn't get out.

The second time he was moved on by an irate householder with a yard-broom who chased them all the way down the street, yelling at the top of her voice, "Be off, and take that ugly monstrosity with you!"

When finally he got parked and they all tumbled out, Kathy realized they were right outside the café that Mabel's husband owned. She couldn't understand it. The place was closed down.

While Jasper was locking up his precious "Dorothy," she spoke to a passer-by, who told her, "His wife left him, then he went off with some floozy. Mind you, he won't get much money for that place. It's not been the same since poor Mabel moved away."

Kathy nodded. She had heard how that bully of a husband of hers was not doing so well, especially since the news got out of how he beat poor Mabel senseless. Serves him right, she thought. I hope the floozy gives him a run for his money.

After traveling for most of the day, Tom was on the last leg of his journey.

Disembarking from the train in Weymouth, he glanced up at the station clock. It was already quarter to five. He had a half-hour wait for the bus and another half-hour journey before he got into West Bay. The one and only thing on his mind right now was Kathy.

When the bus arrived he climbed on board, gave the conductor the required fare and took his ticket with thanks.

Hitching his ticket-machine higher up his shoulder, the conductor walked on, stopping at each seat to see if there was anyone else wanting a ticket. When there wasn't, he came and sat down opposite Tom, eyes closed and for all the world looking like he might be having a crafty kip.

Tom smiled. The poor bloke looks done in, he thought. So when they stopped to collect more passengers, and he spied the familiar uniform of a bus inspector, he gently tapped the conductor on the leg. "Time to wake up," he whispered, and by the time the inspector got on board the conductor was wide awake and tending to his duties "like a good 'un," as Jasper might have said.

When the bus stopped at West Bay, the inspector got off just before Tom. "Thanks for that, mate," the conductor told him. "If it hadn't been for you, he'd have caught me good and proper."

Tom told him it was no problem, and that he was glad to have been of help.

When the bus moved off, Tom was still standing there, his gaze reaching across the street to Barden House. For a time he savored the sight of the house. In his mind's eye, he could see Kathy lying on the rug in front of the fire, and his heart leapt.

Quickly now, he made his way past the harbor and across the road, the sweet, salty tang of sea air filling his nostrils. Oh, but it was good, he thought.

At long last, he was home—and soon, thank God, he and Kathy could begin to make plans.

Inside the house, Kathy was alone; just as Tom had pictured her, she was lying across the rug in front of the fire, fascinated by the bright, leaping flames as they danced and wove themselves into a frenzy.

Tom was never far from her thoughts and now, as she wondered about him, she made a decision. "I'll call him in the morning," she murmured softly. "I miss him so much. I need to hear his voice. I need to tell him how much I love him. I won't tell him about Samantha, not yet. I'll just ask him to come home as soon as he can. I need him here, with me."

Coming up the path, Tom saw that the curtains were open. Stepping onto the lawn, he peeped through the window. There she was, arms folded beneath her head and her face turned toward the fire. He smiled. "As I thought," he whispered, "just the same." There was something very comforting in that.

He knocked on the front door.

It was a moment before she answered.

The door opened and there she was, silhouetted in the soft light coming from the hallway; a small, familiar figure, sending a rush of contentment through his senses. In the background he could hear a song from the film, *Singin' in the Rain,* playing on the wireless.

"Hello, darling." His voice was soft, his eyes adoring. "You look wonderful!" In the pale blue dress with white collar and fitted waist, she seemed so young, he thought, so vulnerable.

For a brief second she stared through the semi-darkness, her eyes taking in his face, a momentary look of confusion in her gaze. "TOM!" Suddenly she was in his arms, and he was swinging her around. "Oh, Tom, thank God you're back!"

Laughing and crying, she held him by the hand and led him inside. It had been the worst time of her entire life, but now that Tom was here everything would be all right.

Standing there, the room wrapping its warmth about them, tight in each other's arms, they held each other close. For a time they were silent, just content being together. The light was dimmed, the fire crackled, and they were so much in love. There was no need for words.

In that precious moment, it was as though they had been through the darkness of a long frightening adventure, and now they were through it together, still safe, more in love than ever.

There was a need in them, a deep, trembling need that would not be held back any longer. Momentarily releasing her, he crossed the room and quietly closed the curtains, shutting out the night and its prying eyes.

She waited, her heart fast with anticipation, her eyes following his every move, until he was back with her, kissing her on the forehead, on the mouth, down the curve of her neck. And she, with uplifted face, offered herself to him.

Reaching down, his dark eyes enveloping her, he slid her dress away, then her undergarments, gasping with amazement as he unfolded her nakedness. "You're so beautiful!"

Discarding his own garments, he drew her down to the rug, the heat from the fire playing on the skin of his back as he leaned over her. "I love you," he murmured, his face so close to hers she could imagine herself melting into those dark eyes and being lost forever.

Now, as he entered her, she clung to him, afraid he might be disappointed in her, afraid he might not find her to be the woman he believed she was. But she need not have worried, for she was everything his heart desired.

The lovemaking was not a frantic thing, nor was it soon over. This was another adventure, a most beautiful, wonderful experience: discovering each other's bodies, touching, exploring; the exquisite binding of two lonely, desperate souls.

It was the long-awaited realization of a love that had grown from the heart and was now blossoming to fulfillment.

When it was over, they lay there, content in each other's arms, eyes closed, faces uplifted, their glistening bodies gently washed over by the heat from the fire.

They lay there for a while, side by side, with Kathy rolled against him, her arm over the expanse of his chest. Drawing her close, Tom stroked her arm, his senses lulled by the smooth softness of her skin, and the gentle rhythmic warmth of her breath against his neck.

Some time later, when they were dressed, he brought her a drink and they sat together, talking of their love, making plans. As yet, neither of them was ready to break the moment by revealing the darker things on their minds, of jealousy and murder, and all those things that have no place in a quiet heart.

Yet, at some time, they had to be said.

After a while, he held her at arm's length. "I telephoned you a few times," he revealed. "I left messages, but you never rang back."

Dropping her gaze, she answered, "There is something I have to tell you. You know my sister, Samantha, came to see me."

Tom nodded. "Of course, she was here when I left for London."

"She wanted to take this house from me. She said Father should have left it to her, because she was the eldest."

Tom knew now why she hadn't called him. He had sensed the tension between the two women, and now he knew the cause of it. "And you didn't call me because you knew I'd be straight back on the next train, is that it?"

Kathy nodded, taking a moment to break the awful news to him, her voice trembling. "Something happened," she whispered. "Something *terrible!*"

"What do you mean?"

The horror of it all was overwhelming. Kathy shook her head, unable for a moment to go on. Even now she had not come to terms with the sudden, terrible way in which Samantha had died.

Taking her gently by the shoulders, Tom softly urged her, "Go on, darling. What happened? Tell me."

And so she told him about how Samantha had refused to leave until Kathy had signed papers that would give her half the value of the house, that she and Samantha had fallen out over the whole issue, and that she had asked Samantha to leave that day he had left for London, but she wouldn't. "It was just after you'd gone, dark, pouring with rain," she explained. "Samantha had started out to the pub. She just grabbed my coat and went." She paused, swallowing hard, her hand shaking as she wiped the sweat from her forehead. "She never got there. They came to tell me." Her voice broke. "She . . . oh, Tom!"

"Easy now. Take it slowly."

With Tom's kind urging, she continued, telling him how Samantha's body had been discovered in the water. "She was wearing high heels—she always loved the latest fashions. She must have slipped on the wet stones and fallen into the harbor. They think she knocked herself out somehow— on the wall or a boat—and she . . . oh, Tom." Kathy could not go on any further.

Tom took her gently in his arms, his mind in turmoil as she wept softly. How could it be? Dear God! What a terrible thing to have happened.

While he was going over what Kathy had said, a frightening thought came to him.

Kathy had just described how Samantha had "grabbed my coat" and gone out into the night . . . it was pouring with rain. My God!

Could someone have *mistaken Samantha for Kathy?*

He recalled what Dougie had said in those last few minutes. "I killed them . . . *all.*" That's what he'd said . . . *"You had everything. I killed them . . . all."*

No, it was an accident. Tragic, but an accident.

"Tom?"

He was startled from his thoughts. "What, darling?"

"Are you all right?" She had seen how pale and pensive he'd become.

"I'm just sorry that you had to go through all that alone," he said, his voice somber. "You should have told me!"

"I know."

"What about Jasper? I'm surprised he didn't let me know."

"He wanted to," she confessed, "but I asked him not to." She kissed him on the mouth. "But you're here now, and that's all that matters." Nestling into his arms, she asked gently, "What happened, Tom, back there?"

Wisely, Tom told her only as much as he thought she needed to know. About Dougie and the outcome of the police investigation, and what a stroke of luck it had been that the owner of the breaker's yard should be selling up and discover the car. He explained how his own brother had been the one who drove them over that cliff-edge. When she reacted with horror, he took her back into his arms. "It's over now," he said. "We have to look forward, you and I, together."

*Together.* It had a wonderful sound, thought Kathy.

For her own sake, he told her just enough. He had to be strong.

The rest he kept to himself . . . about Dougie's last words, and the fact that the son he had adored was not his son, but Dougie's.

He did not tell her about Lilian's obsession with him, nor that she was a sick woman in need of help. There would be time for all that in the future, when their lives were more settled.

When the clock struck ten, there came a knock on the door. It was Jasper. "Glad to see yer back, Tom, lad," he said, shaking Tom by the hand. "I was in the shop having a tot o' the good stuff with my dear old friend, when I saw you get off the bus. I weren't sure as to what you might be doing . . . whether you'd want the cottage warmed, or if you had any other ideas, like?" He looked from one to the other, delighted to see the love light in their eyes.

"Good to see you too, Jasper." Tom thought the sight of that old hairy face was reassuring.

"Anyway, here's the key. I've lit the fire and you'll find a hot-water bottle in the bed . . . them sheets get icy cold once the weather turns."

He smiled at Kathy. "All right, are yer, lass?"

"I'm better now that Tom's back," she answered. "Thanks all the same, Jasper."

"Aye well, I'll not keep yer." Tipping his cap in his usual fashion, he gave a long yawn. "I'm off to me bed." He gave Kathy a wink. "I'll see youse both tomorrer, eh?"

Tom thanked him. "If you call in at the cottage first thing, there's something I'd like to run by you," he suggested.

Jasper nodded. "I'd like a chinwag," he said. "I'm sure we've a lot to talk about, you and me." He glanced at Kathy, comfortable in the crook of Tom's arm. "But right now the two of youse will have *more* to talk about. You don't need an old geezer like me standing on the doorstep."

He tipped his cap at Kathy once more before ambling away, whistling in the dark, the tap of his boots echoing against the pavement.

An hour later, Tom asked Kathy if she wanted him to stay the night. Even though he knew she had been here on her own for the last weeks, he was worried about leaving her alone.

Sensing his concern, Kathy was tempted, but she decided against it. "Best not," she said. "You get back and settle into the cottage," she said. "Jasper's lit a fire up there, anyway." And besides, "If the locals saw you coming out of here in the morning, there'd be tongues wagging all over West Bay." She chuckled. "Not that I'm too worried about that."

"And will you be all right . . . on your own?" He hated himself for saying it, he knew how independent Kathy was, but he couldn't help but be concerned, even now.

"I've been safe up to now," she answered.

"All right." Kissing her goodnight, he told Kathy to get a good night's sleep, because he was taking her boating tomorrow. "We'll go right out, where nobody can find us. Just you and me . . . out there, with only the wind and skies for company."

It sounded wonderful, to him and Kathy both.

Liz and her son were outside in the garden when the postman dropped the letter through the letterbox. "Look, Mummy!"

Thrilled with his new dragon-kite, Robbie let it loose, laughing and leaping about when the sharp breeze picked it up and carried it high above the garden. "It's flying!"

Liz came to watch, mesmerized like a child as she followed its maiden flight. "That's wonderful!" she cried. In truth when she bought it that morning she had never really believed it would take off, let alone fly through the air like that.

Dipping and diving, it soared above the rooftops, and for a moment seemed as if it would escape the boy's clutch, but then he tugged it back, calling frantically for Liz when it got caught up in the top of a birch tree.

Taking her broom, she reached up, wrapping the handle around the string. She gave a hard tug; the string broke and Robbie fell backward, disappointed but not beaten. "If you hold me, I'll climb up," he said, so she did, and within five minutes the kite was safely back on the ground.

"Bring it inside," Liz told him. "We'll have to retie the string and mend that tear." The dragon had a gash right through his mouth.

"He looks like he's smiling." Robbie laughed, and Liz had to agree.

Once inside the kitchen, Liz took out her sewing basket and, with a few deft moves of the hand, she stitched his mouth and wove the string back together. "There!" Presenting the boy with it, she declared proudly, "He's as good as new, but if you let him escape into the trees again I might not be able to mend him so easily."

While Robbie went back into the garden, she began making her way upstairs. "Best change the beds," she muttered as she went. "Going to the early market has made me late."

Usually by this time on a Saturday she had the beds changed and the washing blowing on the line, but today she and Robbie had got on the eight o'clock bus to Leighton Buzzard, and now, what with the excitement of that kite and everything, she was way behind with her chores.

As she passed the front door she caught sight of the letter lying on the mat. Stooping, she picked it up. Straightaway she recognized Jasper's handwriting: large and scrawling, it was peculiar only to that dear old man.

Tearing open the envelope, she began to read:

*Dear Liz,*

*I hope you and the boy are well. I have two reasons for writing to you. Firstly, I would like to thank you for the wonderful time I had, and for the kind way you and Robbie looked after me.*

*The other reason for me writing is to tell you about a shocking thing that happened in West Bay.*

*Robert's oldest daughter, Samantha, paid a visit to Kathy. There seems to have been some disagreement about the house.*

*Kathy asked her to leave and she refused. By all accounts it seems to me that Samantha wanted her out. She demanded that the house be sold and that she receive half the proceeds.*

*Of course, Kathy refused, especially since she knew that Samantha had been given a very expensive property belonging to her mother, which, like everything else, was wasted on Samantha's extravagant lifestyle.*

*All that aside, though, and remembering that these two were sisters, what happened came as a terrible blow to Kathy. While in West Bay, her sister Samantha fell off the harbor wall and drowned. Forgive me if I shock you with this news, but there is no other way to say it.*

*They reckon she hit her head on something; it was just very unfortunate.*

*Kathy has been devastated. Her mother came to see her, but not with a mind to console her. Instead, she was very cruel and spiteful, blaming Kathy because she did not bend to Samantha's wish regarding Barden House.*

*You can imagine how this has affected her.*

*Knowing what a kind and loving person you are, and how devoted you were to Kathy's father, I wonder if you would find it in yer heart to come and see her, as a friend? I know this won't be easy, lass. But I'm sure it would mean so much to Kathy. You would love her, Liz. She's so much like her father in manner and nature.*

*If you feel this is beyond you, then don't worry.*

*Yours affectionately,*
*Jasper*

Shaken by the awful news, Liz had to sit down. Holding the letter in her trembling hands, she read it for a second time. "Dear God! What a terrible thing to happen . . . and to one of Robert's daughters." It was inconceivable.

Lately, she had been toying with the idea of going to meet Robert's daughter, Kathy, but now she didn't know what to do. Would Kathy feel that she was interfering? What if she took offense at her turning up out of the blue . . . taking it upon herself to feel she had a right to console Kathy?

And what about the way she and Kathy's father had set up house together? It would be understandable if Kathy bore some kind of grudge.

Unless, as Jasper had pointed out, Kathy was made in the same caring, sensible mold as her father.

Wailing and moaning, Robbie came running in. "It wasn't my fault! The wind took it out of my hands!" he cried. "It's got stuck in the tree again. Come and see."

"What am I going to do with you, eh?" Affectionately, she ruffled his hair. "Come on then. We'll try and get it down, shall we?"

The boy saw the letter as she thrust it into her skirt-pocket. "What's that, Mummy?"

"It's a letter, son."

"Who's it from?"

"Jasper."

Robbie danced on the spot. "Is he coming to see us again?"

"No, Robbie. He wants us to go and see him, in West Bay." She did not tell him why. There was no need for that.

"Oh, can we, Mummy? Please!"

"I don't know, son. We'll have to see."

"I love Jasper," he said. "He's my friend."

As she led him out to the garden, her arm around his small shoulders, she looked down. "He's my friend too."

The boy glanced up, his dark eyes smiling up at her, melting her heart.

He was so like his father, she thought. More and more of late, there were times when she imagined Robert was looking at her through the boy's eyes.

She thought maybe she should go and see Kathy, if only for Robert's sake.

Then she wondered. He had kept them apart all that time. Maybe he didn't want her to meet his other family.

She was torn.

Should she go, or should she reply to Jasper and say she wasn't able to, for whatever reason?

If she decided *not* to go, she believed Jasper would understand her motives. He was a good man. A friend of Robert's too.

But there was time for her to think it over.

In the end, all she wanted was to make the right decision for them all.

# Twenty-two

KATHY WAS ADAMANT. "YOU GO AND DO WHAT YOU came to do," she told Tom. "I need some time alone in the church."

"Are you sure?" Tom didn't like to leave her there in the big London church alone. He knew how, within the hour, her mother would arrive. Soon after that, her sister would receive the blessings before being laid to rest. "I can always tend to my business afterward."

"No." Reaching up, she kissed him firmly on the mouth, "I'll be fine. I just need to be alone for a while. Come back as soon as you can, and don't worry about me."

"I don't like to leave you . . ."

"Go!" She gave him a friendly shove. "Like I said, I'll be all right."

Before hurrying away, he told her he would be back in no time. "So don't think you're getting rid of me that easily!"

Inspector Lawson had agreed to meet him nearby at his request. "I've done everything you said," he told Tom when they were seated in the pub. "I've been in touch with the case-officers in Dorset . . . they can't tell me anything I didn't already now. I've sifted through all your brother's belongings, and I've scoured his diary. But there is no mention anywhere of either Kathy or her sister, Samantha."

Tom's heart rose with hope. "So, Kathy's sister's death was an accident?" It would have been so hard for him to tell Kathy that his own brother was Samantha's killer.

The inspector shook his head. "No, Tom! That's *not* what

I'm saying. What I am saying is that we have no evidence to show he even knew Kathy or her sister. The last entry in his diary was made two days *before* she died. So, we can't say it was him, and we can't say it wasn't."

Tom thought about all of that before asking the question, "What do *you* think?" Leaning forward, he looked the other man in the eye. "Was Samantha's death a straightforward accident?"

The inspector thrust out his hands in a gesture of helplessness. "Who knows? The post-mortem was inconclusive. They couldn't find hard evidence of foul play, apparently. But, whatever the truth, and for what it's worth, I don't think it was your brother who did it."

Somewhat relieved, Tom thanked the inspector. "I'd like to think it wasn't Dougie," he murmured. "When he gets where he's going, he'll have more than enough to explain to the Almighty."

"Considering everything . . . it was good of you to see he got a decent burial, even if you weren't there to see it."

Tom's features darkened with loathing. "I didn't do it for him," he said gratingly. "I did it because there was no one else. I can never forgive him for what he did. But I've done my duty, and, as far as I'm concerned, that's an end to it."

"I wish you well, Tom. You must put it all behind you now."

"I know."

"If I hear anything, I'll let you know."

They shook hands and Tom left.

Outside, he hailed a cab, and went to meet Kathy at the church.

When he arrived, she was kneeling in a pew at the back of the church, head bent and eyes closed. She didn't hear him until he was right beside her. "Are you all right, darling?"

She nodded, but didn't reply.

Tom gave her a comforting hug, before going to the altar where the candle Kathy had lit was already burning. Quiet as a mouse, he lit four candles beside it: one for each of his children, one for his wife, and one for Kathy's sister.

He then lit a fifth candle which he distanced from the others. As he put the light to it, he muttered harshly, "This one is for those poor, tortured souls who've lost their way." At the back of his mind was his own brother, Dougie.

In moments of flashbacks he could see them as children, playing and laughing; as he thought of it all, the tears rimmed his eyes.

Angry, he wiped them away and returned to Kathy, who had seen it all, and was made to wonder.

A moment later, they came, one after the other, side by side, her mother and Richard, friends, colleagues; all come to pray for Samantha's soul.

They went to the front of the church and didn't see the two at the back.

With Tom beside her, Kathy watched them come in. She saw the four somber-suited bearers bring Samantha to the altar; a long white, beautiful coffin atop a golden trestle; it was Samantha's style, she thought. It made her smile . . . made her sad. This was her sister, her beautiful, headstrong sister. And she was no more. No more!

Holding Tom's hand, she heard the service, and then they left.

Outside, she held onto Tom, and he kept her safe, until she broke away at a run, fleeing down the path and into the road, where the taxi was still waiting.

Tom followed her.

As they moved away they saw them come out, heads bowed, eyes moist, filing behind Samantha, as they did in life.

It was as it should be.

Later that evening, when the patients of the mental home gathered for their evening meal, Lilian sat sullen and unresponsive at the far end of the table.

The nurse came to speak with her. "Aren't you hungry, my dear?" Soft-spoken and portly, she was a pleasant lady of middle years.

Lilian pushed her hotpot away.

The nurse pushed it gently back. "Just eat as much as you can," she urged. "You ate nothing at all yesterday. You can't go on like that. Remember, you've a baby growing inside you. It needs its nourishment."

Lashing out, Lilian sent the hot stew all over her. When the nurse reeled backward, her arm scalded and calling out for help, Lilian came after her. There was murder in her eyes. "I don't want your food!" she screeched. "I don't want this baby!"

Terrifying everyone there, she grabbed a knife from the table. "SEE!" Slicing the blade across her stomach, she began tearing her clothes. "I'll kill it," she cried. "You can't stop me! You can't make me have it!"

At the nurse's shouts, the helpers came from nowhere, holding Lilian down, trying to calm her.

One minute she was like a crazy thing—kicking out, spitting and snarling; in the next she was like a child—cowering and whimpering. "It was *me*. I did it!" Snatching off her shoe, she held it high in the air, laughing through her tears as she brought it down again and again on the floor, the sound echoing through the room with a sickening thud. "I pushed her . . . shoved her in the water." Her eyes grew wide with wonder before she began laughing . . . mad, abandoned laughter. "I pushed her . . . she fell in . . . it was funny."

Her laughter was insane. "I can do it to this baby as well . . . you can't stop me!" She punched her stomach so hard with the shoe that she actually cried out in pain.

When they tried to stand her up, she fought like a wild thing.

After a while, when she was quietly crying, they took her to the rest room, where she would be shut in for a time, until she had reflected on her behavior.

When they locked the door on her, she could be heard shouting, "The water killed her. It wasn't me!"

One nurse looked to the other. "Mad as a hatter!" she said.

"Talking gibberish!" said the other.

But Lilian knew what she had done.

She could see it all in her head . . . the darkness, the rain, and *Kathy* all alone, walking in the dark. "That woman had no right to him!" she yelled. "He's mine! He'll *always* be mine! I don't want this baby!" Her screams could be heard well into the night.

Until at last she fell asleep.

Even in her vivid dreams, she knew what she had done.

But she was not sorry. Given the chance she would do it again.

# Twenty-three

AFTER ALL THAT HAD HAPPENED, KATHY DIDN'T WANT a big wedding. "As long as I've got you, that will be enough," she told Tom.

On this morning, two weeks before Christmas, they had taken the boat along the coast. It was one of those wintry days, when the chill in the air was muted by the sun's watery rays. The breeze was sharp enough to make their ears burn and their noses slightly pink, but it didn't matter. Well wrapped up, out there with only the sea and sky for company, they were never happier.

Later, as they gentled their way back to harbor, Tom took her in his arms. "I love you," he murmured, kissing her face and hugging her tight.

"I love you too," she told him, laughing out loud when a freak wind rocked their bows to send him staggering away. "If you don't watch where we're going, we'll end up on the rocks."

Coming into harbor, they saw Jasper merrily waving at them from the quayside. "I expect he's after us going for a drink with him." Tom steered the boat in through the narrow tunnel. "I think the world of him," he said, "but I'm glad we could get away on our own just now, aren't you?" He looked at her then, at her small face with its pink nose and the ends of her hair playing out from beneath her woolly cap, and he thought himself the luckiest man on earth.

She came to him then, her arms around his waist, her face nuzzling into his back. "I want us always to be as happy as we are today," she whispered.

Tom turned to kiss her. "And why shouldn't we be?" he demanded with a twinkle in his eye.

"No reason," she answered thoughtfully.

They both knew how life could turn on you like a wild beast when it took a mind.

But they had weathered the storm, and now, God willing, they were home and safe.

A week later, the snow came. Covering the landscape with a layer of squashy white, it hung from the boughs of trees and rolled up in the hedges, but it wasn't cold. Instead, on the day Tom and Kathy were married, it was a warm and beautiful winter's afternoon.

It was only four days before Christmas. The snows were beginning to melt. Through every window the Christmas lights twinkled and sparkled, and children laughed and played in the snow. Soon it would be gone and a New Year started.

"By! Yer look a treat, lass." Jasper was at the house when Kathy came downstairs wearing the cream-colored suit she had chosen for her wedding. With the blue blouse, pretty shoes, and the darker-blue hat with its tiny veil, she looked dazzling.

Having helped her to dress, Rosie came down the stairs behind her. "Ah, but yer don't know what she's wearing under her skirt," she teased the old man.

Jasper laughed. "Go on, then . . . I'm sure you're itching to tell me."

"It's a *garter!*" Winking at Kathy, she said, "Sure, ye might think this gal is all prim and proper, but there's a little devil lurking under there, I can tell ye!" Rushing across the room, she gave Kathy a nudge. "Go on then! Show the man!"

Winking naughtily at him, Kathy lifted the hem of her skirt and there, nestling just above the knee, was the prettiest, pinkest, frilliest garter you ever did see.

Jasper laughed out loud. "Well, yer little hussy, you!" he chuckled.

Kathy's smile deepened. "I'll give you two guesses as to who bought it."

"Ah, sure, it's only right!" Rosie was in her element. "A feller wants to see a little wickedness in his woman. Isn't that so, Jasper?" Linking her arm with his, she gave him a loud smacker on the side of his face.

"Hey!" Jasper gave her a playful nudge. "You'd better watch it, lass. I've been known to sweep a woman off her feet for less than that."

"Well, then . . . sweep me off my feet, why don't ye?"

"What!" He blushed to the roots of his beard. "D'yer want me to crawl in that church on me hands and knees, do yer?"

When she pretended to come after him, he headed for the door. "Come on then, Kathy, lass. We'd best be off . . . the car's waiting outside."

Frantic now, Rosie looked at herself in the mirror. "Ah, look at that! This dress makes me look fat, so it does!"

"You don't look fat at all," Kathy chided. "You look lovely." She had never seen Rosie so dressed up before, and it was a real eye-opener. With her fiery red hair tamed into a bun on the top of her head, the wayward curls dressed with the slimmest of bands, she looked so different. The dress was light blue, to match Kathy's blouse; the style was slim and fitted with a long-sleeved bolero to match, and, in spite of Rosie moaning and complaining, Kathy knew she was quietly pleased with herself.

Jasper grew impatient. "Come on! Hurry up, you two!"

A moment later they were out the door, being waved on and wished all the best by a few of the locals. "You look lovely!" one woman told Kathy. "God bless you!"

When Rosie scowled at her, she told her the same. "You look lovely, too," the woman said, her genuine compliment putting the smile back on Rosie's face.

The registry office was packed to the hilt. There were people from West Bay, neighbors and acquaintances, the site manager. And Kathy's old and dear friend, Maggie, in a bright blue coat and the highest heels Kathy had ever seen.

Alongside her was her newest boyfriend, the owner of a night-club and, as Maggie proudly put it, "Not short of a bob or two."

As Kathy came in, Maggie waved and smiled and told everyone how she had known Kathy for a long time and what a lovely person she was. It was only when her boyfriend gave her a nudge that she sheepishly fell silent, though she and Kathy exchanged a few knowing glances and warm smiles. There was a bond between them that went way back. Whatever happened to one or the other, these two were friends forever.

The service was short and dignified. Tom and Kathy were joined together as man and wife, and when they came out into the bright wintry sunshine, everyone clapped and smiled. It was the happiest day.

As they walked toward the spot where the pictures would be taken, Kathy saw two figures standing a short distance away. *When now the woman smiled at her, Kathy's heart turned over.*

Slowly, unsure, she went to her. In her mind she could see the photograph her father had left behind—she had only recently found it at the back of the drawer—of himself and the boy on the beach, collecting shells with Jasper. There were other photographs, too. "You're Liz, aren't you?"

Liz nodded. "I hope you didn't mind me coming here. I did so much want to see Robert's daughter get married." Her eyes filled with tears. "Oh, Kathy! He would have been so proud!"

For a long, emotional moment, Kathy gazed at her, then at the boy, her brother, who reminded her so much of her dear lost father. "Hello, Robbie," she whispered. "Jasper's told me so much about you."

Suddenly, without warning, he slid his hand into Kathy's, for now he knew she was his sister, and he wanted her to love him.

Openly crying, Kathy threw her arms around them both.

"I'm glad you came," she murmured. "Oh, I'm so glad you came."

Now, as Tom came to hold her, Kathy thought of all the bad things that had happened. They were over now. She had a real family at last. And it was the most wonderful gift of all.

From somewhere behind them Jasper called out, "That's enough malarking, you lot! There's pictures to be tekken. Hurry up! Afore we all freeze on the spot!"

Laughing, they made their way over.

While they waited for the photographer to line the others up, Tom slid his arm around Kathy's waist. "Are you happy, darling?"

Kathy looked around: at Liz and young Robbie, her brother; then Maggie in her ridiculous outfit; and at Jasper, that wonderful, darling old man.

She looked up at Tom with smiling eyes and a heart filled with love. "I'm happier than I've ever been in my life," she said.

She glanced up at the skies, her mind alive with memories of her father. She imagined him smiling down on her. "Thank you," she murmured.

He had given her a new start. A new life.

With Tom and her family.

No woman could want more.

New York Times **Bestselling Author**

# PATRICIA GAFFNEY

## *Flight Lessons*

0-06-103144-5/$7.99 US $10.99 Can

From the extraordinary Patricia Gaffney comes
a poignant, funny, and wise story of truth and
loyalty, of the bonds that shape, sustain, and
ultimately uplift us.

"Women's fiction at its finest."
*Library Journal*

## *The Saving Graces*

0-06-019192-9/$7.99 US $10.99 Can

"A jewel of a book and every facet sparkles."
Nora Roberts

## *Circle of Three*

0-06-109836-1/$7.50 US $9.99 Can

"Gaffney's depictions of female friendships
are right on the mark."
*New Orleans Times-Picayune*